KINGSHOLD

D.P. WOOLLISCROFT

Created with Vellum

For Haneen and Liberty, who are everything to me.

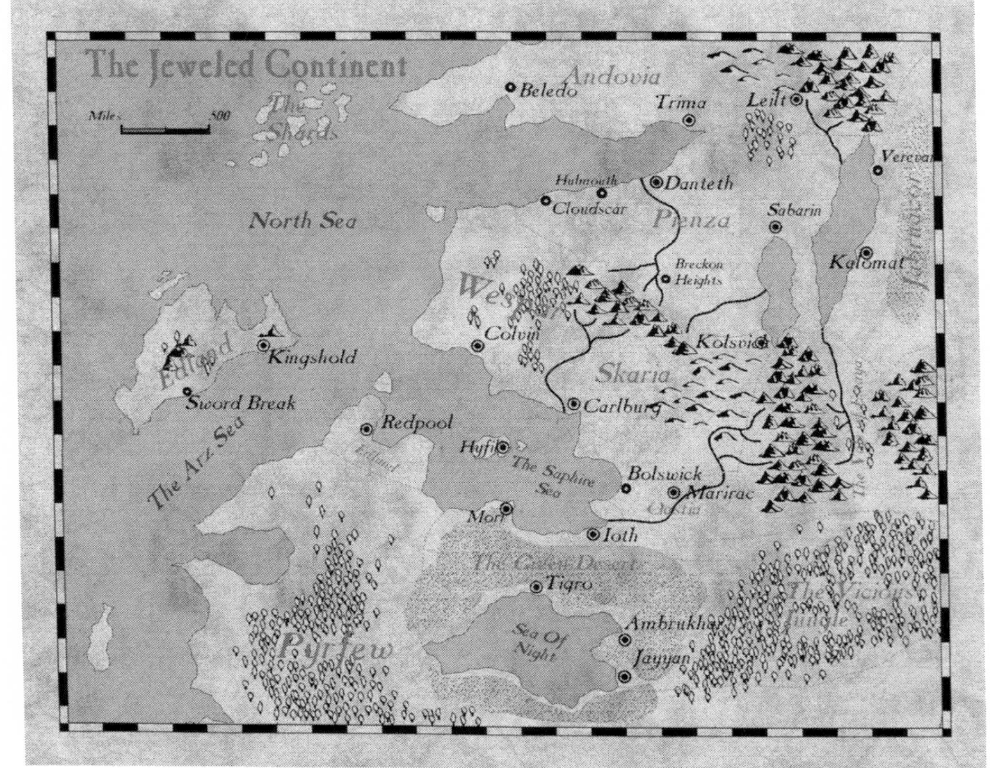
The Jeweled Continent
Miles
500
The Shards
North Sea
Andovia
Beledo
Trima
Leilt
Vereval
Hulmouth
Danteth
Cloudscar
Sabarin
Breckon Heights
Kalomat
Colvin
Kingshold
Kolsvic
Skaria
Sword Break
Carlburg
Redpool
The Arz Sea
Hyffi
The Saphire Sea
Bolswick
Marirac
Mori
Ioth
Tigro
Ambrukhar
Sea Of Night
Jayyan
Pyrfew

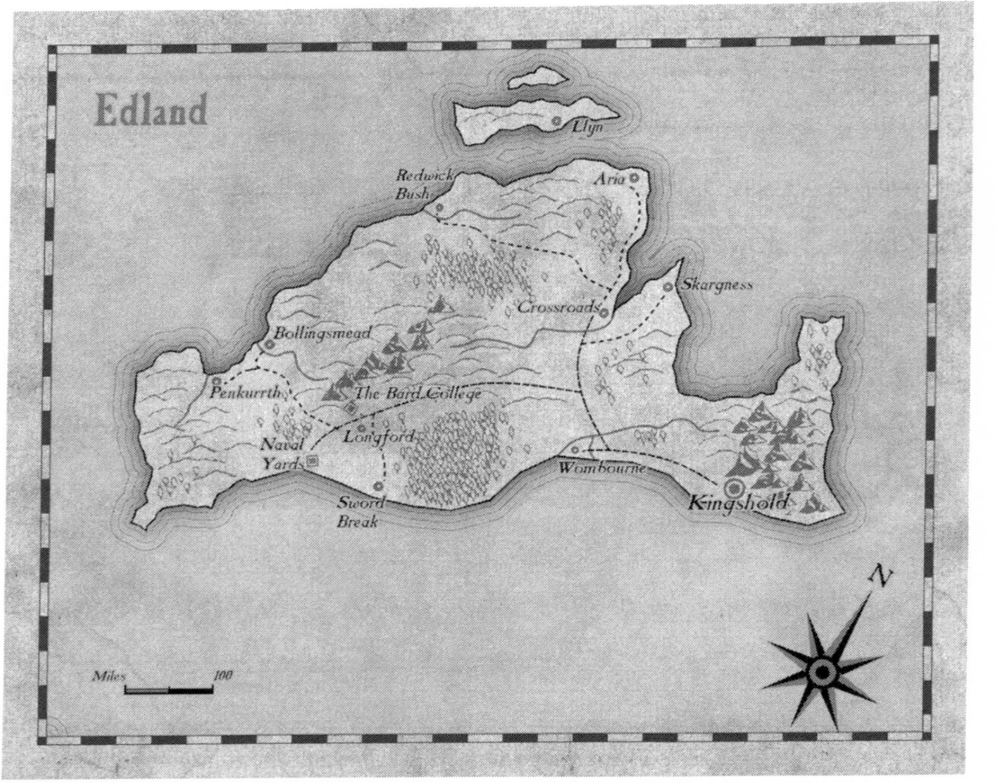

Edland
Llyn
Redwick Bush
Aria
Skargness
Crossroads
Bollingsmead
Penkurrth
The Bard College
Longford
Naval Yards
Sword Break
Wombourne
Kingshold
N
Miles
100

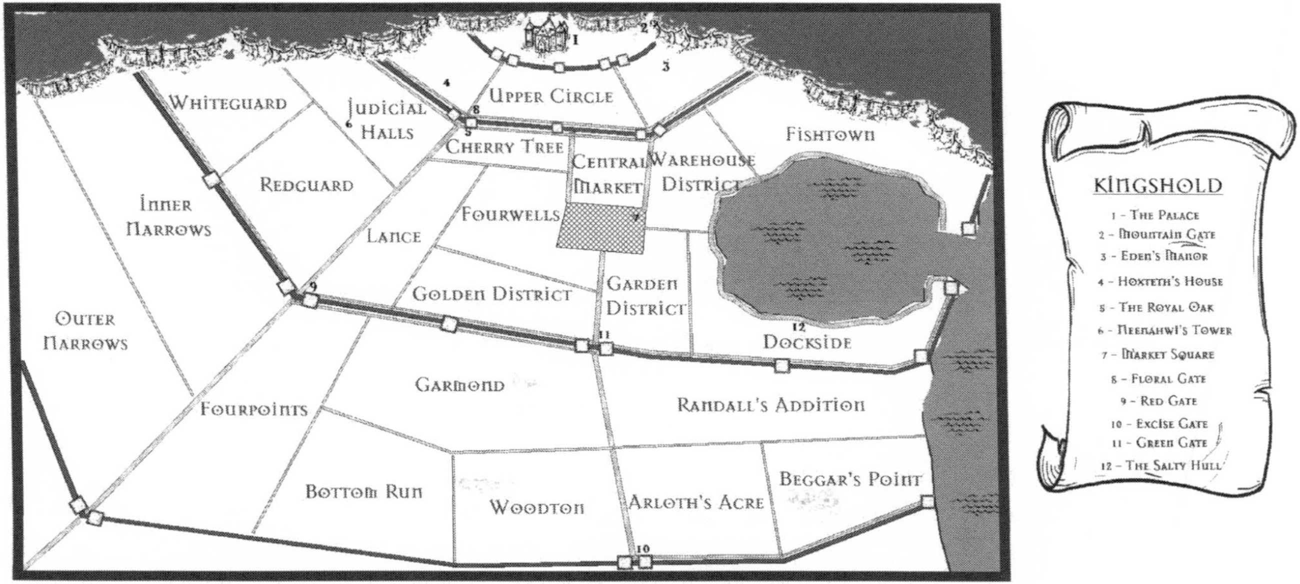

KINGSHOLD
1 - The Palace
2 - Mountain Gate
3 - Eden's Manor
4 - Hoxteth's House
5 - The Royal Oak
6 - Neenahwi's Tower
7 - Market Square
8 - Floral Gate
9 - Red Gate
10 - Excise Gate
11 - Green Gate
12 - The Salty Hull
1
2
3
4
5
6
7
8
9
10
11
12
Whiteguard
Judicial Halls
Upper Circle
Fishtown
Cherry Tree
Central Market
Warehouse District
Redguard
Inner Narrows
Fourwells
Lance
Golden District
Garden District
Dockside
Outer Narrows
Garmond
Fourpoints
Randall's Addition
Bottom Run
Woodton
Arloth's Acre
Beggar's Point

INNINGS

I ... d down from the Floral Gate, their features bereft of emotion as the people of Kingshold celebrated in the street before them. Mareth stood at the side of the cobbled road known as the Lance (both for its arms and armor merchants and that it stretched in a dead straight line from the Inner to the Outer Wall). Considering the scene around him, he gave passing attention to the ache behind his eyes. Another late night at the Swallow and Sixpence.

It was said, when King Roland had wed the then Lady Tulip, that Kingshold had really partied. Hundreds of bonfires, minstrels, dancing. Good old cavorting. Unfortunately, Mareth had missed out on that particular celebration, not being in the city at the time. That was back in his adventuring days, but he had heard about it on his return; after all, it was his job to gather stories as a Bard from the College of Longford. Mareth had just woken up to the impromptu party across the city (outside of the Upper Circle, of course; the rich preferred their parties indoors); it promised to make the royal wedding look like a harvest festival.

But the king did not smile to see such joy in his subjects. And the queen wore her distinctive frown of disapproval. She was known to detest the sight of *commoners*, as she would put it.

Five years ago, the king's reign had begun with much enthusiasm from the general populace—nobility to royal servant, merchant to thief—what with Roland being the beloved son of King Randolph, widely regarded as one of the wisest rulers of Kingshold in a thousand years. Mareth didn't know if things went downhill because Roland married Tulip, or if it just took him a little while to get into his incompetent stride, but after a year, the honeymoon was over. The hike in taxes, the associated crucifixions for non-payment of said taxes, and the stories of excess that seeped from the palace like pus from a boil created a hatred of the royal couple not experienced since the Red Queen killed hundreds of citizens over one weekend centuries past.

Mareth looked up to gaze at the royal couple in the evening sun. It was nearly the summer solstice, and the days were long. Long enough where he would wake up in the light of the afternoon—usually hung over as he was now—stay up through the night, and head back to his flop house after the sun had risen. But he had told himself many times, those were the hours of a bard. When people drink, they want to hear song and story, and people drink through the night. He didn't need the ale, or the whiskey, but no one wanted to mix with someone in a drinking room who wasn't drinking. Obviously. And so, the occasional headache, and maybe some nausea, were just professional hazards. He shielded his eyes as he looked up, considering how he liked the royal couple much more today than he had yesterday, or even the day before.

It seemed like that was the opinion held by most of the throng around him. One man—obviously drunk, with a scraggly black beard over a pockmarked face—shouted something incomprehensible in the direction of the royal couple, and then hurled a turnip. It whistled past their faces with nary a batted eyelid.

It was always amazing how a head or two on a spike could improve the mood of so many. And it wasn't every day that the king and queen were the crow food.

Of course, this could be a short-lived exuberance. Who knew what tomorrow would bring? Would they be trading one turd for a big steaming cow pat?

Mareth took a rolled cigarette out of his pocket—half smoked already—and asked a smith's assistant for a light. As he leaned against the wall of the smithy, the smoke made his head spin and his throat rough. He closed his eyes, lights dancing against his lids. His dream from last night resurfaced. In it he had written a poem, which was so eloquent, so vivid and heart wrenching, it started a civilian rebellion. Thousands of common people rose up against the king and the nobles of Edland, all motivated by his words like the bards of old. Mareth didn't necessarily think of himself as a revolutionary. After all, he'd grown up in relative comfort compared to most. But it had been a long time since he had left his father's house and made his way out into the world. What he had observed since then—literally and figuratively—stunk. No, not a revolutionary, more of an agitator or a herald of what could come.

And then he had woken up today—later than probably nine tenths of the city—to find the object of his hatred cast down! How inconvenient! He considered it a shame he had not finished that poem. One particular stanza caused many lost months and numerous visits to the Giant's Toe in Four Points to lubricate the words to the page. And now, someone else would take the plaudits for the deaths of the twisted pair. But who? There had not been street fighting, or fires in the palace, or other evidence of a coup, to accompany the deaths of the royal couple.

The cigarette had made him feel ill. Mareth dashed around the corner into an alley and vomited, but nothing but bile was forthcoming.

He should have eaten.

He should stop smoking.

He needed a drink.

He needed more to his life than this squalid existence!

When Mareth had completed his studies, the dean had high hopes for him, even offered him employment at the college, but adventure had called. Back then it wasn't enough to tell the stories. Mareth had wanted the stories to be about him. These days, Mareth still desired the fame of epic bards like Garm the Glorious and Malia Silk Tongue, those whose portraits adorned the walls of the great college dining hall, and who had also been once-in-a-generation Song Weavers like him. But now he'd be content for his stories to be about anything but him. The adventuring life had proven too painful.

Still, the question lingered. How did the heads of the king and queen magically appear on spikes without any violence elsewhere? There had to be a story here that he could be the one to write. It might not be as big as something to ignite a peasant rebellion, but a bit of fame, fortune, and maybe a companion for the night would be better than his current situation. He considered this to be a good plan. But where to start?

Wiping the spittle from his beard with his sleeve, and walking back out onto the Lance—the contents of his stomach left behind—he considered where he was and the viable options. The royal couple now called the Floral Gate home, so Market Street was just up there, and the Royal Oak couldn't be more than five minutes away. There was always a better class of drinker in the Royal Oak, and Mareth considered that would be quieter than the streets right now. Not that he was planning on having a drink. No, he just needed to eat. And where better to gather research for his new tale than in a tavern, the place where the gossip of the city flowed before circling the drain. Lovable rogues with rumors aplenty. Traders with secrets fresh from the palace ready to confide in him after sharing a tankard or two. But that was just part of the job, too. He loosely retied his shoulder-length auburn hair behind his head and checked his green trousers and jerkin to make sure there weren't too many visible stains. After all, he didn't want to look out of place.

Mareth, feet already moving him in the direction of the Royal Oak, stopped in his tracks. He remembered he would need to apologize to Jules for what happened last time. He couldn't recall the details of what it was he had done, though he knew it was something. But she'd forgiven him at least three other times in the past, so he was sure it would be alright.

And so, he continued on his way, passing a broad tree, snapdragons sheltering underneath. A small taste of nature's color in the stone-grey city. Mareth gathered up the yellow flowers, a gift to ease admittance into Jules's good graces once more.

CHAPTER 2
THE PRIVY COUNCIL

The big old man rapped the table with the ring adorning his right hand, stopping the murmuring and bringing attention back to him. He looked in sprightly health; clear skin with strong arms, broad chest and barrel-like belly. His white hair long, full, and tied back, with a close-cropped white beard. A pendant—a large blue stone surrounded by strange sigils—hung around his neck, drawing Hoskin's gaze. The Amulet of Jyuth, worn, of course, by Jyuth himself, the title given to all of the magi who had stood behind the throne of Kingshold for as long as the records went back. Some people said Jyuth was one man, but how could that be when there had been someone with that name as long as Edland had existed?

Hoskin knew the scholarly debates well. He had read every record in the palace he could lay his hands on during those interminable childhood summers when he and his mother would leave their estate and journey to Kingshold. They would stay in the palace because he was son to Huth, lord chancellor to King Randolph. Being son of the king's right hand opened almost all doors in the palace, and few people cared about the dusty rooms housing the histories of Edland, and so, Hoskin had frequently escaped to his places of solitude to read of histories, good and bad. He remembered thinking how marvelous it would be to merely observe life and record it for future scholars without having to be involved.

But he was involved. Up to his armpits, as the animal doctor at the family estate would say. Hoskin sat at the far end of a long wooden table—newly constructed by order of the former King Roland, who had taken a disliking to the ancient one before it—from where stood Jyuth. Hoskin's appearance, a stark contrast to the wizard, appeared rather like a malnourished donkey: long, skeletal and decidedly grey. But this donkey was now chancellor instead of his father.

Another rap on the table and the other members of the privy council turned their attention to the old man.

"Stop this chattering and nattering. Stop this gurgling of worries and whinges." Jyuth did not raise his voice, but the tone boomed deep in Hoskin's bones. "You all know as well as I, Roland was an evil shit, not even one tenth the man of his father. And you are better off without him."

Hoskin had noticed Jyuth had been agitated since he had returned to the city not five days past, after a long absence from the court at Kingshold.

"And you, Cockhead, or whatever your name is. I know what you are thinking. You're new here. I can see it bubbling up in your brain, the way your eyes keep shifting from one of your friends to the next, wondering who will be first to ask who the fuck said an old man has the power over the throne." The wizard leaned forward over the table to stare down his target. "Am I right?"

"Err...my name is Sir Penshead...your honor?" said the knight, dressed in neck-to-toe chainmail under a green tabard emblazoned with a white shield bearing the crest of Kingshold. The newest addition to the privy council was young and dashing, but still finding his place in court after winning Roland's Golden Tourney last year and claiming, in the eyes of Hoskin, at least, the worst job in the whole kingdom as a prize. "I am the knight commander of the city guard. I know it is Lord Beneval who is the commanding officer of the royal guard, and so, I don't have the right to say anything here, but I don't understand why you haven't been clapped in irons. How can a ceremonial title—"

"Ceremonial! Hah! Boy, you don't know anything. You're from some upland sheep-bothering backwater, and you're too dim-witted to take the cue of one of your elders and betters around the table here." Jyuth walked around behind the knight and leaned over his shoulder to whisper in his ear. To Penshead's credit, he didn't flinch. "I am this city. I am this kingdom. If it weren't for me, you would all be the thralls of Pyrfew or slaves in a southern land by now. And if it weren't for me coming along every couple of hundred years and resetting the clock on whichever royal dynasty inevitably becomes so corrupted they do ugly things to dogs or small boys, then you would understand what it's like to live under a mad king."

Hoskin had heard Jyuth referring to himself as one person through history before, but he considered it an affectation. He would not have argued that the man who was holding the balls of everyone around this table was indeed much older than he looked, but it boggled belief one person could be centuries old. Jyuth walked back to his position at the head of the table. Penshead shrank back in his chair slightly. He would likely never admit to being afraid of an old man, but Lords Beneval, Uthridge (the general royal) and Ridgton (the sea marshal) were keeping their mouths closed, and so, it must have finally occurred to him it might be wise to follow suit. As the wizard saw the reaction he was hoping for, he switched his attention and his eyes swept across the other men in the room. Hoskin crossed his fingers under the table and hoped he wouldn't be called out. He sat in his usual position at the other head of the table, typically opposite the king, but today the wizard had that place. Hoskin had the three martial privy council appointees to his left. To his right sat two men who couldn't be more different.

Lord Hoxteth was a small, thin man—not an ounce of excess on his frame—widely regarded as one of the canniest merchants in the whole of the Jeweled Continent. This was how Hoxteth had risen to the privy council, initially as the representative of the Merchants' Guild, and then most recently taking on the role of treasurer to the kingdom.

Next to Lord Hoxteth sat Aebur, a tall, fat man who perspired so much it was possible to see lines of dampness in his shirt, and though he artificially enhanced his scent, the sweetness of the flower water and the sour stench of sweat created a cloying smell that irritated Hoskin from two seats away. Jyuth's gaze settled on the fat man, and, for once, Hoskin's finger-crossing had worked.

"So, it's Aebur, right? The new spymaster." Jyuth paused and only proceeded once Aebur slowly nodded. "I know about you, Aebur. I know the things you did for Roland, and let me make it clear. I. Don't. Approve."

Aebur mopped at his forehead with a silk handkerchief while he tried to remain calm.

"I don't approve, but I will give you the benefit of the

doubt you were only following orders. But you've been warned now, and I only warn someone once. Now, prove to me your worth and tell me what your ears are telling you in the city about the current situation."

"M'lord, there are some rumors amongst the populace, from foreign assassins to sex play gone wrong, but the story most repeated is the wizard is back, and he has brought the true king's heir to replace the tainted couple who died yesterday. Of course, this story has actually occurred at least three times in the past, so no wonder it's so quick to be repeated. Is this true, my lord Jyuth? Do you hide an illegitimate son of Randolph ready to take the crown?"

"Aebur, let me let you in on a little secret. There has never been a true king's heir. Each time, there has never been a blood relation who wasn't crooked." Jyuth walked around the windowless room as he expounded, passing in front of hunting scenes caught in tapestry that served to make the privy council chamber less oppressive. "So, I find a genuine soul with a smart head on their shoulders, and then I teach them how to be a good king or queen. They usually do a passing job of raising their children in the right way, but by the third generation, it often goes to pot. And so, no, this time I do not have a child hiding behind my robes."

"What?" exclaimed Hoskin without realizing he had done so out loud. "I mean, you don't have the new heir? Then what is the plan, my lord?"

"I have decided I obviously don't have all of the answers. A millennium of repeating the same mistakes is enough even for me to realize something is broken. So, what do you all think I should do? How should we choose the next leader of Edland?"

"A tourney!" blurted Penshead.

Hoskin rolled his eyes at the knight's typical answer for any problem. Jyuth gave a little shake of his head.

"It should go to the closest blood relative of Randolph. I think that is the Duke of Northfield, the old king's brother." Beneval's suggestion was sound, but Hoskin knew the Duke of Northfield. He was seventy, had no heirs, and was unlikely to conceive any after a hunting accident when he was a teen —a boar destined for a sausage casing instead skewered Northfield's.

"We should declare martial law," interrupted Uthridge without waiting for a response. "A leadership vacuum will lead to chaos. Our enemies will look to take advantage of this situation. I can lead the country in the interim, ensure it's safe, and then transition to a new ruler in a year. However you choose to do it, I don't mind as long as we have someone who's fit and proper."

"What about you, Lord Jyuth? Why don't you lead us now?" Aebur's simpering tone and toadying up to whoever was in charge had begun already. He had been Roland's favorite. Hoskin was having trouble keeping his breakfast down.

"I've heard about something called elections in the city-states of the Green Desert," began Lord Hoxteth, "a situation where the people as a group choose the overseer."

"Exactly!" Jyuth wheeled on one foot and pointed at the treasurer. "I don't have faith in my ability to make decisions, and I don't trust you six. So, we're going to broaden the decision-making group to all able heads of household."

"What!" exclaimed Ridgton, aghast. "Are you saying all will be able to vote? Even the pond scum past the second wall? Preposterous. People won't stand for it. Those animals don't understand what this means and what their responsibilities would be."

Jyuth walked around the table to stand behind Ridgton's chair and placed his hands on the shoulders of the sea marshal. Ridgton went as stiff as a board. "Admiral, we've known each other a long time. You know I don't want to see the great unwashed involved in this process any more than you. So, there will be an entrance test. Something objective and easy to administer. Anyone who wishes to take part in the election will deposit one thousand gold crowns with me until after the election results have been counted. Should separate the wheat from the chaff, don't you think?"

Ridgton nodded, eager for the wizard's attention to move on.

"In exchange, each voter will receive one of my little demons. They will tell these pyxies their vote in the strictest secrecy, and the pyxies will then bring the overall tallied results to me."

More murmuring around the table, except for Hoskin, who stayed deathly quiet and kept looking at his hands resting on the table.

"Gentlemen," barked Jyuth, "my will on this is final. Four weeks from today, when we have the new moon coinciding with the solstice, there shall be an election for a lord protector of Edland. All men, women, and other races may stand for election, but the one who receives the most pyxies shall be declared the winner. All heads of household within three leagues of the royal palace shall be able to vote if they present themselves personally to me before the election day and deposit a thousand gold crowns into my safekeeping. And that is that. So, get back to whatever you were doing and make this happen."

Hoskin rose, and as he pushed his chair under the table, Jyuth called out, "Hoskin, get the message out. Posters and town criers before the end of the day. And, Hoskin? You others listen up, too." He regarded Hoskin's peers as they got up from the table. "Until after the election, Hoskin, you're in charge. I don't have the patience to do this every day, so you can instead. Don't fuck it up. I would like there to be something left of the place to hand over to the new guy."

CHAPTER 3
SNAKE BELLY VISIONS

The journey south and east from Kingshold—over the Arz Sea, and then across the northern reaches of Pyrfew, the independent city states of the Green Desert that clung to the edge of the Sea of Night, to eventually arrive at this sweaty, stinky jungle—had taken roughly a week. Neenahwi's preferred form for a long journey like this was a goose, the wing span and aerodynamic body making the flight smoother and less arduous than if she was to take one of the other forms she used for shorter distances or for hunting.

In the days when she lived on the plains of Missapik, what seemed a lifetime ago, the arrival of geese heralded the beginning of winter. The large birds weren't native to the prairies or the hills bordering the lands of her tribe. They came from the east and disappeared to the west, only pausing to rest and take on water. Those would be a frantic few days each season, to see how many birds the tribe could take down with arrow and spear, while remembering to be respectful of the strength in those wings and what it could do to a hunter if they got too close.

Years later, after the destruction of her clan, the death of her parents and the estrangement of her brother, Neenahwi had noticed many of these large brown geese spent much of the year around Kingshold, her new home.

As she had mastered the ability to change her form, the goose had been the second one she had sought to master, so she knew she could always fly home at any time. The first being the wolf, to be able to remember the spirit animal of her tribe.

Nearly twelve years had passed since then, and she had yet to make the long journey back. Who knew what was left of her homeland since Pyrfew had started the steady shipment of slaves and resources from what these easterners called the Wild Continent? But that land still called to her, still drove many of her actions. If she were to trace her steps, even this journey was driven by her need to one day go home and right wrongs.

Neenahwi sat cross-legged on the damp earth by a campfire she had coerced to life, using magic when the humid air had foiled traditional means. She could tell her destination was close, but she meant to find out more.

She wore a simple silk robe of purple, wrinkled from being in the pack she had carried as she flew. Transformation only affected her physical body, so clothing was always an issue, and Neenahwi had decided a few years ago that being naked often created problems when dealing with easterners. So, she had crafted a small leather pack to use for travel, wearable over her neck while in the form of a goose, and able to carry a few small essentials. The silk robe being chief among them and the smallest item of clothing she could pack.

Her hair reached down to the middle of her back. When in Kingshold, she would braid it to keep it out of her face. Here in the jungle, she settled for the old methods and used fresh mud from the bank of a small stream to slick it back and hold it in place. Neenahwi's skin was olive brown with thin scars slightly visible on her arms and face from a life that had held a certain number of challenges.

One of the snakes she had caught after landing, constrictors that were far from fully grown, was already dressed and roasting over the fire. The second squirmed in her grasp as she moved one hand closer to its head.

"Stay still! Bloody snakes!" grunted Neenahwi through clenched teeth. They were always much harder to handle than rabbits or squirrels or raccoons. The squirming (and the fangs on some) was unwelcome, but the results were frequently worth the effort.

One hand held the snake below the head, pushing it close to the earth, while her other hand gently placed a large rock on it to keep it belly up. A second large rock pinned the tail down, and she pulled out the small steel knife she had brought with her. She had learnt how to read the entrails at the feet of Greytooth, her clan's old shaman, how to answer questions or see shadows of the future. She had loved her old teacher once, but now his memory was fractured like an image on running water, and her skills greatly surpassed what the shaman knew.

Shaman, witch doctors, hedge wizards. They were all the same. They all had some connection with the unseen energies that powered this world and connected all living things. But they relied on crutches to make their magic. Ceremonies or drugs to set their minds at just the right angle to grab hold of the threads and weave.

What set real magicians apart was mental discipline, even though she had to admit she didn't know many (mainly just her new father). Magician, mage, wizard, sorcerer. She had heard all the labels applied to her father. But it all came back to the confidence to grab the world with a metaphysical hand and mold it, and the practice to be able to use the mind like a tool that was readily available and didn't require a roomful of acolytes singing in harmony to get in the mood.

She brought forth her concentration, quickly releasing other unrequited thoughts, and then divided her consciousness in her meditating mind. Two Neenahwi's in one shell, both calm and at peace. One aspect of Neenahwi held the knife over the exposed lighter skin of the snake belly that continued to squirm away from its bound position. The other aspect of Neenahwi saw the energy of the nagual, the little ball of red light hovering around its heart.

It was an odd fact: certain energy sources were better for certain tasks than others. She didn't know why, but snakes, calves, and virgins had long been the sacrifices of choice for the uncultured magic worker; their selection, chosen by experiment or even luck, did not dim their suitability.

She watched detached as her arm struck down and drove the knife into the snake's body, and as she did so, the red ball of energy leaked out in tendrils from the wound. Greytooth would have used invocations and chanting to channel and spin this energy into the needed Thread, but she knew those words did nothing.

Her mind was in control, and it seized the living mana, pulling it forcefully from the beast's body and stretching it into a long, fine filament. One end connected to her forehead, and she cast the other out before her as if she was fishing with a rod. The thread flew through the air and appeared to catch on something in the distance, the end wavering in her sight...

...the jungle camp disappeared, and a stone door, hidden beneath overgrowth, appeared...

...now a dark cavern, lit by torches; two humans, naked with tattoos on their arms and faces, feeding a captured jungle cat kept in a bamboo cage...

...across to the other side of the cavern where two tattooed naked women knelt before another woman, almost blue from ink inscribed in her skin...

...something hung around her neck...

...a red stone on a dull iron chain...

...tainted green meat forced into the mouths of the kneeling women...

...smoke from censers, stinging the eyes...

...a wet red mist exploding into the air...

The vision was brief but useful. Neenahwi knew they had what she wanted, and a few foolish demon cultists should not pose much trouble.

Nevertheless, she wouldn't take anything for granted. An approach in stealth at night would be best. And so, she looked forward to having a good long sleep on a full belly of snake.

Shit, I'm not ready for this. Neenahwi's mind raced. No one had been on watch when she had entered the caverns through the stone door she had seen in the snake vision. That in itself was not too concerning, so she had crept down the tunnel, walking barefoot and able to feel every contour of the floor. She sidestepped three different alarms: crude but effective bone and string contraptions that would create quite a racket for anyone blundering through them in the dark. Neenahwi did not make a habit of blundering around.

No one was on guard at the end of the passageway either, which seemed more unusual; someone should be on watch during the night, especially with five of them. She wondered if they were even more amateurish than she had anticipated, which wouldn't be a bad thing; five cuts of the knife in the dark were better than a fight any day.

That was when she saw a glistening darkness on the wall opposite, by a tunnel leading from the chamber. As she stared, it became apparent it was blood, and what she had first mistaken for lichen and mold on the rocks was bits of flesh and hair.

Shit! What did those idiots do?

Neenahwi's hand went to the quiver tied to her waist by a thin cord. She pulled out three identical arrows: sleek pointed tips without barbs, a foot of thin steel, flights made of sharp razor blades instead of feathers.

Stepping slowly forward, she crossed the chamber and into the short tunnel, being careful not to be heard. From the dark, she could see the cavern beyond, a large hexagonal space, apparently carved by some sentient creature, with tunnels at each angle. She counted three bodies around the room and saw a fourth cultist leaning against the wall across from her. He moaned, pawing at his pale face, losing blood from a leg that ended without a foot.

In the middle of the room, contained within a circle protected by runes, stood a large figure, female from the waist down with the broad chest, long-taloned arms, and the head of a jungle panther. The demon—because that was clearly what the cultists had done, gone and summoned an actual demon, and likely a queen by the size—paced her circle of confinement looking for ways of escape.

It seemed like the cultists had set the circle warding correctly, a pentagram with a binding rune at each corner, but they must have done it with them on the inside. And once the demon had appeared and attacked, the cultists had been tossed across the cavern. The remains of the one Neenahwi had seen on the wall would have been smashed into it with tremendous force.

The type of mistake you only make once.

The blue-furred face of the demon sniffed at the air, eyes turning to where Neenahwi lurked in the shadows. "I see you, mortal. I have no fight with you. Come out into the open and let me free. I will bring you such wealth you never dreamed of." The voice was deep and proud. The *R* sounds vividly reminded Neenahwi of her cat at home, the sound it made when she rubbed behind its ear.

"Demon," Neenahwi called, "I am not as foolish as those scattered about this cave. I have imprisoned and killed your brethren before, and I have no interest in doing so today. You are bound, and you can stay bound for all I care."

Neenahwi stepped out from the tunnel and ambled toward the runed circle. The cat beast turned to face her fully and proceeded to bang her claws against the shimmering shape of force surrounding her. She spat and snarled at the affront of being caged.

Oh shit.

Around the cat's neck was the gem she had traveled such a long distance to obtain, the object of years of research. She was not going to let it stay imprisoned with the demon. So now the question was, would she have to do this the hard way or the really hard way?

She split her mind once, one aspect staying focused on the demon, the other focused on the cultist at the back of the room who was not yet dead but getting close.

In humans, some thought the equivalent of the red ball in the snake as the soul, and it might well be, but it was still the same basic magic that could be used by someone skillful enough. And as Jyuth had taught her, all magic had to come from somewhere, and it was better it came from someone else other than you. So, she weaved a thin thread of mana from the cultist to her, and then back to the cultist, creating a delicate lattice across all of his body, the blood flow slowing from the wounded leg as it became encased by the invisible energy.

"Maybe I have been too hasty, oh queen of lies, countess of codswallop. Tell me what you will give me. Tell me how you think we can make a deal..."

The rage in the demon subsided, and the feline head tilted to one side as it considered Neenahwi afresh. The look it gave her reminded her of the camp cats from when she was a child—hoping for a treat from the dinner bowl. She needed to stop thinking this thing was like a tabby.

"Your words are mocking human, but you should know, in your language you would consider me royalty. I have thousands of minions who do my bidding and fight my wars. I'm not to be fucked around with—"

"That may be, but you seem to be short of minions right about now," interrupted Neenahwi, "and I'm pretty sure they don't know where you are. It won't take long for one of your ambitious captains to see there's an empty throne that needs keeping warm." As she spoke, Neenahwi twirled one of the arrows nimbly in her fingers, the other two clasped in her left hand.

"What are you going to do with that, girl?" asked the demon. "You have no bow! And these walls that stop me from getting out stop you from getting in. If I were free, you would only have time to loose one before I would be upon you. But, of course, if you were to free me, I would guarantee your health. And I would grant you one wish. You can name any item, any amount of money, and nothing in this world could stop me from bringing it to you. I, Barax, would be your ally against any foe."

"How will you bind this oath, Barax? I don't trust you, and I'm sure you don't blame me for that. I know what I would have for payment, but I still call you a liar."

"I swear with blood," said the demon. A claw raked deep furrows across her chest, brown ichor seeping out. "With eye"—a yellow nail put out an eye from the panther's socket, and then pulled a canine from her mouth—"and with fang, and that I will be permanently banished to this annoying mudball for all eternity if I break my word. Your health is safeguarded, and your reward is assured. There, I have spoken binding words; now free me!"

Neenahwi considered the situation for a moment and gave a shrug. That little show was more than she had expected. Maybe it would turn out fine after all.

She nodded toward the body her other aspect had been concentrating on, which, even though she had stanched the bleeding, was rapidly nearing death. The cultist lurched upright as if a marionette, a small whimper coming from him, but his eyes not opening. The unconscious cultist stumbled over to the side of the circle imprisoning the demon, and then began rubbing out the runes with his one remaining foot. He balanced on the other stump of a leg, the shuffling action looking like a drunkard trying to dance at a wedding.

"It seems I underestimated you, girl. You have talent..." The demon stared intently at the man as he danced in place, eventually rubbing away at the rune until the shimmering translucent wall around the demon disappeared. "Ah, freedom!" Barax stretched her arms wide, and she seemed to grow in height and width. "So now, my liberator, what is it you would have?"

"I'll take the amulet around your neck."

"No. I will not give that up. Choose something else." The demon took a step forward past the cultist who had slumped over but remained upright.

"I'm afraid that is all I want. And you made an oath, Barax. Do the oaths of demon queens mean nothing anymore?"

"I made you an oath on my freedom, on my ability to go back to my world, and my home. I need this bauble to do that. With what you ask, then I am cursed either way."

Shit. Neenahwi knew this demon was not the brightest, but Barax was catching up now; she was cornered. Facing off against a cornered panther was not a fun way to spend a weekday. Doing the same with a panther demon is a death sentence for most. Neenahwi knew she likely had five seconds to be ready for the assault, and be ready with her offense. Withdrawing further into her mind, she fractured it once, twice, three times more, ready to—

—on the three-second mark, the demon roared and leaped toward Neenahwi, teeth bared, claws outstretched, a look of madness on the crazed feline visage. However, the cultist had snapped to attention and a fighting stance a second before, no longer the shambling laughing stock. The cultist stood on the blind side of Barax, and so, the demon did not see as the cultist dove to tackle it to the ground.

The demon spun, and with one claw, ripped the head from the cultist, his body thrown across the floor. Barax got to her feet, but so did the body of the cultist, only a little blood bubbling up from its broken neck, and the walking corpse positioned itself between Neenahwi and beast.

On the count of five, the three arrows Neenahwi held in her hands lifted into the air, twisting to point toward their target. A separate aspect of her mind controlled each missile, creating a thread from her own oh-so-valuable and oh-so-finite life force to enable the deliberately constructed items to ignore the laws of gravity. Each arrow paused for a split second and pointed at Barax before flying off in various arcs.

The demon moved forward intent on rending the former cultist limb from limb, to stop this annoyance so it could move to kill Neenahwi.

She realized it was always going to end this way. The demon was cursed now, forever bereft of its home, and now it just wanted to get at the bitch which had caused it. She didn't blame it.

It took one step forward, and then the first arrow flew down from the cavern's unlit ceiling, moving at tremendous speed and hitting it in the breast. The arrow pierced the demon's skin, and without a reduction in speed, continued to travel through its torso, exiting around the small of its back. The sharp razor flights on the arrow inflicted greater damage as the missile sliced through. The demon roared as the second arrow came from behind and punctured a kneecap, bringing it to the floor. The third bolt adjusted its flight as its target fell, and it came down to bury itself in the back of the panther's skull, a metal on stone *snick* as the arrow tip made contact with the smooth granite surface of the floor.

Moments passed. The demon's chest heaved. Brown blood oozed onto the floor around its chest and knee. In the momentary lull, Neenahwi became aware of a sound coming from elsewhere underground, a distant rumbling. Hopefully it was nothing more than an underground river she hadn't noticed before because there was still life in Barax.

The demon clambered to its feet, lower leg below the broken knee impossibly twisted but still, somehow, holding the weight of the beast. Feline teeth clenched around the arrow head piercing the back of its head. A clawed hand reached up and gripped the tip of the arrow, opened its jaws, and pulled the arrow through, not seeming to notice the damage the sharp tail of the missile caused in its passage. Grasping the shaft in both hands, the demon snapped it in two.

"Nice try, little woman, but a wasp sting will not kill a panther. It's just going to make it pissed off."

The dead cultist moved once again to block the demon's progression to Neenahwi, but the demon was truly upset now. A powerful blow sent the body flying back to hit Neenahwi and knock her against the wall.

Her concentration on the connection to the mangled cultist's body wavered as the last of its life force flowed away. The magical forces moving the body disappeared along with the containment energies that had been keeping the body largely in one piece. Blood erupted over Neenahwi from the multiple wounds released as one, blinding her to the demon's deliberate advance on its injured leg.

The demon continued to track the two remaining arrows in the air, swatting at them as they neared it. Once or twice the arrows were deflected onto the floor, with a metallic *ting*, only to lift again into the air and buzz around Barax.

Shit.

Shit.

Shit.

Neenahwi couldn't see a way out of this without using a serious amount of personal mana. The barren cave offered no other sources of energy. *This gem had better be worth it.* It could take a long time to recover, and as she considered the thought of recuperating in the hot, humid, bug-infested jungle, it didn't please her.

But the noise from the tunnel to the south of the cavern was definitely growing louder. Not a river then. Something was getting closer.

The sound turned out to be not so much an *it* as roughly two hundred *its*, the *its* being a whole tribe of jungle goblins, armed to the teeth with bows, curved swords, and notched daggers. Neenahwi sighed.

If she could bring those cultists back to life right now, she would do it in a heartbeat. Just so she could show them how stupid they were to pick a hideout in the annex to a goblin hive where they were planning to summon a demon to do their bidding while on the wrong side of the protective wardings! She would bring them back to life, and then kill them again just for really screwing up her day.

The appearance of scores of upset goblins did not improve Barax's mood either, though it did distract her for a moment, especially as the first goblin arrows arced toward her. The body of the cultist provided some cover for Neenahwi, so the goblins had yet to notice her. Taking advantage of the demon's new shift in focus, she sent the two remaining arrows toward the demon at the same time, the first parried away, but the second striking the chain of the amulet, causing it to snap. The necklace fell to the floor.

The first arrow swooped around and threaded through the clasp of the amulet to lift it into the air and deposit it into Neenahwi's hand. The demon tried to scramble after the amulet, but the first wave of goblins hit her at the same time. The goblins were no match for the demon: each swing of a furred, clawed arm smashed into three or four of the grey, scrawny humanoids, only for more to replace them.

Neenahwi finished wiping the blood from her eyes and considered which way to run, because running was definitely the best course of action. She could sense some stirring of fresh air from the corridor to the north of this room, hopefully a way out and not just an air duct. She crouched, collected the aspects of her mind so she would be fully present, and then sprang from her place of cover, running for the passageway ahead.

More goblins had joined the fight against the demon, but a few had also realized it was not a good fight to get into if you were a goblin that valued its scrawny neck. The appearance of a new figure running across the cavern that was definitely not goblin—and equally definitively, and more importantly, not demon—caused a score of goblins to break off in pursuit of Neenahwi.

As she ran, she stole one last look at the demon that was carving its way through an entire goblin village, a demon now trapped in this world by her, and which was probably not going to die of its current wounds. But her feet pounding into the hard stone of the passageway reminded her that would be a problem for tomorrow.

The tunnel went upwards and upwards, twisting left and right—so there was no clear shot for a goblin arrow—until it eventually reached a breach in the wall. She dove into the crack, squirming her way forward, and for the first time that day, she had some luck as she burst out from a fissure in a rock face covered in jungle growth.

She could hear the pursuing goblins scrabbling through the breach, so Neenahwi turned to run again. But with her first step, the ground fell away from her, and before she knew it, she was sliding down a muddy hillside on her backside toward an impending edge, and then into the blue of the open sky.

Shiiiiiiiiiiiitttttttttt.

CHAPTER 4
MEETING THE WIZARD

Alana was a slip of a girl: sparrow-like in frame and motion, head twitching to keep aware of what was happening around her so she could train her full bright eyes on what occurred. It gave her the appearance of being afraid of her surroundings, like a cat mistreated by a previous owner and becoming mistrustful of strangers; but, in fact, she was fascinated by the palace world around her.

She had been born in Kingshold, in the area outside the second wall known as the Narrows, where the buildings were built so close together they were separated by narrow, crooked alleyways in place of roads. The unwary—who might not be familiar with that part of town, and who might stumble down those narrow passageways—would likely as not find themselves at a dead end, only to turn around and find themselves face-to-face with a few stern individuals eager to help them understand how a dead end got its name.

But Alana had grown up in the Narrows, and she was known there by most, if not all. Known for two reasons in particular. First of all, she was the sister of Petra, the striking sort of young woman who set the hearts racing of many a red-blooded lad (or lass). The second was that folks realized Alana was smart and she could tell which way the wind was about to blow.

If someone was to go to the building where Alana and Petra lived alone—as their parents had died some years ago of plague—and see Mrs. Skrudd, who lived next door, then she would say, "That girl, Alana, she'd make anyone proud to be her mum, she would.

"Do you know she saw the head cook on the first day when she went to the palace? She arrived at the trader's gate just as he was kicking out the last poor sod who had made a mistake or dropped summing, and so, she got a job scrubbing pots.

"And then within a fortnight, she helped the head maid get rid of a mouse in her rooms, and so, she got a job cleaning above stairs. Sitting pretty she was for six months with that job.

"Then, one day, when she was cleaning outside a room of a guest, she heard a coughing and a gurgling, like someone choking, and then you know how her eyes narrow a little when she is concentrating on summing, I'm sure she did that. She realized it was a guest in the room she was standing outside of. Me, I'd have scarpered, let me tell you. I wouldn't want to be around when an ambassador or some hobnob kicks the bucket, but she ran in and squeezed this big man around the belly until a bit of chicken bone popped right out of his mouth. Saved his life, she did. He said he wanted to marry her, even though he was already married!

"And then she came back here with so much food and wine from the chief steward that we had a street party! And not just that, she had been made a real maid, too, to look after guests and other important nobs. And all in less than a year. And what has my Tina done? Nuffin..."

And so, that was how Alana came to be tidying up after breakfast in Jyuth's room as he returned from the meeting of the privy council. Her hand was on the teapot, lifting it to her tray a moment before she looked up to stare at the doors out to the palace gardens that were the entrance to the wizard's apartments. Jyuth walked in, his girth giving him a slight circular motion in his gait that made Alana think of a skittle unsure whether to fall or not. He wore sky blue pants and tunic, which apparently was his style.

She hadn't known that before last week. The other servants had sourced great amusement in her not realizing the man she had drawn the short straw to look after was the very same one from her history lessons in the one-room school she had gone to while her parents still lived.

He wore a brown, leather belt around his middle, many pouches and containers of glass or shining silver along its length. And above each hip, attached to the belt with a unique fastening Alana had not seen before, were the two coppery metal disks she had heard could fly through the air at the wizard's command. So sharp, they could split a hair or take a head off its shoulders...

When Jyuth arrived at the palace a week ago, he had been dusty from the road and immediately requested a bath. Alana was drawing it when one of the king's guards, the tall one with the long scar from elbow to thumb, had appeared at the doorway and commanded the presence of the wizard before the king. She could tell Jyuth had not been happy to be summoned in such a way, and he was positively furious on returning to his chamber a little over an hour later—by then the water for the bath had turned tepid, and Alana had to bring hot water again. For each of the next four days, she attended to the old man's needs (she had calculated he was at least 958 years old, even though he didn't look a day over fifty) in between his times meditating in an antechamber or meeting with other prominent people. Daily, he would meet with the king, and it would leave him incensed or have him muttering and shaking his head on his return, which would then require a period of meditation to bring him a certain measure of calm.

And then on the sixth day, when she had arrived in the morning with his breakfast, she had found the room empty, and it had remained so all day. That was the day before yesterday. Yesterday morning being when Jyuth had returned to the palace and strode directly to the king's quarters without being summoned. Alana had heard from Sarah—who knew one of the palace guards a little too well (especially considering he was betrothed)—that the old man had calmly strode up to the king and queen at their breakfast table. They always began their day with wine and a smoke while the lord chancellor—that empty man who wore the robes of his father, according to Sarah—read to them the news from the city and the realm beyond. The way she told it was Jyuth whispered something to the king and queen, their faces changing from indignation at being interrupted to that of shock and fear. And then, those very same copper circles he wore at his belt had risen in the air before moving so fast they were a blur of orange, and then red as they sliced through the necks of the royal couple.

The guards on duty, taken by surprise, had apparently hesitated, caught between protecting their liege and his wife—which they were too late to do anything about—and protecting their necks. Luckily for them, it gave the lord chancellor enough time to order them to stand down.

Alana had heard of this many hours after the fact, of course. She had heard the hubbub elsewhere in the palace, but she had known to remain in this series of rooms in a separate building in the palace garden, where the wizard resided. After she had heard about the fate of the royal couple, the first thing she had thought of was she was glad it hadn't been her that would need to clean it up.

Jyuth had come back to his rooms shortly afterward, and he had looked positively cheery, a smile on his face as big as those her dad would have when he had come home with a few pieces of gold and gifts for the family after being away at sea for months at a time. Yesterday was when Jyuth had looked her in the eye for the first time and asked her name.

Today, the wizard dropped himself onto a sedan chair and crossed his feet atop a small mahogany table. He'd stopped whistling, but again seemed to be in good spirits.

"Ah, Alana, there you are. Your presence makes me happy! Do you know why?"

Alana shook her head.

"Because you're going to fetch me some good bread and cheese and some warm beer. And maybe some ham, too." He gave a little laugh and patted his rotund belly to pantomime where the food was going to go. "You know talking to these fools makes me hungry, but by Krask, it's fun. I feel younger already."

She smiled, nodding, but avoided eye contact while she backed out of the room before running to the kitchen. When she returned, he was sitting in a different chair by the unlit fireplace, a book in his hands. She placed the tray on the small side table next to his seat.

"I hope this meets your needs, my lord," she said, giving a little curtsy like Bertha the head maid taught her.

"Excellent, excellent. And you brought apples and those fine olives from Faria, I see. Excellent! I do love independent thinking." He grabbed a piece of cheese, tore off a chunk of bread from the loaf, and waved his arm at the seat opposite him. "Please, sit. Now tell me, Alana, where do you hail from?"

"I am from Kingshold, my lord," replied Alana. Some may have thought the tone of her voice to be timid, but that wasn't her. Wary, like the sparrow, too smart to be caught. "The Narrows."

"And do you know who I am?"

"Yes, m'lord. You are the kingmaker, protector of Edland. Jyuth the wise and terri... er, terrific."

"Hah! It's quite alright, dear. I have heard people call me terrible before. And do you know? They're right." A glint briefly appeared in the old man's eyes, then he leaned back in his chair and blew out a sigh. "Or at least I used to be much more terrible in years past. Our enemies knew it, and so did the kings I made. It seems the reputation of my terribleness stopped at Molly Brown's sweet shop at the edge of the Narrows. Is it still there?"

Alana nodded.

"They had marvelous sugar mints, if I recall correctly. Excellent. Anyway, it looks like that reputation has not made its way up to the palace in the past five years."

Alana sat quietly, unsure of what to say.

Jyuth was quiet, too, apparently thinking about something. "And has news of the king and queen made its way down to the Narrows? I killed them, you know. Not the first king I've killed, but I intend it to be the last. I'm quite weary of it."

"Yes, m'lord. Everyone heard the news very fast about the king. There were some who were saying it would happen as soon as you walked back into the city. They probably had a few coppers on that happening and have done quite well for themselves." She answered his question, and she was beginning to feel more comfortable. It made her daring enough to ask a question herself. "If it makes you so weary, m'lord, why did you do it?"

"The details are of no concern of yours, girl," he said, not unkindly. "Suffice it to say, they were doing something that displeased me greatly. And so, I stopped it at the source."

Jyuth put the last of the ham into his mouth, wiped his lips with his forearm, and pushed the tray away from him. "I'm done. And now, I'll need quiet contemplation time, good for the mind and the digestion. I thank you, Alana, for your refreshments and company. You'll hear more news back in the Narrows later today. I don't want to spoil the surprise, though. Keep your eyes and ears open, and then tell me tomorrow all the juicy gossip. I do love gossip."

Jyuth smiled, stood, and walked to his meditation room. Alana was still melded with her chair, processing the conversation she had just had with one of the most powerful men in history.

"Go, girl! Be off with you! Go and read a book or something. I have no further need of you today."

Alana snapped out of her thoughts. She rushed to the tray, tidied the things on it, and turned on her heels to leave the room. Closing the door quietly behind her, she stole a glance through the crack at Jyuth going through his stretches.

The wizard had spoken to her! She wondered if Petra would believe it when she told her. But then it occurred to her: would the wizard approve, or would he strike her dead, too, for tattle telling? It seemed like he wanted to talk to her tomorrow, and she wanted to do so, too. She resolved to be safe and keep this to herself. Now, what was the last order he had given her? Oh yes, read a book. Where should she go and get a book to read?

Alana traveled home that evening with the sun still shining brightly in the sky. She loved the long days as summer approached. Alana had received no further duties from the wizard all day, and so, waiting an hour after their conversation just to be certain she had truly been dismissed, Alana had gone in search of a book.

She knew of the palace library, and she was quite sure the books in there weren't for servants like her. But Jyuth had ordered her to read a book. And he must be the most important person left in the kingdom, so if she didn't get a book to read, then she would be ignoring his command, which would mean big trouble. At least, that was how she had justified it to herself so she could trick her sparrow instincts to enter the library with confidence. She knew it would not do to be seen sneaking around.

The library was as deserted as it had been on the other occasions she had walked past it, but the walls were full from floor to vaulted ceiling with leather-bound tomes. So many books!

She had only ever read two books in her whole life. *The Formation of Edland*, the history book on the creation of the kingdom that all students at Ms. Grange's schoolhouse used to practice their words once they had moved beyond the slate.

And secondly, *The Merry Man of Mincester*, a book her father had given her when he had returned from one of his stints onboard ship. That book differed considerably from the history book, mainly revolving around a young man who loved drink and loved women and was probably not the book a father would give a daughter, but her dad could barely read. It was her most treasured possession, and she had read it cover to cover hundreds of times. Now, though, she could choose whatever book she wanted.

Her fingertips gently touched the spines of the books as she strolled past the shelves, scanning the titles. Here was *A History of Ducal Cavalry Engagements*, next to *The Flora and Fauna of Underground Caverns*, and below it *Collected Poems of the Purple Night-Women*. She stopped and pulled out one book called *A Treatise on the City-States of the Green Desert*.

The cover had a simple drawing of a building, which looked like a palace in grandeur, but instead of the hard, solid lines that made up the Palace of Kingshold, this structure was all circles and sweeping curves.

She opened the book to look inside at the contents when she heard a scratching noise around the corner. There must be someone in the desk nook, and she hadn't thought to check!

Her heart in her mouth, she crept forward to peer half an eye around the bookshelves and see who was there.

Alana felt a crushing pressure on her shoulders as she realized who was in the library with her. It was Lord Chancellor Hoskin.

If anyone might hold more power than Jyuth, it would be

him. Bertha had told her earlier he was in charge now. If she got caught, she knew she would be fired or even thrown into the cells, and then anything could happen to her. And what would happen to Petra without her to look after her? Alana exhaled a steady stream, stopping her mind from racing away from her.

It didn't look like he had noticed her yet. His writing into a large blue book consumed his attention, and she, thankfully, was used to being as quiet as a pallbearer. Alana stepped backward, trying to remain on tiptoe at the same time, until she reached the doorway and made her escape, taking the quiet passages known to servants. Then, as she stopped to catch her breath, she realized she still had the book in her hands.

And now she gripped the book under her old grey cloak as she walked through the Floral Gate from the Upper Circle, out into the Middle.

The Middle was the space between the Inner and Outer Walls, which stretched from the guard barracks built into the walls of Mount Tiston that protected Kingshold on two sides, all the way down to the busy docks and the harbor with its deep-water entrance to the sound and the seas beyond. The Middle had many districts, most of which Alana had no business with. Merchants were all over but concentrated closer to the warehouses and main market square; and the Justicery included the City Gaol, Court, and Lawyers' offices, as well as many places of residence for people of different means. All of whom were a class or two, or three, above Alana.

For her, the Middle was just something in between where she worked and where she lived in the Narrows, and it was the Lance which was the most direct route home for her.

The stores and shopfronts were either closed or packing up for the night as Alana hurried down the street, dodging other pedestrians and carts and wagons that came perilously close to the pavement. As she walked, she kept careful eyes on her surroundings, nervous about the package she carried.

She noticed a few spotters from the Twilight Exiles, Charlie, Tam, and Gammy Pete. The Exiles were the largest crime organization in Kingshold, not an official guild, more a pyramid hustle for the older members on the youngsters, but still better able to police illegal activity than the city guard. They, in turn, paid her more notice than they normally would, but no more than a few seconds each as they went back to scanning the crowds. *There must be some job underway*, she thought, but Alana knew better than to have any interest.

Eventually, Alana came to the Red Gate in the Outer Wall, passing through it, and out into the Hub, the area that had grown over the past few hundred years beyond the Outer Wall.

The Lance became the Pike here (a commoner might have a pike, but only a knight would have a lance), wider and busier than within the Middle, all the way out to the final wall that now surrounded Kingshold. Carndall's Curtain, named after the king who began construction of the wall that should have been three times longer than the inner and outer wall combined. But that would be expensive. That was why some of it had yet to be completed, particularly in the back of the Narrows, where the wall was thin enough that light was sometimes visible through the cracks.

Alana crossed the street and ducked through a crowd at the entrance to the top alley of the Narrows, where roads navigable by beast and cart stopped and the buildings leaned on top of each other for support. In many places, the alleyways became tunnels as the wood and stone houses reached across to touch each other. The evidence of the mass of humanity that was the Narrows assaulted the senses for those not used to it; laundry hung from windows, smells of cooking from simple kitchens, sounds of arguments and the successive agreements filling the air as Alana dodged the porters with their hand carts of produce.

Many people called out to Alana as she walked; she took care to wave with her free hand, as she headed back to the small home she shared with her sister on a small stone courtyard. A crowd of fifteen or so people gathered by the Dumb Crier (the wooden notice-board, which had replaced the Town Criers who used to come into the Narrows to spread official news), and Alana realized there had been three or four similar groups on her walk home. Elbowing her way to the front, she saw the freshly written notice, and now she knew what Jyuth had been referring to earlier that day.

ATTENTION, GOOD CITIZENS OF KINGSHOLD. WE THANK KING Roland and Queen Tulip for their years of service acting as stewards of the realm. Their unfortunate demise in a court-related accident, having passed on without heirs or a clear line of succession, has now created an opportunity for you, the people, to decide on a new lord protector of Edland via an election or counting of votes. The rules of this election shall be as follows:

I. Any person of good standing can nominate themselves as a candidate for lord protector

II. The candidate who receives the most votes will be named lord protector

III. The election will take place twenty-eight days from this announcement, on the day of the summer solstice

IV. Each head of household in good standing will be able to cast a vote in the election. Once cast, their vote cannot be changed

V. To meet the requirement of being a person in good standing, any individual must own property within three leagues of the palace of Kingshold, present themselves in front of the lord wizard, who will ensure impartiality of the vote, and place one thousand gold crowns on deposit until after the election.

I AM SURE YOU LOOK FORWARD TO THIS EXCITING PROGRESSION in the development of the realm.

LORD HOSKIN
Chancellor of Edland

CHAPTER 5

MERCHANT GOSSIP

"Mareth!"

Mareth's eyes opened slightly, and though he meant to say, "Who is that," it came out more like, "Mmmmo ffss vvhrrt?" His face stuck to something solid and stopped his mouth from moving.

With a wrench, he jerked upright, pain exploding behind his eyes. "Where am I?" Mareth focused on his surroundings; the large common room full of customers, at long tables, in private booths, and seated in front of a great stone fireplace came into focus. And so did the memories of last night. This was the Royal Oak.

"Mareth, you need to get up from that bloody table and let me clean up. It's dinnertime. It's busy. And I need the table for punters who actually pay me in coin, not song." The woman who spoke was of middle years, wearing a simple well-cut dress of cotton, lavender in color (which as an uncommon pigment showed her wealth), with a leather apron worn over the top tied at her trim waist. She had a handsome face and dark brown hair pulled back into a bun on the top of her head, a few lines of grey showing. But that didn't matter to Mareth, he found the landlady of the Royal Oak to be quite alluring.

"Why, hello, beautiful Jules," he said, trying to make himself somewhat presentable, acutely aware the beard on one side of his face had become rather matted and stuck out at an angle. "How are you this morning? It seems like I dozed off."

He smiled at her and considered her appearance further. Yes, she was a few years older than him, but those years had been kind to her. Some would say that was the product of hard work, and owning this place was surely hard work. It made her lean and strong. He had seen her extract many a drunken trouble-causer herself over the years, even though a bouncer was usually on duty. She was not a woman to be trifled with, though he often tried. "Wait. Did you say it was dinnertime? How long have I been sitting here?"

"How much of last night do you remember? Come to think of it, how much of the night before can you remember?" she asked.

Mareth held up two fingers in a pinch, indicating not much.

"Well, last night you were still telling tales and singing songs when I went to bed and left Garth in charge. That was two or three o'clock. And then you were still in the same place when I woke up to make sure breakfast was being made." She shook her head. "I was at least glad to see you'd managed to keep more than a dozen punters here all night with you. Folks who actually paid their tabs..." She let the point hang there for a moment, the meaning all too clear, before continuing. "Anyway, when I came down, you were all telling me how you created these hilarious new songs about various lords and ladies, I think. I suggested you write them down while you could still remember them. So, I brought you parchment and pen from my own collection."

"You did, Jules? You are truly an amazing woman." Hope rose in Mareth. Maybe this would be it, his start of something more important in life. It almost made him ignore the queasiness climbing up from his stomach. "Do you have the notes?"

"Hah! I don't have anything, you sweet fool." Jules patted him on the cheek, as one might a boy on his way to his first day at school. "There is the paper on the table in front of you. And the only thing you managed to put down is six hours of drool."

Mareth clapped his hands to his head and stared down.

"You can't remember anything about those songs now?"

He shook his head. "No, I can't. Again." The need to vomit rose in him. Somebody stoked a bonfire in the space behind his eyes. The combined smell of flower water Jules used on her hair with the leather of her apron was not helping matters.

She bent closer and whispered gently, "You've gone white as a sheet, Mareth. Come over here, and you can sit at the bar. I'll get you something to eat. Something nice and greasy with a beer to wash it down." She helped him to his feet. "And then I can have a whole party of folks at this table, too."

She smiled and winked at him. His stomach flipped; as a result of the smile or the after effects of the night before? He considered it to be too difficult a question to answer at that moment, so he followed her back over to the long oaken bar.

~

"...I HEARD THAT EDEN IS GOING TO STAND TO BE protector. Him and Hoxteth. Also, Jimmy said a woman down the wash house told his wife that Lady Chalice is going to sign up at the palace. Oh, yeah, and Chancellor Hoskin, too, but who'd want that miserable toady as lord protector?"

Mareth had recovered enough to be able to focus on devouring the plate of greasy pig, bread, and gravy in front of him, but his ears were drawn to the conversation of two merchants along the bar. From the looks of them, they were reasonably successful, doing better than a single store owner, but not one of the ones with a handful of warehouses to their name. The first one who spoke was fair-skinned with a beard of blond whiskers kept short to match his trim haircut, apparently the style right now, though Mareth had no truck with that.

"Where'd you hear that rubbish? Eden and Hoxteth, I'll buy, but Chalice ain't going to get in the middle of this. Except for a contract. The Hollow Syndicate will make a mint." The second who spoke was dark-skinned and clean shaven, and he had a leather satchel on the bar in front of him next to the bottle of wine they were sharing.

Mareth topped a nice piece of gravy-soaked bread with a lump of fat and popped it into his mouth. He knew a little about Hoxteth. Self-made merchant, some said by running goods through the embargo with Pyrfew, avoiding the customs officers and the navy until, one day, he went legit and married into a family with a title. Became guild leader, and now treasurer of the realm. Gambler, odds-player, and coin-counter. Maybe not the traditional stuff of legends, but he was a winner.

Eden, on the other hand, people thought he was a hero already. Five years ago, he led the Second Company to liberate the city of Redpool, Edland's only holding on the mainland of the Jeweled Continent. The governor of Redpool thought he could test the new king and switch sides to the emperor of Pyrfew, taking the city with him.

Mareth had held many a commoner rapt telling the story of how, in parley, Eden was able to rile the governor so much he marched back behind the walls of the city, roused his fighters, and rode out to meet the Second on the field. Eden, though, had hidden his cavalry a good ten miles away from the city walls. The occupying army thought the infantry in front of them was all they faced. But the cavalry came when they saw the signal fires, and half an hour after stepping out of the city, those foot soldiers had two thousand cavalry smashing into their rear. They officially changed the name of the city to Redsmoke in Eden's (and the signal fires') honor, even though everyone still called it Redpool.

Eden was already rich and well-connected—you don't lead the Second without the connections to begin at captain when others start digging the latrines—but he made a pretty penny out of the liberation. King Roland levied an extra copper on the crown in customs charges that went straight into Eden's pocket (another example of Roland's brilliant new taxes). Probably made the liberator the richest man in the whole kingdom.

"Yeah, you're probably right," said Blond Beard. "Wonder who will make it to the end of the month?"

"Good question," replied Dark Skin. "My vote is going to be for Hoxteth, of course. He's one of us. Got to be good for business. You know, I started working for him as a warehouse hand—"

"Bullshit," interrupted Blond Beard. "You ain't going to be voting. That'll be all your coin. And you've told me a hundred times if you've told me once about how you learnt everything at the knee of Hoxteth. And we all know you got the boot for having your fingers in the cash drawer. Got the boot and only just avoided a blade to your fingers, too."

"Hey, that ain't true."

Mareth mopped his plate with the bread and took a long draught of the ale. He was beginning to feel human again. Like he could talk without heaving over his shoes or sounding like a dull-witted idiot.

"Excuse me, sirs. I hope you don't mind me interrupting. My name is Mareth. Some call me Mareth of the Melody, perhaps you've heard of me? No? Well, I did overhear you talking while I was eating my meal. Are either of you obvious men of means going to take part in this selection of the new protector?"

"Yes, I am," said Dark Skin. "I've wanted to have a say in this country of mine since I was a boy. I've worked hard every day, but never thought to have this chance."

"I say bullshit again," said Blond Beard to his friend, then he switched his attention to the bard. "Begging your pardon, Mareth, for the bluntness of my words. You may not know the price of admission to vote is one thousand crowns." Blond Beard turned back to his fellow merchant. "As I said, that has to be all of your worth. At least your liquid capital. And you're really going to hand it over to the palace?"

"Aye, I am. In fact, I already did. They give it back to you after the election, you know, and who's safer than the crown, or whatever they're going to call it now. Anyway, it was the wizard who I gave it to. I got to meet him in person and shake his hand." Dark Skin shook his head in slight disbelief at the memory. "And look, I got my demon. It's in my bag. You want to see it?"

Dark Skin reached into the leather satchel, taking out a pink creature and placing it on the shiny wooden bar. Mareth and Blond Beard leaned in to get a good look. Five inches of naked strangeness, with smooth, unblemished skin, a tuft of shocking yellow hair on the top of its head, and tiny fangs sticking out over its lower lip.

"It's a pyxie," said the merchant. The creature scurried over to his tankard of ale, and using the handle as a step, climbed up the side of the mug to take a drink of the contents.

Mareth couldn't conceal his surprise at the little demon. He had heard the wizard was using them for the election, but he thought it was a joke, or a case of too many people twisting a story as it passed along. "How does it work?" Mareth asked.

"When I've made my mind up, I tell the pyxie, and then he'll disappear back to the palace. And, apparently, on the solstice, all the pyxies get together and tally up the votes. Probably with some kind of magical chalkboard."

"Truly remarkable, sir," said Mareth.

The dark-skinned merchant clearly enjoyed the attention. "Yes, indeed. These are remarkable times," said Dark Skin.

Blond Beard looked as if he was chewing on a wasp, likely considering how he, too, was going to be able to scrape the coin together for his own little pink demon.

"And apologies if you think I was eavesdropping, but did I happen to hear you know Lord Hoxteth personally? And you'll be voting for him? As I mentioned, I'm a bard of some renown, and I intend to document this fabled time in our realm's history through song and poem, and you, dear sir, could be part of the story."

Now it was time for the merchant to lean in. He had

been enjoying showing off to his friend and the rest of the bar, and he visibly salivated at the thought of being in a famous song.

"What's your name, good sir," asked Mareth, "and can I enlist your help?"

"I am Master Gonal. It's a pleasure to meet you," he said reaching over and shaking Mareth's hand. "What help are you thinking? I do believe it's very important to support the arts. However are we to have a history if not for our stories and songs? And the citizens of the realm far from Kingshold, they need to have confidence in this process, too. They won't get that from the message delivered by the criers, that's for sure. Everyone knows they're just the mouthpiece. No, sir. It requires people like your good self to tell the real story. So, what can I do to help?"

"It's such a small thing. Very slight for one such as yourself, I'm sure." Mareth smiled and patted his new friend on the shoulder. He'd always been good at making friends. "I'd like to meet with Lord Hoxteth."

Mareth stared at the ceiling of his room. Damp stained the whitewashed plaster, and the paint hung from the walls like an old crone's skin. He gave little mind to his surroundings, though. Mareth had lived much better in the past, but also in worse circumstances, too. He considered the rest of last night, putting the pieces back together that were causing him to lie awake in bed. There was the merchant Gonal. And then the blonde girl...

His memory was imperfect, but Mareth recalled Gonal buying him more ale while they talked about the merchant's childhood in the city, growing up as an only son to a tailor in the Middle. Not rich, but not struggling for food like many in the city, until the day his father died from the pox. His mother ran the business then, and probably did a better job than his father, but it left Gonal with a lot of time to himself.

That was when he discovered a young merchant working his way up from a single stall in the market to owning many stalls, to then securing his own warehouse after winning a month's rent at the card table. That was Hoxteth, of course, the canny lord treasurer getting a foothold in life via his wits and ability to count cards.

Gonal said he shadowed the young Hoxteth, whining for work and taking any errands he was given, until, one day, he was taken onboard as an apprentice bookkeeper. Mareth struggled to remember the exact details of what happened next, but there was definitely some falling-out. It was something like the senior bookkeeper had been dipping into the cash deposits and hiding it in the books, small amounts, difficult to find. But Hoxteth reviewed the details himself, and so, one day, some of Hoxteth's hired guards brought Gonal into the office and questioned him. The merchant actually cried into his mug as he had told the story to Mareth.

Gonal had been so ashamed when he was fired and told to leave, with a scolding that he should have noticed the theft himself ringing in his ears. But an unsigned letter came a week later, informing him of an opportunity to buy a delivery of wool from upland and deliver it to a crew from Pyrfew—not strictly legal at the time, but Gonal took his opportunity, borrowing the seed capital from his mother. Gonal swore blind the letter had to have come from Hoxteth, and it had started him on his way.

A month after being fired, Gonal learnt the bookkeeper

had never been seen again, he hadn't reported to the office, and he hadn't been seen by his neighbors. Mareth wondered whether he had been tipped off and fled, or if Hoxteth had taken care of business in another way. Hoxteth wouldn't be the first merchant to know how to take care of business permanently.

The stories of how Hoxteth and Gonal had made their way in the city were good backstory for Mareth. He did not yet know how these details could be crafted into the telling, but it was always better to have more material to call on.

Gonal had left him around midnight, but he had secured the promise to meet this very day, so they could see Hoxteth together. Mareth remembered there was even some talk about Gonal being his patron. The merchant had settled his account for the evening and even some days past, which Mareth greatly appreciated, but he knew he could aim higher than a cloth merchant.

He had left his reputable family behind to join the Bard's College, and he needed to be mindful of his reputation. However, Mareth prided himself on not being a man to take advantage of another, and so, he resolved to talk to him once Gonal had followed through on his introduction. Of course, Mareth would still include him in the tale, which would be payment enough.

Once Gonal had left, he recalled singing songs again for the common room crowd. Eventually, it became the reserve of the usual faces, and they had called his name, patting him on the back and asking for more. He had made them laugh with the tale of *Old Edward's Finger* and some had cried with *The Shipwife's Lament*. There must have been other songs, too, but he struggled to recall them as the tankards of ale had accumulated.

But one thing did stand out. At the end of one song, as he had raised his head from his mandolin, he had seen a beautiful vision. A young woman with blonde hair and eyes as green as the meadows of his home. Her name was Penny or Petra or Ponna.

Her name was not the important thing to Mareth at that moment. It was that he was lying there alone. He remembered her appearing somewhat smitten with him. And he had heard from some women in the past that he sang as a siren would, attracting women to the rocks of his bed. Mareth also considered himself to be quite handsome, though he might have lost some of the luster of youth he once had. So, why was he on his lonesome?

He had many things to think about.

A girl and the thrill of the chase.

A story to be written.

Who knew purpose traveled in pairs?

CHAPTER 6
UNCERTAIN RETURN

The ship had been making good speed since they'd broken through the storm two nights past, the Arz Sea now giving way to the Grey Sound and the entrance to the port of Kingshold, sheltered in the bluffs of the Mount Tiston. Motega would usually be ecstatic about time onboard ship almost coming to an end, his stomach having only just recovered from the tempestuous crossing. He was born to run, preferring solid ground beneath his feet to wooden decking, and so, usually, he would be the one lining up at the railing with a pack on his back.

But coming back to Kingshold created mixed feelings for him, feelings he knew were to some extent mirrored in his companions.

Motega wore brown leather traveling trousers and a hooded jerkin over a rough cotton shirt, with well-worn leather boots on his feet. Under his open jerkin was a bandolier of slim knives and pouches across his chest, but he wore his hood up to hide his skin. His complexion was mixed. Some would call it piebald, as most of his skin was a ghostly white with brown patches that, on his face, resembled the wings of a bird, and it attracted attention. His black hair hidden under the hood was cut short, no longer down to the middle of his back since that last escapade of theirs back in Carlburg.

Motega had not been back to Kingshold for ten years, even though it had been home for some time for him and his sister before then. His sister fit in at Kingshold, but he knew it wasn't the place for him. He was supposed to wander, and a few small adventures in the city hadn't taken away the need to be free.

At the time, he had warred with himself about what to do because it had only been him and his sister for most of his life. And so, it had been difficult to make a break and a separate life for himself. So difficult, he maybe didn't say goodbye to her before leaving.

"There it is. Looks even bigger than when we left. How can they pile more shit into that space?" said a man who had walked up behind Motega. He wasn't much taller than Motega, but he was nearly twice as wide. That was Florian: friend, veteran of three wars and more than twenty battles, many as a mercenary, and famous for the two mismatched long swords strapped to his back (famous at least if you moved in the right circles). Florian was ready to get off the ship, chainmail hauberk over leather trousers with grey traveling cloak fastened around his neck by a small silver pin. He dumped his pack on the deck.

Coming up behind him was a tall, athletic, dark-skinned man, traveling cloak worn over close-tailored cotton clothes. Motega knew Trypp didn't like to have any excess weight or fabric get in the way, especially in his line of work. Trypp always thought the coin spent on a good tailor was an investment worth making; he was one of the best extractors on the whole continent.

"There's always room, Florian. Look to the starboard side. New shanties outside the Curtain Wall stretch nearly a mile now, and the wall is probably still not finished. More people come all the time to Kingshold to get their share of the cream, not knowing it turned sour long ago..." Trypp shaded his eyes. "Do you see? It looks like the flags over the customs' house are at half-mast. You think the king is dead?"

"By pox or poison?" added Florian, chuckling. "You know, I believe you're right. Mot, what do you see?"

Motega's eyes rolled up into the back of his head. His vision was weak over distances, the result of a curse from a sorcerer when he was a child. But of the three of them, he still had the best eyes, because perched on the crow's nest at the top of the mast was a small peregrine falcon, his spirit animal.

Only once a generation would a spirit animal select one of Motega's tribe, and when his tribe was destroyed, and he had been separated from his homelands, he thought that dream of one day being selected had died, too. The falcon was not a traditional bird for his tribe, but it was native to Edland, and for reasons he had yet to discover, one of his tribe's spirits had traveled across the ocean to be with him. With practice and concentration, Motega could see with the falcon's eyes as if he was inside its tiny skull, and so, he focused the sharp predator's eyes on the dockside.

Trypp was right. The flag over the customs house was at half-mast. The docks were crowded with people, too, many of them in groups. The falcon glided on the winds. Its eyes shifted further into the city where a conspiracy of ravens clustered in the air, attempting to land on something, but being waved off by someone with a spear. Heads on spikes. Traitors or assassins, more than likely, if the king was dead.

Motega's eyes returned to normal, and he looked at his friends, his surrogate family since he had left his sister. "You're right, something funny is going on. There are a lot of people dockside. Not sure if that's going to be helpful for us or not. Let's be careful. Keep it quiet." Motega paused, thoughtful, his friends not interrupting the silence. "Or we could just turn 'round and get out of here. Are you both still sure about this?"

Florian nodded. He was no nonsense. They had already given this much thought, and he wasn't one for turning back. Motega couldn't imagine a more solid and dependable friend.

Trypp had the most to consider in coming back to Kingshold; he had been born in the city, but was raised by an Order orphanage until he left at the age of eight to escape the beatings. Months spent on the streets, surviving by his wits, would be followed by more beatings when he was inevitably recaptured, only for the cycle to repeat itself. And then at the age of fourteen, he was accepted to join the school for the Hollow Syndicate, the most exclusive assassins group in the Jeweled Continent.

He took to the quiet work killers need to do, the skulking in shadows and the scaling of walls, but the killing part was tough for him. Especially as the customer chose the target, and the customer was always right even when it was obvious they were wrong.

Unfortunately, nobody got to quit the school. Winnowing happened via the dagger or the poison bottle, not by students going back home and talking about what they had learnt. So Trypp had to fake his death before the first winnowing.

Back on the streets, he eventually made connections with the Twilight Exiles, Kingshold's band of thieves, burglars, muggers, extortionists and all-around shady characters. Trypp's unique skills were put to good use.

But all of that changed when he met Florian and Motega. Trypp had been caught for the first time in his career, by Motega and Florian, while he tried to sneak into the home of Motega's sister. Somehow, he had talked his way out of being handed over to the authorities. As Motega remembered it, it was quite likely he had relented simply out of boredom. Having the chance to personally find out who had requested the job seemed like much more fun at the time.

Unfortunately, the Twilight Father, the leader of the 'family', did not think the three of them infiltrating his safe house to be quite so amusing.

Motega knew Trypp was considering all of this. He felt he could almost read the minds of his friends now. That was what made them such a good team. And so, when Trypp nodded his confirmation and gave a big smile to his companions, Motega felt they'd all come to terms with it being good to be home, no matter the consequences or how short this sojourn might be.

"Good," said Motega. "I'll get my stuff together. Let's see what insanity we have to look forward to."

THE HARBOR WAS WALL-TO-WALL WITH PEOPLE. MANY ships had arrived around the same time, the storm of a few days past being a leveler in their arrival times. Motega and his companions had bid farewell to the captain of their ship —a salt-weathered woman out of Redpool, who had been lined up by their contact here in Kingshold—and then they walked down the gangplank to join the throng on the quayside.

Per, as Motega referred to his spirit animal, took flight from the ship and circled above the crowds in the direction of where the threesome wanted to head. Motega kept his hood around his head, and Florian took his arm while they walked. With his face hidden and his friend guiding him, he was able to use the eyes of his spirit animal to scout ahead.

Various parties in the city always watched the docks well, and even though Motega had not been in Kingshold for many years, many of the usual signs of those lookouts were the same, especially for the ones less experienced.

So, the three men walked through the crowd, avoiding the spotters that were, in turn, spotted. Of course, Motega was most concerned about the ones who were more professional in their line of work, but new enough where he wouldn't be able to recognize them by sight.

Florian carried two packs, the larger bag on his back being the one that had accompanied him across many leagues and full of the tools of their trade. The second bag he held in the hand that was not guiding Motega; a leather case carrying the fruits of their recent labors.

All three of them liked to think of themselves as adventurers. Some weeks would entail hunting down lost treasure in a faraway catacomb; other weeks, it might be helping villagers with a particular monster problem they might be having; and then, of course, other weeks, it might be an extraction job commissioned by a wealthy individual.

And was it their fault they were good at that latter category of work and had become particularly well known for it?

The threesome walked through the docks and up the

incline of Ships Row past the warehouses housing the trading goods of the merchants who called Kingshold home. Porters pushed carts; a drayman led a wagon with spices and fabrics brought from other corners of the continent; laborers sweated in the summer air moving crates and barrels, all contents destined for shops in the city or back onto other ships bound for foreign ports.

As they walked, they saw crowds of citizens gathered around town criers, listening to the news, but they steered clear. City guard were thin on the ground, and a chaotic air only intensified as they entered the market square, skirting the outside of it to lead them toward the beginning of Market Street.

"Stop, thief!"

Motega switched his attention back to his own eyes and saw a well-dressed merchant ahead call out in their direction. A small figure zigged and zagged between the townspeople, pursued by armed men who must be the merchant's bodyguards. A boy clutching a purse and a small knife ran past them toward the crowds of the market, the heavy footfalls of the three bodyguards getting louder as they approached the three companions.

A woman pushing a cart of roasted nuts made an obstruction of herself to two of the guards, who slammed into the vendor, causing her wares to scatter to the filthy floor. The lead guard avoided the cart, turned to see what had happened to his colleagues, and not looking where he was going, ran headfirst into Florian.

Trypp had once described Florian as a small movable mountain and, unsurprisingly, the guard came up much the worse for the collision, bouncing off the fighter and sprawling on the floor.

"You! Ox! Why didn't you stop that urchin? Or at least move your lumbering carcass out of the way!" It was the same voice that had called moments earlier, a sweaty well-dressed balding man who had been jogging behind his guards.

"Good sir, are you referring to my friend as an ox? That does not appear either friendly or wise," said Trypp, looking the merchant in the eye and speaking for the three of them. "I also don't see what your business has anything to do with our business. We're just passing through."

"Of course, that's what you'd say. You're probably in cahoots with the little shit, much like that woman. Men, grab her. We'll take her to the city guard, and we'll see what they have to say."

The merchant's guards picked the woman off the street, and as she squirmed to escape their grasp, one punched her in the stomach, while another grabbed her hair.

Motega sighed. He knew his friends. Trypp would wince, but walk by the scene, knowing they'd agreed to keep a low profile. Florian was different. Merciless in a fight, but a good soul at heart, and even though it could be problematic, Motega loved him for it. That goodness rubbed off on him.

Florian stepped forward. "Leave her be, sir, or you'll regret it." Motega flipped his cloak over his shoulders to free his war axes holstered at his waist. Trypp took a step backward and melted into the crowd that had begun to gather around the disturbance.

"Oh, now you want to be involved, do you?" said the lead bodyguard, a big bastard who wouldn't have looked out of place standing at the door to one of the dockside grog taverns. "Well, fuck you. We have numbers on you, and the guard will be here any minute."

Florian looked at Motega and nodded a little to the right. Florian took one step forward and, with his left hand, drove his fist into the chin of the guard who had punched the nut vendor. Still gripping the leather case in his other hand, unwilling to put down their prize, he kicked the lead guard in his jewels, and the man fell to the ground, eyes bulging.

Motega grabbed one war ax and threw it at the guard holding onto the woman's hair. Handle spinning over the blade, blade over handle until the steel-shod grip struck the guard in the face, nose exploding. He staggered back, hands to his face.

The woman was free, and without waiting to thank her saviors (or pick up her nuts), she pulled up the hem of her rough-spun dress and ran for it.

Trypp stepped up behind the merchant with a cloth in hand and set it to the rich man's face. The fat man attempted to struggle, but before the count of three, Trypp had gently laid him out on the floor, still breathing but unconscious.

So much for an inconspicuous entrance, thought Motega. He retrieved his ax, hung it back in the loop on his belt and looked at his friends. "Split! You know where to meet. Two hours."

"I ASSUME, GENTLEMAN, AS YOU ARE HERE, YOU HAVE THE books?" Artur Danweazel, the proprietor of the store Motega, Trypp, and Florian had come to with their package, peered over his glasses as he spoke. Florian stepped forward and put the case on the counter.

"Artur, when have you ever known us not to get a job done?" asked Trypp. "But why the cryptic message about meeting here instead of Redpool? We didn't know you had a place here, too."

"Young man, I have establishments in a good many cities, which you don't need to know about, as it's none of your concern."

Artur was probably in his early fifties, grey hair around his temples, and feathering at his eyebrows (which were waxed to a point). His eyes were a bright silver grey; his complexion olive brown, with lines around his eyes and on his forehead from his characteristic frown. Which he had been doing since they arrived, until he took a deep breath and visibly relaxed a little.

"Sorry, I don't like people prying. But you gents are the right kind of trustworthy, and by that, I mean I have a lot of secrets you'd rather not be told, and you have the good sense not to ask. But, by the by, I spend every summer here in Kingshold. I find it to be better for my temperament, what with it being less hot and humid than Redpool. But we've all walked into some messed-up situation right now."

"What has been happen—"

"I'll tell you afterward, but right now, let's look at the goods." Artur opened the laces on the bag and took out, one by one, three books and placed them on the counter. "*The Sexomnicon*, all three volumes in their original bindings, and none of the pages are stuck together. Excellent!"

"So, those books are just what they look like? A bunch of dirty hand-drawn pictures?" Trypp leaned over while the old shopkeeper leafed carefully through the pages. "There aren't any magic spells or treasure maps hidden in the pictures?"

"This collection of etchings by Runeau is exceedingly rare and is a quite sought-after set by a particular kind of collector. One with a finer taste in all things, shall we say. So yes, for once, this item does not possess any magical power or intrigue."

"Well, fuck me. I guess the coin is the same no matter what. Hey, Motty," Trypp turned to look at Motega with a toothy grin, "so you lost your hair all for a few books of lovely arses! Does it make you feel any better?"

Motega didn't feel better for this. His hair hadn't been cut once in his life until this particular escapade had given him the option of losing his hair or his head.

The job had gone perfectly all the way up to the point where they were making their escape with the books. And then his hair, which he had always worn the traditional way of his tribe—a long ponytail with a series of ties along its length to keep it contained—got caught on the window frame as they were leaping from the study of the mark's house to the rooftops across the street.

Motega had jumped from the window like Florian and Trypp, but while they had made it to the rooftops, their planned escape route, he had come crashing back into the wall of the building they were attempting to leave. His hair caught above him, and no matter how much he wriggled, it would not release. Motega had hung there for what seemed like minutes, trying to work out what to do—his comrades already disappearing across the rooftops—and knowing he couldn't risk calling out and potentially drawing attention to himself.

For a Wolfclaw clan member, the hair was a physical manifestation of the ability and honor of the warrior, but as Motega hung there, pain in his scalp, he realized he wasn't a warrior anymore. He was a thief. And so, with tears in his eyes that had little to do with physical pain, he had pulled a dagger from his belt and cut his hair just above his scalp.

The three-story drop from the window had also done little to improve his mood. And so, Trypp bringing it up again and tying his dishonor to the theft of a few dirty pictures stuck in his craw.

The rabbit-punch into the kidneys of Trypp, who doubled over and onto his knees, helped to cheer him a little.

"Now, now, gentlemen. No brawling in my establishment, please. Here's your payment as agreed." Artur handed a coin purse to Florian, and then went on. "So, as I was saying before about this messed-up situation..." Artur explained how the king had been murdered by his own wizard and how the same wizard had called an end to the monarchy. No more kings or queens. Instead, there would now be an election for a new lord protector.

"I'm going to be heading to the palace to sign up and get my pyxie just as soon as I have passed on those books you brought me. I think I know who I'll be voting for: Lord Uthridge. Yes, he's a general, so probably not the smartest at running a country, but he has two things going for him. One, he won't be able to go five minutes in charge without some war, and war is always an opportunity to make profit. And second, he hates Hoxteth almost as much as I do. That jumped-up little pumpkin peddler."

Motega and Florian exchanged looks. Talk of the wizard and Uthridge had brought back memories for the pair of them, but Artur wasn't the only one who wanted to keep some secrets.

Artur paid no mind to the reaction of the two men remaining standing in his shop. "I assume you gentlemen are now unemployed and looking for work?"

Trypp pulled himself off the floor, using the counter for leverage, and gave Motega an evil stare, before nodding to

Artur. "Depends on the job, as always. But I'm listening, at least as long as I don't start puking..."

"There are no rules in this election. All that matters is getting the people who can afford to cast a vote to be on your side. Many people are siding with those they've had relationships with for all of their lives, while others are going where there's an opportunity to make money.

"Hoxteth is getting more joy from the traditional lords and ladies of court than I expected, and it's all because he's offering them a slice of the action if he's in charge. However, there are rumors that back in the last war with Pyrfew, Hoxteth was running both weapons and intelligence to their demons. If we had evidence to prove it, then that would really put the turd in the bath, so to speak. That's where you guys come in. What do you think?"

"Sounds reasonable," said Trypp. "So, we have to figure out if there's any evidence and then acquire it. How much?"

"Five hundred crowns. But you've only got ten days to get it done or the deal's off. Time is of the essence, gentlemen."

Some hours later, Motega, Florian, and Trypp exited the shop after gathering as much intelligence about their new mark as they could from Artur.

They were on a quiet cobbled street, known for the curiosity shops that had clustered together like mismatched birds huddling for warmth. Per had been resting on the top of the chimney at Artur's store, and Motega's mind sought that of the bird as he walked out. As he feared, there had been a small succession of individuals who had been watching the door they had entered this morning, all hidden in the same spot in shadows across the street.

Motega nudged Trypp and indicated the spy's direction with a glance, the dark man understanding without words. The threesome walked out onto the narrow street, not paying any mind to the hiding spot of the spy until they were upon it. Motega switched directions quickly and made a grab for where he expected the man to be. He missed. A small, agile figure ducked under his lunge and dove through Trypp's legs, looking likely to make a daring escape.

Except Florian was waiting for him.

In particular, Florian's fist was waiting for his nose. Blood burst down the weaselly man's face as he fell on his arse, tears welling in his eyes. Florian picked him up and pushed him against the wall, feet dangling in the air. Trypp approached and lifted the spy's left hand, revealing the tattooed crescent moon in his palm matching his own. The Twilight Exile mark.

"I have a mind to dump you in the sea. I don't like being spied on," said Motega, coming up close to the man's face. "What do you want?"

"Don't hurt me," stammered the man, blood and snot streaked across his chin. "I'm just following orders. It's Mother Sharavin. She wants to see all three of you. Now, she says."

CHAPTER 7
TIME TO STOP PROCRASTINATING

"Good morning, Lord Chancellor. I trust you slept well," said a young man, back rod straight with greased hair in a side parting and dressed all in black. Hoskin yawned as he looked up from his largely untouched breakfast.

"Percival, you know perfectly well I have not been sleeping. You come and bring me various tinctures and draughts during the night, and still I can't sleep for long." It had been three days since Hoskin had declared the election following the wizard's instruction, and so, it had been three days he had been responsible for the realm.

He had previously thought of himself as being the person who ran the country, but it had never occurred to him how rare it was for him to make the final decision. The pressure of being the one who was responsible had hit him on leaving the privy council meeting, when people came to ask him what they should do about important matters, like what to do with the body of the former king and queen (dispose of quietly in the palace grounds), the guild of shipwrights asking if the funding for Admiral Uthridge's new flagship was approved (no), and a request from the Ambassador of Pyrfew to meet to discuss the status of Redpool given the change in rulership (definitely need to avoid this meeting...).

And then, since that day and those quick-fire decisions, he had been unable to sleep. Questions came one after another, and as the days passed, he was deferring more and more decisions, until last night when the wizard paid him a visit in the library.

It was a strange meeting with Jyuth because it seemed like the wizard was trying to be positive and encouraging.

In fact, he said Hoskin should trust in himself to make better decisions than the old king would have made. Now, that conversation had not helped his sleep last night, but it had encouraged him to face up to his life for the next twenty-something days and address some of these meetings he had been procrastinating.

The past few days, Hoskin had been trying to catch up on writing the histories of the last five years, and he had been enjoying himself for the first in a long time. Now, there was a glimmer of hope this election would bring a new leader, and a new chancellor, and then he could do something else with his life.

"I'm sorry, sir. It's a matter of habit. Would you care to know the latest about the election?" Chancellor Hoskin nodded, so Percival continued. "There are now a total of seven individuals who have nominated themselves to be candidates: Lord Eden, Sir Penshead, Lord Hoxteth, Lord Uthridge, Lady Kingsley, Lord Fiske, and Lady Orlan."

"Good grief, Percival, that is a strange group, and no mistake, one of them is so dimwitted I'm not sure he can put his trousers on without help, and another believes herself to be so smart she can't converse with anyone outside of the university. And Fiske is quite dull. Can you imagine having a judge as lord protector? We would have more rules saying what we can and can't do than people would be able to keep straight."

Hoskin shook his head. At least he had not been foolish enough to add his own name to the list. "And what did the tax rolls tell you about how many individuals in the country could be involved in this election?"

"Well, sir, my estimate is a maximum of one hundred and fifty-two, all being individuals who own their property and would have the funds to meet the wizard's deposit. So far, there have been thirty-nine voters who have paid the price of admission."

"So, thirty-nine thousand gold crowns are just sitting around in the palace? Please ask Captain Grimes to triple the guard. Don't bother asking Beneval; he'll forget it after five minutes, the senile old boot. We're going to have every thief in the Jeweled Continent coming to town to see if they can crack open this egg. It's not like we're a bank with a vault. People are forever coming in and out of the palace. Where is Jyuth putting all the gold?"

"It's actually in his rooms, sir. He had a few large chests brought a few days ago to collect the coin. Maybe that's the safest place in the palace, sir? The wizard scares most people. But I'll pass the message onto Captain Grimes. Are you ready for the day ahead?"

"I'm not so sure," said Hoskin, pushing back his plate of unfinished sausages. "But there's no point hiding anymore. Where do we start?"

~

"Firstly, my lord, may I introduce the Duke of Northfield." Percival opened the door to his office, stepping in, and announcing his first visitor.

Hoskin stood out of politeness for the old man who walked uneasily into the meeting room, even though right now he technically outranked him, Regent of Edland to a minor Duke of Pienza. It was impressive this old man had moved so fast, it being two days sail from Pienza to Kingshold, but the sight of his young bride at the door explained everything. It takes a particular ambition to marry an old fart like this and to put up with however many years he had left to get his Northfield holdings, and having a chance to be a queen was obviously too good an opportunity to pass up.

"Your Grace, how lovely of you to visit at this time of year. Would you care for tea?"

"Yes, certainly, Chancellor." The duke collapsed onto the cushioned armchair across from Hoskin with a sigh. "I heard something had happened to my nephew, and I, of course, rushed as fast as possible to see what I could do to assist. And now I hear he's dead. Is this true? Can I see his body?"

"I'm afraid that won't be possible, Your Grace," said Hoskin, hands clasped on the desk in front of him and with what he hoped was a concerned look. "There is not going to be a funeral. The monarchy has been dissolved. At Jyuth's insistence, you understand. The body has been disposed of."

"The warlock is behind this, then. I thought as much. I remember the day when he took my brother away. We were both children, you know. He made him king. And he only had one son, who is now dead, so hereditary law states I'm next of kin and I'm legitimately king."

"Dear Duke, you must have misheard me. The monarchy has been abolished. No more kings or queens, princes or princesses. I believe Jyuth dearly loved your brother, but now he refers to all kings and queens as arsewipes. So, no more throne for you to go after, I believe, and if you disagree with that, then it's best to bring it up directly with the wizard. I'm sure Percival here could go and find him—"

"That won't be necessary, Hoskin," interrupted the old man. Funny that no matter how indignant someone was, it always disappeared when faced with the prospect of actually talking with Jyuth. "I...er...don't deign to talk to the murderer of my kin. Don't think you've heard the last of this, you know. I'm on my way to meet with the father of Queen Tulip and pay him my respects. I'm sure he'll boil with anger at the fate of his daughter—"

"Actually, Jyuth sent him a note himself, offering his condolences and explaining the evidence of what he had discovered Randolph and Tulip were doing. And how he would personally ensure that none of the evidence would become known to other families of significant station. And do you know, the Duke of Breckon Heights sent a note back actually thanking Jyuth for cutting off his own daughter's head. Said it saved him doing it himself!"

The duke's pallid features went even more pale. So much so, he looked like a ghost. He gasped for air, white turning to purple, and he banged the floor with his cane. A manservant and his blushing bride ran into the room and helped the duke to his feet, Hoskin assumed to administer some assistance or take him to a doctor. As they were walking out of the room, the young woman turned back to look at the chancellor, her scowl perfectly practiced.

"You despicable man! You haven't heard the last of Northfield, I tell you. He should be your king!"

"Goodbye, girl," said Hoskin with a sigh. "Be careful of what you wish for."

~

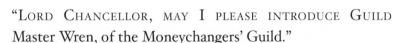

"Lord Chancellor, may I please introduce Guild Master Wren, of the Moneychangers' Guild."

"Chancellor Hoskin, thank you for making time to see me today. I have dire news indeed. Dire news that threatens the very fabric of our city! The economy is on shaky ground!"

Hoskin leaned forward in his chair and looked across the table at the chief banker of Edland, and the second successive prune of a man. Wren had led one of the most prominent banking houses when his father was chancellor, and he had been guild master for the last twenty years. Proximity to ledgers was obviously a good preservative. Though the banker's face was creased with wrinkles, and he had small wireframe spectacles perched on his nose, his eyes were alert, and he was still renown for being a shrewd judge of character in his business dealings. But here again was a man who was not one to pass up an opportunity.

"What is it, Guild Master?" asked Hoskin. "I had heard business is booming."

"Oh no, my lord. It's hard these days to be in the banking business." Wren shook his head, his features channeling a widow asking for money to feed her starving family. No doubt with plenty of experience on what that looked like having spent a good amount of his career turning down such requests. "We have a run on the banks, my lord! All the noble houses and the richest merchants are withdrawing gold from the vaults. It has to stop!"

"But is it not their gold, Guild Master?"

"Well, of course it is! But they can't take it all out at once, can they? We loan that money to business opportunities, to finance construction, to loan to the crown, Chancellor. If everyone takes out their deposits, then how can we make investments with which to make a return! Our vaults are running low, Lord Chancellor. We need new laws so we can have adequate time to give people their money when they ask for it. Let me see, ten days should be appropriate."

"I find it hard to believe your vaults are running low, Wren." Hoskin considered the old banker over steepled fingers. "In fact, I've heard that some lending houses, including your own, have been executing on *demon loans* to finance...how shall we refer to them...middle-income traders and tradesmen. I heard the going rate is fifty crowns for a one-month loan. It seems like you have enough gold to strike these deals, sir."

"Slander! Fifty crowns interest? Never, Chancellor." Wren assumed a look of indignation. "I believe the rate is only twenty-five crowns, and we are only accepting the best collateral from the best individuals who are challenged from a liquidity perspective. You understand."

"I do understand. And I have every confidence you'll figure out your own liquidity needs to meet your responsibilities to your depositors." Hoskin sat back in his chair and smiled. "Tell me, Guild Master Wren, how much does the crown owe to your member houses? I don't believe I have that number on hand."

"I believe it's around three hundred thousand crowns, Lord Chancellor, and I'm sure you remember we've provided those loans at only the best interest rates."

"Of course, Guild Master. I do remember the good friend the crown has always had in the Moneychangers Guild. Tell me, did you read the announcement of the elections with your usual attention to detail? You do understand Jyuth declared the abolition of the crown, not a process to declare a new king, but the dissolution of the crown and its institutions. I'm fully expecting I will not have a job in twenty-three days' time. Have you considered what it could mean for you?"

"..." The old guild master turned pink, and then red and purple. "..."

"Wren, I do believe you've forgotten to breathe. Percival, would you mind patting the guild master on the back to see if you can bring the old man back to life? We can't have more prominent individuals of the city dying in the palace, can we?"

Percival walked behind the old man and gave him an open-handed *SLAP* between the shoulder blades, and the guild master quickly drew in a deep breath. Hoskin flicked his eyes toward the exit, and so, Percival grasped Wren under the armpits to help him to his feet and guide him to the door.

"So nice to see you, Guild Master," called Hoskin to his retreating guest. "Be well and good luck with your conversations with all of the candidates. I'm sure they'll all soon be getting a lot of your assistance."

Hoskin leaned back in his chair and gave himself the pleasure of a little smile. He was quite enjoying himself.

~

"Lord Chancellor, may I please introduce Ambassador Egyed of the Deep People, KeyBearer of Unedar Halt."

Through the door walked an incredibly pale-skinned man, his complexion almost translucent, a foot shorter than the average Edlander, but broad in shoulder and chest with biceps as big as Hoskin's thighs. His long white hair and beard were both plaited into braids, and large gold hoops hung from ear helix, lobe, and nostril. This visitor also wore spectacles, but bigger than the guild master's, with dark purple glass contained within the rims.

As befitting all parties to meet with the lord chancellor, the ambassador was not officially permitted to bring any weapons into the palace; however, the ceremonial rod he carried, made of steel and with rough uncut gems of red and green embedded in the balled end, looked like it could cause some serious damage in his hands.

Egyed walked over to the desk, gave a small bow, and sat in the chair opposite Hoskin.

"Welcome, Ambassador. How are our favorite neighbors?" asked Hoskin. It went unnoticed by many in Kingshold, but the people of Edland shared the far eastern edge of their country with the dwarves of Unedar Halt. The deep people had lived under Mount Tiston for centuries before Kingshold was founded as just a keep and few surrounding hovels. Thankfully, they had generally been good neighbors, the last hostilities being many years ago. "What do we owe the pleasure of this visit?"

"We are well, Chancellor. Our caverns are dry, the fish in our lakes are teeming, and our new seams are plentiful. We heard about the passing of King Randolph, so I came to pay our respects." Egyed betrayed little emotion as he spoke. Hoskin had always considered him an opponent to avoid at Picket for fear of losing his shirt. "And then I understood the little prick was killed by the wizard, and it made me smile.

He was truly a terrible king, Chancellor Hoskin. But we have always found our dealings with you to be sound."

"Yes, he was rather full of himself, even though everyone else thought him quite empty," remarked Hoskin. He was only just beginning to realize how grateful he was the king and queen, with their attendant whims, were no longer around. "I'm sure you've also heard about the transition we're going through to select a lord protector, but I want to reassure you no matter what happens, I think all in Kingshold see the mutually beneficial relationship we have. And many of us remember that much of your city sits under ours, and I don't think anyone wants the ground to fall out from under them." Hoskin laughed. "That was a joke, Ambassador."

"Are you sure it was, Chancellor?" Hoskin detected the beginnings of a smile at the corner of the dwarf's mouth. "I did hear about the election, and I'm familiar with a number of the candidates. Most of them seem to be motivated by gold, even more so than my kin. Why is it only people with money get to have a say? All of our elders have a say in the selection of the forger, and all must agree. It's been known to take weeks before a decision is made, but then all stand behind that leader."

"Ambassador, your ways work for your people, but our belief that some people are better than other people is deeply entrenched in our society. Those people lucky enough to be born as the privileged few fear it could be taken away from them at any moment. I've read about more egalitarian societies in other parts of the continent, but that's not going to be our lot, I'm afraid. Is there anything else I can do for you today, Ambassador?"

"Chancellor, I think you know I wouldn't have made the

trip above surface without other items that need to be discussed." The dwarf now truly cracked a smile, showing off a few gold teeth, one embedded with a diamond. "I do believe we still have the outstanding issue of effluent runoff, the price of wheat, and this summer's exercise in drake elimination. Our historians believe this year is going to have a significant migration back to the mountain for roosting."

Hoskin didn't try to hide the sigh. Just when he thought the day was going to be all fun, the world came along to remind him of his place.

THE REST OF THE DAY PROGRESSED IN A WAY CLOSER TO the meeting with the ambassador than his early successes against elderly men. Various nobles or representatives of institutions with some concern or another.

He was going to have to talk to Percival about how one young lordling had managed to gain an audience to demand damages because the king and queen would not be attending his solstice ball after his family had made some significant *contributions* to secure their presence. Hoskin fully intended to have the city guard visit the little turd and, at the very least, scare him and his father about the implications of making threats to the lord regent, even if he would only have the title for a little more than three weeks.

And, unfortunately, Percival had saved the best meeting for last.

"Lord Chancellor, may I please introduce Gawl Tegyr, Bearer of Light, Bringer of Peace and Ambassador of Pyrfew."

"Gawl, please be seated. It's been a long day, and I'm not

sure I want to hear the peace you have brought me." The ambassador of Pyrfew intensely irritated Hoskin.

He was clearly of middle years, but imbued with a sickening amount of vitality and good health. He dressed well, in bright expensive colors, that complemented his trim frame, and always accessorized with a broach or chain of exquisite delicacy. He irritated Hoskin even before he opened his mouth. And the fact Edland had been in a hot or cold war with Pyrfew for hundreds of years didn't generally help matters.

"Chancellor Hoskin, it's been a long day for me, too. Your man here has kept me waiting since nine this morning." Hoskin smiled internally at that news. Percival had redeemed himself the folly of admitting the party boy if only to keep this odious man waiting longer. "But I'm pleased to be seeing you now. How are you enjoying your new station?"

"I'm living the dream, Gawl. I can assume it's no coincidence you present yourself here mere days after the change in control in our fair land? Come to pay your respects, have you?"

"Emperor Llewdon was extremely saddened to hear of the demise of King Randolph. Yes, he may have once again stolen Redpool from our lands, but we thought he was someone with promise and someone to bring our nations closer together. What a shame it was to hear the mage thief had once again intruded in the proper running of your land. How do you even stand for his continuous meddling?"

"I'm sure Lord Jyuth would not be happy for you to refer to him as a thief, Gawl," said Hoskin. "At least our wizard hasn't been the one placing the chokes at our necks for the last six hundred years as your emperor has done to your people. All are grateful for his protection and wisdom and that of his forebears. Would a father abandon his children when they need help?"

"Father or puppet master? The answer to that is a matter for your faith, and how you sleep at night, Chancellor. It's a bold move opening yourselves to so much chaos, experimenting with letting the people choose a leader in these troubled times. I do hope the decision is a wise one, Lord Hoskin. Will the new Protector understand the delicate balance in the world today?"

"I have every confidence that any likely victor will see the snake at the door, and they will surround themselves with the appropriate experts. And I can assure you our navy will continue to be the best on the seas and will not allow any challenge to our dominance." Hoskin decided to play his hand a little. "Our master of ships is an admirer of the yards in Ioth, where we know they're building your new fleet. In fact, he says they've recently mastered designs he learnt as an apprentice. You can have your empire of empty land and squalid cities, but we own the seas, and so, we own the trade. And let me make this clear, Redpool will remain part of Edland."

"Yes, I'm sure you're right, Lord Chancellor, but you misunderstand my questioning for threats. We mean you no harm. We're only concerned for the populace of our friends across the narrow seas which separate us. If you believe we once coveted this island realm, you can rest assured our discovery of the Wild Continent is the greater focus of our expansion. Why settle for a stepping stone in the river when we have the whole of the far bank for our own?"

"I'm well aware of your adventures in that place, and the despoilment of the land you're carrying out in your emperor's name. We've seen the slave ships coming back to Pyrfew, and we turn them away from our ports when they seek harbor, as we want no part in that foul practice. And you forget we have one of those people you call savages living here in the city. She has provided us with many perspectives on your actions there."

"I forgot your sensitivities to slaves. It's strange to us when you have thousands of souls living in squalor outside the protection of your walls, with disease and no food. You're obviously by far our superior." Sarcasm dripped from his pores as he spoke. "And we remember the witch fondly from her stay with us. I do hope you pass on my regards when you see her next. As you said, we're both tired, so I think we've spoken enough." Gawl Tegyr got up and walked to the door, talking over his shoulder as he strode confidently away, "I shall leave the city at first light. Good luck with this election. I think you'll need it."

CHAPTER 8
FOOLISH OLD MAN

Flying cleansed her mind, the focus on the flapping of her wings, the soaring on updrafts to conserve her energy, in a way not even her trances could do. She was one with the World, and not troubled by the petty affairs far below her.

As Neenahwi journeyed back to Kingshold, she sometimes joined flocks of other migratory birds heading north for summer breeding grounds, allowing herself to warm in the pure comfort of a family that would surround her, even though she suspected the other birds wondered who this newcomer was. She took her turn at the front of the flock, as well as slipstreaming behind. Geese could be terrible gossips, and as long as she did her part, most were fine without much chatter.

She flew over jungle, plains, forest, desert, and sea, signs of human habitation below, but Neenahwi stayed away from all intelligent life.

She could fly through the night if needed, but she typically found a sheltered and quiet place to land and camp.

During these times, she didn't sleep so much as meditate, recharging her mind and body while her eyes stayed open and alert to keep watch.

Each time, after reverting to human form, she pulled her silken robe from her pack to cover her modesty, and then took time to study the treasure she had recovered from the demon Barax. The gem had been hard won, the battle with the woman-panther had drained her, but it would have required expelling much more hard-earned energy if it wasn't for the appearance of the goblins.

She had never been thankful for a goblin war party before, and she was sure the appreciation would have been tempered if they had caught up with her, but it had been a boon.

The fall over the cliff was not enjoyable, though.

She had a few contusions and scrapes, a nasty knock to the head from the almost sheer drop, before she had been able to gather her will and slow her descent (transforming shape in midair being much too risky). The few goblins, who, in their exuberance, had forgotten the location of their own backdoor, didn't have the benefit of a magically induced updraft, and they had fallen past her to the ground.

Yes, the appearance of the goblins had been helpful. Barax was a particularly powerful demon, and it troubled her she had left a loose end untied. There were documented histories of demons with goblin armies at their backs, or other intelligent races for that matter, but, hopefully, the creature and the goblin war party had injured each other so much they both had retreated to lick their wounds. It was too much to hope the demon had been dealt with.

The gem she had retrieved, from what had turned out to be a goblin warren, had proven to be perplexing in the brief periods of study she had each night before her rest. She knew from Jyuth of these objects, outcasts from the other worlds demons called home. He had collected more than one and had obliquely referred to them as being the source of his long life, but it was a tough nut to crack.

Neenahwi could create threads to any living thing to drain their energy—from a blade of grass to a human being—and though sentient creatures typically resisted more, they had a greater source of energy available. The injury to the cultist in the chamber had weakened it so much it could put up no fight as she used its life force to turn it into a living shield for her. That was typically more trouble than it was worth with a healthy man. But in all instances, she was able to see the energy that was available, and with rock, or sand, and even water, there was nothing to tap.

The point of power she saw within the gem was small in size, but of such a dark red she conjectured it was a thread to a major well of magical energy. But it was inside the gem, and she could no more make a connection with this particular stone than she could a pebble on the seashore.

For the past three nights, she'd spent some time considering the problem. And each night she'd decided to put it aside until she returned home where she could spend as much time as she needed to solve it, only to then pick up the challenge again the next night. As much unable to leave it alone as she could resist picking at her scabbed wounds.

Now, she was flying across the Arz Sea, and she'd be home before nightfall. The peace of embracing the bird form ebbed away as she saw the city of Kingshold, nestled at the foot of Mount Tiston, anticipating being back in the hustle and bustle of the city.

She began a slow descent over the sound, the harbor, and

then the inner wall, sweeping over the grand houses of lords that surrounded the palace and the home of the king. She circled there for a moment before gliding on the winds that swirled in the cradle of the mountain, back out over the Floral Gate, and toward her home near the Judiciary.

Neenahwi noted the carrion birds atop the Floral Gate, her bird brain warning her of getting too close even though she was four times larger than any individual raven, her human brain noting some lord must have done something to annoy the king, as the heads of commoners ended up on spikes around the marketplace. Never the most appetizing scenery, as the citizens of Kingshold would gaze upon the remains of criminals, mainly poor individuals, who had been caught trying to feed themselves or their families, while shopping for their tables.

She flew through an open glass window into a tall round tower attached to a two-story wood and plaster house.

Her home had once belonged to a neighborhood loan shark, not accredited by the Moneychangers Guild, and he had favored the tower as a way to keep a good watch all around his place of business. That still hadn't stopped the city guard from arresting him once the guild discovered him and wanted the enterprise shut down. At least it had given her the chance to buy the tower and get out from living in the palace.

Neenahwi kept the rooms she used in the tower. The rest of the building, though furnished, went mostly unused. She returned to her natural shape and immediately warmed a bath full of water, transferring the energy from the lit fire in the fireplace to the large copper tub. Neenahwi allowed herself the help of one person to keep the place spotless, ensure there was always a bath full of clean water, and a fire lit in the hearth, though weeks often passed between the time she saw the girl, Sarah (who incidentally was paid way above the market rate for such a low-maintenance mistress.)

Lying back and relaxing in the bath, the knots in her muscles unwinding, she began to drift off to real sleep for the first time in more than a week. The noises of the city infiltrated her room from the open windows, essential in the summer heat, especially with a fire always lit.

"Hear ye! Hear ye! Gather round for news of great import from Lord Eden!"

A town crier. There were hundreds of them across the country to communicate the news to all corners of the kingdom without bias. A simple, yet effective innovation from one of Roland's predecessors, though she didn't understand why they chose to talk in such archaic language. *Tradition?* And at certain times, the network could be employed by others who could afford it—and Lord Eden could definitely afford it—even though she couldn't remember him doing so in the past.

"Lord Eden shall be arriving in Kingshold in two days' time from the province of Northshire. Lord Eden has declared his intent to stand for lord protector of the realm of Edland and intends to root out the evil infesting this fair city!"

What!

Neenahwi sat up in the bath, sloshing water onto the stone floor, her full attention on the crier. She climbed out of the tub and ran to the window, not aware of her state of undress, and looked out to see the crowd gathered around the messenger at the street corner across from her house.

"Lord Eden shall defeat our enemies! Lord Eden will reduce your taxes! Lord Eden will introduce a new annual festival once he's elected!" At the end of each exclamation, the gathered crowd cheered. It was by no means uproarious, but Neenahwi had never seen the citizens of Kingshold cheer for anything other than a public hanging. "Lord Eden will arrive in two days through the Excise Gate, and there will be gifts for all!"

She had been away from the city for less than two weeks. What had happened in the meantime?

HER PACE WAS QUICK AND HER STRIDE LONG. THE impression she was aiming to present was one of *storming* as she threw open the doors of Jyuth's apartment in the palace grounds. A servant Neenahwi didn't recognize swirled around and made to head her off.

"Good morning, ma'am. How may I help you? Are you lost?"

"No, I'm not fucking lost," she snapped. "I'm here to see the old fool. I suggest you move out of my way and go back to whatever you were doing before you regret it."

Usually, that would have done the trick with any of the palace servants. This one apparently didn't know who she was—and she was braver than the common breed employed—as she began to call for the guards.

"It's alright, Alana. This whirlwind is my daughter, and by the looks of things, I'm in trouble again." Jyuth had appeared at the threshold between the entrance hall and his sitting room. Neenahwi hadn't seen him for many a month, but he looked the same as always. The sight of him was generally a comfort, so she had to remind herself she was pissed off. "If you could bring us some lemonade, it would be greatly appreciated. And then you are excused."

"Yes, my lord," said the servant, and she hurried out of the room, keeping a watchful eye on Neenahwi as she went.

"Daughter?" screamed Neenahwi. "Why didn't you inform me of your plans to commit regicide? I thought you trusted me!" Neenahwi thought of this man as her father even though they weren't blood-related. He had saved her from a different fate, taught her how to master her control of magic, and she had believed he thought of her as an equal. It stung she was discovering his plans later than everyone else in the whole city.

"First of all, I don't think of it as regicide," explained the wizard calmly. He gestured for Neenahwi to follow him into the sitting room and join him on the couch. She followed, but shook her head at the offered seat.

"I dissolved the monarchy, and a couple of roadblocks in the way needed tidying up first. And before you interrupt, yes, I do think I have a right to do it. This country wouldn't exist if it weren't for me. I put the first kingly arse on the big chair, and it's only fitting I dispose of the last one. You know I've had to be something of an interventionist in the past, and this was one of those occasions. Though you may not believe it, it wasn't something I had planned before you went gallivanting around. New information came to light."

"Gallivanting! I've been fighting demons and goblins, you old fool. And then I come home, looking forward to a good rest to find all this out!" Neenahwi belatedly processed what she had heard. "Wait, what new information?"

The servant Alana came back into the apartment carrying a tray with a copper pitcher and two glasses. They quietly waited while she brought it to the table, placing the tray down with care, then left.

"What new information?" Neenahwi repeated at a lower volume.

"You don't need to know. Randolph was a turd of the highest order, and everyone will be better off without him."

"What new information?" Neenahwi said through clenched teeth, her moment of calm evaporating before her frustrating father.

"We all knew he had increased taxes on the citizenry, and it was being pissed away somewhere. We also knew he and his wife had peculiar tastes in individuals to join their bedtime activities. What I didn't know was what was connecting it all and how. It was Llewdon and slavery. That's why I wasn't sure if I was going to tell you."

Hearing the name of Llewdon, the Sun Emperor of Pyrfew—a wizard in his own right and the person who had kept Neenahwi and her brother enslaved for eighteen long months—made her blood boil. She tried to keep a tight rein on her anger. "Go on," she said.

"Randolph and his queen had been smuggling slaves into Kingshold. They had purchased a number of houses near the palace where they'd created brothels for the use of them and their friends. The workers at those brothels were people from all over the Jeweled Continent, held against their will. Pyrfew was gathering those people and bringing them to Edland for the king. The gold was all being frittered away on those houses, decorating them, paying people to keep quiet. In exchange for the slaves, the king was trading dwarves from Unedar Halt, live prisoners he had captured in secret over the course of the last two years. I don't know who did it yet, but I have my suspicions. There have been three in total, and each dwarf was worth fifty of the slaves coming back in the other direction."

Neenahwi's hand came up to her mouth at the shock of what had been transpiring. She sat next to her father.

"What, daughter, do you suppose Llewdon wants with them?"

Neenahwi considered the information she had so far and what she knew of the machinations of Pyrfew. "A number of things come to mind, Father. Understanding of the war machines that the dwarves have created for our army and navy. Conscription to help with the mining of iron or gold in their territories; the efficiency of those slave mines must be appalling. And, it could be information about Unedar Halt itself, how to access and use it to gain entry to Kingshold!"

"Yes, my thoughts exactly, and my concern is that it's the latter that interests him. If he could access the dwarven city in secret, take it before an alarm was raised, then Pyrfew would be able to prepare a force that could invade Kingshold from the inside. The defenses around the mountain door used to be considerable, but there have been three hundred years of peace and cooperation and what is there now isn't sufficient to stop any significant force. What silver lining do you see to this cloud?"

Neenahwi noted, but didn't comment, on the fact her father couldn't stop being the teacher, always probing her thinking. "There have been three dwarves traded, presumably over a period of months. That means at least the first two haven't talked, or they haven't divulged enough information. Who knows about the third, though?"

"I do, thankfully. I discovered the plot in time to stop the last dwarf from making it aboard ship here in the harbor."

"What did you do with him? If the Forger discovers the

king of Edland was kidnapping and trading his people into torture, there will be war."

"Yes, I thought of that. I took the dwarf to a safe house I have in the city, and I gave him a draught of Thoughtwart. Once I confirmed he remembered nothing of being captured, I left him in the mountains where his people could find him, the lost memory explained by a fall, evidence provided by a bonk from my trusty staff." The wizard smiled as he pantomimed the swish of a stick.

"And after that," he continued, "I came back to the palace and dethroned the royal couple." He let the words hang there for a moment, the joy had fled from his face. Neenahwi was silent, too, intently focused on this old man she loved, mind racing with implications of Llewdon's intentions.

"Why, Neenahwi? Why does it always come to this?" said the wizard. "No, don't answer, I don't need you to help me feel better. I know why it happens. I have to intervene because the kingdom has come to expect me to do something when things go wrong. Even those who think I'm a different Jyuth than the original one still believe that." He shook his head, considering how some people couldn't accept the evidence right in front of them.

"It sounds crazy, I know. The kingdom is just a group of people, most of whom don't live long enough to see more than one or two changes in the throne. But the collective? That is ever-living.

"And then why are the kings getting shittier much quicker? At the beginning, we went hundreds of years with one bloodline; now I'm down to the next generation being one of the biggest royal arseholes there has ever been, and he was the son of a great king!"

"Father, this makes no sense. It's not your fault if Rudolph didn't raise his son correctly."

"No, you're wrong. I've given this much thought." Jyuth's face was set, and she could see he had made his mind up about something. Experience told her Mount Tiston was more flexible than her father in this mood. "My presence is woven into the history, the fabric of this realm, and it's expected. And. I. Am. Tired. Of. It." He paused for a moment and looked into her eyes. "I need to go away for a long time."

His words took her breath away. "What do you mean? Where will you go?"

"I mean, I'm done with this place. I leave it to you to be its guide." And he gave a seated bow in her direction. "Seeing through this transition of leadership is the last thing I'll do for Edland. This country I founded. And then I'll move away. I'm not sure where yet, but far away from here, from Pyrfew. Somewhere warm. You, dear girl, are the only thing I'll miss about this place, but I won't ask you to come and live the life of an old man. You have your own stories to write."

She stood, her ire rising once more. "You're leaving it to me? You mean you're leaving me with your self-confessed fuck-ups and then you're abandoning me! You arsehole! I don't need you! I don't want your help!" Neenahwi pulled her hair in frustration as the old man in front of her sat helpless.

With a flick of her fingers, the pitcher of lemonade flew into the air and dumped its contents over the wizard's head. She turned on her heel and walked briskly toward the door.

The wet wizard remained in his seat, dripping with lemonade as his daughter stormed out.

~

Even though it was dark, she recognized it immediately as her tribe's village.

How was she here?

She could hear shouts of alarm and warning coming from up ahead. The darkness didn't help with navigation. Unseen rocks and other obstacles caused Neenahwi to stumble as she ran.

Her parents' house came into view, and she made for it as the shouts turned into the sound of battle. More of the tribe's men and women were appearing, armed with spear or ax or bow. Everyone fought when they were under attack.

Neenahwi remembered this night, the night when everything changed.

In the past, she'd been too young to fight, but here and now, she was an adult with real power. Power to change the outcome.

She ran to the house of her parents, looking for her brother, thinking of how to protect him from the dangers around them as she had eighteen years ago. She slid to a halt when she saw him, the little boy who was nearly nine, bow and arrow in hand and looking blurry eyed as he emerged into the night air. A hand grabbed his shoulder and pulled him back inside.

"No, Little Hawk, you must stay here with your sister. I'll be back." The tall figure of her father's champion stepped past her brother and ran into the dark. It had been so long since she had seen Kanaveen. She had to follow him.

Neenahwi set off at a run after this warrior from her past, and in an instant, she found herself in the middle of the chaos. Soldiers in plate and chain armor, with full helms and long swords, were cutting through her tribe.

Wolfclaw weapons were made of stone and bronze, most

arrowheads made of sharp flint, and they did nothing against the armor of the troops attacking. And while they tried to fight bravely, the steel weapons of the attackers were too much.

One of the friends of her mother fell from a blow that severed her leg above the knee (Neenahwi had sat in her lap when they listened to Greytooth's stories).

A boy not much older than she had been on this night—his name was Cadawa (a playmate on the plains around their camp) —charged a soldier with his stone spear. The spearhead ran off the breastplate of the soldier and slipped upwards, ramming into the soldier's neck below his chin. A lucky strike, but Cadawa's fortune had run out. The trooper's arm was already descending, and the flat of his sword bashed the boy's brains out as the soldier fell.

The destruction inflicted on her people, her friends, brought tears to her eyes and a pain to her chest. She began to run again, away from the current battle, in the hope of finding Kanaveen. She tripped and fell and found herself looking into the open eyes of one of her father's hunters, blood running from his mouth and deep wounds to his chest.

A scream came from ahead, and looking up, Neenahwi could see a tall silhouette, half as tall again as the tallest of the tribe's warriors. Tears streaked her cheeks, sooty from the fires lit in the village buildings, as she crawled toward the screaming. She saw her father, and over there, her mother, caught in the grip of an oversized taloned-hand at the end of a bony multi-jointed arm attached to the tall figure. A demon.

This demon had an insectile head, human male body—but with the legs, feet, and claws of a bird of prey. It was saying something to her mother, but she couldn't hear what.

Her mother screamed, "No!" repeatedly and tried to wriggle free as the demon's claws pierced her legs and arms.

Her father ran past her and leaped at the monstrosity with his steel sword (one of the few in her tribe, handed down for generations), but the demon was too fast. It used the figure of her mother to parry the blow from her father while the other taloned-hand reached out and picked him up by the head and threw him away.

Her father's body skittered across the floor as the demon released the broken doll of her mother, falling in a tattered lump on the ground. Sobs racked Neenahwi's body as she saw this unfold.

How could this happen to so many good people?

Kanaveen appeared from the shadows, shouting at Greytooth, their shaman and her teacher, who was pushing the warrior away. She could see the look of anguish on Kanaveen's face as he turned and sprinted away from where her parents had fallen. She knew he'd been sent to escape with her and her brother.

Greytooth turned to face the demon, and his deep voice filled the air, "I'm here, beast. I'm the one you want. I'll be your doom."

The demon ambled forward, the mandibles of its face clicking together as a high-pitched laugh escaped its mouth. "No, paltry wizard, I haven't come for you. You served your purpose years ago. I'm here for your daughter."

"You shall not have her, demon!" The shaman lifted his arms, and blue arcs of light leapt up from his chest and swirled about his arms before coalescing around his fingers. The light gathered, and then streamed out to strike at the demon, but it danced to the side, faster than he expected, and dodged the attack.

A second arc of light caught a multi-jointed arm, which withered black and smoldered, but it didn't stop the creature. Neenahwi could see Greytooth was using all of his power, all of his own precious limited life force against the demon, all self-preservation gone.

She stood, and a fire in her chest exploded into deep purple flames that surrounded her without burning, her tears became rivers of flame down her face. The demon had closed on Greytooth, and its one remaining good arm flashed out to pierce him in the stomach with its clawed hand. Greytooth cried out and doubled over, agonizing pain visible on his face.

Neenahwi screamed in shared pain, and the fire rushed out from her in all directions, scouring the land, the demon, her village, and her people from the world. All was purple and red fire.

All was cleansed.

She didn't know how much time had passed since the flames had died down. She was on rocky terrain, the peak of a mountain to her right. Scrub and mountain bushes were aflame; boulders glowed red in the night.

Where was she?

Neenahwi turned, winds buffeting her, and she saw the lights of a city below her. Kingshold. That meant she was on Mount Tiston, not the plains of her homeland.

Her heart was pounding, her breath came shallow and quick, and her hand hurt where she had been gripping onto something for too long. Opening her fingers, she saw the demon gem nestled in her palm.

CHAPTER 9
HOXTETH

Those mercenaries!

Mareth scowled at the town crier hollering at the crowd around him. In the short walk through the middle district, three of them had announced the arrival of Lord Eden the following day. Three! He didn't agree with them simply peddling their services to whatever rich noble had the coin. They were supposed to be in the employ of the crown, as well as serving a higher mistress—the truth. He couldn't understand how these Criers could abide to be nothing more than a mouthpiece for whomever came along and bought their voice.

Mareth couldn't help but shake his head a little to himself. And to think that now people relied on them to understand what was happening in the realm instead of bards like him.

"Mareth, have you been listening to me?" asked Master Gonal, walking slightly in front of him. "Is it something I said that made you have such a dirty look on your face?"

In his indignation, Mareth had lost track of where he was for a moment.

"I'm sorry, Master Gonal, for my wandering attention," he replied. "I was simply aghast at this news about Lord Eden. It's being announced like he's a savior riding into the city." He knew Gonal was not a fan of Eden; he had already made up his mind on his candidate and that was where they were heading. So, Mareth made sure not to say any positive words about the noble arriving on the morrow, though he did have some respect for Eden's style. He was sure his entrance would be a spectacle.

"Ah, yes, I share your distaste for Eden," said the merchant. "It'll be an opportunity lost for the people of our kingdom if the new lord protector is one of the establishment. The richest man in Edland, what can he possibly understand about the everyday person? Where would his priorities lie, eh? Well, I'll tell you. War. That's how his family made their treasure, and how he gathered more. Now, war can be good for business, but I don't want my son getting fancy ideas about becoming a knight or another kind of hero. Peace, that's what we need, so our children can focus on making money."

It was a little past noon, and the sun was hot on Mareth's face. A boy had delivered him a message that morning to meet the merchant at noon, by the fountain in the Square of Queen Linn. They hadn't met the day before, and he'd been concerned his connection had fallen through. Mareth had been gathering himself to search for the merchant when the messenger had arrived, so that had been a blessed and timely relief.

But now, meeting at a public place, and then walking to the meeting (no carriage), raised alarm bells about Master

Gonal. His blond-bearded friend at the Royal Oak the other night was likely correct in questioning how he was able to vote. He either lived like a miser, or getting the little demon had cost him every penny he owned. But he couldn't fault the fact that he'd followed through on bringing him to the meeting. Assuming it materialized.

"When we arrive at Hoxteth's mansion, I need you to make sure that I do all the talking," explained Gonal, Mareth nodding along. "I'll introduce you as my bagman—a place of respect, you understand—that will allow you to remain with me during the meeting. There will be some business that needs to be conducted, but you'll get to observe and have your view of the man we hope will be our first protector."

Mareth suppressed recoiling at the mention of him being a bagman. He vowed he would never stoop so low in reality. An assistant in commerce? Was there no other title he could be given? But it really didn't matter. How else would he be able to create his chronicle if he couldn't judge the mettle of these men and women? He needed the meeting.

They arrived at a stone mansion house, four stories high and twice the size of the Royal Oak, leaded windows with a steep sloped slate roof and turrets at each corner. Outside the thick reinforced front door stood two professional-looking guards, clean shaven, with untarnished chainmail under tabards emblazoned with Hoxteth's sigil of an unbalanced scale. Rumor had it the judiciary was not too pleased with Hoxteth's choice of sigil—their balanced scales referring to justice, his unbalanced ones meaning he got the better end of any deal.

Master Gonal introduced himself to the guards and showed them the pyxie in his pocket (which blew a raspberry in the guard's face). The entrance routine was successful, to

Mareth's immense relief, and they were escorted into a waiting room. Three other people sat there, whom Mareth pegged as merchants by the hungry looks in their eyes.

The two of them took seats in the tastefully decorated room. Wood paneling lined the walls with green-velvet couches and individual chairs in clusters about a space that Mareth considered to be nearly as big as his father's great hall. Tapestries of great skill hung from the walls. One depicting a dragon fighting a knight on horseback. Another of a broad oak tree with golden apples and children sleeping in its boughs.

They sat without talking, silence in the air, with only the sounds of the household to be heard. Every ten minutes or so, one of the other men waiting was met by an officious-looking steward to escort them into an adjoining room. Mareth found himself tapping his hands on the arms of the chair or his feet on the floor, which would draw unhappy glances from Gonal.

"Lord Hoxteth will see you now." The steward had approached without Mareth noticing. He had been working through a particularly troublesome rhyme in a long-time work in progress regarding a giant he'd once met. The steward addressed Master Gonal, "Thank you for waiting. As you can see, it's been a rather busy afternoon. You may leave your associate here and collect him once your business has concluded."

"Thank you, Master Bales, but this is my bagman, and he's present for all of my business conversations. I'm sure you can understand the importance of being on hand to execute on any business. He's new in my employ, but he's proven himself to be quite exemplary."

The Bales man looked Mareth up and down and didn't

seem to be particularly impressed with what he saw. Mareth wasn't particularly impressed with what he saw, either, but he did suppose that he should have dressed more for the role he had to play.

He wore the finest clothes he now owned—perhaps a little tight around the middle—but they still vied for quality with that of his supposed master in this charade, which would mark him as unusual. It was hardly his fault, though. He hadn't been given any warning. Bales gave a little snort, said, "Very well," and escorted them to the door at the far end of the room where all of the previous attendees had also been led.

The room they entered was dark and candlelit while the waiting room was bright with light from the many windows, and so, it took a moment for Mareth's eyes to adjust. They were in a library with a large wooden desk in the center, a man seated behind it with a stack of parchment in front of him, and shelves of leather-bound books lining the walls. The man was small and of middle years, grey hair cut neatly close to his skull, and lean in the face and the waist. Mareth was happy to see he had not succumbed to the typical predilection of the rich to show their wealth in their girth. He wore clothes of black silk with an elegant black, woolen cape, which in the diminished light of the room gave the impression of his pale face floating disembodied in the air. This was obviously Hoxteth.

Behind him, next to the unlit fireplace, sat a handsome woman in an attractive purple gown, some ten years younger (or her life had been ten years kinder) with black hair braided down her back. She didn't look up from the book she was reading as Gonal sat down in the chair across from the lord treasurer.

"Well, well, well. Master Gonal. What a pleasure to see you here." Hoxteth smiled a thin smile as his guest got comfortable. "It must be what, fifteen years since you last sat opposite me? I trust your bookkeeping skills have improved in the intervening years?"

"Ha-ha. My lord, it's a pleasure to see you again. I learnt so much from you. Your kindness in teaching a young man has been immensely valuable to my success today. Nothing to rival you, of course, my lord." Mareth's eyes rolled at Gonal's nervous laughter. He stood by the closed door, a few strides from the action where he thought Gonal likely to pledge his undying love any minute now. "I want you to know you're the man for me to be the lord protector of our realm. You'll bring peace and stability and the right environment for business."

"Excellent. I'm pleased to hear it. I shall count on your vote in the coming weeks. Was there anything else?"

"Well, Lord Hoxteth, you taught me that every opportunity is a business opportunity and never to trust anything freely given." Gonal was quickly trying to dig himself out of his self-made hole. It had looked likely they were going to be ushered out as soon as Gonal had gotten comfortable. "So, yes, you are my favored candidate. But business is business after all. I have a pyxie, and you and your competition want them to call their name at the tally, and so, that has to be worth something..."

Lord Hoxteth looked directly into Gonal's eyes without speaking a word. The silence extended, but his face remained impassive.

"Yes, that's correct, Gonal. Maybe you did learn from our brief time together. If I understand rightly, you're still in the wool trade. How would you like to diversify into silks?"

Gonal's head bobbed up and down in acceptance. Was his brief moment of courage fading away? "In that case, I'll give you two options, and you must choose now. Option one, I'll give you free use of one of my ships and crew to acquire your first consignment of silks. This is guaranteed at the time when your vote is cast. Option two is dependent on my successful election, but in this case, I'll grant you a ten-year license from the realm to create and operate a market dedicated to the buying and selling of silks. All business would pass through your halls. Which option will you choose?"

"My lord, they're both very generous offers, with obviously different risk and rewards. But I'd be foolish to pass up the opportunity you propose when you become lord protector. I have every confidence you'll be chosen. How can the civilized population not see you're the right candidate? Let's put this in writing, and I'll cast a vote here in front of you."

Hoxteth nodded to the steward standing beside Mareth, who went to a stack of papers on a nearby table and pulled out a pre-prepared parchment. Bales went about inscribing the specifics of the deal while the bard remained motionless.

Mareth had a newfound respect for Master Gonal. The deal he'd struck would deliver a great return on the investment he'd made in the pyxie. But was that the limit of the conversation? It was hardly the stuff of tales to have a succession of votes bought by favor.

He noticed Lady Hoxteth was looking at him quite intently, and when he met her gaze, she didn't look away. She seemed to consider him further before giving a brief smile and returning to her reading.

Gonal and Hoxteth had now signed the agreement, and the former took the little pyxie out of his traveling pocket and placed it on the desk in front of him.

"I wish to place my vote for lord protector for Lord Hoxteth," said Gonal, slowly and carefully.

"Please state your name." The pyxie's voice was rough and gravelly. He wasn't sure why, but Mareth had expected a high-pitched squeak.

"I am Master Alborz Gonal." And with that, the little demon gave a nod, smiled a smile of a pin cushion, and then disappeared in a *pop*, leaving a faint smell of sulfur behind.

"Thank you, Master Gonal. I'm pleased to have earned your vote. Master Bales will see you out now. More eligible voters to meet. I'm sure you understand."

Hoxteth stood, shook Gonal's hand, and was guiding him toward his steward and the door. Mareth was disappointed this was it. His window of opportunity to do something, he was not sure what, was disappearing.

"Wait," called Mareth, all eyes turning to the man that the rest of the audience had considered to be a temporary part of the furniture. "I mean, Lord Hoxteth, let me introduce myself now that you've finished your business. I'm Mareth, a bard of some renown in the right circles, and I've taken it as duty to chronicle this historic moment for Edland."

"Gonal, what is the meaning of this?" Hoxteth directed his ire toward the man he had just been thanking. "You bring a minstrel into a meeting with us in disguise?"

"Er, I... was only trying to support the arts, my lord," Gonal stammered as he gave Mareth a look of combined disgust and anger.

"It's my fault, my lord. I asked Master Gonal here to help. And he's familiar with my work, which helped him understand the cause I serve. I know, my lord, you're the favorite to be our new lord protector, and if you'd do me the honor of sharing with me your firsthand thoughts in this saga, then I'd be eternally grateful. And I would, of course, immortalize you in song."

Lady Grey had walked to stand shoulder-to-shoulder with her husband. He looked close to anger, but she was more contemplative.

"You look familiar, Mareth. Have we met before?" she asked. "Where are you from?"

"I don't believe we've met before, my lady. I'd remember a face so beautiful." Mareth's attempts to curry favor with the woman seemed to land on fallow ground with Hoxteth, so he quickly moved on. "But I'm from Bollingsmead. Son of Tomas and Prisanth."

"That's it! I knew you looked familiar." Lady Grey clapped her hands. "Doesn't he, my dear? A younger, more dashing version of the fuddy-duddy Tomas Bollingsmead. So, you are a bard, are you? I'm sure your father doesn't approve!" Mareth didn't go around calling out his heritage. He *knew* his father wouldn't approve.

"He doesn't, my lady. But we all have to make sacrifices to achieve our calling, don't you think?"

"Yes, of course, very astute. We have all made sacrifices. Dear, follow me for a moment." Lady Grey led her husband by the arm to the far corner of the room to confer in whispers, glancing over at Mareth, considering him appraisingly, like livestock or the latest fashion.

While they spoke, Mareth became aware that Bales the steward was behind him, accompanied by two guards, both of whom looked as professional as the guards at the main entrance. Professional enough to see him go the way of a certain senior bookkeeper if this parley didn't go well.

After a few minutes, the pair walked past the desk and round to face the bard.

"Mareth, I don't approve of how you came to be here," said Lord Hoxteth, the anger gone from his features, "but after due consideration with my lady wife, I have a proposition for you. I'll be your patron. Secretly, of course, and in return, you'll do your work to cast me in the most favorable light and disparage my competitors. You will, of course, have to take your performances to the most reputable establishments in the inner district for the right people to listen to you. Eden is going to throw his considerable wealth at this campaign, and I don't desire to try to fight him coin for coin. He may have a reputation as a military tactician, but I haven't gotten where I am today without understanding people. And people believe what you tell them."

CHAPTER 10
ERRANDS

Jyuth had said she was free to go.

Instead, she'd waited just outside the door to the wizard's apartment, by the rose bushes that framed the entryway.

She told herself she was only doing so in case he needed something else. But the truth of it was she was intrigued by the tall, beautiful woman who had strode so purposefully into the wizard's rooms without the typical fear she saw others display around him. And then he'd referred to her as his daughter. They didn't look alike, but she did seem to share his confidence.

Alana could hear the two of them shouting at each other, in the way only family members tend to do. And then the voices returned to a normal volume, and she couldn't hear what they were saying. It was too much for her conscience to put her ear against the door to listen better, so she picked at some dirt underneath her fingernails. Then the woman's voice erupted again.

"You're leaving!"

The doors swung violently open into her face, and she saw the woman's figure receding down the garden path. Alana had seen that hurried shuffle and hunched posture before. That woman was crying and not trying to hide it.

"Girl. Don't stand there with your mouth open. I thought you were dismissed. Get in here." A wet wizard was standing in the doorway, picking slices of lemon out of his beard and off his robes.

Alana hurried into the room, secured the entrance, and took a deep breath before turning to face the wizard.

"My lord, I'm very sorry. I-I-I was just waiting in case you needed me."

"I told you I didn't need you, Alana." The wizard's face softened, and he sighed. "Bring me a towel and some water. I'm starting to feel sticky."

"So, Alana, what did you hear?" asked Jyuth. "And tell me precisely. I have ways of knowing the truth you'd rather not become accustomed to."

While Jyuth dried his face, Alana recounted what she'd heard as completely as she could, finishing her tale with what the wizard's daughter had screamed before she left the apartment.

Her stomach churned at the possible implications of her actions. Was she going to be fired? She and her sister depended on the income from the palace; the options weren't good for people in the Narrows. Or maybe she was going to end up like the king and queen with her head on a spike! She looked at the floor, but her eyes grew wide as her mind raced with all of the terrible alternatives.

"Thank you for telling me everything, Alana. And I'm glad you didn't hear all of our exchange. For your sake." Jyuth finished drying his hands and face and threw the towel on the sofa. "Now, I'm sure you have some questions..."

"Questions, my lord? No, I don't have any questions; that's not my place." Alana couldn't believe she was getting away with what she did. She just wanted to get out of there now.

"If I asked you if you have any questions, then I'll be disappointed if you don't have any questions," said Jyuth. "And even though you try to hide it, I can see you're intelligent. And I like to nurture intelligence, wherever I find it. So, ask away. And do sit. I hate to talk and stand at the same time."

"Yes, my lord." Alana wasn't sure if this was some kind of trick. Maybe she should just ask some inane questions and still make good her escape. But she might not get the chance to have a conversation with Lord Jyuth again. Curiosity won out. "Who was that?"

"Ah, yes. You haven't been in the palace long; otherwise, you'd know Neenahwi. She was my apprentice, and I have long considered her to be the daughter I never had. We have a somewhat complicated history. She's from the Wild Continent, you know. I'm sure you noticed her distinctive appearance."

"Why is she here? I mean, what brought her to Edland from the Wild Continent?"

"That's her story to tell, not mine," he replied, "but she once resided here in the palace with me, traveled with me in my studies, and now she lives in the city. Next question."

Alana took a deep breath before asking the next question. The answer was what had made Lady Neenahwi explode and it could be a touchy subject with the wizard.

"She said you're leaving. What does that mean? Everyone knows you come and go. Sometimes you're gone for years..."

"Alana, what I tell you now you have to promise me you won't tell another soul." At the nod of her head, he continued. "Good. Well, I plan on, how shall I put it, retiring. Yes, retiring. It's time I let this kingdom stand on its own two feet, or at least let someone else meddle in it instead of me. Such as my daughter. I want to go somewhere quiet and have peace to study. Oh, how I need to have peace and quiet. And I want it to be warm all year round. I'm tired of snow!" He said the last words with a smile on his face, and it was apparent he was trying to make a joke, but Alana just frowned at him.

"Don't worry, Alana. This city isn't going to sink into the ocean without me. And it's probably going to do better with whatever lord protector is elected than any king I install. I'm not going to leave Edland in the lurch and disappear."

"Is that why you wanted there to be an election? So you couldn't be blamed for a bad leader after you were gone? Are you really going to just leave it up to the people?"

"I see the dam blocking those questions has burst, and the torrent comes out!" The old man let out a deep laugh that came from down low.

"And I also see I was right about your quick mind, Alana. Call it an old man's ego, but that's exactly the reason why I thought an election would be the right course. Mind you, I want you to understand the king and his queen didn't die because of me wanting an election. There were much more severe issues I had to address that led to that outcome. The election was simply making the best of a bad lot. And what was your last question?"

Jyuth paused to think back, and a mischievous look crossed his face. "Oh, yes, as if I, Jyuth the Wise, Wizard of Kingshold, would tamper with the election!" And he laughed again, Alana uncertain what his response had meant. "You do remind me, though, I have a few errands in the city where I need your help."

JYUTH HAD MADE HER MEMORIZE THE TASKS HE GAVE HER along with the addresses in the city she had to visit. He'd given her two sealed messages and two gold crowns and an additional warning for her to watch her back, which had now made her the tiniest bit twitchy.

First stop was the Stonemasons' Guild just outside the Inner Wall to deliver a message to Guild Master Ballard. The guards at the door to the guild house were a rough-looking lot, more like professional slouches than professional guards, but they did still stop her from entering until they saw the royal seal on the documents.

Alana had asked the wizard why he was using a royal seal when the monarchy was no more, which seemed to amuse him greatly. He said it should at least get the messages read. She delivered the message to the guild master personally as instructed, and she waited in the antechamber outside his office for a response. Ballard came out himself to hand her a rolled-up piece of parchment, sealed with the crossed chisel sigil of the guild. "Tell him I'll be there tomorrow, around noon. For lunch!"

The next stop took her all the way down to the end of

the Lance, and along the Outer Wall, until she saw the compound, a wall enclosing three buildings and a courtyard visible through the gate. This was the home of the Hollow Syndicate, an ancient group of assassins, apparently completely legal even though their business was murder. She'd heard stories of how trainee assassins were typically bonded with the guild as small boys and girls, where they then, eventually, graduated or were *released*.

The school for trainees shared the compound with the house that was home to the members, though novices weren't allowed entry. Apparently, non-Syndicate members weren't allowed either, as the doorman wouldn't let her in. But he did promise to convey the message to Lady Chalice, the leader of the house.

Jyuth had warned her she likely wouldn't be able to enter, but she was still disappointed all the same. The stonemasons' guild house was the first she'd ever seen from the inside, and while it didn't have the grandness of the palace, it had a feeling of *sensible elegance* and a certain coziness that appealed to Alana. And though the Hollow Syndicate wasn't an official guild, she wondered how their house would compare, especially as their members were regarded with higher status.

She didn't have to wait for a reply, and so, she was left to her daydreams of what it'd be like to be trained as a killer, as she walked back out onto the busy city streets.

Her third stop was to a smithy, not on the Lance where most of the blacksmiths who created arms and armor for knights, lords, and ladies were located. This smith was on the other side of the Outer Wall, Garlick's shop near the Narrows.

She knew the place by sight and reputation. Garlick tended to horse's shoes and iron for carts and building materials, and she didn't know why Jyuth would have business with him. But she followed her instructions and introduced herself to the smith as a messenger from Merchant Harwich.

Garlick retrieved a sealed message from a room adjoining the smithy itself—the private rooms of the blacksmith and his family, as evidenced by the sounds of children playing—and handed it over with little discussion. She made her farewells and moved onto her last stop.

Out in the streets, she tried to stay close to the afternoon crowds, wary of the wizard's warning about being followed. As she neared the Narrows, the number of people she recognized increased, many saying good afternoon and stopping as if to pass the time of day, but Alana made her excuses in each case and hurried on her way.

As she passed one alleyway, a hand reached out and grabbed her arm, pulling her off the main street. Alana's hand went to the little knife she carried in a pocket. Screams were of little use if someone was willing to attack in broad daylight.

"Alana, it's me, Davith."

"What are you doing, Davith? I was just about to stick you. You want to end up like your dad?"

"No! Look, you need to know, there's someone following you." Davith was small for his fifteen or so summers, but that's what happened when you grew up on the streets and had to fight for every meal. He was part of a small gang of similar street kids. They did a little petty theft, mainly of people outside the neighborhood, and Alana had something of a soft spot for Davith and his friends. She sometimes thought about how she and her sister could have ended up on the streets when her parents died.

"Who?" she asked, anxiously looking over her shoulder. "What do they look like? How do you know?"

"We saw you come through the Redgate an hour or so ago, and we tagged this solo man just after you. Looked like a tradesman, but not one we recognized. So, we were going to see if he'd like to make a charitable contribution, you know, but he was never out of eyesight of you. He didn't tag us, I swear. He was hanging around when you were at Garlick's, and then as soon as you left, he moved, too. We thought you should know."

"Shit," she exclaimed. Alana wasn't one for swearing. She got that from her Da, who never swore even though he was a sailor. Her Ma, though, now she could swear. This seemed like one of the occasions when her father would forgive her. "I mean, thanks, Davith. Maybe I can lose him in the Narrows."

"You want us to help?" he asked excitedly. "We could create a little diversion to would give you enough time to slip away."

"Davith, if you weren't covered in filth I'd kiss you. Instead, you do a good job, and I'll give you this shiny gold crown. You know where I live. You can come and get it tonight after the ninth bell."

"A crown!" he exclaimed, a desperate craving visible in the boy's eyes. He and his friends could live for a while on a crown, as long as they didn't get robbed themselves. "We could take care of him permanently for that if you like. Just give me your little knife and we'll—"

"No thanks, Davith!" she said hurriedly. "The diversion will be just fine! And if it works, you'll have earned the fee."

~

She set the tray of crusty pies down on the table in Jyuth's apartment.

The fourth errand had been to buy a batch of blood pies from Mama Batty's in the Narrows. Getting the pies and making it back to the palace had been uneventful, the diversion having worked a treat. But to call it just a diversion seemed unworthy; it was a masterful display of street-urchin theater, the actors ad-libbing on the same frequency without a formal plan.

There had not been time to go through a dress rehearsal, but Davith had only needed to let his friends know the rough objective using hand signals they had developed, and then everything clicked into gear.

As Alana entered the Narrows, she was roughly aware of the presence of the man who was following fifty strides or so behind her. Once the alleyway became tight, she ducked behind a jutting corner so she could watch what was going to happen, whether she'd have some breathing room or would need a plan B. That, and she wanted to watch the show.

Her shadow approached the entrance to the Narrows, when one of the street kids leaped off a nearby building onto a cart, whipping the horse into a charge with the rope that normally held his trousers in place. The horse and cart swerved into the entranceway to the Narrows, smashing into a watermelon salesman and sending the fruits spinning across the ground.

The wagon became stuck while, at the same time, the horse went berserk from the impact and being trapped in a confined space. The man had to stop then. He couldn't enter the Narrows through this gate, and while he pondered his next move, the other kids pounced.

A tomato—hurled with the accuracy of a lifetime of practice at throwing stones at pigeons to get food to eat—smashed into the back of his head, red juice exploding around him like a halo. He turned and another kid materialized and threw himself at the back of the man's knees, causing him to fall face first into the street. And before he knew what was happening, a score of street kids swarmed over him, holding him down, stripping him clean like ravens on a dead rat.

That was all she needed to see, and all the time Alana needed to make it into the heart of the district she called home, walking quickly through the confined streets.

"Ah, blood pies," exclaimed Jyuth, as he entered the sitting room. She could see how he had gained his physique, this man clearly enjoyed his food. "Excellent, Alana. How did everything go?"

Alana told the wizard about her journey, handing over the messages from the stonemasons' guild master and the blacksmith. He opened the letters and nodded as he read them, all the while eating the blood pies. When it was time to talk about the person tailing her, Jyuth put the pie down and paid his full attention.

"Did you see who it was?" he asked. "Would you recognize him again?"

"I'm sorry, my lord. I didn't get a good look. It was Davith who told me I was being followed. I felt it before, but I could never catch a glimpse of him."

"Hmmph. I bet that long slimy shit, Aebur, is trying to stick his nose into my business. Well, we'll need to be smarter next time, right, Alana?" Jyuth flashed a mischievous smile, not unlike Davith's when she had promised him the gold crown for his work. She found herself smiling right back at the old man.

CHAPTER 11
TIN MAN

It seemed as if half of the city had come out to line the Farm Road from the Excise Gate up to the Outer Wall, and many of them had been waiting since early morning. Though Eden's criers had proclaimed which day he'd be arriving, they'd been less specific on the actual time.

Mareth was standing in the garret window of a ramshackle apartment building, the home of an old lady he had just met. He'd chosen this particular window as it was ideally suited to have a view down the road to the gate from where Eden would approach. Mareth took little pride in charming a little old lady in a small hovel—that wasn't much of a challenge—but he was glad she'd made her guests a cup of tea while they all waited. You see, Mareth wasn't alone in this endeavor. He had a new best friend: Dolph.

Dolph had come as part of the deal with Hoxteth, with the explanation he'd be helpful to the bard. He'd make connections at the right kind of inns and meeting halls and protect him in case of any trouble if he was to say anything to anger a supporter of a rival candidate.

And what went unsaid was Dolph could keep an eye on their investment of ten crowns in advance and five a week. Dolph came without uniform, nor visible armor (though Mareth thought he had chainmail under his jerkin given some jingly noises when he walked), and he wasn't the hulking type of guard someone used when they were obviously guarding something. More the type that managed not to attract anyone's eye, but then when someone did notice him, they'd sense the confident menace. This was a man who broke fingers in the evening—for fun.

But still, Mareth was sure the old lady was so accommodating because she liked him.

It was a bell or so before noon, and the crowd on the Farm Road was mainly made up of commoners from The Edge of Kingshold, the collection of districts that existed in between what was still called the Outer Wall and the Curtain Wall, which was now the true boundary of the city.

The population of the city had exploded in the last few hundred years, and most of the growth had taken place in The Edge, and now the vast majority of the city's population lived there. They were the working poor, the destitute and the forgotten. Those in positions of power and nobility gave them little thought, except in times of war, plague, and famine. But Mareth had spent most of his life with people like that since he had left the Bard College. He'd seen how even in their daily struggles, they often had more moments of happiness than those with two coins to rub together. He knew whose company he preferred now, including that of his own family.

From his vantage point, Mareth could see small groups of cutpurses roaming the crowd, but it was slim pickings for likely targets, like vultures descending on the victims of starvation. Across the street stood a priest of Arloth declaring blasphemy for the temerity of having the people choose a ruler, calling out at the top of his lungs, that it was the responsibility of the gods.

The sound of horns blowing a fanfare came from the direction of the Excise Gate. Mareth squinted to see to the end of the road, just making out the beginning of the procession coming into the city.

White horses led the way, their riders flying the emblem of Eden, crossed swords over a sheaf of wheat on a burgundy background. Behind the vanguard were a handful of knights on horseback, one of them a giant of a man, all wearing shining plate armor. Following them were ten ranks of household guard marching in formation.

It seemed like Eden had arrived with a small army, the crowds going wild as they approached. Following the house guards was a single figure on horseback, wearing ceremonial armor of silver and gold with burgundy inlays, and then another group of infantry behind.

So that was Eden, keeping all of the attention on himself. *Got to love his style. He knows everyone likes a military procession.*

Drummers beat the rhythm of the march, booted feet meeting the tempo, and the sound reverberated down the street. The cheers from the crowd had increased steadily, but then it changed. Cries of welcome giving way to shouts and even some screams. Mareth could see the crowd moving backward and forward like a pumping heart, calls for help from those trapped by the shove of the crowd.

As the procession reached halfway down the road, he could make out people on either side of Eden throwing small objects that glinted silver into the crowd. It caused the throng to scramble at the ground and grab at their neighbor's hands. Scuffles broke out, and children nearest the street were getting pushed out in front of the procession, and then pushed back by Eden's guards.

Mareth could hear chants of "Eden's Silver" from below. *Was that fool throwing silver coins into the crowd?* The people below certainly thought so as, all of a sudden, the group that lined the street in front of the procession broke from their waiting positions and rushed toward the mounted knights, afraid all the silver would be gone by the time Eden reached them.

A shouted command went up from the group of guards, and they stepped forward to create a perimeter around their Lord and the mounted knights. Shields up, swords drawn. From the front, and then from all sides, people smashed into the shields and looked to push their owners down to the ground. The guards struck at the crowds with sword hilts or the flat of their blades, but some used the sharp edge, and the real screams began. People at the mercy of the guards' impenetrable wall were shoved continually forward by people at the back of the group, themselves safe from harm but desperate for the silver coins.

"Oh my, I'm glad I didn't go down there," said the old lady standing next to Dolph and looking out the window. "These things never end well, you know. My nan always said, 'Change is a demon with a smiling face.'"

Mareth looked at Dolph. "We should do something."

"There's nothing we can do, Bard," said Dolph. "And I'm not paid to be a hero."

Mareth was about to declaim the absence of the city guard when a regiment approached from the Outer Wall end of the Farm Road, dressed in chainmail and leather and holding long wooden sticks. The crowd were now trapped between Eden's men and the city guard, who began cracking skulls and dragging citizens away. Some men and a few women tried to stand their ground and trade punches, perhaps laying a city guard out on the ground, but then they'd be tackled on multiple sides and dragged away kicking and struggling.

Beneath their window, Mareth saw a group of children trying to avoid the chaos: a teenage girl corralling younger children and stopping them from scrabbling on the ground.

"We have to help them!" Mareth cried and moved for the door, suddenly relieved to be doing something, even though he was running into a riot.

Dolph grabbed at his jerkin and pulled him back, but Mareth turned and drove his fist into his minder's stomach. Mareth caught Dolph by surprise, who released his grip but, in truth, his stomach had been as hard as unflinching stone, and Mareth's hand throbbed.

"Come back here, you arse!" called Dolph to Mareth's retreating form. "You'll get yourself killed. Or arrested!"

Mareth dashed down the three flights of stairs, hearing the hammering of Dolph's steps behind him as he made it out of the front door and into the street. The noise assaulted him immediately: cries of pain, horses stomping, the *bash* and the *thud* of sticks and shields on flesh. The crowd had scattered. Most who could, ran for safety, but some were still trying to get at Eden or find the silver on the ground. Mareth turned on the spot, taking it all in, and he saw the children who initially attracted his attention as Dolph burst out on the street.

"Children!" Mareth called, attracting their attention. "Quickly, come into the house." He ushered five children of varying ages toward the door. Dolph stepped toward him, arm back, and fist clenched.

"Duck!" shouted Dolph.

Mareth threw himself out of the way as Dolph planted his leather-gauntleted fist right into the nose of a city guard who'd been approaching from behind. His nose smeared across his face, and he fell to the ground with a clatter. They both rushed into the tenement house behind the children, barred the door, and pushed everyone up the stairs and back to the old lady's room.

"Thanks, Dolph," said Mareth. Getting brained by a guard's cudgel would have definitely impacted his new work arrangement.

"Look here," said Dolph, his finger pointing in his ward's face. "I did it because it's my job. I'm not going to hit you because that's my job, too. But you got one lucky punch. Now, remember I'm a man with skills very much in demand, and given enough incentive, I can find another job. And then I don't have certain restrictions. Get it?"

"Er, alright. Got it," said Mareth.

The old lady clucked around the children, making sure they didn't have any more severe wounds than a few bumps and scrapes. Mareth stepped away from his angry minder. He thought a little distance between them might be wise, so he went over to inspect the children, too.

"Do you know them?" he asked the old lady.

"Yes. These were Maggie-from-around-the-corner's kids. Look at 'em. All different dads. But she died a couple of months back. A bad customer done it." The old lady turned to address the oldest child. "Where you been, girl?"

"We didn't have nowhere to go, Agnes. Been living in the alleys. But now we've got silver, we'll be able to get our old place back and eat something warm!" Tears were in her eyes, but a broad smile brightened her face as she raised her hand to show the silver coins they'd picked up off the street.

But something was wrong. Many of the coins had bent in half from her tight grip. Mareth reached over and took one from her hand to examine it.

"I'm sorry, child. These aren't silvers," said Mareth bitterly. "They have Eden's face stamped on them for starters. And then this looks like tin, not silver. That's why it bent so easily. Eden wasn't giving away money; he was giving out fucking souvenirs!"

THE FOLLOWING EVENING, MARETH WAS AT THE Griffon's Beak, an inn in The Upper Circle. It wasn't a place he typically frequented. He found that this place—and more generally, the other inns and taverns in the most well-to-do area of Kingshold—lacked the character and the characters he'd find elsewhere, not to mention the ability for him to drink on credit. Also, there was a distinct lack of women in these particular establishments. Mareth was dressed in new finery that Dolph had picked up from the tailors, part of his package from Lord Hoxteth to make sure he looked the part.

Mareth had been up late writing, and with hardly any ale, too, which he had been proud of. Seeing how the people had been treated earlier that day, and the needs of those children in particular, had both saddened and inspired him. He'd left a few silvers behind with Agnes in the hopes she'd give a home to the orphans for at least a time, but he knew something bigger had to be done to make a real impact.

And so, for the first time in a long time, he *really* worked, through the night, until he was proud of something.

Then he slept most of the day.

By the time he arrived at the Griffon's Beak with his Dolph-shaped shadow in tow, he was freshly bathed and had only just broken fast.

On arrival, he met with the landlord of the establishment to discuss proceedings. Their resident minstrel, a man by the name of Carney, whom Mareth was aware of by reputation, had come down with illness two nights before. And so, the landlord was grateful to Mareth for being able to stand in. Fortunate timing.

At eight o'clock, Mareth was to start playing, and the landlord would tell him when to call it a night, usually around midnight when most of the well-to-do merchants or lordlings had drifted off home to bed. He began with some of the classical fair, walking around the common room to get a feel for the crowd. Mostly small groups, Mareth could tell many of the younger men were unmarried and probably ate most meals at the Griffon, but there were also groups of older gentlemen with whiskers, who were more serious in their drinking.

After the classics, he moved onto comic verses as the drink did its work on the customers, and their voices rose to join in when they knew the words. Mareth was carefully gauging the audience. He wanted to be able to time it perfectly.

And so, when he felt he had the attention of most in the room, he banged his mandolin with the flat of his hand. The room grew silent as all eyes became fixed on him.

"My lords, gentlemen. It's a pleasure to play for you this evening." There was a strong round of applause, and Mareth knew he had them before he started. "We live in changing times, and it's the solemn duty of the Bard to document history. And so, my next piece is a new song. You'll be able to tell your family and friends you were here. This song is called, *The Fable of the Tin Man*.

He won the day with curse and smoke,
let the ego of the man work,
its wicked revenge on his-self,
and he came along to sweep it up.

E-den, E-den,
Free-er of Pool.

He reaped the reward of the king's gift,
taxes he levied on all you do buy,
lines his pocket with gold,
and he comes along to sweep it up.

E-den, E-den,
taxman for you

The king is gone and his income may, too
disappear, and so, with his criers,
he announces his return to Kingshold,
so he can sweep it up.

E-den, E-den,
Player of fools

He rode through the tax gate

with his army around,
cheering crowds plucking silver from the air,
and sweeping it up off the ground.

E-den, E-den,
spreader of coin.

But this was no silver, it was only tin,
tin for cracked heads and crushed children,
tin for the realm and tin for you, too,
so, he can sweep you all up.

Tin-man, Tin-man,
protector of none.

CHAPTER 12
TWILIGHT EXILES

It was incredible how from city to city, country to country, that resident groups of thieves and ne'er-do-wells always ended up living in the sewers. Or, at least in some long-forgotten buried part of the city, one usually accessed via sewers. If someone were to build a new city, would they have to put in secret tunnels so thieves could hang out there?

Those were the thoughts that kept Motega's mind off the smell of piss, shit, and rotten matter as they followed the little thief who had finally introduced himself as "Gneef." Of course, the broken nose was messing with his enunciation, so it could be his name was Keith or Leif, but the three of them found it more fun to keep calling him Gneef.

They could easily have walked away from Gneef when he told them Sharavin, current mother and leader of the Twilight Exiles, wanted to see them, but there would be no escaping for long unless they got out of town. And that wasn't in the cards right now. It seemed like there was excitement and potentially some coin to be had in this election. So best to get it out of the way and see how Trypp could talk his way out of trouble this time.

Now, if Gneef had said Father Silas had wanted to see them, then they might well have just turned around, packed their bags, and headed back to the docks. Back before he had earned the "Father" honorific, they called him Psycho Silas, and it was right on the nose. But life at the top of a pyramid of cutthroats and purse-snatchers is a shaky one; not many reached grey hair.

So far, their journey had been through a pie shop run by a man called Dibbler, his basement leading to a passage that led into one of the underground sewers that ran the length of the Inner Farm Road from under the market square to the Green Gate. They were wide round tunnels, open at the apex of the arch along the length of the sewer. If anyone stood underneath, he could see fifty feet up to the street above.

Of course, if that person stood underneath, he was likely to get a bucket of shit on his face.

Gneef walked ahead with a lantern he'd taken from the pieman's basement. Even though some light filtered down from above and even without Per's eyes (he had stayed above ground), Motega noticed at least three lookouts hidden in the shadows. After a few hundred yards, six big heavies came to meet Gneef. Enforcer types who made sure everyone paid their debts or the kind to make sure no one tried anything while being escorted to a secret criminal hideout.

Motega wasn't worried about these six. They were big men, but he doubted they were used to fighting someone armed. The three of them might get a scratch or two, but they shouldn't be a problem if there needed to be a scrap.

Trypp had been babbling to Gneef during the walk, and now he was trying to talk to the thugs, too, making some joke or other about where they bought their matching clubs. If he didn't know better, he'd think Trypp was nervous.

Florian and Motega walked along in silence, Florian in front, posture alert and hands near two knives he kept at his belt. They turned into a new tunnel off the main sewer line that thankfully became dry quickly, and then descended along a long slope to an iron reinforced oak door. This looked familiar to Motega now, though it had been more than ten years ago the three of them had broken into this place to find out who had commissioned Trypp to steal his sister's journals.

After they entered through the door, the interior looked much like any other house of reasonable stature in the city; it was just a few hundred feet underground and so lacked any windows; instead, painted scenes of bucolic landscapes adorned the walls. Though this wasn't the only Twilight Exile safe house in the city, it was the grandest and the oldest, many others being little more than disposable hovels. This organization of thieves was equivalent to a lesser guild in wealth and influence. It put food in the mouth of many an urchin, and made good coin for a few at the top, but they rarely held those places for long.

They walked down the hallway and past the offices where, last time he had been here, Motega had discovered surprisingly good records of the Exile's activity. As yet, no one had tried to relieve them of their weapons.

Another door led them into a large, circular, two-tiered meeting room, and it was evident why they'd been allowed to keep their weapons. They wouldn't be any use.

Twenty family members, each armed with crossbows, spread around the balcony encircling the room and ensuring every angle was covered. The bar on the outside of the door through which they had entered fell into place with a thud.

"Trypp. You're looking well, for someone who should be dead." The woman on the balcony in front of them was striking: long curly hair held loosely behind her head with features sharp as a fox. She wore a tight-fitting waistcoat over a shirt of silk, her empty hands rested on the railing. She stared intently at Trypp.

"Hello, Sharavin," said Trypp, "you look...well, too."

"Life as Mother suits me," said Sharavin, raising her hands in the air to include the other grim-looking adult thieves around the room, "and it's been good for the children, too."

"What happened to Silas?" asked Trypp.

"Father Silas was becoming...inconsistent. For example, why he didn't kill you and your two friends when you were captured is confusing to me as Mother."

Trypp couldn't hold her gaze any longer. "You asked him yourself to spare my life, banish me instead..." he mumbled.

"Yes, I did! And you didn't even come and say goodbye!" She was leaning on the balcony railing now, looking like she could vault it at any moment. "I would have gone with you, but you slipped into the night before I could find you. Oh, I've heard about you since then. Some excellent jobs, I must say. But I thought you'd have more sense than to come back here."

Motega realized they were in more trouble now than he'd anticipated. Trypp and Sharavin had been together. Not only had he betrayed the family, but also the Mother. *Trypp's not going to be able to talk himself out of this one.*

Motega stepped forward. "What do you want with us, Mother Sharavin?"

"Hello, Hawk. I didn't realize you could speak." Sharavin's attention moved to Motega as he'd hoped. "I want to set an example to the guild of what happens to those who turn their back on their brothers and sisters. How do you think I should do that?"

She was playing with them now, like a tarot reader turning over one bad omen after another. There was only one hope.

"Mother, you *could* kill us to set that example." Trypp turned to face Motega and gave him a what-the-fuck-are-you-doing look. "You could easily kill us, with all of your crossbows. But we would kill many of you first. What do you think, Florian? Ten, eleven?"

"Twelve," said Florian, fully focused on their situation. Motega knew he'd be on the balcony before most would be able to respond.

"The man says twelve. So, what would you achieve?" asked Motega plaintively. "You've killed us, but you've lost twelve of yours, and all because Trypp here was a steaming turd and did wrong by you. Now, I understand that doesn't sit well. But I know something to make it feel better for all of you."

Sharavin had noticeably relaxed. She stood straight with her arms crossed over her chest, staring intently at Motega. "And what, little bird, is that?"

"Coin, of course," he said simply. "We buy our way out. Make reparations. What's your price?"

She considered the offer in silence for a moment. Motega worried that maybe she wanted a piece of Trypp more than gold. And then she spoke. "I want a demon. I want a say in this election. I'm the head of this household. But a thousand crowns is a steep price. Buy me a pyxie, Hawk."

MOTEGA HAD CASED THE LORD TREASURER'S ABODE FROM the safety of his room at the Royal Oak. His view from the falcon's eyes being sharp and clear, with the added benefit of it being much less conspicuous than him walking around outside.

Hoxteth's home was a four-story building with a pitched roof and expensive windows secured with iron bars on the lower floors and iron latches on the upper floors. There were only three doorways: the grand central front doorway, a side door leading to the carriage house and the walled courtyard, and a door to the kitchens for staff and tradesmen. All of the doorways were heavily guarded throughout the day and night, with regular changing of shifts to avoid boredom and lack of concentration.

It wasn't possible to see from the street or sky, but there were likely to be numerous cellars, and the sewers were much more substantial in the upper quarter, so that was a potential means of entrance, but required some specialist knowledge.

For the past few days, he and Trypp had been working the inns and taverns to gather information on Hoxteth's house from loose-lipped servants and low-scruple merchants. The challenge with this job was they had to acquire *incriminating evidence*, but they didn't know what it would look like and where it would be. The only thing they could go on was the assumption any documentation would likely be in an office.

Some sources had confirmed the presence of Hoxteth's primary office off a waiting room near the main hall on the ground floor. Intriguingly, they'd also heard from a former carriage man that there was a second room where he worked adjoining the bedroom Hoxteth shared with his wife. This former employee had never seen it, but he'd been present in the kitchen when there was a request to take up refreshments in the early hours one morning.

Six days had passed since they took the job from Artur and that meant they still officially had nearly four days to figure out the rest of the plan, but Sharavin had changed that.

Motega had taken the offered price of freedom, but they only had half of the money, and that took everything they had from Artur for the last job, along with what coins they had in their pocket on arrival in Kingshold and the small emergency stashes of gems they each had sewn into their clothes. And Sharavin wasn't willing to wait ten days for the second half of the money; a week was all she'd give them.

So now they had to get into Hoxteth's well-fortified house, find something they didn't know existed, and do it all in the next two days to be able to pay on time.

They weren't out of the frying pan yet, but as usual, Motega found himself enjoying the pressure and the thrill of being in a scrape.

Outside, it was dark, it being two bells past midnight. Motega and Trypp were now staying up all night and sleeping during the day. They'd decided pretty early this was going to have to be a night job. There was practically zero chance of being able to infiltrate the house during daylight hours.

Florian had yet to switch to the late shift. He'd been gathering various items of equipment they'd need, as well as working on a particularly important component of the plan, and so, he was asleep in the bed opposite Motega in their shared room. Trypp, meanwhile, had been out and about for some hours.

Per had continued to be Motega's eyes to reconnoiter the house, and from the lights in use during the night, he was pretty sure where Hoxteth's sleeping quarters were and where the second office was. That was the good news. The bad news was Hoxteth didn't seem to sleep very much. The upstairs room stayed alight until around this time each night, and given the time of year, dawn would break before the fifth bell.

"Mot, Florian!" Trypp burst into the room as Motega re-centered himself into his own body. "We're doing it today. Got to be today." Trypp looked excited and a little out of breath.

Florian was a light sleeper and now sat up on his bed, hand automatically on a sword he kept close by. "What's up, Trypp? Close the door and come in."

"I was at The Eagle's Nest chatting with Lizzie, that bar lady with the big... Anyway, I heard this woman talking about her night off getting shifted. Because Hoxteth is throwing a party tomorrow at the merchants' guildhall, or they're putting it on in his honor. Either way, he's going to be out until late. I went over to the Crooked Weight, too. Heard the same thing there. Shindig's not going to start until after dark."

Motega smiled and nodded. "Should give us a lot more night time to play with, but there's risk around when he'll come back. What if he's not the partying type? Just shows his face and heads home?"

"Well, my friend," said Trypp with a bright white smile, "let's just hope he's like Florian here and can't stop at one drink."

~

THE THREE FRIENDS HAD WALKED ACROSS THE ROOFTOPS TO the building opposite Hoxteth's mansion, dressed in black and moving soundlessly and confidently over the pitched slate roofs. Per flew overhead, but Motega needed to be sure of his feet, so he relied on his own eyes. Opposite them was a fourth-floor window, three feet high with a small ledge at the bottom.

Motega unslung his bow from its berth across his back, strung it, and prepared the arrow he and Florian had designed some years ago. It had four barbed hooks extending forward from a typical sharp arrowhead, and an eye through which he threaded a braided rope of silk. He fired the arrow into the wooden ledge and then pulled on the rope to confirm it had buried itself securely, before tying it off on a metal staple Florian had secured in a nearby chimney.

Trypp tested his weight on the tightrope before dashing across to the window high above the street, arms out slightly to keep his balance. At the window, balancing one foot on the ledge and the other on the rope, he pulled a small roll of implements from a pocket at his waist.

First, from a metal vial attached to a thin tube, he applied Drakic acid onto the window, dissolving a small circle of glass with a slight hiss. Then Trypp fed a long L-shaped instrument through the hole in the glass to flip the window fastener, and finally used a small crowbar to pop open the window. All of this done while balancing forty feet above the cobblestone streets. Trypp was a master of his craft.

The thief quietly climbed through the window, disappearing from view for a minute before reaching back outside to quietly hammer in two staples to secure the trip wire for his heavier companions. He gave a signal it was safe for Motega to come next, who darted nimbly across the tightrope and disappeared into the window, with Florian to walk last.

The room Motega entered was small with a simple oak desk in the middle, a leather chair pulled up close. Stacks of parchment cluttered any available surface: some in rolls and others piled flat. The desk looked like it'd been in use for many years, perhaps something sentimental for Hoxteth.

Motega checked the single exit from the room as Florian climbed through the window. So far, their research seemed to be correct. The next room was the bedchamber. Thankfully, it was empty; however, the sounds of staff in the house were audible above the silence of the night.

Trypp searched through the papers on the desk, scanning the contents for any mention of Pyrfew or Emperor Llewdon. Florian did likewise with the documents stored on one side of the room, and Motega took the other. Motega saw letters of credit, shipping manifests, warehouse inventories, even correspondence from a number of banks regarding the financial security of the realm, which didn't seem that secure, but nothing that appeared to be related to Edland's ongoing struggles against Pyrfew.

Trypp clicked his fingers once to beckon Motega over to him.

"Have you found something?" asked Motega.

"No documentation, but look here." Trypp showed him a small chest he'd discovered in the desk. The lock was already picked, and he opened it carefully. Inside were many diamonds, rubies, and sapphires—a small fortune beckoning them.

"Trypp, we're not thieves," whispered Motega. "Well, we are kind of thieves, but we're not thieves like that. We need nobody to know we were here. So lock it back up and put it away. Then let's find what we came here for." Trypp did so grudgingly.

They continued their search by the light of small lamps worn on their foreheads. Some years ago, when they'd been exploring a forgotten barrow to acquire one particular treasure, they'd discovered a type of moss on the walls that gave off a dim light, equivalent to a candle or two. Motega had taken samples of the plant and kept it alive with a diet of beer and honey, enough for it to grow steadily. Trypp had the idea to fashion a small glass container for the lichen, with one side mirrored on the inside to help reflect and focus the light, which he was then able to fasten to a leather strap worn around the head. It wasn't very bright, but in total darkness, it provided him with enough light to do a job like they were doing now, and, most importantly, it enabled him to keep his hands free if any trouble arose.

Minutes passed, and the search of the documents turned up nothing of interest. Motega wondered if they were missing something obvious. The use of a code name or something, but there wasn't the time for a more thorough study.

"Trypp, Florian, I have nothing," said Motega, calling a halt to what they were doing. "We have to go check the other office."

Motega had been hoping this wouldn't be necessary. Breaking into the upstairs room undetected didn't worry him, but descending three flights of stairs when the household was still up was going to be much more challenging and require a good deal of luck.

Trypp led the way out of the office and into the bedchamber, closing the door behind them. It was a long room with three more doors at the far end. Two of the rooms connecting were in darkness and looked to be dressing rooms for the lord treasurer and his wife, Lady Grey, but the third led into the rest of the house, brightly lit with many wall-mounted oil lamps.

The stairway was wide and made of oak, and the first stroke of luck was the thick green pile carpet muffling their steps. They descended two flights of stairs before they saw anyone.

Seated on a chair opposite the main entrance, and in front of the waiting room, was a single guard. Most of the others were either outside the house or had departed with Hoxteth an hour or two earlier. Trypp signaled his two friends to stand still, and he walked silently to the banister of the landing above the guard, pulling from his cloak a little pouch. Motega nodded to himself in agreement with Trypp's plan.

He placed powder from the bag into a thin metal tube, no longer than a handspan, and with the pipe to his mouth, Trypp leaned over the banister and blew the dust down in front of the guard's face. The dust was hardly perceptible as it fell and went unnoticed as the guard inhaled. Before a count of three, the guard's eyes had closed, and his chest rose and fell steadily. Crumian powder, in higher quantities, could cause a coma, but in small amounts, it just generated a deep sleep. The guard would probably be fired for sleeping on the job, but better for him than a knife in the back.

They descended the final flight of stairs and could hear laughter and singing from the back of the house in the direction of the kitchens, the staff enjoying the time their master was away. Across the hall, through the waiting room, and into the office was a good forty feet to travel in the open, and with servants so close it would be a challenge for most others in their profession. But this was easy compared to their other jobs.

Motega remembered how one time they had moved so silently through the shadowed eaves of a temple to Mother Marlth, while the pews had been packed with the congregation; no one heard or saw them. They had spiked the oil used for the ceremonial lighting of the Mother's body with diluted liquid fire. Paid work, of course, not just for the enjoyment of seeing hundreds of people quiver in terror when the explosion greeted the end of the service; it made them think Marlth was passing judgment.

Lamps lit the downstairs office, and once again the three companions began their search of the room, opening drawers in desks and dressers, paging through books lining the shelves and reading the most recent correspondence resting in trays on the largest desk in the center of the room.

"This is going to take too long." Trypp was holding up a bound leather book three inches thick. "This one book alone could take me a whole bell to go through it properly. We could have completely missed what we're looking for already!"

Trypp was whispering, but an edge was coming to his voice. He'd not spoken much about the meeting with Sharavin when they got back to their rooms at the Royal Oak. All three had become focused on the job, but it was evident to Motega the sentence weighing over his head was now getting to him. "Do the best you can. Scan," said Motega. "Hopefully, we still have an hour or two before Hoxteth returns."

And that was when their luck ran out.

A bell rang out from the courtyard along with a repeated cry of "Master returns!" The sounds of the street came into sharp focus: horse's hooves and carriage wheels on paved road, the turning of the iron wheels on the gate to the courtyard as it was dragged open. The laughter of the household staff abruptly stopped, and the sounds of feet as they rushed back to their positions to welcome their master home.

"Mot, we're fucked," Florian stopped leafing through the pages he had in his hand. "Too many people moving all around the house. I don't want to have to cut my way out of here. You need to do it, now."

Motega's eyes rolled into the back of his head, and he could see through the eyes of Per, looking down on the street below and the black carriage of the lord treasurer waiting to enter his compound.

The falcon leaped from its perch and picked up a leather loop attached to a glass bottle where Motega had left it by the tightrope. The bird beat its wings to climb up over the house before circling once, twice overhead before descending to fly over the courtyard and release its grip on its package above the carriage house. As the bottle hit the roof of the carriage house, it erupted in flame. Undiluted liquid fire, flammable on contact with air and a bastard to put out.

Now the bellman shouted, "Fire!" and the cry was picked up and repeated by multiple voices in the house. Footsteps turned heavier as the household staff ran, hopefully to the fire to start a bucket chain to try to extinguish it.

Motega's eyes refocused on the room around him while the three friends waited for the sounds of footsteps to die down. Trypp opened the door from the office to the waiting room and gave them the nod to move out.

Silence was still necessary, but their pace was fast as they climbed up the stairs. On reaching the landing of the first floor, they heard from below, confident, measured footsteps and a voice calling out, "Keep an eye on them, darling. Don't let them burn the bloody house down. I need to change." Hoxteth was right behind them and moving up the stairs.

Motega followed his friends up the stairs, steps muffled by the combination of the carpet, their soft-soled leather shoes, and years of practice, staying one turn ahead of the owner of the house. They made it to the bedchamber as Hoxteth gained the top floor, and Trypp realized they weren't going to make it across to the open door of the office without being seen, so he ducked into the nearest door, which Motega closed behind them.

From the light of their head lanterns, they could see they had entered Lady Grey's dressing room, and now Hoxteth was next door, between them and escape.

Motega took stock of his surrounding while Trypp listened at the door. There was a small fixed window in this room, probably just large enough for him and Trypp, but Florian's broad shoulders would never squeeze through. Rows of gowns, tunics, and trousers hung from rods around the room, a full-length mirror fixed to the wall next to a dressing table, two portraits on the far wall and framed map hung close to him. The chart was of the Jeweled Continent, nicely done, but it looked different somehow, though he couldn't place what it was. On a hunch, he took a knife from his belt, cut it from its frame and rolled it up to tuck under his belt.

"Who's there?" The voice from the bedroom made Motega stop his exploration of the room. He and Trypp exchanged glances. Had Hoxteth discovered them?

"No! You don't need to do this!" The voice from the bedroom sounded terrified. "I'll double whatever he's paying you!"

Trypp opened the door a crack, each of them peering an eye around the door frame just in time to see a figure dressed head to toe in black, only his eyes visible through a gap in the tight-fitting mask. The figure took two quick steps forward and pushed a stiletto through the lord treasurer's eye and into his brain. Hoxteth had begun to cry out as the assassin had stepped forward, but ceased as he fell to the floor.

The killer bent to retrieve the knife, wiped it on the victim's shirt, and then stood. After admiring his work for a moment, the assassin looked directly toward the erstwhile thieves peering through the crack in the door and blew them a kiss.

CHAPTER 13
ASSASSIN

Motega stood in shock as the slim figure, unsure if it was a man or woman, turned and moved quickly into the adjoining office.

"Fuck!" He shout-whispered, remembering seeing the office door open when they'd been racing back upstairs. "I knew we had closed the door. Bastard used our break-in. Move! Now!"

Motega threw open the changing room door and ran full tilt to where the assassin had disappeared into the darkness, leaping over the bed with all semblance of stealth now discarded. Motega reached the window as the killer came to the end of the tightrope and the safety of the building across the street. He had his knife in hand and was about to cut the line, royally screwing them, when his head became the target for the outstretched talons of Per.

Waving his arms in the air, he beat at the bird, giving Motega enough time to bridge half the distance across the tightrope. The assassin landed a good blow on the falcon, knocking it to the rooftop with a screech, and looking up, saw the figure of Motega bearing down, his eyes blazing and lip turned up in a snarl. The killer turned tail and ran across the rooftops.

Once the solid slate was beneath his feet, Motega glanced to make sure Per was fine and picked up his bow and quiver. Florian reached the rooftop as Motega sprinted up and over the pitched roof in pursuit of the assassin.

Two figures in black, running at close to full speed at the crown of the pitched roof, chased the other dark figure who'd managed to build a thirty-yard lead while Motega had paused. Motega pumped his arms and tried not to think about the slipperiness of the slate roof, hearing Florian coming up behind him. They were gaining on the assassin, but the masked figure continued to run even though the elevated highway was about to end.

The impending street didn't stop the fleeing figure. Without a pause, the assassin leaped from the edge of the building out across the twenty-foot gap, landing on a lower, long, flat roof, rolling to manage the momentum from the drop.

Florian was almost alongside Motega now. "Are we jumping, too?" he called over their pounding feet and rapid breaths.

"Yes..." Motega leaped into the air, arms spinning for momentum, landing in a roll to come up sprinting, Florian doing the same a second behind him. He would love to have been able to stop and get a clear shot with his bow, but at this pace, in the dark, and without Per's eyes to help, it would never work. They were gaining on the assassin, though, as they leaped from one building to the next in pursuit: twenty yards between them.

The reason for the assassin's slowdown became abundantly clear as a sharp pain went first into one heel, and then into the ball of his other foot. Motega fell to his knees, unable to run or even walk. Bloody caltrops. The soft leather boots they were wearing for stealth work were perfect to muffle their steps, not so good to stop an inch of sharpened steel. Motega pulled the spikes from his feet as Florian, noticing what had befallen his friend, jumped over the trap and continued pursuit.

MOTEGA HAD BEEN DOWN FOR A MATTER OF SECONDS, BUT was now trying to catch up. Pain from his feet made him grimace and grunt as he tried to get back up to the same speed as before, but not quite managing it, effectively double-limping. He considered it fortunate that, at least, it seemed the caltrops weren't poisoned. But then again, it could also take a minute or two for any substance to reach his brain or heart when entering through his feet. Probably best not to think about it.

Now, he could hear the clash of steel on steel as he trusted his ears in his pursuit and jumped between two buildings over a narrow alleyway. The assassin had run out of runway.

Ahead of Motega, the buildings ended and were now surrounded by wide streets on three sides, as they had run all the way to the Inner Wall.

Florian had both of his swords drawn and was engaged with the assassin who had a long, thin knife held in each hand. Motega didn't know a better swordsman than Florian. He was stronger than most, faster than anyone would expect for a man his size, and, wielding a long sword in each hand, he was truly ambidextrous, able to adjust his stance and attack with either sword equally well, not just for showing off. And in the dark of the night, the thin sliver of moon shining down on the combatants, Florian's blades were a blur as he pressed the attack, and Motega was struck by the beauty in his friend's movement.

But the assassin was clearly skilled. Dangerously so. He danced away from each blow, a thrust sidestepped or a cut deflected with a knife to fall inches away from his body. Motega had his bow in hand, and an arrow notched and drawn, but the combatants were too close to each other and moved too quickly to be able to get a clean shot even at this short distance.

Florian feinted to lead with his right, but switched his weight and went low with his left. The assassin jumped the blade and Florian was waiting to hit him in the head with the hilt of his right blade. It wasn't a clean shot. The masked figure managed to sway back while in midair and then convert the deflected momentum into a tumble.

Now, he came at Florian. Thrusts and slashes parried on twin swords, a transparent feint to the right shoulder followed by a stab toward Florian's thigh. That Florian parried, but he had opened himself up on the inside, and the assassin moved into the space, driving his forehead into his chin from below. Then the right knife came in to punch into the bigger man's belly.

Motega dropped his bow, pulled his war axes and charged, a war cry from his lips drawing the attention of the assassin. In that split second, a long sword flashed, nearly cleaving the killer's skull in two, but again he dodged in time, though the blade caught his mask and ripped it in half.

Shoulder-length red hair, suddenly free, blew in the night breeze.

Florian was alright. The chainmail he wore under his jerkin stopped the strike, and now he advanced on the assassin with Motega spreading out to his left to attack her flank.

She, and it was clearly a woman with her face partially revealed, stepped back to the edge of the wall, a three-story drop behind her. With a flourish, she pulled off the remains of her mask, revealing a thin, lightly freckled face with grey eyes and a broad, thin-lipped smile.

"Thank you, sirs, for the welcome mat you laid out for me this evening. And for the workout, of course." Then she stepped backward and fell from the roof, feet first.

Motega and Florian rushed to the edge and looked over, seeing the lady assassin push off a ledge two floors below, no more than three inches wide, and somersault backward to land on her feet. She turned and ran off down the street.

Florian looked at his friend. "Can you do that?" he asked.

"No," said Motega. "Can you?"

"I don't think so," said Florian, shaking his head. "I jumped off three floors once into a hay cart. That was fun, but there ain't no hay cart here."

"Nope. I guess we lost her." Motega shrugged. They stood there for a moment, both gazing off in the direction where the assassin had run.

"She was good," said Motega, breaking the silence. He looked at his friend. "I thought she had you there for a minute."

"It was close. How are your feet?"

"They hurt like hell. Hey, where's Trypp? Wasn't he behind you?"

"Shit. I thought he was," said Florian, looking around. "You want to go back and look?"

"Hey, you up there!" A voice called from below. "Stay where you are, you're under arrest!"

Four city guard had arrived at the foot of the building where they stood. They must have seen the acrobatics, and then it had taken them a moment to notice Motega and Florian standing on the roof with weapons in hand.

Obviously, their luck was well and truly spent.

Motega secured his axes while Florian sheathed his swords. Grasping his hand and looking his friend in the eye, he nodded and spoke one word.

"Split."

THE SUN WAS UP, AND IT HAD BEEN FOR SOME HOURS. Motega and Florian lay on their beds on opposite sides of the small room at the Royal Oak Inn, staring up at the ceiling.

"He must have been captured," Motega sat upright to fidget with the bandages on his feet, "How long have we been back?"

"Six hours since you hobbled in," said his friend, eyes still intent on a small patch of damp plaster.

"Right! Six bloody hours," said Motega. "So, has he been captured by the city guard? And are they going to pin the murder on him?"

"If they've got him," began Florian, as he rolled into a sitting position and looked at Motega. Florian was shirtless, bandages wrapped around his stomach, a small spot of blood seeping through, which he kept checking to see if it had stopped bleeding. "And I do mean *if*. Then yeah, he's going to take the blame. The lord treasurer killed in his own home, and Trypp either stuck in there for some reason or running across the rooftops away from the scene of the murder dressed all in black. And the syndicate won't own Trypp if asked, won't even admit to the existence of a contract. If they got him, then I hope they just decide to turn it into something public."

"What do you mean something public?"

"You know. Do it by the book," explained Florian. "Put him before the justices. Hang him in public."

Motega regarded his friend, confused. "Florian, why do you want to see your friend hang?"

"Not so he can hang. So we can rescue him," said Florian in a way that made Motega think he'd been the one to say something stupid. "I read this book once about outlaws who saved some of their own on the gallows by shooting the nooses with an arrow, and when they fell, they escaped. Could you do that, Mot?"

"Depends on how thick it is. I can hit the rope easy enough. But if the rope is too thick, then it's not going to be cut with one of my arrows, and it will be up to Trypp's weight to see if it'll snap. The arrow head is too small and pointy. I guess I could use two, but the element of surprise might be lost."

"So, what's your idea then?"

"I think we'd have to break into the jail, use a disguise to get us in, like washerwomen or guard uniforms. Then we could slip him some tools to get out or we could try to escort him out if it's dark enough."

The door to the bedroom started to open. "Remind me never to get caught because your two escape plans have to be the worst I've ever heard."

"Trypp!" Both the injured friends got up from their beds to grasp him by the hand and squeeze him in a bear hug. They noticed he was unharmed and looked unruffled and, actually, he seemed to have a big smile plastered across his face.

"Hey, where have you been?" asked Motega. "We were worried sick."

Trypp went over to the third bed they'd asked the landlady to squeeze into the one room—funds being a little tight since their meeting with the Twilight Exiles—and sat down. "You both went so fast after the assassin. And I was so close to jumping right behind you, honest I was. And then I thought about Sharavin, and we wouldn't be able to give her money, which would mean it'd be rough for you Mot, and me, of course."

"Why me?" asked Motega. "You were the one she wanted to kill."

"Because you're the one who negotiated it. As far as she was concerned, it was your debt."

"Was?"

"Let me finish the story. So, there I was, one foot on the window sill waiting for that dainty little fellow," Trypp gestured to Florian, "to get across the tightrope before I set foot on it. And then I thought, well, Hoxteth is dead now. So all hope of secrecy around our job was gone. And, of course, our employers' plan to discredit Hoxteth wasn't going to be necessary anymore. So, I went back to the desk, and took the chest of gems." Trypp held up both hands in mock surrender. "Look, before you say anything, I'm not proud of it. Burglary. Not our usual style. I know. But desperate times and all that."

Florian walked over to Trypp, hand outstretched. "So,

where are they? Let me see?" Trypp dug around in his pocket and dropped a purse of clinking coins into his hands. "These aren't gems. Feels like gold to me."

"You'd be right about that, my fine friend. By the time I had the little chest out of the desk and got across the tightrope, you both had gone, and I wasn't sure where. So, I went straight to Mother to give her the present. Here's the good news: your debt is lifted, Motega. The bad news is she already knew about what had happened in the Inner Circle last night.

"She believed me when I said we didn't do the killing, but she knew I wasn't going to be able to fence these gems for months, as no one would want to touch them. So, she gave me a terrible price on them. Debt cleared and fifty crowns for all those gems. It's not a win, but I'll take it right now."

"And so, how long did all that take, Trypp?" asked Motega. "It's been hours."

"All taken care of before the sun came up, Mot," said Trypp, the big grin appearing again. "Sharavin wasn't too happy about me waking her up in the middle of the night. But there was one more bit of good news, at least for me. All those gems, the sunrise, being back to my usual charming self. Well she could hardly resist, could she?"

"You bastard." Motega punched his friend playfully on the arm. "Florian and I take a beating, almost get caught, and then we sit here waiting up for you like your old mum, and that's what you've been up to for hours?"

"I see you two have been in the wars," Trypp said, looking over the injuries they were both carrying. "So, did you catch her?"

"Her?" asked Florian. "I thought it was a man until we

got her mask off. How did you know when you only saw her for a couple of seconds?"

"I put it together. There's only one person I know of in the Hollow Syndicate who could get away from you both and still give you a hiding. That, my friends, was Lady Chalice."

CHAPTER 14
THE DIMINISHING PRIVY COUNCIL

Hoskin entered the privy council chamber and took his seat at the head of the table. Hoxteth's place was empty, but around the table sat Lords Beneval, Uthridge, and Ridgton, Aebur the spymaster, and Sir Penshead. And at the other end of the table was Jyuth, the first council meeting he had decided to join since the king's death.

"Lords, gentlemen. Thank you for coming today," said Hoskin, opening the meeting. "Our first order of business will be what you've all already heard, the untimely death of our friend Lord Hoxteth. Sir Penshead, please provide a report of what is known."

The knight rose from his seat, dressed in ceremonial tabard with a long sword belted at his waist. He coughed to clear his throat and began to pace around the table, hands clasped behind his back.

"I spoke with Lady Grey, Hoxteth's widow, and she informed me they had been out that evening at a party held at the merchants' guild house, where they were courting potential demon-holders from ten o'clock.

"Around midnight, Lord Hoxteth grew tired of the company and wished to return home, and so, they traveled to their house in the upper district by carriage. They noticed a commotion in the courtyard as they arrived, a fire in the carriage house they assumed was caused by one of the men who lived there. The household staff and guards put out the fire while the lord treasurer went to his room to change.

"Lady Grey remained to see to the fire until she heard a woman's scream from inside, and then a call for her to come quickly. A maid, who was described as being hysterical, found the lady and brought her to the bedchamber, where she discovered her husband, dead on the floor with a single stab wound through the eye and into the brain."

There was much muttering and tuttering around the table, a shaking of heads as Penshead continued his circle and his tale.

"There was no sign of a struggle, so he was apparently taken by surprise. An open window was discovered in a room adjoining the bedchamber with indications of a break-in. The manner of the killing and the lack of witnesses, theft, or collateral damage make me confident it was an assassination.

"One patrol near the Inner Wall reported seeing two figures dressed in black on the rooftops after a third person was seen fleeing the scene, but, unfortunately, no one was apprehended. I have a captain waiting at the Hollow House now in the hopes of talking to Lady Chalice to receive confirmation it was one of their contracts. If so, then the case is closed. If not, then as usual, Lady Chalice will ensure the unlicensed perpetrator is hunted down and dealt with."

"Another assassination, Hoskin!" said Lord Beneval, looking nervous. He was commander of the palace guard, but it was more of a ceremonial title for the old man. Once he had been a talented knight, but one battle too many had destroyed his nerve. "Last week, it was Lord Garret, who had not even announced his standing for lord protector. Now, it's Hoxteth. It could be any of us next. I'll be increasing our protection."

"Lord Beneval, I think you're safe, and most of us around the table, too," reassured Hoskin, thinking it was time for Beneval to be put out to pasture. "You're not a candidate, and it seems likely all of this is a winnowing of the field by one of the others. At least assuming there is no outside involvement?"

"There won't be any interference from outside of Edland." Hoskin's question had been directed at the spymaster, but it was Jyuth who answered. "I made it clear to Chalice I will get involved if I discover her house taking any contracts paid for by foreign money. And she knows she doesn't want me involved. Look, anyone who becomes lord protector is going to face assassination attempts. Best to think of this as part of the selection process." The wizard smiled and looked at the men who sat around the table, daring them to disagree.

"I appreciate your opinion, Jyuth," Hoskin broke the silence. "A smaller field is probably called for. I only hope there are not any further candidates winnowed from this room, seeing as we have still two candidates remaining at the table. I don't want to lose any more of you, as finding competent, temporary replacements isn't easy. But that does bring me to the next point. Who are we going to have fill our empty chair?"

"Well, Lord Chancellor, I believe Lord Ginwood and Lady Halton are both competent in running their lands and have good connections with the banking houses. Both would be quite suitable," said Ridgton. Predictable. As far as Ridgton was concerned, any role had to be filled by someone of nobility, even if they weren't sure which hand they should use to wipe their backside.

"A fine proposal, sir. But I'm afraid they're at their holdings. By the time we would have a bird fly with a message and expect them back, I fear there would only be a week before the election is called. That hardly seems worth it. Is there anyone who is in the city right now?"

"My lord, what about considering Lord Eden?" drawled Aebur. Every word from him seemed to ooze out of his mouth, sending shivers up Hoskin's spine. "He does have considerable wealth. In fact, I think he's already a lender to the crown."

"Ahem," Jyuth cleared his throat, "you said the crown. Just to be clear, the crown doesn't exist. What that means for the debt of the prior administration, I think, is for others than me to decide."

"Yes, good point," said Hoskin, nodding to Jyuth, but looking to bring the conversation back to the point he wished to solve. "I don't believe it's appropriate for Lord Eden to take on the role. Already I have Lord Uthridge and Sir Penshead here not focused on their vital jobs for the realm. I don't need another case of that, especially for the one person who keeps the gold flowing and the wheels turning. No. We need someone else to do the job."

A few seconds of silence stretched out; Hoskin scanned the faces of the council members. It looked like Uthridge was about to say something, so Hoskin carried on talking.

"No other suggestions from you either, I see. Good. So, I propose Percival; my assistant will fulfill the technical aspects of the role on my behalf, and of course, he'll then transition to the new permanent appointment after the solstice. I assure you he's very competent. Any concerns? No. Settled then. Now, let's move on."

"As we discussed a few weeks ago, my contacts in Ioth have confirmed the contract between Pyrfew and the shipwrights of the city." Aebur spoke without referring to the sheaf of papers on the table in front of him as he provided his weekly intelligence briefings to the council. "Work on the fleet is well underway. It's apparent that eighty warships of varying classes have been commissioned and are currently under construction."

"Eighty ships!" Ridgton looked aghast. "That's twice again their current fleet and will make for a bigger force than our own. Lords, our command of the Arz Sea will be tested if this fleet takes to the open waters."

"I bow to your assessment, my lord," fawned Aebur. "My sources tell me that for a construction effort of this size, the fleet isn't expected to be ready for another two months to sail to Pyrfew."

"It's only a matter of time. I'd expect the Ioth shipwrights will sail them with a skeleton crew for delivery, but they'll have an escort. We have to destroy them before they're crewed and deployed." Ridgton was animated, clearly concerned.

"What are the options, Admiral?" said Hoskin.

"We could attack on the open seas, but that'll require

fighting whatever escort Pyrfew uses. Alternatively, we can destroy the ships in the yards before the escort arrives. I've received no reports of an escort from Pyrfew currently sailing. They'll probably wait to leave until the ships are ready. With the typical summer winds, it'll be two weeks to sail from Kingshold to Ioth."

"So, we can conceivably wait two or three weeks before deciding a course of action?"

"Yes, we could do, Lord Hoskin," Ridgton begrudgingly agreed, "but the time for action is now. Are you afraid of making a decision?"

Hoskin felt his cheeks grow warm. The admiral would never have spoken to the king in this way, and he could feel the eyes of the other privy council members on him. He was damned if he was going to let this one bully him.

"Lord Admiral, I'm neither king nor lord protector. My job is that of caretaker, to ensure there's something to hand over to the next poor unfortunate soul who has to look after this realm." Hoskin held Ridgton's gaze. "Be assured, if action was required now, then I would choose. But I will not unnecessarily commit Edland to open war with Pyrfew or raid a neutral city like Ioth, which, may I remind you, is an important trading partner for us. I'd suggest you ready plans for both courses of action, and also consider alternatives, so we're ready to respond. And Aebur, I expect daily briefings on this situation going forward."

The lord and the spymaster both nodded, Ridgton visibly bridling at having to take direction from Hoskin. He knew the admiral saw him as simply an administrator, who knew nothing of the matters of war. "Anything else to report, Aebur?"

"No, my lord."

"Hoskin, I'd like to say something to our spymaster."

Hoskin was taken aback for a moment. That sounded like Jyuth asking for permission. Hoskin gave him a small nod to continue.

"Aebur, I know you have your eyes in the city, and that's what you need to fulfill your responsibilities. But let me remind you, those responsibilities are for the protection of the realm. I don't want to hear of you meddling in this election. You hear me?"

"Of course, my lord Jyuth. I had no intention to do anything of the sort." The spymaster's face was devoid of expression, but Hoskin didn't sense sincerity in his words. He was going to keep an eye on him; he didn't need Aebur to have delusions of being a kingmaker.

"Anything else to report, gentlemen?" asked Hoskin, his patience for this meeting at an end and wanting to get on with the day.

"I have one more thing," said Ridgton. "It may be trifling, but could have an impact on trade over the coming months. The summer fogs from the north are coming earlier than we've ever remembered. They're already further south than last year. If they continue at that pace over the next month, then they could reach Kingshold and the mouth to the Sapphire Sea. Commercial ships will be impacted by longer journey times. And, of course, pirates like the fog. We've never seen anything like it, nor have any records of anything similar."

"You may not have records, Ridgton," said Jyuth, "but I've seen it happen a handful of summers, the last time probably close to a hundred years ago. The streets of Kingshold cloaked in fog for a week. Makes your life complicated, too, Penshead; folks can get up to a lot when you can't see further than the end of your fingertips. I thought I had worked out the pattern for when it happened. I guess my calculations must have been off..."

"Thank you, Uthridge," said Hoskin, letting Jyuth's reference to his age pass once more. He'd have to discuss that with him at some point. "That's valuable information. I'll be sure our merchants' guild is aware of this information. I expect they'll be able to turn it into a profitable opportunity somehow. I call this council adjourned."

"HOSKIN, A WORD PLEASE."

The lord chancellor was next to last to leave the privy council chamber. Only Jyuth remained sitting. Lord Hoskin closed the door to the room, resumed his seat, and forced a smile.

"Yes, Lord Jyuth. How can I help?"

"I wanted you to know I think you're doing a good job."

Hoskin nearly fell off his chair at the unexpected praise.

"It looks like you've realized most of the council is worthless for you to do your job. Worthless, or in the case of Aebur, to be treated with caution."

"I know you have misgivings about him, my lord. Can you share them with me?"

"I'm afraid not, Hoskin. If they're proven unfounded, then you'd know something; it's best you didn't know." The wizard leaned back in his chair, appraising Hoskin in silence. "Have you considered standing for lord protector? It would be refreshing to have someone guide the kingdom who is both capable and not power mad."

Once again, Hoskin was flabbergasted. "My lord, I don't

think so. I'm not well-liked amongst the nobility. And with Hoxteth's death, Eden probably has a third of them in his pocket already, the rest split between the other five candidates. I wouldn't be able to overtake Eden."

"Well, now there are only four other candidates. Lady Orlan has withdrawn for fear of a knife in the dark. But don't overestimate the impact of the votes cast only by nobility. More pyxies are in the hands of the merchants and non-noble landowners now than nobles. Granted, I'm sure a number of other nobles are planning on traveling here before the solstice. How many votes do you estimate will be cast?"

"From the tax rolls, we estimated around one hundred and fifty. Two-thirds of them nobles."

"Your estimate is logical, but who tells the tax collector the truth?" Jyuth laughed at his own joke. "You'll be surprised, Hoskin, at the coin circulating in the shadows of the city. The nobles will be relevant, but I think this vote will be driven by more than just the Inner City."

"Well, thank you for the vote of confidence, my lord. But I don't have any intention to run. I'm actually looking forward to being done with Kingshold and going back to my family. Some quiet time to write my histories."

"I understand, Hoskin. This place does wear you down," said Jyuth, deflating for a moment. "But you remind me, I've seen you in the library a fair deal recently. Very commendable. Could I ask a favor of you, Hoskin? Could you find a book called *The Trials of Bethel*?"

Hoskin didn't realize he had now become the royal librarian, too, but thought better of arguing the point. He could get Percival to do it, of course.

"Are you referring to Queen Bethel the Red? I don't recall seeing that book before, but I will find it if we have it."

“Thank you. Very much appreciated.” Jyuth got up from his chair and walked toward the door before turning with a big smile visible through his beard. “And keep up the not-fucking-it-up!”

CHAPTER 15

NEWS TRAVELS FAST

The sun rose above the city as Dolph and Mareth walked through the streets of the Middle back toward the Floral Gate and the Royal Oak.

Mareth knew Petra would be starting work there by the time he returned; the blonde-haired vision from the night he met Gonal was a new serving girl for Jules, who worked the late shift. He remembered thinking she was besotted with him when they met; though he now recognized he might have had that backward.

Each evening that week, Mareth had performed in a different inn in the Upper Circle; *The Ballad of the Tin Man* joined by other new songs like *Who Judges Us*, about Lord Fiske, and *Can You Tell Me The Way To The Battle*, a comic song about the lord general. The crowds had been steadily growing. Mareth would see familiar faces night after night, young nobles even singing along now.

Each night, after finishing, they went to the Hub or the Middle and played through the night for throngs that would likely never see the money needed to vote in their lifetime, but Mareth found their engagement invigorating. The citizens wanted Hoxteth to win. They wanted someone who started off as one of their own in the palace, even though he was now a lord.

And though it was the early morning, Mareth walked through the streets without stumbling, no need for Dolph to hold him up. Mareth had rediscovered his original addiction, the adulation of the audience, and it had greatly reduced his booze consumption. And like every morning for the past week, he had walked back to the Royal Oak where he now had a room using Hoxteth's money; it was important for him to appear reputable now. Like most days, Mareth's stomach was in knots about seeing Petra again, and if he was honest with himself, Petra might also have had something to do with his new choice of home.

He knew Petra liked him.

Or he liked to reassure himself that was the case. Each morning, she would greet him as he entered and seat him at a table while she brought a breakfast of fried bread and black pudding. Petra would always sit with him while he ate, interested in the stories of the night before and how the people reacted to the songs.

At least she would until Jules told her to get up and back to work.

He liked to watch her move around the common room going about her business. She had such grace—her lithe body clothed in a simple green dress (which brought out the green in her eyes) with a white apron, talking to the tradesmen who came to eat before the day ahead. Laughing at their jokes, maybe touching their arms to make them feel welcome.

Mareth reassured himself Petra really did like him.

He really should make sure.

He needed to write the poems that had been circling his mind since he met her.

Dolph walked side-by-side with Mareth, matching his stride and scanning their surroundings for signs of trouble. Mareth had to admit he had become bearable, perhaps even a reassuring presence. He gave thanks Dolph wasn't a talker. The performances each night would leave him energized, but also spent, and so, he was glad of the silence while they walked.

Mareth walked tall, feeling good he was doing something of value. Not simply a historian viewing this time of change for Edland with detachment, but being involved, changing people's minds.

And he realized for the first time in many years, in truth, since his friends had died, that he was having fun.

They were approaching the Red Gate, but turned to avoid the Lance and the shops that were beginning to open, heading through less busy streets. Some people recognized Mareth as they walked by, and they'd sing a line or two of *Hold My Cock* (no need to explain who that one was about) or *The Tin Man,* which brought a smile to his face and stoked the rekindled love he had for the city.

Maybe there would be a brighter day for all?

Dolph lightly grabbed his arm and whispered out of the side of his mouth, "Don't look. But we're being followed."

He couldn't help himself; without thinking, he turned and saw three rough-looking men walking twenty paces away from them.

"I said don't look! And there are three more in front. Is the sword just for show?" asked Dolph, nodding to the saber Mareth wore at his belt. He had been encouraged to wear a sword to complete his new costume, like a troubadour of old, and so, he'd dug out his old saber and oiled away the rust.

"Oi! You!" The lead thug of the three in front was an ugly lump of meat, only half of his left ear remaining, the top half looking like it had been chewed off. "You! You're that bard. Haven't you given up? Haven't you heard the news?"

The three in front and the three behind stopped about ten feet away from Dolph and Mareth. Calmly stepping to the wall, Mareth lent his mandolin against it. No point in it getting damaged if there was going to be trouble. And it looked like there was going to be trouble. He and Dolph were outnumbered. Mareth hoped he'd remember which end of the sword to hold.

"I think you must be thinking of someone else," replied Mareth, keeping it civil. "I don't think we've met."

"Nah, you're the one," said Half Ear. "You're the one who's been singing all those songs about everyone except Hoxteth. So everyone knows you work for him. Or at least you did. Ha ha ha." And the other thugs laughed along with him.

As far as Mareth was concerned, Half Ear wasn't making any sense. What did he know? "Who do you work for? Do you know them, Dolph?"

Dolph had turned to have his back face the wall so he could see both groups, but he shook his head in response.

"That's none of your concern, bard. All that's important is our boss is alive, and yours got a knife in the brain last night." The thug was enjoying himself, goading his prey while he had his thug friends with him. "I'm sure that's very saddening for you, so here's the deal. We're either going to cave in your skull, or you can promise to stop the singing, and we'll just give you a good hiding to help you remember."

"He's dead?" Mareth asked in shock. Hoxteth was meant to be lord protector. "He's dead..." Mareth considered the news, steel forming in his belly from who knows where. "Here's my answer, and you can tell Eden this, too. Fuck. You."

And he drew his sword. Dolph already had his long sword in hand and wordlessly moved to cover the left. In front of Mareth were Half Ear, Nail (his weapon of choice being a club with nails driven through the end), and Shortarse (five feet tall, but nasty looking). Half Ear had a sword; the rest of his crew had clubs of various sizes, but he still waved them forward first.

The years of inactivity, slouching by tavern fires and at bars, slipped away from Mareth. He found himself back in his adventuring days. Living by his wits, fighting side-by-side with his friends, always looking for the next song. It made him feel good!

He breathed in deeply. For many, what would follow would be a war cry or a shriek, but when he fought, Mareth sang. The thugs momentarily looked confused as he belted out the *Battle Song of the Clayborne*.

Shortarse came in first and swung at his head, which Mareth ducked easily and returned a vicious cut to the thigh, putting his assailant on his backside. Ha! One vanquished!

Mareth felt his blood rising as the excitement and the song seeped deep into his bones.

Nail came in jabbing with his club, looking to rake him with the rusty nails at the end, but he batted off the blows. Half Ear raised his sword and took an uncultured swing at Mareth's arm. He had to pivot and parry the blow, but Nail was able to hit him in the back, the wind knocked out of him in a rush and sending him forward into Half Ear.

Half Ear wasn't expecting it. It took him by surprise as much as Mareth, and the pair ended up in a heap on the ground. Mareth untangled himself from the scramble and picked up the song again at the chorus, readying for Half Ear to come at him with his sword. But he saw his saber had gone through Half Ear's gut when they collided, and now the thug was bleeding out on the street, a look of horror on his face as he tried to hold the blood in.

Lucky, thought Mareth. He hadn't felt lucky in a long time.

And then the lights went out.

PETRA WAS BENT OVER THE NEAR-NAKED MARETH, stripped to his underwear and lying on his bed. She washed the cuts and scrapes on his body. It felt delicious, though his head throbbed from the blow that had knocked him out, and his back stung from the gouges carved by the nailed club.

Dolph had dragged him back to the Royal Oak, apparently his last service to him before disappearing back to Hoxteth's compound to see what the situation was. Dolph had dispatched the other thugs just after he'd been hit from behind, but not before Nail could lay the boot in a few times. Mareth had learnt all of this when he'd regained consciousness just a little while ago. Now, he winced as Petra guided him into a seating position to bind his bruised ribs and the cuts on his back.

"I'm sorry, Mareth. You can lie and rest in a moment," said Petra gently. She looked even more beautiful to Mareth as she administered her care. He admired her long, blonde hair, tied behind her head to be out of the way of her face, allowing him to see the pale curve of her slender neck. And, slightly ashamed of himself, as she bent over, he'd steal a look at her cleavage.

"Thank you so much," said Mareth. "You didn't have to do this. I could call for a doctor. Jules must be mad you aren't working."

"Shh, don't worry about it. A cutter will probably only make things worse. Jules gave me the morning off, anyway. She cares about you like a younger brother, you know."

"I know. I don't know how I came to deserve it," said Mareth, truly not sure why Jules had always been so welcoming when he'd always been so worthless.

"You're a good man, Mareth." She paused from attending to the bandages to look him in the eye. "I heard how you helped those kids on the farm road. Don't forget that."

He gave a half-hearted smile. His recent optimism was slipping away. He found himself craving a stiff drink. Hoxteth was a promise of change, and he'd felt he was changing people's hearts and minds to see that. Now, Hoxteth had been taken away by an assassin's blade.

"Why did they have to do it, Petra?" he asked.

"They were wicked men, Mareth, who do it for coin all the time. I know Carl, the one you said had half an ear. He's from the Narrows. He's a real nasty piece of work."

"I know. But I didn't mean that. I meant Lord Hoxteth. He could have been something different." The futility of the situation, of life, struck him. "You didn't see how Eden treated the people who came to meet him as he rode in. Full of contempt, riling the crowd with the fake coins, and then the way his soldiers attacked unarmed men and women. Twenty people died there, Petra, and there were no repercussions for him."

"I know. Some of my neighbors were there that day. But ask yourself, would things really have been different? Hoxteth may have been one of us early in life, but he was still a lord at the end. Didn't he care most about profit?"

"That's true, but he would have left that behind him if he was lord protector. I can't believe he would have forgotten how he dragged himself up from the Hub. Now we're doomed to have one of those warmongers who see people like you and me as fodder to press into service, or someone like Eden who thinks we're little more than cattle. Maybe it's time to move on again. Go somewhere new. Would you come with me, Petra?"

"Mareth, I'd love to, but I have a sister. It's only been the two of us for so long. I couldn't leave her."

He didn't know she had a sister. He realized there was so much he didn't know about her.

"But why give up? Fight! Maybe there's another candidate you can support. Don't just give up, if it's something important to you. Why don't you organize?"

"Organize?" he asked. "With whom?"

"The guilds? Other merchants? The district supervisors? I don't know. It was just a thought."

Mareth considered this. He had heard some of the guilds were beginning to organize how they'd pool their resources to buy their pyxies; some of the richer guilds were able to fund more than one vote. And he hadn't considered the district supervisors. Each area of the city had their unofficial counsel of responsible citizens who judged minor squabbles and tried to keep the peace. Could they be used to get the message out? Maybe there was something that could be done.

"You're incredible, Petra! I could kiss you."

She bent close and whispered, "You can, you know."

Their lips began to touch, her soft, smooth flesh brushing his as she leaned in. Then the door opened, and she stood with a start, both of them looking at who had intruded.

"Dolph!" Mareth snarled.

"Heh. Did I interrupt something?" Dolph found his untimeliness to be quite amusing. Mareth didn't. "Wanted you to know I'm back. Or to see if you were dead yet." More chuckles. "Lady Grey is in charge now. She told me to stick with you and to say you're still employed. She said do whatever you like, just cause trouble. She thinks Eden paid for the knife, and she wants even."

"Understood," said Mareth. Maybe it wasn't all going down the drain, but coming up with a plan could wait a little while. "Thank you for telling me. Now, would you be a good fellow and leave me alone for a while?"

"Sure," Dolph said, making to leave the room before ducking back inside. "Wait. One other thing. You handled yourself pretty well back there, better than I expected, to be honest. But what was with the singing? I thought it was going to be a bloody annoying way to die, having to hear you warble on, but you know what? I felt stronger and faster, like the warriors you were singing about were inside me. How'd you do that?"

Mareth looked at him, steely eyed. "I don't know what you're talking about. Now. Fuck. Off!"

CHAPTER 16
WE THE PEOPLE

Alana sat at the rear of the back room of the Royal Oak, observing the gathering that was assembling. She'd never seen her sister so excited or passionate as during the last couple of days. She often became enamored with new boyfriends, but this was different; she was enthused about *something*, not just someone.

And Alana saw the fruits of Petra's labor. More than thirty-five individual requests to join a meeting in the back room of a tavern, a well-respected tavern granted, but more than a dozen attendees was frankly amazing for just two days' work.

She counted ten district supervisors in all: men and women from Fishtown, Cherry Tree, Warehouse District, Fourwells, Lance, Red Guard, Inner and Outer Narrows, Bottom Run, and Randall's Addition, along with four guild representatives from the bakers, brewers, butchers, and tanners houses. True, most of them were men, old men at that, and so, it wasn't every day they had someone like Petra arrive on their doorstep and make a request to spend time with them.

Petra sat at the front of the room with her new boyfriend, a bard called Mareth, who Alana had only just met, and Jules, the owner of this inn and also the supervisor of Cherry Tree.

The supervisor was an interesting and important role in how the city worked. Officially, they didn't exist, of course, but in actuality, they managed a large number of matters the rulers of Kingshold had only a passing interest in: from new building construction in the poorer areas of town to negotiations with the criminal families, most notably the Twilight Exiles, if a district's inhabitants were being hit particularly hard.

The position was usually elected by a show of hands at a community meeting, and then once someone got the job, assuming no one noticed if he was corrupt, then he'd usually have it for life. Cherry Tree was one of the most respectable districts in the city, and so, when Jules took her seat at the front of the room after everyone else had arrived, Alana could see how it put the others more at ease. Petra had probably been the reason why many of them had come this evening, and then they saw her hand-in-hand with a semi-infamous bard, who looked as if he'd been pounded on a kneading table by the representative of the Bakers' Guild; so it was Jules keeping them in their seats.

Mareth stood and smiled. "Thank you for joining us here this evening, fellow citizens. Let's get down to business. Hoxteth is dead, as you know. He could have been a good lord protector for all of Edland. He understood the needs of the poorest citizen and that of the richest nobleman. Now, we're left with a choice between the richest man in the country—who squeezes the tenants on his land so he can expand his coffers—or men of war who can't be trusted to govern a country at the heart of trade across the Jeweled Continent. I'm saddened and afraid for our city and our nation. So, I ask you, what are we going to do about it?"

"Mareth, I appreciate your concern," said Master Gonal, the supervisor of the Warehouse District, who seemed acquainted with the bard. "You know very well I supported Hoxteth. By Arloth's beard, I already cast my vote! I don't think you're going to find the coin in this room to put a contract out on Eden. And as you said, we'll just get one of the other bastards then."

"Aye, they're all shit for us in the Narrows," Dyer from the Inner Narrows spoke.

He sat next to Lud from the Outer Narrows. Alana knew them to be boyhood best friends, but they'd still spent a good part of their lives warring with each other about whether the Inner or the Outer Narrows was best and where to draw the line separating the two. As far as she could see it, the answers were neither and didn't bloody matter.

Dyer continued, "There ain't no king that wanted the Narrows to be there, and we still half expect them to come down from the palace one day and torch the place. So, what are we going to do? Nothing."

Alana listened in silence as the rest of the supervisors made similar declarations about their inability to do something.

Finally, Jules stood and addressed the group. "I refuse to give up." Her voice was strong and confident as she addressed the room. "This city is good to me, but I'm one of the lucky ones. I see everyday people living like dogs, kids dying before they grow up, good men and women hanging because they're trying to put food on the table. It's been a rare king that's cared about those issues, but it's time someone did. We had a candidate we believed in before, for all of his flaws. Now, we need a new candidate, someone who's not a noble, and then we have to get people to support our candidate! There are still more than two weeks left until the solstice. We can do this."

Some of the supervisors sat back in their chairs and looked at the floor; others shook their heads—and not in the way you respond to your mother telling you not to do something, more what someone does when daunted by a big job they know they should just stop whining about and get on with.

Mareth took that as his opportunity to pick up his mandolin and began to play.

The rock looks over the water
and shelters Edwards town
Caravans of wheat and lamb
feed those Edland grown
Ships of spice and silk to trade
in the marketplace
peace and festivals and life without duress
for the people of this place

The rock looks over the sea
and bids farewell to the fleet
Young men and women of Edland
on their way to defeat

boys and girls of other lands
Fields sown with grief and tears
Rations on ships to supply this waste
leaving them hungry except for fear
The people of this place

Stand up, stand up, Edlanders
Stand up, stand up
How do you choose?
Stand up, stand up, Edlanders
What can you lose?

ALANA SAT IN HER SEAT, TEARS ROLLING DOWN HER CHEEKS as she gazed at her feet. Mareth's singing had conjured such vivid pictures in her mind. She'd seen the warships leaving with her friends. She'd seen them dying outside foreign walls and the sadness left in Kingshold. She'd never experienced the like from other singers in the past.

She found herself on her feet, and she saw she wasn't alone. The old woman from Fishtown, Eldrida, broke the silence. "Marlth's tit, boy. You have a voice and then some. I guess we've chosen."

"Aye," said Win from Fourwells, "you've hooked us now. So, what are we going to do?"

"May I speak?" Alana had raised her hand.

Her sister Petra smiled and nodded for her to continue.

"I know the guilds are pooling their money to be able to vote for a candidate. Why can't we do the same? Master White, can you explain what the Bakers' Guild is doing?"

Master White was in his middle years, but he still looked

healthy from years of kneading bread. The white beard on his face couldn't hide his look of concern and confusion. "Who are you, girl? How do you know this?"

"That's Alana, my sister," said Petra, "and she's the wizard's personal assistant."

"More servant than assistant, Petra," corrected Alana, "but I do work for Jyuth. And I know he wants this to be about more than nobles picking amongst themselves."

"Fine then, Alana, servant of the wizard. We in the Bakers' Guild are combining our resources to vote. We each contribute an equal share, and then the guild master will have a pyxie cast our vote after we've had a show of hands about who we shall support. Most of us were leaning to Hoxteth too, Mareth. Now, we don't know who the candidate will be."

"Thank you, Master White. By the way, I think your crusty cobs are the best in the city," said Alana, flashing him a smile. "What if instead of doing it by guild house, we did it by district? The entry fee shared amongst many, and the supervisor casts the vote. The entry fee is returnable after the election, so the people won't be without the coin for long."

"Girl," interjected Eldrida, "even split amongst many, it's still a lot to ask our people. There are fewer than a thousand families in Fishtown. That's more than a crown each."

"I know, Mistress Eldrida. It won't be easy for all to do it. But I know many would sacrifice to feel enfranchised. We'd need to organize how to help you collect and redistribute with minimal pain."

Alana shot a look at Mareth to see if she was overstepping her bounds, but he had a broad grin and nodded for her to continue. "And maybe there's something we can do to help those who want to be involved. Dyer, don't you think our neighbors would want to be involved? It's all anyone is talking about in the Narrows."

"Alana, you've got your mother's smarts. Yes, I think they would, and though we're poorer than those in Fishtown, we have many more," said Dyer. He didn't look sold yet on this plan, though. "If we do this, is it going to make any difference?"

Alana was grateful she had paid so much attention to the conversations she had recently with the wizard. She found the topic fascinating, visualizing in her mind all of the various players. She knew these facts without the help of notes.

"Jyuth has told me there are around 150 families in the realm with the declared wealth to vote. If all of the districts and all of the guilds participate, that would be nearly forty additional votes. And more than half of the 150 are merchants, who will hopefully be more rational than the nobles."

She stopped talking for a moment to make sure everyone was following along as they turned around in their seats to see her. "And you don't have to get half of the votes to win. Just the most. Because there are so many candidates, forty could be enough to win on its own, though Eden is the clear favorite right now. The way I see it, our biggest problem is we don't have a good candidate to back yet. But we can work on that, too!"

~

"It's getting late," said Alana, pushing back her chair to get up from the table. "I have to get home so I can be at the palace in the morning to attend to Lord Jyuth."

It had been a few hours since the supervisors and guild masters had left after they'd collectively worked through how they were going to organize. Alana had then had dinner with Jules, Petra, and Mareth to further discuss their plans.

A voice in her head was asking if she knew how much work they had just signed up for with her harebrained scheme, but her face wasn't listening, as she'd had a silly grin plastered to it all the way through their late meal.

"Are you sure you have to leave? You can stay here," said Jules. Alana liked her. She was a successful businesswoman and still cared about her community. But Alana shook her head. "Would you at least like someone to escort you home? I can have one of the doormen walk with you."

"That's very kind of you, Mistress Jules, but I've been walking in this city since I was twelve. I'll be okay. And I'll come back tomorrow after work, so I can help talk to the other districts who weren't here today."

Alana got up, said goodbye and thank you to Jules and Mareth. Her sister stood and walked her to the door.

"I'm going to stay here tonight, Alana. I hope you don't mind."

"Of course not." She gave her sister a hug. "I like him, too, you know. You make a good couple."

"Thank you, it means a lot to me," said Petra. "You look happy, too. I was so glad you were here tonight. I don't think this would have worked without you. We weren't sure what we would actually do. I'm so proud you're my sister."

Alana's eyes began to water. "Shut up, Petra. You're going to make me all blubbery. It's been a long time since we were happy. I think we deserve it."

She kissed her sister on the cheek, and then stepped out into the cool dark evening, her mind still swimming with thoughts about how they were going to change the city, maybe even the whole country.

Organizing the districts was going to be a lot of effort, but seemed achievable. Getting the people of each area excited enough to vote was going to be a different challenge. But if they could make a buzz in the next few days, then they'd get the other districts on board.

They did need another candidate, though. She couldn't see how they could get people excited with the current options. Hopefully, there would be another entrant to the race.

Alana walked briskly south from the Royal Oak through the Cherry Tree District. Her planned route took her through Fourwells and the Golden District to the Outer Wall, and then through the Red Gate to the Narrows and home. How would they be able to motivate the people of the city? The town criers would be an excellent way to get the message out, but they didn't have the coin to be able to do that, and Mareth had made it known he wasn't exactly approving of their profession. He suggested he could visit each neighborhood to talk or sing, which she knew from this evening would work. But it would take too long, one man to cover the whole city. They needed more Mareths to be effective.

A hand grabbed her arm and pulled her into a side street from the main thoroughfare. Lost as she was in her thoughts, she'd only been half paying attention to her surroundings.

"Aren't you the smart little servant girl," said the man who held her roughly. His face was in shadows, but he was bigger than her, with calloused hands and a firm grip. "I know someone who will want to talk to you, Alana. Come quietly. Or I'll make you quiet."

The voice sounded familiar. Alana could see the outline of the shoulder-length hair and the full beard, and she realized she had heard his voice earlier that evening. "Win? What are you doing?"

"Master Win to you, girly. You know an awful lot about the wizard and what people are doing. I don't think that's normal for a palace maid. I wonder what else you know. So, you're going to come with me and talk to a little someone. He's a very nice man. If you help him, he'll help you. He'll get you out of the Narrows, maybe get you a better job once this election is all done with. But if you're not nice, then he might not be so nice either, if you know what I mean." Win's hand moved to Alana's throat and began to squeeze. "And don't think the wizard is even going to notice if you disappear. There are plenty of other girls to replace you."

Win pushed her back against the wall with the hand around her throat. She couldn't make a sound, struggling to breathe, so she nodded vigorously as if agreeing with Win.

"Good, good. We don't have far to go." Win took his hand from her throat, and Alana bent over to gulp air down to her lungs.

"Aarrgh!" screamed Win.

Alana had straightened and drove a knee into the gonads of the taller man, just the way her dad had taught her. He released his grip on her arm as both of his hands went, by reflex, to cup his balls.

Alana turned tail and ran. Not back the way she had come, as Win was blocking the exit, but further down the side street. The street should head in the direction of the Lance. She just hoped it wasn't going to be a dead end.

"Come back here, girly!" hollered Win. "I'm going to kick you in the cunt when I get you!"

She ran, but heard his footsteps behind her. He was gaining on her. The street twisted to the left, and then to the right. She could see it opening out onto a larger street up ahead, but now she could hear his heavy breathing right behind her.

A hand reached out and pulled at her shoulder, spinning her to the ground feet from the open thoroughfare. The man's body landed heavily on her, driving the wind from her stomach, and a clenched fist hit her above her eye.

Silly girl.

She had always thought of herself as street smart, but this was how it would end. She had known men like Win before, who wouldn't stop hitting a woman once they started.

So close to the Lance.

But there probably wouldn't have been a guard patrol anyway. Another fist struck her cheek, and she was having difficulty seeing, blood flowing from the cut above her eye.

"Hey, you. You should pick on someone your own size."

"Fuck you," said Win without even looking up. He was snarling into Alana's face, strings of dribble splattering her cheek.

And then he was gone. She felt him thrown off her and heard him land with a *thud* somewhere not too far away. Turning her aching head, she could see three figures silhouetted in the entry to the street.

"No, thank you. You're not my type. I suggest you run before I shove your arm up your arse."

The blood and the tears made it impossible for Alana to see clearly what was happening, but one of the men, a big man, had moved past her in the direction of where Win had been tossed.

Another figure moved close to her and spoke in a kind voice. “Young lady, you’re safe now, but you don’t look well. Is there somewhere we can take you?”

“The Royal Oak.”

CHAPTER 17
WHAT WOULD JYUTH DO?

The floor below her bedroom at the top of the tower was Neenahwi's workspace, empty like a priest's prayer cell, straw mat replaced with a soft red velvet cushion in the center of the room. The early morning sun blazed onto her face and arms through one of the two glass windows. She sat cross-legged on the cushion, eyes closed, much as she had done for the past week since her argument with Jyuth, hands in her lap, palms up cradling the red gem while sweat trickled down her forehead.

She still wasn't sure what had happened that night on Mount Tiston. Losing control was not something she was used to, but she was at least thankful her subconscious had guided her out of the city. She remembered the waking dream of that evening, so similar to the visions that had troubled her childhood, but also so different. Never before had she seen the demon up close or her parents and Greytooth die, not in real life or dream.

Since then, she had meditated day and night on gaining control of the demon gem, but the source of power continued to evade her. Her third eye, her magic eye, saw the dark red of the energy source deep inside the gem, but there was still a barrier she couldn't break through.

Yesterday, she thought she had a turning point; holding the stone above her heart, she could feel it inside her, but the threads were still elusive as her mind attempted to grasp them. Her failings made her second-guess whether it was right to remove the gem from the ugly ironwork amulet Barak had been wearing, even though it had been a necessity at the time as it would have been too heavy for her to carry in flight for long.

And now another night had passed without success, the silence beginning to give way to the cacophony of the day.

Neenahwi opened her eyes and rolled her arms, twisting her body and stretching out the stiff muscles from many hours of sitting.

"Shit. Another night wasted," she muttered to herself. "What use is this if I can't control it?" She gripped the gem tightly in her hand. "WHY WON'T YOU WORK!"

She threw the red stone, and it hit the wall. A bright flame of pure red jumped from the stone and encompassed her hand. It didn't burn, just raced from fingertips to shoulder and back. She concentrated and separated her mind in two: one aspect of her mind studied the red flame while the other aspect of her mind reached out to grasp and channel the energy as she'd been taught years ago by Jyuth.

But then it was gone.

All that remained were the goose bumps on her arm and a little static electricity arcing between her fingers.

She let out a deep sigh and walked up the stone staircase to her bedchamber. Collapsing on to the soft feather mattress, she sighed again and lay still until a small furry form leaped onto the bed with her.

"Tuft. You've been gone a long time! I thought you were leaving me, too." Tuft was a long-haired cat. In his mind, ruler of the neighborhood. The many battles to defend his turf and his harem had left visible scars, and his hair grew in clumps in some places. But he was a good cat. He rubbed himself against Neenahwi's face and purred loudly.

"I missed you, too. When you're not here, I talk to myself too much. Even though Jyuth says it's a sign of intelligence. Do you know he's going to leave us, Tuft? He's throwing all the cards up in the air, and he's not even going to stay to see how the hand plays out. Can you believe him?"

Meow.

"Of course, everyone needs to get away, Tuft. That would be okay. But he says he's not coming back this time. It's my turn to sit at the table."

Meow, meow.

"I'm not whining. I'm processing. There's a difference." Neenahwi paused. "Are you ready for the big time, cat?"

Meow.

"Yes, yes, you're already king. So, what would you do? Besides marking your territory, of course. I'm not sure I can be squatting all over the city." Talking to Tuft was already improving her mood.

Meow, meow.

"You're right. It's probably better to think like Jyuth. Hmmm. You're such a smart cat." Neenahwi reached over and pulled a small dried fish head from the drawer and gave it to the cat. He jumped down to take his prize into the corner while Neenahwi paced. "That's right. Jyuth wouldn't just sit to one side to see what hand he gets dealt. He'd be stacking the deck at every opportunity, working out the weaknesses of the other players!"

Picking up a pen and parchment from her desk, she quickly scribbled out four notes, sealing them with wax and her sigil of an arrow's fletching. Down the steps of her house and into the street, she found two street children, familiar faces who she sometimes fed but was wary of accidentally adopting.

"Jill, Gill, I want you to do some work for me today. You deliver these letters for me and wait for a reply. Two each. Do that for me, and I'll give you both a silver. For each letter."

The children's dirty faces broke into big smiles, and they rushed to hug Neenahwi, and then, before she could respond, they both ran away, letters in hand.

~

"Ms. Neenahwi Wolfclaw, my lord," said the overly starched secretary as Neenahwi was escorted into the grand office, flanked by two bristling guards.

"Please, take a seat," said Lord Eden from behind the desk, still yet to look up and greet his guest. Smooth and shiny, he reminded her of a slippery eel and had remarked as such to Jyuth last time they had met. Her father had warned her it was important to be able to tell an eel from a snake.

Eden continued to scratch at a piece of paper with his pen before drying the writing with sawdust and shaking it loose onto the floor. "Have we met before?" he asked. *Hardly welcoming.* "How should I address you?"

Deep breath. Focus. No need to be afraid of an old, white man. He's just another demon.

"Good morning, Lord Eden. Yes, we've met once or twice before. I was apprentice to Jyuth. I'm sure you remember him," she said and smiled excessively. "And King Rudolph always used to call me Lady Neenahwi."

"Lady? Are you noble born?" Eden looked visibly affronted.

"I was the daughter of the chieftain of my tribe and would have been chief myself in time. And I'm the adopted daughter of Lord Jyuth."

"Yes.... Ms. Wolfclaw it is then. And how may I help you today?"

Neenahwi was sure he wouldn't have helped his own mother out of a bathtub, let alone anyone else.

"I'm trying to work out how to cast my vote, and I don't know where to start," said Neenahwi, deciding to play up to his expectations about her. "Why should I vote for you, Lord Eden?"

"Ah, you have a pyxie. Why didn't anyone say? Well, let me assure you I'm the ideal person to be lord protector and guide this realm into a new golden age. I've always loved Kingshold, but it's become so squalid, as I'm sure you've noticed. I can hardly bear to spend time here, if I'm honest. We need to make Kingshold the shining jewel of the world it once was."

"It sounds fantastic, my lord," fawned Neenahwi. "How will you do that?"

"Well, we must build new strong walls around the city! We need to have monuments to our achievements! We need to explore this Wild Continent, too, and see what riches await us. We need to demonstrate kingly power in the world."

"I thought we didn't have a king anymore. Hasn't the monarchy been dissolved?" reminded Neenahwi.

Eden cleared his throat. "Er, yes, of course. I meant we need to show the power of Kingshold and expand Edland. Do you know one in two foreigners would like to be an Edlander? We shouldn't deny them the privilege."

"I don't know your sources, Lord Eden, but I think that means they'd like to live here in Edland."

"What? No! Too many bloody foreigners here already. Present company excepted, of course, heh. No, they can be part of Edland, staying where they are. We can bring civilization to them, and they can pay taxes to build our walls."

"What a fascinating outlook you have, my lord." Neenahwi made to stand up, considered reaching over to shake Eden's hand, but thought better of it because the gesture might not be reciprocated. "You've helped me a great deal and can be confident in my decision."

"Wonderful, Ms. Wolfclaw. You won't be sorry. Good day."

"LADY NEENAHWI, HOW NICE OF YOU TO JOIN ME TODAY." A lady of advancing years stood to shake her hand in greeting and ushered her to an armchair, tea arrayed for them at a table between their two chairs. Once a beauty, now she reminded Neenahwi of a long-thorned, yellow rose, petals starting to grey.

"Lady Kingsley, you honor me. It's a pleasure to meet you finally," said Neenahwi.

"Please, sit. Can I offer you tea?" She poured the tea herself into delicate teacups. "How is Lord Jyuth? I haven't seen him for a long time. He and my great-grandfather were quite close, you know, when he was chancellor for King Dumar. I'd see him at court when I was a child, and he'd make coins appear from thin air. Wonderful. Of course, he hasn't aged a day, has he, dear?"

"I'm sure he hasn't, my lady."

"Now, I believe you wanted to talk to me about your vote." The old woman's eyes bore into Neenahwi's face, the steely gaze matched by the color of her eyes. "It's time we women cleaned up this mess made by men. There has been a long history of queens in Edland, you know, but there hasn't been a lady on the privy council for more than a hundred years. And just look at what a mess everything has become! We need to clean house, young lady."

"I can only agree with you, Lady Kingsley." Neenahwi liked this stiff old woman so far. She could tell she didn't suffer fools, and she rather agreed the men had made a pig's ear of most things. "Where would you begin the scrubbing?"

"Isn't it obvious? Merchants!" Neenahwi sank a little in her seat. Not the response she was expecting. "This city, this country has become enamored with profit. The merchants and the bankers wield all the power. The former treasurer was a merchant! Talk about letting the fox into the hen house," Lady Kingsley tutted and shook her head. "Nobles were put on this land by Arloth to rule, but that's being taken away, eroded like the cliffs, financiers washing away the rocks and taking power for themselves. And many of the profiteers are foreigners! We must arrest the tide, young lady, before we find the foundations washed out from under us."

Neenahwi took a sip of her tea, sweet chamomile, to let the old lady continue. All expectations this woman knew what she was talking about were now gone.

"So, we must take back the royal orders that have devolved the marketplaces. We can have good men and women appointed by me to run those institutions. And we must build alliances with countries similar to ours. Pienza has a grand tradition of nobility and chivalry, and so, we must shift our gaze north from the trading cities to those where we share a mutual heritage. Together, we can form a bulwark against the darkness of incivility."

"That's a...very interesting perspective. One I must consider further. Don't you think that trade has increased the wealth of Edland?"

"Yes, you're right; it has! That's the problem. We have peasants leaving the estates to come to the cities. They were happy before, my dear, not having to worry about their future. For an honest day's work, they had protection by their lord, and they had the festival holidays to relax. This is a rot inside Edland that needs to be removed."

"I'm sure you're right, Lady Kingsley. Thank you again for your time. I must be away; one appointment after another. I'm sure you can relate."

"Yes, dear. Thank you for coming by, and I hope I can count on your support. I sense a smart head on those shoulders. I'll need women like you in the future. I hope you remember that."

"My lady," said Neenahwi as she shook Lady Kingsley's hand in farewell. "Everything you have said I have committed to memory."

~

"NEENAHWI, IT'S WONDERFUL TO SEE YOU! COME AND SEE this."

Neenahwi disengaged from the strong hug and allowed herself to be led by Uthridge over to a table longer and wider than two grown men. A model of the lands around the Arz Sea depicted in miniature.

The lord general had been one of the first people she'd met when Jyuth brought her and her brother to the palace thirteen years ago. He was a major then, and he spent a lot of time with her and her little brother, showing them the city, helping them both to hone their skills with bow and blade. At the time they'd thought of Uncle Uthridge as a great friend, even though his real reason for spending so much time with them was to protect them from a possible reprisal. And more than likely to try to worm any information out of them about Llewdon and his forces.

"It's a lovely model, Uncle; very realistic."

"It's precisely to scale girl!" He beamed, proud of the craftsmanship. "But that's not what I mean. This is what I worry about at night. Look how Pyrfew is circling us."

Neenahwi studied the map. The Empire of Pyrfew at the center bottom of the table stretched up close to Redsmoke on the west of the Jeweled Continent and the border of the Green Desert to the east. There was a great expanse of sea to the west of Edland before a new land mass perched on the edge of the table. What these people called the Wild Continent, but what she knew as home. And this land, too, was colored a bright scarlet like Pyrfew.

"They lurk within a week's march of Redsmoke, new bastions under construction. I believe they'll swallow the city-states of the green desert in the next five years. Meanwhile, they are plundering your home, Neenahwi, at our rear. If this were a battlefield, then we'd be caught in a classic pincer. And let me tell you, this is a battlefield. It may take longer to move the pieces, but your father understands this."

"So, what do you propose we do?"

"We need to go on the front foot to have a proper defense, just as I taught you when we fenced. We need a bulwark to protect Edland. We have to secure Redsmoke for a generation, create a new border here," he said, pointing to a line five hundred miles south of where Pyrfew forces were today. "And here, we need to bring the Sapphire Sea cities into the realm. We cannot afford to lose them and their shipyards and trade routes to Llewdon."

Neenahwi was stunned, processing what her uncle was telling her. "You can't be serious. This is ten years of war! It took every professional soldier we had to retake Redsmoke. For this, you'd have to muster every able-bodied man and woman in the land!"

"We can supplement the professionals with mercenaries, but, yes, that's right."

"And here," Neenahwi said, pointing at the Emerald Sea. "How are you thinking of bringing these cities into Edland? Sending them a friendly invitation?"

"That's what we would try first, but they, too, are likely worried about their independence. If necessary, we can choke their trade routes. We own the Arz Sea still. Our navy is the largest. An embargo will soon have them change their minds if they decide to hold out."

"That would be after thousands of people had starved, Uncle! This isn't a game."

"I agree this isn't a game." He looked at her forlornly.

Only now did she see the deep sadness in his eyes, the joy he shared with her and her brother gone. Was it simply old age or something else?

"This next generation is going to be a dark one, girl. I worry for my grandchildren and the world they'll inherit. Commitment is going to win this war."

Holding in a deep breath, and then slowly letting it out, Neenahwi regarded the man she considered to be family and finally shook her head. She moved close, kissed him on the cheek, and whispered, "Uncle, I love you, and you're a great field tactician. But I hope, for all that is good in the world, you're wrong about what needs to be done..."

"Good afternoon, Lady Neenahwi. I'm sorry to keep you waiting. We've had a full day of hearings today, and let me tell you, the hangman will be busy next week." Lord Fiske, head judge of the realm and still Law Guild master (who better to argue away any potential conflict of interest?), sat behind a long, dark oak desk in his private chambers at the House of Scales.

He was dressed formally with a high, starched collar that was tradition for judges, and bushy, white-whiskered mutton chops reached down his cheeks. On his nose, a small pair of spectacles were perched that Neenahwi suspected he used to look down on those in front of him.

Two clerks were in attendance, but they busied themselves at separate tables. "I got your message, and I don't typically meet with potential voters during the day, I'll have you know, but I made an exception for you. Unlike some others with responsibilities granted by the realm, I think it's important to work when it's time to work. I'm sure you agree."

"Well, Lord Fiske, I appreciate you making the exception." Neenahwi smiled and bowed her head in thanks. "And I do agree with you. I was recently thinking about how it was time to go to work. As your time is precious, I'd like to know why I should vote for you."

"Of course, my lady. At least I know you aren't here to try to make some deal, eh? Some of the offers I've heard!" The judge tried to laugh, but it came out as more of a cracked bark. "Look, I've been an arbiter of the king's law for thirty years and, yes, I know it's not the king's law anymore, but an old dog takes a long time to learn new tricks. I've passed down judgment on nobles and commoners alike. Who better to make the right decisions for our country than me?

"We need to do more to root out those less savory elements of our society. Why should criminal families be tolerated? Why is murder allowed? The Hollow Syndicate operates with impunity just because their services are expensive? I believe if people are honest with each other, then they'll be happy."

"And what do you think of overseas concerns, Lord Fiske?" asked Neenahwi.

"I say leave them to it, my lady! We need to focus inward to Edland. Get our own house in order and be a beacon to other countries. Pyrfew doesn't care to conquer Edland anymore. It's occupied with the Wild Continent, and let them have it as far as I'm concerned."

As the attention turned to talk of Pyrfew, Neenahwi noticed from the corner of her eye that one of the clerks looked up. He was a human chameleon, blending in with his surroundings because nothing was interesting for the eye to notice. She turned her attention back to Fiske. "How do you intend to stop this crime wave, as you see it? Are you going to be increasing the city guard and the local marshals?"

"Oh no. Trust me, they're in the middle of all of this corruption. If I add more guards, all I'll do is add more expense. What we need is for the people to come forward with intelligence. They know what's happening and who the miscreants are. We'll pay for information that leads to convictions."

Something was bothering Neenahwi, and it wasn't the blathering of this old fool. Paying for rats, indeed. No, something was nibbling at the corner of her mind.

She focused her third eye.

Someone was trying to probe her mind, a magic user, and they must be in this room with her; one had to see his target to be able to infiltrate someone's thoughts. This person wasn't skilled enough to penetrate the protections Neenahwi had built over many years of study and vigilant reinforcement, and she could sense that foreign attention darting around trying to look for a weak point.

Fool. Don't they know who I am? I came here announced.

As the grizzly bear to the salmon, she swatted at the intruding presence with a flick of her mind.

Wallpaper man slipped off his chair to the floor in a faint.

"Of course, we'll need to expand the work camps. Harold! Wake up, boy!" shouted Fiske as he noticed his man hit the floor.

"I think he's fainted, my lord. Maybe his collar is too tight?" asked Neenahwi in mock concern.

"Too much gin last night more like." Fiske pushed his chair back and walked around the desk heading for Harold the clerk, but then remembered himself and strode over, hand extended to Neenahwi. "I'm dreadfully sorry, Lady Neenahwi. I'm going to have to attend to this lazy boy. Thank you very much for coming. I greatly enjoyed our conversation. Remember, order equals safety when you come to cast your vote, eh?"

EASING INTO THE HOT BATH, NEENAHWI LET THE scalding water relieve the tension from her muscles. The cat jumped in from the open window and began to prowl around the bedchamber, looking for a good place to curl up. Tuft didn't like water, so stayed clear of the bathtub and any potential overspill that might occur.

"Ah, Tuft, there you are. We have both had a long day patrolling our territory, I see."

Meow.

"Yes, I met with them all. And what a sorry state they are. I'm troubled. They're all flawed. Uncle Uthridge I have a relationship with, but his worldview troubled me most. He may be right about what is necessary, but I pray he's not."

Meow.

"Eden is a self-centered bastard. If he wins, I'm leaving, too. And don't worry, you can come with me. The other two are irrelevant at this moment. I don't know how they'll appeal to more than a handful of other nobles. But should I choose one to align with and make them into something possible?"

Meow.

"I know you're a cat, Tuft. You don't have to tell me. I guess there's only one person I can talk to."

CHAPTER 18
DEMONCRAZY

Florian opened the door to the Royal Oak, Motega walking in behind him, carrying the limp body of the girl they had just saved. She had slipped into unconsciousness after asking them to bring her to the inn, which was their destination in any case.

The common room was busy with customers, enjoying dinner and a quiet drink. Their entrance was unremarked until a voice called out, "Alana!" and then everyone turned to see what was going on. A blonde-haired girl ran through the tables. Another man followed her with his hand on his sword. And the landlady of the inn stepped out from behind the bar, wiping her hands on her apron.

"What have you done to her!" screamed the blonde girl.

"Put down the girl, sir," said the man who came to the blonde girl's side, his sword now halfway out of its sheath.

"Hey, hey, hey!" said Motega. "We're the ones helping here. If it weren't for us, she'd be smeared on the cobblestones of the Lance."

"She's going to be fine," said Florian, stepping forward

and reminding the man and the girl he was considerably bigger than both of them. And he had two swords. "She took a bit of a beating and now she needs somewhere to lie down. We can help get her cleaned up."

"Thank you, gentlemen; we can take care of it." The landlady had threaded her way through the common room tables, calm as you like, having seen much worse than this in her line of business. "If you could bring Alana this way, then we'll see to her."

Motega muttered minor thanks for calm heads and stepped out from behind Florian to follow the innkeeper up the stairs and to an unoccupied private room. It was a simple chamber with a feather bed, washbasin, and a chest, lacking windows, but with hooks on the walls for the hanging of clothes. Motega lowered Alana to the bed and stepped back. Her eyes opened weakly and took a moment to focus.

"Petra. Jules. I guess I should have just stayed here after all." She gave a weak smile. "They saved me. It was Win. He was waiting for me..."

"Hush," said the landlady. "Let's take a look at you, and then you can tell us the story." She turned and faced Motega and his friends. "Thank you for your help tonight. I can handle it from here. You're staying in room twelve, correct? Please ask the serving girl downstairs for any food and drink you may like. And then I'd like to talk to you later, if you don't mind."

"Yes, ma'am, and thank you," said Motega.

"And, Mareth, you can go, too. Petra and I will handle it from here. We're getting to be quite experienced nurses," she said. "You make sure these gentlemen are looked after."

The landlady ushered the men out of the room and closed the door behind them.

"I'm sorry if I was hasty there at the front door. I'm Mareth," he said, reaching out to shake hands with Motega and his friends. "That girl is the sister of Petra, who's dear to me. And Alana is quite exceptional in her own right. Would you join me at my table?"

"No problem, Mareth. We understand how it's easy to jump to conclusions in these situations. I'm Trypp; this here is Motega, who carried the girl home, and the walking wall there is Florian."

"Well met. Come, let me get you an ale for your efforts." Mareth led them back down to the common room and a table at the back big enough for six. He called over the serving girl and ordered ale for his guests, along with plates of the roast pork and potatoes and a cup of unfermented apple cider for himself. Mareth noticed the look he got from Florian at his order. "I'm trying to cut down on the ale. And the wine. And the brandy. Good to take a break every now and again."

"I agree. I haven't had a drink since breakfast," said Florian, his deep laugh matching his deep voice.

"So, Mareth," said Motega, "what's going on? Do you know this Win character?"

"It's a long story. Are you sure you want to hear it?" Motega and Florian nodded as they took a drink from the tankards set down before them. Trypp didn't respond, just focused on his beer. Motega knew he believed business was private unless there was a contract involved.

Mareth recounted how he'd wanted to chronicle what happened after the king had been killed, but found himself working for Hoxteth, initially as a way to be involved in the process and to get a unique angle, but when he saw Eden enter the city, his mindset had shifted.

The traditional crop of nobles wouldn't help the vast majority in Edland. It would only happen with someone who had grown up like everyone else, and so, he helped to create a buzz about Hoxteth's candidature throughout the city. And then, when Hoxteth was murdered, he was despondent at the realization that the monied people of the city would ensure the status quo.

But Petra and Jules convinced him they could collectively do something, and so, that evening, they had met with district supervisors and guild masters, and they had decided to try to bring a voice to the everyday people of Kingshold.

As Mareth told his tale, Motega found himself being sucked in. By his ancestors, this man could tell a story. Like the shaman in his old tribe, he felt magic weaving in his voice, he was sure of it. When the bard had mentioned the death of Hoxteth, Motega made certain not to look at his comrades, but he could sense them shifting slightly in their seats.

"Thanks for the tale, friend, and thank you for the meal," said Florian between mouthfuls. "It's delicious."

"This whole place has gone demon-crazy," said Trypp, rolling his eyes. "Now, we have commoners and thieves all wanting to get their hands on a pyxie."

"There's something contagious about this change in power. Is it crazy or is this a breath of fresh air? I don't know." Motega turned from his friend to address Mareth. "And so, this Win guy was one of the supervisors? Why would he attack the girl when it sounded like everyone agrees with her idea?"

"I don't kno—"

"Because he's a spy." Jules had walked up unnoticed behind Mareth. "Alana is going to be fine, by the way. Some big bruises that'll only go bluer, and a few cuts and scratches. But she'll be fine. She intends to go to work tomorrow, but for now, Petra is trying to get her just to relax and go to sleep."

"Well, that's a relief. But a spy! Who for?" asked Mareth.

"It doesn't matter. Another candidate? A noble? The government? We don't want him blabbing to his boss or poisoning the well with the other supervisors." Jules pulled a chair and sat at the table, leaning in conspiratorially and looking at Trypp, Motega, and Florian in turn. "You gentlemen look like you're men of certain diverse talents. I've noticed the odd times of your comings and goings, but, of course, that's none of my business. You know our business now, though. And I don't like people who beat up on young women. Would you be willing to do some work for us tonight? I'll clear your tab, and you can stay here as long as you like if you can stop Win from blabbing. And give him a little lesson in manners."

Trypp nodded along as she spoke. "Just to be clear, you're not asking us to kill him?" he asked.

"Not as a first choice. Is that easier for you?" asked Jules.

"Well, it can be much cleaner if we're talking about killing someone. We know we have met our customer's expectations when the body stops breathing; things in between tend to be shades of grey. But it also usually costs a lot more than our tab is likely to be." Trypp looked at Motega, and then Florian. They both gave little nods. Trypp reached over to shake Jules's hand. "We'll do it."

MOTEGA WALKED SOUTH FROM THE FOURWELLS AREA WITH

Florian and Trypp flanking him. The streets were quiet. It was the time of the early morning where most everyone was in bed, but too soon for the serious drinkers in the taverns to be stumbling home.

Win had been exactly where Jules had said he would be. Lying in bed in his own house without a care in the world, evidently able to sleep peacefully shortly after beating a defenseless girl.

Nice man, that Win.

Trypp had popped open the lock to the back of the house with no fuss. Motega had covered his mouth, while Florian readied the gag. From there, it was all a quiet game of whispers making it clear about what was acceptable behavior and what wasn't, and strongly suggesting he pass the baton as supervisor to someone else who'd be able to talk.

He looked confused at that point, but when Florian punched him with one of his brass knuckles and broke his jaw, everything became a little clearer.

Trypp then pointed out that, though he might not be talking for a couple of moons, he could still write. Which was true. So Motega broke his thumbs using an ax handle.

And now they were walking back to the inn, but going the long way. No point in being too obvious.

"So, are we going to do it?" asked Florian.

"Do what?" said Trypp.

"Yes, I think we will," said Motega, looking at Florian.

"Do. What?" repeated Trypp, looking at his two friends.

"Well, we're going to go back to the inn now, tell them we did the job with minimum fuss—" said Florian.

"—and while we've been gone, they'll have been talking about how they need to be ready for anything with what they're trying to do—" interjected Motega.

"—and how they're going to piss important people off. And so, they're going to ask us to work with them through the election," finished Florian.

"What? You were both thinking that? How do you do that?" asked Trypp, incredulous. "And wait a minute, you said yes to this, Mot? And what do you think, Flor?"

"I say yes, too."

"I'm repeating myself now, but what?" Trypp stopped dead, and so, Motega did likewise. This was the response he'd expected. He'd been through this dance before with his friend. "They don't have any money, you know, or not a lot of it, so why should we help them?"

"Trypp, my friend, it isn't all about coin. Sometimes, we must go to where the current is strongest and see where the river takes us." Motega rested his hand on his tall friend's shoulder. "The people of this city have no balls! For hundreds of years, they've let a few rule them when they have the greater numbers. A chieftain on the plains of my home would be challenged and killed for being as useless as these kings and queens. Now, the people are growing balls. Finally. And no surprise it's three women at the center of it for this growing of balls. So, we should be there at the heart of it. I think it'll be fun." And Motega smiled a big toothy smile at Trypp.

"I agree with our grinning ranger here," piled on Florian. "And here's one other thing for you to think about, Trypp. What if they win? If they help a candidate become lord protector. That will mean we helped, too. How much future forgiveness do you think it buys us to have the protector of Edland behind us? Think of it as a wager, a bet on a long-shot outcome, and all it'll cost us is a little time."

"I hadn't thought of that." Trypp rubbed his bearded

chin, the motion helping him to align his thoughts. "A lord protector of Edland could probably even get us out of jails in other countries. That would be a lot of forgiveness. So, here's the deal, boys. If they offer us the job, then we'll take it in the end, but you've still got to let me negotiate to the point where I'm pretty sure I'm getting half of everything they've got. Alright?"

"Deal," said Motega.

"Deal," said Florian.

"This is going to be fun," said Trypp.

Motega knew he would come 'round.

CHAPTER 19
A WIZARD'S ANGER

"So, you've forgiven me, daughter?" Jyuth wore a long robe of purple velvet over his nightgown, looking more like the old man he was than she remembered seeing him before. It was a little after seven in the morning, and he had just woken before Neenahwi had arrived at his rooms.

"Not entirely, but I don't want to lose these last few weeks with you, Father. I can wait to be angry with you all over again."

"That's a small pleasure to me, and I want to take all of those I can get." The old man smiled and embraced Neenahwi. "Now, where is that girl? Alana knows she's to wake me earlier than this and bring me my breakfast. I'd offer you coffee, but I don't know how to get it myself. Let's sit, and we can have some of this wine from last night."

They sat in Jyuth's bedchamber, and he poured two cups of red wine, picking out some small insects which had drowned a happy death in the uncovered jug. When they both had a drink in hand, Neenahwi explained what happened that night on Mount Tiston, the release of the demon gem's power, but then its reticence to release its gifts after. She shared her thoughts on the potential future rulers of Edland, too, providing a colorful commentary on their relative merits (or demerits, as was mainly the case).

"Two critical topics, my dear," he said, nodding, having allowed her to talk uninterrupted. "With regard to the first, I have some knowledge to share, though it may not sit easily. For the second, I have no magical insights, but maybe history can help?"

"Let's start with the demon gem. What am I missing? Why can't I use it?" Neenahwi was eager for answers.

"Well, you've figured out more than I did a week after discovering my first stone of a similar heritage. Now, let me caveat that my knowledge may not be complete, so don't think of it as the end of your research, but it's practical in some sense.

"I know of two ways to access the energy within the stones. The secret is you cannot connect a thread to the stones as you would a living thing, as there's no way to penetrate it. And I tried to cut them, drill a hole even." Her father chuckled at the memory. "The stone has to make a connection to you, and that's where I know of two ways.

"The first is through anger. Because these stones aren't of this world, they seek out what they know, and the great demons are creatures of rage and hatred. So, when the holder is angry, it's like the dam bursts and the mana flows. And like a burst dam, the torrent that comes out can sometimes be uncontrollable. That's why people generally don't like it when I become angry."

"In both cases, it was my anger that caused it, then. First, my anger at you, and then at myself not being able to make the stone work."

"I'm glad to see I was useful for something, dear. The second method is through blood. When a stone comes into contact with the holder's blood, there's a slow seep of magical energy from the stone to the wizard. It adds to your life force, so you can use it at will without leeching on your reserves. Look here." Jyuth rolled up his sleeves and opened his robe and nightgown to bare his chest. "See these small scars? That's the mark of my using the stones. I have three such stones, and I've had them set in trinkets I can wear, but in each case, there's a sharp edge or point which agitates against my flesh and causes a small wound. The blood and the stone come into contact, and a connection is made."

"Ingenious. How did you discover that?"

"By accident, of course, like most great discoveries. Now, here is the *but*. You have to be very aware of how long you stay in contact with the gem. It'll corrupt you if you use it too much or wear it too long. It'll fill you with anger, and your aspect will change. You'll become more akin to the creatures who used these stones in their home world. And with too much anger, you can release too much power for your body to contain. It wants to destroy, and it might not mind if it's you. So be sparing. And your meditations become even more important to purge any anger on a daily basis."

"You talk about the stones as if they're sentient. Do they have a mind of their own?"

"Not all things need to have a mind, Neenahwi, to have a nature. Rivers flow down to the sea. Trees reach up to the sky. This is why they exist, and this is what they do, and you can't change it. Think of the stones in the same way. I can help you design a necklace, or a torc that will serve your need, and I know of someone who can craft it for you." Jyuth reached over to the table and refilled their cups, pouring out the last of the slightly sour wine. "And so, to the second topic."

Neenahwi was grateful and relieved to have the secret to the demon gem, and so was content to move onto the second of her worries. "Father, these candidates are all different kinds of useless. Or downright scary. Even Uthridge worries me for what he believes is coming. What would you do? Who would you support?"

"Well, I'm not going to tell you what I'd do, and don't get angry with me!" He smiled and held up his hands in surrender. "We don't want you melting down the palace now, do we? No, I'm not going to tell you because, if I did and you followed my thinking, then it's no different than if I did it myself. If it went wrong, then you'd feel it was my fault, not yours. And I might, too. And this old man wants to be free of guilt.

"However," he continued, "I'll give you two pieces of advice I've learnt over the years, and I'll also tell you a story. One I have probably told before, but you might not remember it. So, here's the advice. Firstly, no one is perfect. I've realized not everything will be done the way you want it to be done, and most of the time I accept it. Only when there's something truly egregious, despicable, or threatening to the empire, do I intervene. And that's been the only way I've found to be able to live with a bearable level of guilt and not turn into a tyrant like Llewdon."

At the mention of her former captor and emperor of Pyrfew, she wondered what made these two men different, even though they were both so long-lived. "Have you ever thought about just taking over? I can't imagine you ever being a tyrant."

"A few times. Especially early on. And so, even though I just counseled patience when others were making decisions, I know I'm not patient when in the middle of things. If I were to rule, then I'd rule everything. Even though I'd have good in my heart, I'd still be laying out a maze for the people of Edland, where every twist and turn had been defined by me. I don't think people want to have their whole journey planned out for them, especially for those where it may result in a dead end. Tyranny, in my eyes, is not when the ruler does injustice on their own people; that's plain and simple evil. Tyranny is the taking away of choice, the enslavement of all, even if some of the subjects may have jewel-encrusted manacles."

"My second piece of advice is brief. Trust Uthridge. He has the sharpest military mind I've seen in a long time. The risks he sees are real. But that doesn't mean he'll make a good lord protector."

Neenahwi nodded. In a way, she was relieved to know the other old man she cared for was not losing his mind, though she needed time to ponder the broader repercussions.

He took a big sip of wine and continued. "And so, this brings me to my story. Once I was young, though you may find that difficult to believe. I had barely seen fifty winters, but I had studied and gained power in many different places—"

"Where did you study magic?" interrupted Neenahwi. "You've never told me."

"And I'm not going to today, and I may never," Jyuth reached over and patted her hand, "but I have taught you almost all I know. Trust me in that. So, as I was saying, I had just returned to the land of my birth, what we now call Edland. Back then, there were twenty, thirty kings. I can't remember precisely how many. All squabbling over various patches of dirt. They called themselves kings, but they were indeed little more than war chiefs with wooden forts as their homes.

"I'd traveled to other lands and cities where I'd seen what I thought of as civilization, and I wondered why it hadn't evolved with my people. I chalked it off to the island we live on, isolated from other countries and other influences, but big enough that there wasn't a desire amongst most men to see what the rest of the world held.

"Why venture across the unknown sea when you could fight who was in front of you? I spent many years traveling from one shit-hole fortress to another, taking stock of these men who called themselves kings, and they were not impressive. Oh, some of them could fight, fight like the heroes of old they were, but they weren't leaders of peace, which is much more challenging than being a leader in war.

"But on a visit to one dunghole—fifty miles north along the coast from Kingshold it was, but is there no more—I came across a warrior called Edward. He was a king's champion, quick with spear and skilled with sword, but he was also aware. He observed things and took an interest in people. He didn't have an ego and didn't benefit from his status. He was to be my clay.

"I spent time with him and befriended him, before I had to leave with some excuse or another. I went back across the sea to the northern kingdoms, traveling in disguise, and I told them about an island with bountiful fields and gold in the hills you could dig up with your hands. It took a while, but that spring they invaded, landing near the settlement of

Edward and his king. I had, of course, warned them, and they were prepared. They met the raiding party from the north on the beach."

"An arrow took the king in the eye, most unlucky for an arrow to fly so far and so accurate, as the king lurked at the rear. And Edward was a hero that day, killing twenty men himself and setting fire to the boats. So, of course, Edward became king of this little backwater, and I became his advisor.

"Over the next year, a full-scale invasion came from across the sea, but they landed on the long shore of this island, keeping clear of Edward's lands. Many fiefdoms were destroyed, and many kings and their people fled their lands. And Edward, smart lad that he was, had the wonderful idea to bring the kings together so they could join forces to regain their lands. I wonder where he got the idea from? At the kingsmeet, after weeks of discussions and tourneys, there was, at last, agreement Edward would command the combined forces.

"He had a brilliant tactical mind, using the strengths of the different people in complementary ways, and so, by the next winter, they'd driven out the invaders. Many of the kings had worked closely with Edward in the field and grew to love him, and I befriended them, too. Unfortunately, many other kings not in this close circle perished on the battlefield. And a week after the last of the northerners were driven from this land, another kingsmeet was held, and the remaining kings begged Edward to be the one true king of this land. There was a traveling priest of Arloth nearby we commandeered to pronounce that Edward had been chosen by God and that was that. They then named Edland in his honor.

"He was a good king, and the start of civilization on this island. He built the original parts of this palace. But he also knew his limits and where to trust others, not just me, but other carefully selected advisors. Back then, we knew we were building something special..." Jyuth trailed off, and silence reigned for a few seconds.

"And?" asked Neenahwi.

"And that's it. End of story," he said, dusting off his hands. "Make of it what you will. Make of this kingdom what you will. And most importantly, make your life what you will."

"You're being rather melodramatic, aren't you? And evasive, too."

"Yes, maybe. I should have disappeared in a puff of smoke at the end of the story like a real wizard would have." Both he and Neenahwi shared a smile. "But I'm so hungry! Where's my breakfast? Where's Alana?"

The door to the apartments opened and in stepped the girl Neenahwi recognized from her most recent visit to these rooms. She wore the simple black dress of palace staff, but she was moving gingerly. A cut above her eye, stitched tidily, and a swollen purple cheek the signs of some assault.

"I'm here, my lord. I'm so sorry I'm late." Her voice was partially distorted by a thick lip that joined to meet the swollen cheek.

"Alana, what happened to you, my girl?" Jyuth ran across the room to meet her, taking hold of her hand. "Come, sit down."

"Thank you, my lord," said Alana as she was swept into the seat Jyuth had just vacated, "but I'm fine."

"You're not fine. Now, tell me, what happened to you?"

"I was attacked last night when walking home. Nothing for you to worry about, my lord."

The old man leaned forward, hands on his thighs to bring his eyes level with Alana. "I'm going to tell you one last time, or I'm going to pull it out of your mind myself. Was this because of me? Like last time when you were followed?"

"No... Yes... Both, I guess." Alana took a deep breath, closed her eyes, and the story flooded out. "I was at a meeting where we were trying to organize for the common people of the city to vote, with the supervisors of a lot of the districts, and I suggested how we could do it. I said I thought you wanted more people to be involved, not just the nobles. I hope you don't mind.

"And then, after the meeting, we were planning how we were going to do it, and when I left to go home, Win—he's the supervisor of Fourwells, but you probably knew that already—was waiting for me. He said he wanted to take me to someone, as I knew too much, and I tried to get away from him when he was holding me, and so, I kicked him in the plums and ran, but he caught up with me and hit me, and he would have killed me if it wasn't for three men coming along and saving me." Neenahwi noted she said all of that in one breath, thinking about how she had missed her calling as a pearl diver.

"Do you know who this Win was working for?" asked Neenahwi.

Alana looked at Jyuth. "It was Aebur. Those men who saved me went to his house to find out. They stopped him from talking. They broke his jaw and his thumbs."

Jyuth paced in a circle. Neenahwi could almost see the steam coming out of his ears. "What is it, Father?" she asked. "Why are you so upset? It seems like Alana has managed to take care of business herself. And without killing anyone, I might add. Maybe you should take note."

"Hah! It's Aebur. I warned him off prying into my business. I warned him about being involved in the election. And I'm sure he participated in that business with the king."

"You think he has an agenda?"

"Of course, he has a fucking agenda! It's being an enormous slimeball, who'll help whoever's paying him the most! And one of his agents doing this to Alana is like doing it to me. I'm going to pop his rancid little head." He disappeared into his bedchamber and quickly changed into one of his typical blue robes, belted with steel discs attached in their holsters.

"I'll come with you, Father," she called to him before seeing to the girl in obvious discomfort. "Alana, you're very diligent coming in today, but you should be resting. Lie down on the chaise there and sleep."

Jyuth, now changed, stormed through the sitting room and toward the palace grounds. "Neenahwi! Stop fucking dawdling! I'm angry. And I haven't had breakfast."

"STAND ASIDE, MEN." JYUTH STRODE QUICKLY TOWARD THE iron-bound oak door, waving half a sausage he'd picked up from the kitchen on the way. The two palace guards standing outside looked in two minds as what to do.

"My lord," said one of the guards, "Master Aebur is currently having his breakfast. I can announce you if you wait a moment."

"I warned you." The remains of the sausage disappeared into the old man's mouth. Her father's hands now free, Neenahwi saw the magical energy gathering in his palms before he swept them to either side, the armored guards skittering across the floor with a scrape of metal on stone. The next moment, the door imploded in a shower of splinters and metal shards. One of the guards struggled to get back to his feet.

"I'd strongly suggest you don't get involved," said Neenahwi.

The guard took one look at the door and his unconscious fellow and ran up the corridor away from trouble.

"Aebur, I warned you!"

The fat spymaster sat at a table gorging on a many-plattered breakfast. His mouth hung open at the shock of the explosive entrance, partially chewed food falling to his lap. A rush of wind swept by Neenahwi and hit Aebur in the chest, throwing him into the far wall of the room.

"I warned you to keep your nose out of my affairs, and that includes the people working for me."

"My lord, I don't know what you're referring to," stammered Aebur. "This is most unusual, barging into my rooms."

"I'll barge wherever I like! I've had enough of your schemes. I'll know the truth."

"I promise you. I'm a faithful servant of the realm," whispered Aebur.

"I grow tired of this." Jyuth's hand reached out as if to grasp Aebur though he was ten feet from him.

The fat pig rose into the air, clutching at his throat as he struggled to draw breath. His face changed from pink to bright red to dark purple as he gurgled away. Neenahwi stood watching from the broken doorway with arms crossed.

"Jyuth! Stop this right now!" A small, thin, bookish man with thinning hair and goatee rushed into the room, stopping a distance away from the angry wizard. Neenahwi knew him to be Hoskin, the former king's chancellor. "What's happening here?"

Jyuth turned to face Hoskin, and for a moment, he didn't seem to recognize him. "Good morning, Hoskin. Arrived in time to see me pop this pimple?"

"I mean it, Jyuth. There will be no more killing in the palace. What's going on?"

"This man is a traitor and cannot be trusted. I warned him to change his ways, and he chose not to listen." Jyuth relaxed his grip slightly on Aebur, and he was able to take small breaths, but he still hung from the air.

"If he's a traitor, then you'll hand him to me. I'll have him interrogated, and we can discover the truth behind this. Jyuth, you placed me in charge. I cannot allow this chaos in the walls of the palace!" Hoskin shook like a leaf, but he maintained eye contact with the old man. "If he's a traitor, then we will find out who he's working for. And then we'll decide his fate."

Jyuth looked begrudgingly back to Hoskin. "Make it stick," said the wizard. The spymaster was still struggling for breath, but he began to float over to hang in front of Jyuth, inches from his face. "I doubt I'll see you again, Master Aebur. You'll probably wish I had finished you here. But Bartholomew shouldn't have to do all of the work, so let me get him started." Jyuth's forehead bashed into Aebur's face, nose flattening with a shower of blood and a gurgled cry. Jyuth turned, and the spymaster dropped to the floor.

Neenahwi stepped aside to let Jyuth out of the shattered doorway and matched his pace past the score of guards standing perplexed outside.

"Really, Father? A headbutt?"

CHAPTER 20
LADY GREY'S PROPOSITION

Dolph came back to the table with four mugs of ale in hand and slid one over to Mareth, Motega behind him with three more. The common room of the Royal Oak was buzzing with the news about the closing of the trading marketplaces earlier that day.

Rumors began to spread two days ago that Lady Kingsley intended to revoke the trading licenses for the markets and bring them under government control, and the response had been unsurprisingly critical. Many of those merchants had made a considerable investment to acquire the licenses and build increasingly lavish operations to attract merchants from up and down the Arz Sea. Closing the markets had caused chaos. Administrative workers and porters, having nowhere to go, descended on Lady Kingsley's estate to heckle and pelt her house with yesterday's vegetables from the Green Market.

Mareth had heard she'd been afraid to leave her house all day, the crowds becoming quite intimidating. Customs officers and city guards were also overwhelmed with demands for recompense from merchants incurring higher docking fees. Typically, they were in port for a matter of days, but the situation meant they were unable to sell the contents of their holds and stock up for the next leg of their journey.

The chaos had spread through the city and had complicated their efforts to put into action those plans developed since the meeting with the district supervisors. Petra sat next to Mareth, looking tired. She'd been trying to keep up with Dolph as they'd roamed the city, Mareth not wanting her to be unaccompanied around the city after what had happened to Alana. He squeezed Petra's hand, almost unbelieving at how his life had improved in the past couple of weeks.

"What progress today?" asked Alana, sitting opposite him. The bruises on her face were fading to yellow, and she'd been back at the palace all day after being ordered to spend two days resting. She and Petra had effectively moved into the Royal Oak as well, now, Jules providing a room in the private part of the building for them to share.

Petra reported first. "We've posted notices all across the Narrows, north and south, and I spoke with most of the gossips, so they can help get the word out. We've arranged meetings in two nights' time, so people can come and ask questions. We'll have a good opportunity, then, to see if people are going to get behind this."

Once Petra had finished, Alana made a few notes and looked to Mareth.

"I've now met with all of the district supervisors who didn't attend the meeting," he began. "They know what we're doing, of course. Word gets around quicker than a whore's pox." He noticed the stern look from Petra and attempted to scramble to safety. "Not that I've anything against whores with the pox, of course. Anyway, they're interested, but they want to see how this is going to work."

Mareth considered how this might have been a little bit of an exaggeration regarding the positive response. Two of the supervisors had laughed in his face, saying there was no way it was going to work, and another had rubbed his hands in greed at the thought of being the custodian of a thousand crowns. They would need to find someone more trustworthy there.

Alana nodded as Mareth finished, and she turned to the men to her left. To Mareth's surprise, Motega, Trypp, and Florian had been with them since they rescued Alana and dealt with Win.

Petra had suggested asking them to help, but he hadn't expected a positive response. Avenging a young woman assaulted in the street appealed to their heroic sense, but they had agreed to be hired when Petra asked, even when he explained how the plan was more similar to a door-to-door knife sharpener than an adventurer. Worn shoe leather and words sowed in hope rather than expectation.

The tall, black man called Trypp spoke for the three friends. He'd taken the lead amongst them even though he'd been mostly quiet that first night until they returned from dealing with Win. Mareth had thought he was little more than a hanger-on initially, but now appreciated he was the business brains of the trio and canny about the city and people. "We had a good day. There will be a dozen people here in the morning from Fishtown, Randall's Addition, and Bottom Run to help. Some of them aren't the smartest, mind you, so think about the jobs you give them."

Alana was keeping notes as each person provided their update, her pen scratching on a large map of the districts she'd drawn. They all looked at her as she studied the chart, breathing deeply in concentration. "We need more people. It's going too slow. We're going to run out of time."

"We'll be able to bring more volunteers tomorrow, Alana," said Trypp, "but they need someone to give them better instruction. There's no one left here at the inn when we're all walking the city."

"And we need a candidate, too, Alana," said Mareth. "Right now, people aren't excited. No one wants to pay so they can choose between a punch in the mouth or a kick in the sack. If we had the right candidate, then others would do the work for us."

"You're right, I know. There may be some news on that to investigate. Jyuth mentioned today that Guild Master Ballard was going to present himself as a candidate. He obviously has the backing of his guild and apparently a few other lesser guilds."

"Excellent," said Mareth, looking around at the others. "Anyone know anything about him?"

"I know of him," said Trypp. "Solid, good reputation like his stonework. Honest, too. And don't ask me how I know."

From the corner of his eye, Mareth noticed a small figure standing beside him, a girl dressed in a house servant's clothes. She looked at the people around the table, recognition on her face as she saw the object of her search and scooted over to whisper something in Dolph's ear. Dolph whispered something in return, and then the little girl ran out of the inn.

"What was that?" asked Mareth.

"I have to go. Lady Grey has called for me at once."

"But I was just about to say we would go and see Ballard."

"I'm sorry, Mareth, but you're not the one who holds the

purse. I don't know what this is about or if I'll be ordered back." Dolph pushed back his chair, drained his mug, and then he, too, walked out the door without further farewell, into the fading light of the evening.

"I'll go with you, Mareth," said Motega. "I'd like to see this stonemason. I can make sure we get there safe."

"I'll go, too," said Alana.

"Thank you, Motega. That's appreciated," said Mareth. "Alana, I think Petra should come. Please don't take offense, but you still look like you've been in a tourney. You should rest, and we can talk when we return."

Mareth was eager to leave, his tiredness from the day of pounding the cobblestone streets slipping away at the prospect of seeing someone who could be their new candidate. "Petra, Motega, let's go."

IT WAS DARK BY THE TIME THEY ARRIVED BACK AT THE Royal Oak, and the time of year meant it was very late. What Mareth considered to be their usual table at the back was unoccupied, but there was no sign of Alana. Motega followed behind Petra and Mareth, and moved off to talk to Trypp and Florian, who played skittles with some regulars. Mareth scanned the room until he saw Jules and waved her to the empty table. Petra left to fetch Alana.

In a few moments, their merry band of electioneers had gathered, all looking eager for the news. Alana jumped right into it as she walked over, stretching, looking like she just woke up. "So, how did it go?"

"It took a long time for us to be able to see him," said Mareth, "but it went well. I liked him..." The words died in his mouth as he saw Dolph striding across the room toward them, a grim, purposeful look on his face.

Mareth had learnt some of his moods with all of the concentrated time they'd been spending together. This was either "doing something I don't agree with" or "I'm tired of walking around all of tarnation and need a drink." Or it could have been a combination of the two.

"Evening, Mareth," said Dolph as he came to a stop at the table. "I know I'm interrupting, but you're about to have a bigger interruption than me. Lady Grey is in her carriage outside, and she wants to talk to you." Then he scanned the faces of everyone around the table. "She wants to talk with all of you. Ms. Jules, I think we're going to need the back room. This isn't something we should do out in the open."

"What's going on, Dolph?" Mareth inquired. "What does she want with all of us?"

"And how many guards has she brought other than you?" asked Motega, his friends pushing away from the table, eyes scanning the room, likely assessing other exits.

"Listen, you three." Jules pointed a finger in Motega's face. "No trouble. No fighting in my inn. I don't want to get shut down. So, bloody relax. Dolph, what does she want?"

"I don't know. I'm not sure if I could tell you if I did know. She's only come with three other guards that could fit in the carriage with her. She didn't want to be conspicuous, so I'd say she means what she says. She wants to talk."

"Alright then," said Jules, "all of you in the back. Dolph, you can tell her she's welcome to come in. I'll meet her at the door. Not every day I have a lady in the Royal Oak."

~

MARETH WOULDN'T ADMIT IT OUT LOUD, BUT HE HAD A thing for older ladies.

For a long time, he'd thought his flirting with Jules was going to get somewhere, but it had never been reciprocated. As Lady Grey walked in alongside Jules and took a seat at the head of a table, the pair of them were almost enough to make him forget Petra.

Jules was Jules. She always looked commanding and put together. Lady Grey was wearing black as befitted a widow of less than a week, who should still be in mourning, but she was wearing trousers and a tunic tailored to her trim figure. Her hair was pulled away from her face, the faintest of wrinkles around her almond-shaped eyes and at the edge of her full lips. She would have turned the head of the old Mareth, but the new one was trying much harder to be a better man. He squeezed Petra's hand under the table, more for his sake to remind him of her presence and how she had been so important in his rebirth.

"Good evening, Mareth. It's a pleasure to see you again," said Lady Grey, inclining her head toward him. "And this must be the beautiful Petra I've heard so much about. And you're her sister, Alana, or should I call you the ringleader? And then we have Trypp, Florian, and Motega. Motega, does your sister know you're here in Kingshold?"

Everyone around the table shifted nervously, even though it was always known Dolph would be reporting back to his employer. Mareth could tell what they were thinking. *Is Dolph her only source or does she have other spies?*

"Lady Grey, it's a pleasure to meet you," said Motega. "And no, my sister does not know I'm back in Kingshold. I'd appreciate it if that remained the case."

"That's a shame, Wolfclaw. Family is critical to all of us. I'm especially reminded of this in recent days."

Nobody spoke, not wanting to interrupt her grief, if that's what the silence was.

"Well, I haven't come here to be maudlin. Mareth, I asked you to make trouble, and it seems you've been more ambitious than I anticipated. And you have a cohort helping you, too. Remarkable."

"Lady Grey, I'm sorry for your loss. It must have been terrible. I assume Dolph has told you our plans," said Mareth. "You should know there's been real disappointment for the people of the city at the news of Hoxteth's murder. We think we have an opportunity to stick it to the nobles standing for the role of protector. They won't see what's coming."

"Now, now, Mareth, let's not call it murder. It was an assassination. I know full well it was a contract, and I'm pretty confident I know who paid for it. Officially, there's been no crime committed." Lady Grey kept even and calm as she talked about her husband's death. "And as for sticking it to the nobles, I, for one, would like nothing better to slide up behind them in the shadows and stick a knife between their ribs. But from where I sit, you have two problems. All of the declared candidates are nobles, and the math is against you."

"We've been looking for a new candidate people can rally behind, Lady Grey," interjected Alana. "Mareth was about to tell us about a meeting he had this evening when you arrived."

"Yes, yes. Master Ballard, of course. Please, do continue with your report to your friends, Mareth."

"Well, he's hard to meet with. He didn't know who we

were, but Petra managed to charm her way into having an audience," began Mareth. She squeezed his hand this time. "We all liked him. He was grounded, understanding of what's going on in the city and the realm, wanting to build a broader relationship across other guilds to be able to govern effectively.

"He also seemed a man of simple tastes, no displays of wealth, which he would have access to as the master of even a lesser guild, and it seems like he cares. He hasn't yet declared, as he's unsure about his chances. He has most of the lower guild houses with him, but that'll be less than a tenth of the vote. So, when we explained what we were doing, he seemed actively interested. We need to organize a meeting with the district supervisors and Ballard."

"Ballard is a smart man," said Lady Grey, smiling. "He should be wary about his chances. He honestly doesn't have any. There won't be a single noble who'll vote for him. And if he continues to be as straight and true as the lines of his stone, then he's not going to make the deals necessary to get the wealthy merchants on his side."

"But if we can bring twenty districts behind him, and he has half of the guilds, then he'll have more than thirty demons right there." Alana looked directly into the eyes of Lady Grey, not shirking the attention that came her way. "We must be able to win over some of the other independent voters who'll want to have a good man lead Edland?"

"Miss Alana, that's wishful thinking. But if you wish to spend the next fortnight pursuing a losing cause, then I'm not one to stop you. Math is against you doubly. With a candidate like Ballard, there are too few votes you can pursue. You would be relying on the vote being so evenly split amongst the nobles for you to have a chance, when we all know the bastard Eden is going to get a majority of that vote. You need coin to organize and mobilize, too. There are only so many favors you can cash in. Once again, math is against you. You need coin, and you don't have it."

"Did you travel here just to warn us we're wasting our time?" asked Mareth.

"Well, I knew I'd do that, at least. I like what you're doing. I, too, want a candidate I can believe in, one who can lead in a way I thought my husband would have. I can feel the ground shifting, and I don't know if this is going to be an earthquake or a sinkhole beneath my feet." *Bang.* Lady Grey slapped her hand on the open table, making everyone jump, sheepish looks from the fighters around the table. "But you need to face reality; otherwise, you'll lose. Ballard is not going to be the candidate you want. As you said, you need someone who cares, but you also need someone charismatic, someone who'll make the right deals and, most importantly, someone with the right family."

"Are you considering standing, my lady?" asked Petra.

"No, my dear. I wouldn't make a good candidate, even if I would make a good protector. I've alienated myself from many of the nobles of this realm through my marriage to my former husband. And I have no obvious connections to the common people, though I care about their plight deeply. No, I'm afraid I'm not the candidate we're all looking for."

Mareth had been grateful to Lady Grey for her employment up to this point. It had been her intervention in Hoxteth's office that had started this journey, and she'd stood by him over the past week, but it was beginning to grate how she was telling them things they already knew.

"If you won't stand, then, Lady Grey," Mareth said, irritation showing in his voice, "where do you think we're going to find someone noble born who's going to turn their back on that? Because we've been looking hard and we can't find anyone!"

"Mareth," she chided, "sometimes we forget to look in the most obvious places." Once again, the smile was back on her lips as she focused her attention on the bard. "Tell me, can you think of a minor noble who might be involved with what could be considered a popular uprising?"

Oh no, she can't be serious.

"You're barking up the wrong tree, my lady," said Mareth.

"Oh, I don't think so. I think you do yourself a disservice." He noticed the others around the table looking at him confused, all except for Trypp, who looked like he was enjoying this exchange. Petra was staring at Mareth with questions in her eyes.

"Mareth, what's she talking about?" asked Petra.

He sighed. "I'm a noble. A minor one. My father is Lord Tomas of Bollingsmead. As his third child, I'm officially of less worth to him than his favorite mare. My father thinks I'm a wastrel, and so, he's hardly likely to pull strings to get other nobles to back me."

"That can all be managed, Mareth," said Lady Grey. "What many care about first is the name you come with. We can build a story around the rest. And I've heard you can tell a *very* good story."

"Mareth, you never told me." Petra withdrew her hand from his. She looked disappointed, which hurt like a punch in his gut. "But if this is all true, then why shouldn't you stand? You told me you wanted to be at the center of the story. What better way? And we'll all support you. I mean, we were already with you."

Mareth didn't know what to say. She still believed in him,

even though he hadn't told her everything. Were they all following him? It might have been his original idea, but it was also as much Petra's. And since the first meeting with the supervisors, he was pretty sure he had just been following directions from Alana and Jules.

He had said he wanted to be at the center of things, but he'd given up the stories being about him. And for good reason. People he loved got hurt the last time.

But he knew this was a once in a lifetime chance for Edland to be better. Seeing the look on the faces of his father and brother if he became lord protector would also be priceless. But, by Arloth, he didn't want to fail again.

Alana confirmed his thinking of who was really driving the cart by addressing Lady Grey while Mareth sat quietly, unsure what to do. "So, assuming he does this, we then have the candidate we need. Are you able to help us address our math problems?"

"Yes. I'll support you," said Lady Grey. "I, too, have considered other options, and you have the best chance, even if it's small. And so, I'll finance the campaign so you can get organized in the districts. You can pay people something reasonable for the next few weeks of work. I can also lead the contacts with select nobles who can be swayed from their current positions or who have yet to decide. And I know all of the deals made by my husband with the wealthy merchants of the city. If we honor those, then we can likely count on their vote if enough see public support by the time we get to solstice."

"Lady Grey, can I ask you a question?" said Trypp. "Speaking as someone who's had an annual vacation in a little town called revenge, I'm sensing there's at least a small element here of wanting vengeance against Eden. Why not just buy an assassin to get back at him?"

Lady Grey looked at Trypp, considering him and his question. "Yes, revenge is a motive here. Eden losing the election is not revenge enough. But the price for his assassination is too high, the guard around Eden is too big, security too strong. So, I need to wait until after the election, but if he wins and becomes lord protector, I can do nothing. So, the bitter part of my soul that wants revenge now has to first of all wait for him to lose the election. Then I can kill him, nice and slow as he deserves. But there's still the other part of me, the part that stayed up for so many nights with my husband working out how we'd make this whole world a better place. That part knows we all deserve something much better."

Everyone deserved better. And everyone deserved a say. It might not work, but Mareth realized he had to give it a shot. What had changed since earlier in the day when he'd been talking from one supervisor to another? Nothing, that's what. The same mission, the same goals, except now, maybe, they had a good candidate. Or, if not good, then at least different.

"I should probably just drink the hemlock now and get all of the pain out of the way, but I'm in," declared Mareth. "I'm in if you're all with me, and you promise to help me avoid screwing it up too bad. I didn't want this. This has been a team effort so far and it needs to be going forward."

There were nods, smiles, a smattering of applause, hugs and handshakes, and all vouched their support. And as a result, they were all responsible for dropping him into it, right up to his neck.

CHAPTER 21
BARTHOLOMEW

The grey stone stairs descended through a torch-lit passageway, shadows dancing on the walls, their footsteps echoing loudly about them.

Hoskin didn't usually have a need to descend to the dungeons. It wasn't his first time, but the occasion usually demanded a traitor of some significance to make the trek into that gloomy hell hole. Hoskin wasn't exactly afraid of the dark—he loved to work late into the night in the library with nothing more than a single candle for light—but that was a comforting light, warm and personal, creating a little bubble in the dark for him and one of his beloved books.

The dark here was different: a cold dark, a dark where creatures of the imagination could consume a person. He was taken back to a time just before his thirteenth birthday. His father was away from home attending the king, and he and his mother were at their estate when his Uncle Gerald came to stay. Gerald was a cavalry captain and had just returned from a fake war against the tribes of the Green

Desert—initially to spend time with his sister, but he quickly bored of that, and so, he'd made it his mission to turn Hoskin into a fighter.

Hoskin had given up drills with their sword master when he was eight—after two long years of bruises, cuts, and blows to his self-esteem—before his mother finally intervened to spare him further misery. But Uncle Gerald wanted to make a man of him, so it became day after day of Hoskin being humiliated by an adult in the castle courtyard. His uncle seemed immune to the words of his sister to stop, until Hoskin had broken down into a wet quivering lump, tears streaming down his face.

The crying made his uncle snap, and he locked Hoskin in the damp cellars of the castle in the complete dark—for what seemed like days, but in reality, was only a few hours. Hoskin huddled in a corner, hugging his knees while he could hear rats scrabbling around in the dark, his eyes conjuring demons and dragons from the swirling colors he saw in the total black.

Even when he'd been freed, and his uncle clapped in irons, his sleep had been disturbed for years to come. His father stripped his uncle of his rank and ordered two hundred lashes in punishment. Hoskin watched every lash, and when he saw his uncle cry, he knew for the first time his father loved him.

A cough brought him back to the present. Oh yes, he'd picked up Percival on the way down, not wanting to delay this particular visit, but Percival insisted there were things he needed to discuss. "Yes, Percival, please do go on."

"Lord Chancellor, I've been working my way through the records kept by Lord Hoxteth, and I must tell you, the financial situation doesn't appear to be at all healthy. The reserves of gold in the palace are little, and it seems there haven't been many taxes collected in the past two weeks. I additionally found that the crown owes money to bankers in Ioth, Carlburg, and Danteth. Oh yes, and it seems the royalty paid to Eden each month has been one of the driving causes of this financial calamity. We've become somewhat hand to mouth, it appears, my lord."

"Is it that bad?" he asked. "Hasn't it always been that way?"

"I don't believe so, sir," said Percival, brow furrowed. "I did give some thought this morning to looking for a new job, as I'm not sure you can pay my salary."

Hoskin stopped and looked closely at Percival.

"I'm sorry, sir. That was supposed to be a little humor. I shan't do it again."

They started walking once again, now through a long tunnel that would take them to the dungeons below the mountain. "The fundamental question, Percival, is do I need to do anything about it?" Hoskin put the emphasis on *I* in his question. "Do we have enough money for the next eleven days?"

"I believe so, my lord."

"Then, in that case, let's move on. Next topic."

"Lady Kingsley had a very intriguing audience last night," read Percival from a new sheaf of parchment. "She called the merchants with charters for the various market houses in the city to her house after the fiasco of the strikes the day before. The good news is she did clarify she'd honor all existing charters, if elected. However, when they were having drinks afterward, she did manage to call one merchant from

Ambrukhar a *towel head,* I believe. And she asked another merchant from Ioth, who was there with his husband, 'Is everyone in that city a sissy?' It seems Lady Kingsley may not be able to hold her gin."

"Well, that's her out of contention, then. Not that she's a quitter; she'll hang on until the bitter end. What else? We're getting close to my destination."

"One last item, Lord Chancellor. Lord Eden is inviting you to a ball in two days. Apparently, it's going to be the social occasion of the year."

"Tell him to shove it, Percival. Politely, of course. Now, I think you should head back to the palace. I wouldn't want to damage your delicate sensibilities with what you might see."

Hoskin was met at the dungeon door by a big man, who wouldn't have looked out of place in the meat markets of Kingshold: rough brown clothes covered by a leather apron with many sharp gouges, pincers, and saws secured on a belt around his middle. His appearance was not that of a monster. He'd seen men like him walking in his ordinary course of life, but Bartholomew rarely saw daylight, choosing to live here in the dungeons.

Without a word, Hoskin followed him to a small cell, door ajar, where, inside, a fat, oily naked man hung from iron chains secured to his wrists. He was bleeding from numerous cuts to his face and body, one eye badly swollen.

"I took the liberty of warming him up for you, Lord Chancellor," said Bartholomew.

"Master Aebur," said Hoskin. "I assume you're enjoying the hospitality of our dungeons? I'm sure you can agree it's much more pleasurable than being a head on a spike."

Aebur was silent, his eyes appearing slightly unfocused.

"If you don't talk, you're of no use to me," continued the lord chancellor. "In that case, I can easily have you dressed and sent back to our good wizard. Tell me, what is it Jyuth thinks you've done? After the king was dealt with, he said he'd give you the benefit of the doubt for something, but what was it?"

"I-I don't know what to tell you," wheezed Aebur. "I'm a loyal servant."

"Not good enough." Hoskin turned his back on the spymaster and waved his hand to Bartholomew. From behind Hoskin came the repeated sound of fist on flesh and groans of agony. After a few minutes, Hoskin said, "That will be enough for now."

"I'll ask one more time," Hoskin said to Aebur's face. "I'm a busy man, and I can't stay down here all day watching you foul yourself. Now tell me, why does Jyuth want you dead?"

"I-I don't know, my lord. I swear."

"Master Aebur, this saddens me greatly. I'm not a cruel man. I could say this hurts me, more than it hurts you, but I don't think that would be true, and I want to set you a good example about how to be honest. I'll be back tomorrow, and I hope you have more to say. Bartholomew, it looks like our guest might be a little cold. Maybe you should light a fire?"

THE NEXT MORNING, PERCIVAL SKIPPED ALONGSIDE Hoskin as he walked quickly to the dungeons. "Percival, why are these tunnels lit with torches when we have oil lamps throughout the rest of the palace?" asked the chancellor.

"I believe it's for mood, my lord," said Percival without a

hint of irony. "My lord, I have some other matters to discuss."

"Everything is urgent," Hoskin said wearily.

"No, sir, there are many things I just handle myself."

Hoskin stopped and looked at his secretary. "Really? Like what?"

"Just this morning, I've already approved Sir Penshead's request to double the shifts for the city guard in the Inner Core in response to the increased levels of protests against each of the candidates. And I asked the commander of the customs guard to step up duty collection once more given our cash flow situation."

"Good...very good. So, what's important enough for me actually to hear about?"

"Well, Lord Jyuth is asking how the questioning is proceeding."

"Tell him it's going swimmingly. Aebur is having the time of his life. Next."

"I've received reports from a number of sources that groups of common people are organizing to be able to buy a demon. To vote, sir. It appears the unofficial district supervisors are part of this scheme, but there are others who are leading the organizing. Should I have Sir Penshead stop this?"

"Interesting," said Hoskin, mulling on this turn of events. What harm could it do? And would they even be able to do it successfully? Getting a thousand crowns would be a challenge for anyone, and who would they trust to not run off with it instead of heading to Jyuth? "No, let them carry on. I'm sure they'll lose interest soon. Next."

"One last thing, my lord," said Percival, shuffling to his final page of notes. "High Priestess Teresa is asking how the

Church of Arloth should prepare for the coronation of the new lord protector."

"Coronation? They aren't going to be king or queen. What about that don't they understand? I can only imagine how it rankles her that the new protector is going to be named by a six-inch pink pyxie instead of Arloth anointing a new monarch," he said, shaking his head. "But it's a good point, Percival. We should probably prepare for some celebration after the announcement of the new lord protector. At least Jyuth chose the solstice, so it's already a festival. Please give it some thought."

"Yes, my lord, of course. Do you have anything for me?"

"No, Percival, I'll see you later."

Hoskin opened the dungeon door himself, the thing thick, heavy and made of oak with a barred window set in the middle. There were no locks on the door other than a deadbolt on the inside. Guests of Bartholomew weren't usually able to walk out under their own steam, so keeping them inside wasn't a concern.

His nose wrinkled at the smell of burnt hair and barbecued meat that wafted through the corridor from the open cell door as a scream ripped through the silence. Hoskin was light-footed, reaching the doorway unnoticed, where he peeked his head around the frame so he could compose himself before going in.

It wouldn't do to vomit in front of the man being tortured.

He saw Aebur hanging in the same place as the day before, but now long, red, angry marks covered his torso and legs, the wounds weeping. He took a moment to compose himself before stepping around the corner and into the room, the heat of the brazier assaulting him, the iron pokers sticking out of it giving it the look of an infernal hedgehog.

"Good morning, Bartholomew. How is our guest today?"

"Good morning, m'lud," said Bartholomew, smiling. Now here was a man who enjoyed his work. "I think you were right that he was cold yesterday because the fire has helped our friend be a lot more comfortable about sharing."

"That's good news. What do you think he'd like to talk about?"

"He has answers to them questions from yesterday now, m'lud. Don't yer! Wake up!" Bartholomew pushed at the spymaster's fat belly with the iron poker in his hand. The end was not red anymore, but by the faint sizzle, it was still hot. Aebur's eyes opened wide, and he screamed again. The torturer kept pushing the end of the poker into the naked man's gut.

"Aaargh...I'll say...I'll say why Jyuth has suspected me; just stop, please." Aebur was sobbing and sniveling, and the words came out in a flood in between wet snorts.

"Go ahead, then, Master Aebur. I'm all ears," said Hoskin, regarding the captive. Aebur was less smarmy in his current position than usual. In the past, Hoskin could tell that Aebur always valued what was left unsaid, what someone didn't know, but he did. Now, it was in his interests to make Hoskin believe he was telling everything.

"I was just following orders, I swear. I was doing what the king wanted. The king and queen. They liked to have others join them in their bedroom. At the beginning, it was all simple enough. I was helping them by bringing the odd whore into the palace. I'd bring her, or him, in through a secret passageway from the Inner Circle. It carried on for a year or so, and then they wanted to be more lavish and more discreet than being in the palace where you and others might hear something. So, they had me buy the house that had the secret passageway. And then they wanted it to be like their own private zoo, whores of every race and color from all over the world for them and their friends."

Snot ran down Aebur's face as he spilled his guts, his eyes imploring Hoskin to provide him with some reaction. He nodded for him to continue.

"But there was only so much money that could disappear from the treasury without Hoxteth getting suspicious at the excuses, and so, they needed another way to get money. And that's what led them to trade things they had acquired for slaves and gold. I had to act as the go-between for all of this activity. The king trusted me, and I thought I was doing the right thing by helping him. And they kept needing more slaves as they began to expire. And I admit it, I liked doing this with you not knowing it was happening. He knew you wouldn't approve."

Hoskin was incredulous he was unaware of this. He was the chancellor, supposedly responsible for running the country effectively, and he didn't know this was happening under his nose.

The story made sense of some of the king's behavior: the increasingly late hour when he would awaken, the bags under his eyes, and the royal guard making sure he wasn't to be interrupted in the night. But still, Hoskin was shocked he hadn't seen any of the warning signs. And if he had, would he have had the courage to act and punish his king for these heinous acts?

"Who was the other side of these deals, Aebur?" Hoskin asked calmly.

"A captain, originally from Pyrfew, but a smuggler now. It

was the ambassador, Gawl Tegyr, who made the introduction."

Hoskin looked incredulous at him admitting to dealing with the enemy, and Aebur saw it in his face.

"I was desperate one day when trying to keep the king happy! He was putting me under pressure, and then I saw Gawl after one of his visits with you or the king. We always talked. I think we liked to see if we could worm information out of the other. I asked if he knew how to obtain something, maybe a piece of furniture the king was looking for, and he introduced me to Captain Nothon."

"You fool. Pyrfew! Any of this would have got back to Gawl. In fact, he was probably orchestrating the whole thing." Hoskin paced around the small dark cell. "What were these things you traded for these slaves? What could have been valuable enough? Secrets?"

"No, not secrets. It was dwarves," muttered Aebur.

"What?" asked Hoskin, unsure he had heard correctly.

"Dwarves. We'd trade one dwarf from Unedar Halt for each shipment of slaves. I-I had to arrange for them to be captured alive. Used different groups of mercenaries to catch them during the annual drake hunt."

Hoskin's face had turned red, and he was inches from Aebur. He could smell the stench of sweat, vomit, and shit. It reached all the way down to his stomach and made him feel unwell. "And you say this was all the king's idea? You were just following orders?" he asked through gritted teeth.

"Yes, my lord. I swear."

"YOU LIE!" screamed Hoskin at the top of his voice. "King Roland was a half-wit! He couldn't have planned his way out of a hedge maze. You did this, or someone else told you to. Who?"

"No...I swear. I was just doing as my king commanded," pleaded Aebur.

"Bartholomew, it appears our guest is getting confused. You should lighten his load so he can remember the truth. Start with the fingernails, and then move on to the fingers and toes."

CHAPTER 22
COMING OUT

Mareth hadn't drunk last night. Well, he maybe had one ale, but it didn't qualify as drinking by his usual standards. But as the sun came through the window of his room that morning, he felt as if he had the king of hangovers, or better put, the lord protector of hangovers.

As he lay there, in those few moments of silence to begin the day, it seemed preposterous he should have thoughts of winning this demon-crazy election. Who would vote for him? What relevant experience did he have? Now, he knew he could sing a good song, and unlike some others, he was sure he could arrange a piss-up in a brewery if the occasion arose, but he had no idea what it took to run a country. Hell, his father wouldn't even trust him running the estate!

It had been very late by the time Lady Grey went back to her estate after they had all stayed up talking and developing the basics of a plan for their crazy goal.

The list had seemed endless. They had to make contacts with the guilds, reach out to merchants, those who had previously made deals with the late Hoxteth and those who had not, and then they had to have a way to get the message out to the city at large that Mareth was now a candidate. All as quickly as possible. He had refused to use the town criers and had come up with another idea instead, though he was unsure whether it would work.

Lady Grey also thought they had to get in front of the nobles. They needed to recognize his candidacy to give it legitimacy. She said it was lucky there was to be a reception the next evening at Lord Eden's mansion, which would be the perfect occasion.

Mareth wasn't too sure about that.

He looked into the small mirror above the water bowl in his room, the bearded face staring back at him. More lines now than there used to be, a few strands of grey hair that hung down past his shoulders.

The other thing everyone (other than him) decided last night was he didn't look the part, that he needed to have the appearance of a lord protector in waiting, whatever that might be. So while everyone else had important matters to be organized this morning, Mareth was to go shopping.

"Petra," he called gently, waking her from where she slept. He moved the only chair in the room to be a foot from the bed, putting the clothes that had been discarded there the night before onto the floor so he had a place to sit.

"What is it? Is it morning already?" She yawned and rubbed at her eyes, sat up in the bed, the blanket not doing a good job of concealing her nakedness.

"I need to ask you a question," he said seriously. These questions had been gnawing at his stomach for the last few hours since dawn. "Are you ready for how different I might look later? Will you still want to be with me if I look like a lordling?"

"How silly, Mareth. Is that really what you're thinking about?" She placed her hand on his knee. "You'll still be the same for me."

"Are you sure? There's going to be a lot of change over the next couple of weeks. They want me to move into the best guest room in the inn later today. I'm going to be dressed in finery. And they're going to cut my hair, Petra. I just know it." Secretly, it was the feared haircut causing the most agita. "And it might only last two weeks, and then back to normality, but I just wanted to know you'll stick through the insanity, and then we can get back to this lovely little bed when it's all done."

"Firstly," she said, holding up a beautiful slender finger in his face, "you have to believe you can win. We all believe in you, and we need this to happen. And secondly," she said as she held up her thumb and forefinger, "I'm not going anywhere."

"Why are you with me, Petra? You're so beautiful you could have your pick."

"Mareth. Let me tell you something about me. My Ma and Da, they did their best to give me anything I asked for. I was their first child. They'd had a number of miscarriages, so I could tell I was their favorite, even after Alana was born. And I grew up pretty, and my parents protected me from what a lot of life in the Narrows is like.

"And then they died. And I didn't know what to do." Petra sniffed, her eyes glistening with barely mastered tears. "I'm the elder sister, but it was Alana who looked after us. She called in favors from neighbors, got good prices for the few things we had we could sell. She was the one who got a job at the palace.

"I've had a few boyfriends, but none of them got to know me, or they had nothing going on upstairs," she said, tapping a finger against her temple. "They just cared about looking big to their friends or getting into my pants. And looking after me. People are always trying to protect me, not listen to me. Even Alana!

"But you listen to me, Mareth." Petra took both of Mareth's hands in hers. "When you came back from your late-night performances, you'd listen as I wittered on about nothing. And you listened to me when I said we could organize. Normally, people would laugh if I said something like that! It made you think. It made you want to partner with me to work this out. I'm still not used to it yet.

"These past two weeks have been a whirlwind, the most fun of my life. And maybe the next two weeks will come to naught, but we tried, and we'll remember them for the rest of our lives together."

Mareth nodded, unable to speak, the words caught in his throat. The tear rolling down his cheek conveyed more than any epic poem.

"So, whatever you look like at the end of the day today, I'll still be here," said Petra, her intense gaze softening as her lips curved into a smile, "but how about you come here so I can make sure I remember how you used to look?" She pinched his nose gently and pulled him back into bed.

"I'M THE MASTER OF WARDROBES FOR LADY GREY. YOU may call me Spinnet," said the man introducing himself to

Mareth in the common room of the Royal Oak. He gave the impression of a peahen, being straight and upright, elegantly dressed, with distinct quality, but he wasn't supposed to be the center of attention. This was a man who was used to being next to the peacock.

Mareth had dressed in his usual clothes, his hair tied back in a ponytail, but in comparison to Spinnet, he looked like a dirty little pigeon—even though after getting pulled back into bed by Petra, he did try to wash off the smell of sex. Nonetheless, Mareth shook Spinnet warmly by the hand, thinking it best to get a potential tormentor on his side early in the proceedings.

"I've spoken with Lady Grey this morning," continued Spinnet, "and she's given me the necessary inspiration for today. We are to think hero! And we have to include some of the latest court fashions." He waved his hands as he spoke more than the actors at the theater on Cheap Street. "I have the day planned out, so let's get moving." This time, he clapped his hands to signal that Dolph and Mareth should fall into line.

Mareth followed Spinnet out of the inn and into the waiting carriage with a sense of foreboding.

HE HAD NEVER BEEN TO A BARBER TO HAVE A HAIRCUT.

He had visited plenty in the past to deal with stitching a wound and, in a few cases, helping some old friends to have limbs removed when they'd gone gangrenous. All the barbers he knew were doctors or cutters after all, the tools they needed were basically the same.

However, the barber that Spinnet took him to didn't look

like those other barbers. This one had tight, curly black hair, made shiny with something, and a tightly trimmed beard, which seemed pointless to Mareth. What was the point in having a beard if you had to trim it every day? You might as well just shave, then.

Curly had him sit in a chair in front of a large mirror, something worth more than most people's houses in this city. He and Spinnet conferred, jabbering so Mareth could hardly follow. Dolph stood off to the side, arms crossed with a smirk on his face, the kind a kid has when their mother is licking a handkerchief to deliver a public face-cleaning to their brother. The conversation bounced back and forth until he couldn't stand it anymore.

"Hey, I'm here," said Mareth, waving, "and you're talking about me, you know. What are you discussing?"

Spinnet made eye contact with Mareth through the mirror. "We've decided that people don't think beards are trustworthy, so we have to lose the beard. We wondered about keeping a mustache—"

"But smooth will suit you better, sir," interrupted Curly the barber.

"You have a beard!" protested Mareth.

"Good observation, my lord. But do you trust me?" asked Curly.

"No, not really," he grumbled.

"And then we must do something about your hair," said Spinnet.

"Don't you think the long hair is heroic?" Mareth asked hopefully.

"I'm afraid not, sir. We must take it short. I think it will enable your eyes to shine and your strong jaw to stand proud."

"We're going to have to cut off a lot of hair," said Curly with a crazy sparkle in his eyes.

Dolph snorted with laughter and had to turn around. Mareth wondered if he could talk with Lady Grey about having a new guard.

THE SECOND STOP OF THE DAY WAS ONE OF THE FINEST armories in the city, the kind that made stuff that was so expensive it was highly unlikely ever actually to come in the vicinity of the battlefield. It was a well-appointed store where a person rang a little bell to receive admittance, and Mareth got the impression if he wasn't the right person, then attendants would have been mysteriously out to lunch. On the walls hung many beautiful swords, ornate breastplates, and helms of so many different shapes it was a veritable bestiary.

"Spinnet, I thought you were master of wardrobes, not master of arms," asked Mareth, who was still rubbing at his bare face and exposed neck. "Why are we here?"

"Yes, sir, very droll. Your sword won't do, I'm afraid. It looks so barbaric."

Mareth looked down at the saber that hung from the worn scabbard at his waist. It was Andovian steel with a simple pommel and crossbar, hardly a beauty, but it had served him well for many years. There were a few nicks, though he had kept it reasonably sharp, even when there hadn't been much call to use it in recent years. Mareth knew he owed it his life in the past, so it deserved some pampering in its retirement. "What's wrong with my sword? And what do you mean barbaric?" he asked sensitively. "It's for, you know, slashing and stabbing. It's not needlepoint."

"Yes, quite. But it's fashionable for lords and men of the court to wield a rapier and parrying dagger. You need to do the same. You can keep this butcher's cleaver, of course, as long as I don't have to see it."

"I don't know how to fight with a rapier. Why would I want a weapon I don't know how to use?"

"Master Mareth, you don't need to fight. You have Dolph over there to fight for you, and more men should they be needed. You need to look... appropriate. We want the right first impression." Mareth could tell Spinnet was trying to remain patient with him, and enthusiastic. His arms pumped into the air with each exclamation. "You are confident in who you are! You are a force to be reckoned with!"

Spinnet tapped his chin while he was thinking, appraising Mareth. "But now I think on it, you probably should be trained how to fight with these new weapons. I do believe this is the standard form for duels today, correct, Dolph?"

"Duels? You just said I wasn't going to be fighting," interrupted Mareth. "When these nobles were learning how to duel, I was fighting with a real sword against real monsters that wanted to really eat me. Where am I supposed to learn to fight with this toothpick?"

"I believe Dolph can help you, sir. He used to spar with his lordship." Mareth turned to look at Dolph, smile now permanently etched on the guard's face. The excitement evident at the thought of him getting to fight his ward under the pretense of it being for his own good. Mareth accepted he would need him after all.

~

When he'd been singing recently in the best taverns and bars in the city, Mareth had noticed what many of the lords had been wearing. And he'd inwardly laughed at the bright colors, the frills at cuffs and collars, the long socks and tight crotches that seemed to be in fashion now. All good fun, just another way for Mareth to enjoy his work.

And now it was proven that Arloth liked nothing more than a good chuckle at his expense. And so, it seemed, did Dolph.

By the third outfit Spinnet had him try on, something he described as a lovely little number that was lavender and decorated with expensive coral buttons, Dolph couldn't hold it in anymore and guffawed. Spinnet looked upset and went back to talk to the tailor to obtain another outfit to be tried on. With effort, Dolph stopped laughing and waved Mareth over conspiratorially.

"Mareth," began Dolph, "don't let him dress you up like a twat."

"What am I supposed to do? Isn't this what I need to wear?"

"Think, man. Did you see Hoxteth dress like this? No. Remember where your balls are. In fact, I can see them, with how tight those trousers are. You tell him what you want."

Looking back, it seemed obvious, but the day had been long and a little distressing for Mareth. His face and neck still felt cold, even though it was summer, and Spinnet had managed to keep a mirror away from him all day—the master of wardrobes insisting it would be better to see the change all at once. Mareth thought he was a little melodramatic. So, wordlessly, he nodded agreement to Dolph and looked around the tailor's store, seeing the pieces modeled on dress forms.

"Spinnet," called Mareth, "what about this dark green coat with the brass buttons? I like it. And it has fewer frills than anything else."

"But, sir, the embellishments are very popular." Spinnet the puppy-dog tried to get him to play with another ball. "What about this white coat with this beautiful pink collar?"

"Would Hoxteth have worn it?"

"No, he had more, er...straightforward tastes."

"Then let's go with the green," maintained Mareth. He squatted up and down, testing his pants. "And let's get some trousers with some room to breathe. I may want children one day."

It was afternoon by the time he and Dolph got back to the Royal Oak, leaving Spinnet in the carriage, refusing his requests to help him prepare for the evening event with Lady Grey tomorrow.

He wore the green long coat with brass buttons, black trousers and white blouse underneath. His hair had been cut back close to his skull, shorter still at the sides which showed patches of grey around the temples. Clean shaven, and shorn of his long hair, Mareth's steely blue eyes drew attention. At his hip was a thin belt of black leather adorned with a silver buckle, gilded rapier handle on one side and carved bone dagger on the other. Mareth had been allowed to see his final look in the tailor's mirror, and he had been surprised to find himself impressed with what he saw.

Walking into the common room, he saw Petra sat at the usual table at the back of the room with a number of men and women he didn't recognize. They must be the workers

Lady Grey had promised. Petra looked up as he and Dolph walked across the room, but then quickly returned her attention to the people around her.

"Is that all the welcome I get now?" Mareth called as he neared the table. He'd been getting used to the special attention from her, and this wasn't the greeting he enjoyed.

Petra looked up again, a puzzled look on her face. She squinted and tilted her head as she regarded him. "Mareth?"

"Of course, it is, my sweet! Do I look so different?" he asked before doubt hit him. "Do I look bad?"

"No, no, no. You look very handsome. Like a lord," she said without the excitement he was hoping for. She sounded full of uncertainty.

"I'm still the same person, Petra." Mareth opened his arms for a hug, and she got to her feet and came over and returned the embrace. He smelled her hair and whispered, "They may have polished off my edges, but I'm still the same rough diamond underneath."

"I know, Mareth. I know." But he could tell she thought he was someone different already.

THE CARRIAGE HAD BEEN SENT EMPTY TO THE ROYAL OAK to collect him alone. Dolph was to stay behind that evening. Mareth rode to the manor house of Lady Grey where she was waiting in the courtyard with three guards.

Lady Grey looked magnificent: a long, black gown down to the floor as befitted someone still in mourning, the plunging neckline, and diamond jewelry probably not quite as fitting. Her hair piled on top of her head and fixed with other sparking trinkets showed her long neck and delicate earlobes. He had to remember to close his mouth and avert his gaze as she climbed up the stairs into the cabin.

As they rode to Eden's city estate—a journey of less than a mile that took considerably longer than walking because of congestion caused by similar carriages—Lady Grey briefed him on the plan for the evening.

She was to do as much of the talking as possible, making the introductions, providing his background, and he would follow things up with small talk. Any questions he couldn't avoid by having her answer on his behalf were to be met with a noncommittal response and a promise to get back to them. And so it was they arrived at the entrance to the mansion house, with Mareth having some comfort of how he was going to bluff his way through his first public appearance.

He climbed out of the carriage first and held out his hand to help Lady Grey from the carriage.

"Thank you, Lord Bollingsmead," she said. Being called "Lord" was going to be a transition for his ears. He hadn't had a title for a long time. "And may I just add, now that I see you in the light, you do look most handsome."

He didn't expect it, but it felt like he'd been waiting for the acknowledgment. "My lady, I am but a moth to your flame."

She gave a somber smile, and they walked up the steps to the large entryway. The sun was dipping over the city, but the mansion house was ablaze with light from gilded oil lanterns illuminating the vaulted entranceway adorned with high mirrors and shiny marble flooring. There probably couldn't have been a more pretentious way for Eden to welcome people to his house: mirrors over a few feet in size were apparently extremely difficult to produce, and marble was not native to Edland at all.

Mareth walked half a step behind Lady Grey, and they swept up the grand staircase to the ballroom, which was even more extravagant than the foyer. Walls adorned from floor to three storey vaulted ceiling with fabric, gilded crown moldings framed a fresco of what looked like Eden riding to save a walled city. Tens of staff loitered around guests with wine goblets and platters of food.

A minstrel played by the entrance to the ballroom, and Mareth met his eyes, nodded, and smiled. It was Zaff, and he was playing the music to his song *Tin Man.*

Earlier that afternoon, Mareth had met with more than a dozen minstrels and bards from the city. Petra and Alana doing the hard work of rounding them up to come and meet with him. He hadn't expected them to come, but they had, and when he asked them for their help to get the message out between now and the election, he was even more surprised they wanted to help.

Mareth felt somewhat ashamed about their enthusiasm to help one of their own, because if the tables had been turned, he doubted he would have even gone to the meeting, unless there were free drinks. He'd always had a problem with others being more successful... But Zaff was there, playing the song he had taught them, and no one noticed.

Lady Grey guided him around the room, arm-in-arm, and with the slightest of pressure, directed him to the next person with whom to talk. The conversations were all similar. They all said how terrible it was about Hoxteth's assassination, half of them quickly following it up with something like "But that's politics for you," or "Venerable institution, though, the Hollow Syndicate, something we Edlanders can be proud of." Then Lady Grey would introduce him as Lord Bollingsmead, which confused a good number of people, who thought he was his father or even his elder brother.

He would, of course, say nothing except for some pleasantries and smile dashingly at any wives of greater years. Lady Grey would then explain he had just announced his candidacy for lord protector, inquire if they could follow up with a meeting, and then move on to the next annoyingly similar weak-chinned target.

He had just been introduced to the lord and lady of Rayburn, when he finally caught sight of Eden himself, standing across the room. For a second, the crowds parted, and there was the host, talking in whispers with a member of his staff before looking over in their direction. A series of tiny bells rang around the room, bringing the conversations and the music to silence, and everyone else turned to face the host.

"Lords and ladies, welcome to my home away from home," said Eden. There was a smattering of applause. He stood in the center of the room, the acoustics of his position under the arched ceiling ensuring everyone could hear without him having to shout. "I wanted to thank you for coming, and I wanted to ask for your help. You, like me, love our country. Edland has long been a glorious bastion of civilization on the Jeweled Continent, but it has decayed. Our influence on the world has waned, though we still have the greatest navy on the seas. Our territory of Redsmoke was stolen, and it was left to me to return it to our control. Our walls don't even keep our whole city safe anymore. And so, I ask you, what are we going to do?"

Eden didn't wait for any response, but plowed on. "I'll tell you what we need to do. We need to expand. We can't let Pyrfew control the southern continent and expand into the

Wild Continent without being challenged. As we expand, we can bring people into the light. Have them pay taxes to the realm, and we'll build our walls and venerable new institutions. As we expand, we'll create opportunities for our sons and daughters to rule new parts of our glorious land." Applause again, more robust this time, and Mareth could see many people nodding around the room.

"Good, good, I'm glad you agree," said Eden, giving a little chortle and clasping his hands in front of him. "So, enjoy the rest of your evening and join me in ushering in this brave new dawn of opportunity. To Edland!" And Eden raised his glass as his call was taken up around the room.

The combined nobility in the room began to go back to their conversations, and Mareth turned to face Lady Grey as he thought they would resume their conversation with the Rayburns. But she nodded toward the center of the room and muttered, "Eden is coming."

Indeed, he was. Flanked by the staff member Mareth had seen him talking to before, Eden walked directly toward them.

"Lady Grey, thank you so much for coming this evening. I didn't expect to see you," he said with faux warmth. This was the first time Mareth had seen Eden up close. The lord was a good fifteen years older than the bard, but he had remained in reasonable shape. The years had taken their toll on his hair, though, and his skull was shaved to shiny, tanned skin, a bushy, blond mustache being the center of attraction on his face.

"Good evening, Lord Eden," replied Lady Grey, the poison in her tone so cleverly concealed.

"I don't think I've ever seen a widow look so ravishing.

My condolences on your loss, of course. I was very sorry to hear the news."

"Of course, you were. I'm sure it came as a terrible surprise," she said, maintaining eye contact with her adversary. Mareth didn't know how she restrained herself from punching him in the face.

"It did, it did. But it looks like you've replaced Lord Hoxteth with a good degree of haste, my lady." Eden spoke jovially, but Mareth knew the topic was wholly inappropriate. "Who is this young man?"

"This is Lord Bollingsmead. He's the newest candidate to stand."

Eden turned to face Mareth for the first time and looked him up and down. His staff member shadow whispered something into the lord's ear.

"Are you indeed? I know your father. It's a shame he's not here tonight to see you. He has confided in me that he'll be here within the week, though, and that I have his support."

"Lord Eden. It's a pleasure to meet you," lied Mareth. "I'm my own man with my own support. I have yet to talk to my father. We shall see if he'll change his mind."

"Yes, quite. Well, it's good you obviously love our country too and want to be involved in this process. I don't think you'll win, of course." And he gave Mareth the biggest shit-eating grin seen outside of the Ioth monkey houses.

"We shall see, Lord Eden," said Mareth, trying to smile, but finding the act was causing a pain in his cheeks. "There are many votes to fight for. And I do intend to fight."

"Excellent. I do love a good scrap. I think I like you. And because I like you, I do want you to be careful. This business is a little dangerous, you know." Eden leaned in conspiratorially. "It would be a shame if something happened to you as it did to Lord Hoxteth."

Eden paused to let it sink in. "Well, I must go. Lots of people to talk to, you know. Very nice to meet you, my boy. And, Lady Grey, it was a very great pleasure to see you again." And with a shake of their hands, he was steered away to talk to someone else.

"Mareth," Lady Grey said as she touched him on the arm to attract his attention, "we should leave now. I think we've made enough of a stir. We can't have Eden take further offense and look to call out a duel."

"A duel? Whatever for?" asked Mareth. He thought he'd been pleasant enough. And he didn't want to have to use the ornaments he was now wearing, even if his opponent could be old enough to be his father.

"Whatever he decides. This room is his tonight, and he'll have enough witnesses to call on if he needs."

Without further pause, they walked briskly out of the ballroom and into the cool dark of the night.

CHAPTER 23
BROKEN

"Percival, you look terrible," observed Hoskin. "Have you even shaved this morning?"

"I'm afraid not, my lord. I do apologize. I was up all night," said his secretary.

Hoskin was taking his now regular walk to the dungeons through the castle and the underground corridors to the little corner of hell reserved for traitors and people of importance who hadn't been taught how to share as a child.

There had been no breakthrough yesterday, Bartholomew reminding him it was important to be patient. But Hoskin felt a bounce in his stride this morning, holding sheaves of papers Percival had handed to him as he left his chambers. "So, you were up all night? Why didn't you call me?"

"I came to see you, sir, but you were sleeping, and so, I didn't want to wake you. When I received Bartholomew's message that Master Aebur wanted to talk to you, I thought I could go in your place. Take copious notes and such." Percival paused. He did not look well, bags under his eyes, but also a haunted look on his face. "My lord, it's a horrible place you have been going. I wanted to thank you for keeping me away from it before. How do you cope?"

"Mainly by thanking my stars it's not me in there. And you spoiled my intention of keeping you out of it." He did feel bad that the impressionable young man had to see the inquisitor at work. He remembered his first time. It wasn't one of those things you could ever un-see. "So, what did the slime-master have to say?" Hoskin scanned the sheaves of parchment, parsing the neat handwriting he was so used to reading. His pace slowed as he read, Percival matching his continually slowing pace until they eventually came to a stop.

"So, he admitted to working for Pyrfew and has done so for some years? And he has been feeding us misinformation these past six months. Just enough truth to be credible."

"Yes, my lord. He became quite talkative after Bartholomew removed his big toe."

"Am I reading this right?" asked the lord chancellor. "Did he say the Pyrfew fleet being built in Ioth is complete, when he's been telling us we had another two months?"

"Yes, my lord. And worse, currently a force is traveling overland through the Green Desert to man those ships. Sailors, captains, and thousands of soldiers. They mean to attack Redsmoke immediately."

"Arloth preserve us. Here it says a land force is gathering south of Redsmoke, too. Using their new forts to disguise troop numbers."

"Yes, my lord. I'm not a military man, but it doesn't sound good."

"No, not good at all. I want you to go and get Uthridge and Ridgton and have them in my office in an hour. We need to attend to this now. And ask Jyuth if he could join us, too."

Percival nodded and turned to leave. "Wait, before you go, did you ask Aebur why he did this?"

"Yes, we did. He was very emotional at that point, so it was hard to understand fully, but he said something about Llewdon being in his dreams. Terrible dreams. And he talked about chess, how he was so good as a child no one could beat him. I might be wrong, sir, but I got the impression he thought all of this was a game he couldn't lose."

Hoskin sighed. "Maybe he would have won if he hadn't done something stupid to piss off Jyuth. If it weren't for the wizard's servant girl, we'd be royally screwed. And we still might be. Wait, one more thing." Hoskin flipped through the pages. "Did you ask about why they wanted the dwarves?"

"Page five, my lord. He didn't have a detailed answer. But he did know each of them expired some months after being taken to Pyrfew."

"Hmm, that doesn't help. I thought they'd be trying to get some information. But what?" He snapped himself out of the little trance he'd entered, considering all of the parts on the board. Hoskin thought he had always been pretty handy at chess himself. "Go and get the lord general and the admiral. I'll be back soon. And, Percival, nice work. Get some rest afterward."

Hoskin set off again, papers held tight in hand, the receding footsteps of Percival behind him as he went to execute his orders. Percival had been working with him for five years now, and he continued to astound. He was essentially a private secretary before, but now he was effectively treasurer and had started to clean up a lot of the messes that the elephant of life would occasionally choose to drop. That young man would go far. Hopefully, not so far as to have Hoskin hanging in a cell one day, though.

Bartholomew sat on a simple wooden chair outside the open cell when he arrived. The inquisitor sat upright, straight as a rod, but his eyes were closed in sleep. His visage almost beatific. It could have been an oil painting of one of the prophets touched by the light of Arloth, though with arms and apron smeared with blood and gore. Hoskin gently took hold of his shoulder and shook him awake.

"M'lud. Sorry, I was just catching forty winks there. Good morning to you."

"Good morning, Bartholomew. I believe you had a busy night. I have Percival's report." Hoskin waved the papers in the air. "Did our guest say anything else after Percival left?"

"Not much, m'lud. I think he's empty. He talked when I took the first toe. Said everything. So, I stopped then. I likes to let them talk when they're going to talk," explained Bartholomew, taking pride in his process as much as a smith explaining how he tempered his steel. "Then when he finished, I recommenced. And there was just a whole lot of crying and pleading, but no more talking."

"Good work, Bartholomew. Take him down and put him in a secure cell. Do you need a healer sent down to attend to him?"

"All depends. How long do you want him alive?"

"I think it prudent to see if we have a use for him in the future. I'll have someone sent down."

HOSKIN SANK INTO THE CHAIR WITH A SIGH AND LET HIS head hang back against the cushioned surface. His office was a small haven of peace and solitude, allowing him the opportunity to arrest his racing nerves. Just when he thought he was getting the hang of running the damned country, he now had a potential invasion to deal with.

Less than two weeks, and then he could get out of this place, leave these responsibilities behind. Why could it not just have been easy?

He could just ignore it.

Only two other people knew this information. Bartholomew hardly saw another a human being, and Percival could be trusted with whatever he told him. If he ignored it, then he could just glide on out of Kingshold and go back to the big empty house where he grew up.

Unfortunately, even though he hadn't been a natural at learning the blade as a child, he had always had a strong moral compass. So strong he wouldn't even sneak an extra cake or two at the wintertide festivals like most of the other children. *Balderdash.*

There was a knock, and Percival poked his head around the door. "Lord Chancellor, may I come in?" Hoskin waved him through.

"I have Lord General Uthridge and Admiral Ridgton outside. I haven't told them anything. I asked Lord Jyuth if he would care to join, but he was with his daughter and said he was busy. He did give me this book to give you, though."

Hoskin took the offered book. *The Trials of Bethel.* Inside the front cover was tucked a note.

"Thank you for finding this book, but I meant it for you. You will find it enlightening."

CHAPTER 24
THE INTEREST OF WIZARDS

Alana hid from Bertha, the head maid.

Bertha didn't realize it, of course. She thought Alana was attending to the lord wizard's needs, and Alana didn't want that perception of reality to change.

It was true; Alana realized she should go and see what else needed to be done after she had completed her morning duties, but frankly, that was less interesting than the book she was currently reading.

Or any book really.

Alana had made a little corner of Jyuth's sitting room into a hidey hole of piled cushions, almost at the wizard's insistence, and now spent her free time reading whatever book had currently caught her eye.

She was no longer afraid of going to the library to retrieve a book to read, though she did try to avoid Chancellor Hoskin if he was there. She had worked out that using Jyuth's name as a reason to be collecting a particular title would appease anyone who questioned her, and she always made sure to identify the name of the next book for the next visit.

For the past couple of days, Alana had been working her way through *Flora, Fauna, and Families of the Wild Continent.* Two weeks ago, she had never seen anyone from the Wild Continent, let alone knew anyone, but now there were two of them in her life every day.

Granted, they couldn't be more different. Motega was outgoing and dashing, and he had saved her from that foul man, Win. Motega's skin was peculiar, what with the white patches on his face, but it was also distinctive. Neenahwi, on the other hand, seemed to be in a state of flux the whole time with her father: angry at him for something, but also frustrated with herself. Oh, she seemed pleasant enough. She hadn't shouted at Alana all of these days when visiting Jyuth. In fact, she'd directed all of her anger at her father.

So, that's why that particular book had caught her eye, but it wasn't keeping her attention. It was a recent work, written by a traveling scholar within the past ten years, copied for the Kingshold library. So far, the book was focused on the flora, whereas Alana was most interested in the study of the people. She could skip to that section, but the luxury of being able to read whatever books she liked was still so new it almost seemed disrespectful to the author, the copyist, and the book itself, not to read every word.

As she read through the entry for the Greater Purple Wort, her mind began to wander again. Sitting there in her little spot with the sounds of Jyuth's and Neenahwi's murmuring coming from the bare meditation room one room over, the book in her hand, she thought about the past two weeks that had not only brought her into contact with new, exotic people, but also brought new opportunities and dangers.

It wasn't so long ago she and Petra struggled to put food on the table after their parents died. Odd jobs and the charity of their neighbors kept them alive and from turning to less savory ways of earning necessary coin.

Alana's job at the palace, and then a steady series of promotions, had brought some stability to their lives and enabled her to pay back the kindness of others. And then Petra had also gotten work at the Royal Oak, and now she'd met Mareth, and it made Alana so glad to see her sister happy. She supposed one day they'd get married, and then Alana would truly be alone.

Not that Petra thought that day was coming soon. This morning some of the happiness had left her, replaced by uncertainty if she was good enough for the newly unveiled Lord Bollingsmead. Alana had laughed when Petra had brought it up after Mareth's return. Not from a lack of empathy, of course, more at the absurdity of how her sister—who had always been the tall and beautiful one—could have discovered anxiety. Alana had reassured Petra that Mareth wasn't like other nobles. She knew the real him.

Alana hoped that was true.

Petra was the older sister, but it had always been Alana who had looked after the two of them. Their parents loved them both, but Alana knew in some ways they loved Petra more. Petra would ask for things, small things, nothing grand, and her parents would try their hardest to give it to her. It had made her confident that if she wanted something, there was no reason why she couldn't have it.

As a child, Alana didn't ask for things; she asked questions, instead. But the answers she received left her unfulfilled for the most part.

Why do we live in the Narrows? Because we're lucky for what we have.

Why can't I keep going to school? Because we don't need to have learning for the jobs Arloth has in mind for us.

Why do we struggle? Because some people are chosen to be kings or lords, soldiers, or thinkers. And some of us are not selected in this life, so we work hard to be chosen in the next.

All of these answers felt wrong to Alana, even as a child. They screamed she had to stay in her place. But why did she have to accept that?

She didn't.

Surely her current situation showed her that was true. Right now, she was being paid to read books! How that would shock her mother. Alana had taken risks to get here, so why shouldn't she take more? Could she leave her current situation behind to follow what her heart was calling her to do? She thought Jyuth would understand, she just needed to bring it up with him.

"Alana!" called the wizard from the adjoining room. "Work has made my daughter hungry and me thirsty. Bring lunch."

Well, if that wasn't a sign, she didn't know what was.

SHE RETURNED FROM THE KITCHEN WITH FRESH vegetables from the palace gardens, a selection of hard and soft cheeses, bread, and two roasted duck legs, along with an opened bottle of ale from the cellar. Knocking on the door to Jyuth's meditation room, she didn't stop for an answer, walking in and placing the tray directly on the floor between the improbable father and daughter.

"Thank you, Alana; it looks delicious," said Neenahwi, looking up into her eyes with a smile. After their first meeting, when Neenahwi was blinded by rage, it seemed as if she had been making an extra attempt to be considerate. Or maybe that was how she normally was, but in Alana's experience, it wasn't true for most palace guests.

"Well done, my girl," said Jyuth with gusto, patting his belly in anticipation of lunch. "A perfect feast to keep the brain ticking over. A thousand thanks."

Alana stood there looking at the two of them. Not sure if she was dismissed, but also not wanting to be. She needed to talk to Jyuth, and even though she could see he was busy, she was afraid she wouldn't have the courage to bring this up again later.

"Yes, Alana? Is there something else?"

"No, my lord. Well, yes. I mean, if you don't mind me taking a moment to talk about something." Alana's eyes flitted from the wizard to the daughter, seeing a kind smile on her face. "Or I can come back later when you are not so busy, of course."

Jyuth laughed and patted the stone floor. "It seems like you have something to get off your chest, my girl. And I have always found it's better to pluck a flower when it's blooming than wait for it to wither on the vine. But sit! I'll have a damnable crick in my neck if I have to keep looking up at you." Alana sat cross-legged. There was no third cushion for her, but the cold stone on her legs and buttocks was calming. "So, what do you have to say?" asked Jyuth.

"Well, my lord, I don't know if you are aware, but a new candidate is standing for lord protector. Lord Bollingsmead."

"Yes, of course," said the wizard, nodding. "I received a message from Lady Grey this morning. It seems like she is quick to align to a new candidate. I don't think I have met him, though. What of him?"

"Do you also remember the night when I was attacked? How I told you I joined a meeting with a bard named Mareth and the district supervisors to see how we could organize the people?"

"Alana, I may be centuries old, but I'm not senile."

"Of course not, my lord! Well, it's just they are the same person. Mareth is Lord Bollingsmead. And Lady Grey and the rest of us convinced him to stand as a candidate we could believe in. He's a good man."

"Well, well, well. I didn't see that coming. I know someone else who's looking for a more decent candidate, too," he said as he looked at Neenahwi and winked. "So, what of this Lord Bard Mareth Bollingsmead?"

Alana took a deep breath and blurted it all out at once, "I want to leave the palace until after the election and help with the organizing because Lady Grey said she would pay me, and I enjoy it so much, and I think I can make a difference!" She had been looking at the floor the whole time while she got her words out there, the weight of them pushing down her head. Once they were released, she felt light as duck down. Looking up, afraid to see anger on the wizard's face, she instead saw a quizzical expression.

"My, two surprises in one day. Two surprises in five minutes! Ha! That's why I like you, Alana. But if you were to go, who would look after me?"

The lightness evaporated. Jyuth wasn't going to let her go.

"On the other hand, though, this Mareth could well do with an advisor like you. You have to spin the wheel to win some of the time," he said. He sat for a moment considering his response. "How about this? You'll come to the palace each morning, attend to my breakfast and lunch and do whatever else you do to make this place inhabitable. And then each afternoon you can do as you wish."

A broad smile grew on Alana's face. "Thank you so much, my lord. I will be in extra early to make sure all is in order."

"Of course. And, of course, you'll be able to keep me informed as to what is going on out there in the city, eh?" Now, it was Alana's turn to receive a wink.

Neenahwi had been sitting there quietly through this exchange, her head turning to look at the servant and the master and their most unusual conversation. "Alana, can you tell me more about this Mareth?"

Alana explained all that had happened the past two weeks, meeting Mareth through her sister, their ideas after Hoxteth's death, to the recent developments of working with Lady Grey. She explained how Mareth had been the center of the group that gathered, his voice truly enchanting at times, but also how his uncertainties appeared as strengths to her. Lady Grey was supporting them financially, with a strategy to attract the merchants and maybe some of the nobles. There was Jules, the owner of the Royal Oak, which had become headquarters for the campaign, and then there were the three adventurers who had saved her the night when she was attacked. Neenahwi listened to it all intently.

"And one of the three who saved me is also from the Wild Continent," said Alana.

"Pardon, Alana. Did you say he is from the Wild Continent? How do you know?" asked Neenahwi.

"Oh, we were talking, and he told me so. But his skin is different than yours. It's piebald."

Neenahwi's eyes widened, and she looked lost for words. Turning to Jyuth, she said, "Did you know about this, Father?"

"No, I didn't think to ask about the people who had saved her. I was more interested in flaying Aebur's hide," he said calmly and with the same recognition Neenahwi had. "Well, well, three surprises all over one lunchtime. I do hope this won't give me indigestion."

"What is his name, Alana?" Neenahwi turned back to face her, even more interested than before.

"It's Motega, my lady. Do you know him?"

"You could say that, Alana. You know, I think it's time I met this bard who would be the protector. Enjoy your lunch, Father. I'll see you tomorrow. I'm going to take your little bundle of surprises with me, by the way. Get started right away on her afternoon-off plan." Neenahwi gracefully got to her feet while Alana remained seated, a little unsure of how this discussion had gone so well.

Neenahwi stopped by the door and looked back at Alana. "Well? Are you coming?" Alana scrambled to her feet and hurried after her.

ALANA SAT AT THE BAR, WATCHING NEENAHWI TALK WITH Mareth at their usual table at the back of the common room. The two young women had walked through the city together, Alana surprised that Lady Neenahwi didn't have a carriage.

Alana answered many questions during their walk, about Mareth, and her life, but she found the conversation to be easy and relaxed.

After arriving at the Royal Oak, Alana introduced Neenahwi to Mareth, but she was asked to give them privacy to talk. Initially, she had felt a little put out at being excluded, but sitting on her perch, a wooden stool worn shiny through years of use, while drinking a cup of watered wine, had given her a few precious moments to relax.

"Who is that, Alana?" asked Jules from behind the bar, walking over after dealing with a group of merchants sitting down for a late lunch.

"That's Jyuth's daughter. Lady Neenahwi." Alana's gaze remained fixed on the two.

"His daughter? Is she a wizard, too?"

"I'm not sure." Alana turned to face the landlady. "I haven't seen her do anything, but I don't know if I would want to either. She does spend a lot of time meditating with Jyuth, so I would wager so."

"And what does she want with our Mareth?"

"I'm not sure. I think she may have met with all of the other candidates. I guess she gets a vote, too. She was very interested in him, and it didn't sound like she was a fan of the others."

Jules made a little noise of acknowledgment, and then carried on looking after her customers. Alana turned back to the talking couple when she heard the door open behind her back.

Neenahwi looked up and over Mareth's shoulder in the direction of the main entrance, maintaining her gaze, clearly distracted. For a moment, Neenahwi didn't say anything, and Mareth, too, twisted 'round in his seat.

"Florian! Trypp!" Neenahwi called across the room.

Swiveling on her stool, Alana saw the tall, dark-skinned Trypp mouthing a curse to the big fighter.

"And where is my brother?" asked Neenahwi. Florian stepped aside, and Motega appeared, flipping down his hood.

"Sis!" he said, smiling. "I was just about to come and visit you."

Neenahwi held his gaze. She wasn't smiling.

CHAPTER 25
REUNIONS

He actually had been intending to see his sister.

At some point, anyway. He wasn't going to leave the city again without at least seeing how she was doing. But he thought he'd have time to prepare himself for that talk.

Motega had played it through his mind multiple times since he'd boarded the ship from Carlburg bound for Kingshold, and the funny thing was the more he thought about it, the worse the twisting in his stomach became. He wasn't one to be nervous before a battle, or fighting some beast, or conducting some daring heist, so it was confusing as to why the prospect of seeing the person he loved more than anyone else in the whole world filled him with dread.

He guessed it was because he was afraid he was a disappointment to his sister.

But when he saw her, sitting there at the table under which his feet had started to feel comfortable, he was only filled with joy. This was his sister, even more grown into womanhood now, but to him, she was still the girl who had comforted him as they'd fled the destruction wrought on their village and who had planned with him how they would have their revenge.

She looked the same, just more so now. More confident. More dangerous. More like she was ready to kick his arse.

"Sis! I was just about to come and visit you!"

"Bullshit, little brother." There never was much hope of tricking her, and that lie was pretty transparent. "You and I need to have words. Stand there and don't move."

Florian and Trypp both turned to look at him, eyebrows raised. The looks on their faces read a combination of 'good luck' and 'you're on your own'. Funny how the pair of them had always been afraid of her, too.

Neenahwi turned her attention back to Mareth. "Bard, thank you for the time. You're an interesting man. I don't know you yet, but I think you might hold some promise. Can we talk again soon?"

"Of course. It's been a pleasure to talk to you, too," Mareth said, giving a little bow, "and I'll do whatever I can to secure your support. We have a lot to do and not a lot of time."

"That's very true," she said, and then walked over to Motega. "Now you. Do you have somewhere here where we can talk in private? Not that it's not lovely to see you two," she said to Florian and Trypp. "I'm delighted to see you both are still in one piece."

"We have a room upstairs. Follow me," said Motega. "Trypp, can you give Mareth the update in case I'm not able to make it downstairs after she's done with me?" Still smiling, he took Neenahwi's hand and led her up the stairs to the room he shared with his friends. "Neenahwi, you are looking radiant."

"Save the flattery. But you are looking well, too. Shit, Motega, you've grown up! You were a stripling when you left." They entered his small room, the three beds distributed around the chamber, with a chest at the foot of each. The beds were made and gear put away. It almost looked vacant. "Well, this is a lot tidier than your room used to be. You have changed."

"Florian's a bit of a neat freak. That's probably a good thing, though. In rooms this small, it can get real messy real quick."

They looked at each other in silence for a moment, and then Neenahwi took a step forward and wrapped her arms around her brother. He returned the hug.

"I missed you so much." She sniffed.

"I missed you, too, Neenahwi," he croaked, a lump in his throat making it difficult to get the words out. They embraced for a while, Motega thinking about all of the times he'd fallen asleep in her arms over the years, how she smelled the same, felt so familiar even after ten years away. Then she pushed him gently by the shoulders and looked into his eyes again, tears streaked down both their faces.

"Now, how long have you been avoiding me?"

Motega looked sheepish. "About two weeks now. We arrived from Carlburg a few days after the king was pruned. But I know what you're thinking; I promise I have not been back here since I left. And I was going to see you. It's just been one thing after another since we got here."

"Really? I know how one thing quite often follows another when you put your mind to it. You could have written and sent a messenger sometime! I've heard various stories I thought might be you and your little friends over the years. I assume it was you three who stole the Bishop of Tigro's golden whip a couple of years ago?"

"How did you know about that?" he asked, genuinely concerned. "If you know, then others might know. And if some of them are the wrong sort of people, it could be very uncomfortable for us."

"Motega, isn't it about time you grew up and stopped this gallivanting around?" she asked as she perched on the edge of a bed. Motega joined her. "It doesn't even look like it's made you rich. You're just avoiding having any purpose in your life."

"We've got some money put aside, sis, don't worry. And what else would I do? You know what you're doing with your life. You've known for years. You're the chosen one of Jyuth, the only apprentice he's ever had. I'm sure you two get up to all kinds of magical adventures together. Father and daughter, dancing with unicorns..." Motega didn't want to get upset with his sister, but she knew which wounds would be sore. And she wasn't the only one who reminded him about his life choices.

"You know he thinks of you as his son, too, don't you?" she said. "I know he would like to see you."

"I don't think so. You were always his favorite. You were the reason he rescued us. If it weren't for you, then I would have been thrown into a pit long ago," he said, but Motega tried to smile. "Anyway, let's not fight. I take it one decision at a time and see where it takes me. You might not like it, but look, we're in the same place at the same time to see the same person. That's got to mean something."

"I guess so. Pattern or plan?" she asked. Motega tilted his head with a quizzical look on his face. "It's something Jyuth and I have discussed. Is there a pattern that links these kinds of events, or is there some grand plan? Destiny, if you like."

"You know what I think, sis. You overthink." Now his smile was genuine, healthy white teeth on display. "Let's just enjoy being together. Why not enjoy being on an adventure with me for once?" The bell of the nearby clock tower struck five. "Speaking of which, we have our daily gathering now. Come and join us, learn more about what we're doing."

MOTEGA SAT NEXT TO TRYPP AFTER PULLING UP A CHAIR for his sister. Mareth, Alana, Petra, Jules, Dolph, and Florian were already seated, tankards of ale in front of them, and it seemed like they had begun without him. Someone he didn't recognize spoke to the group.

"...a number of meetings today. Lady Grey has presented the previous proposals agreed with Lord Hoxteth to each, and they have, in principle, agreed. But they do want to meet with you, my lord."

Motega nudged Trypp in the ribs and leaned over to whisper a question. "Who is he?" He eyed the man. Thin, straight, and with the look of a lawyer. He was the kind of person Motega would usually avoid.

"That's Folstencroft. Sent by Grey," muttered Trypp out of the side of his mouth, trying to pay attention to what the man was saying.

"Please, here at this table, you can call me Mareth. When will we meet with them?"

"Lady Grey thinks it would be best to host a reception in a week," said Folstencroft. "It'll help us gauge the number of supporters, and also let you avoid having to meet with them all at once."

"Has there been any pushback on the agreed terms?" asked Trypp. "It's been a little while since Hoxteth's death, and I'm sure each of those merchants have been to see the others to see what return they can get on their investments."

"There were a few who wished to renegotiate terms, and so, Lady Grey took the privilege of adjusting where she thought it necessary. She was able to strike a better deal in a few cases, I might add. It would seem many of the other candidates don't look favorably on the merchant class."

"I saw it firsthand," interjected Neenahwi. "Oh, I'm Neenahwi, by the way. I'm a friend of Alana. And I guess I'm also the sister to this lump," she said, pointing her thumb at Motega. "As I was saying, I met with all of the candidates, and each of them thought merchants were a boil on the beautiful arse of Kingshold."

"Ahem, yes, I'm sure, Lady Neenahwi," said Folstencroft, visibly uncomfortable and struggling for a suitable response. "Lady Grey will be most interested to know you're here."

"I'm sure she will," she said and smiled at the secretary, "and I'm sure you'll enjoy telling her."

Petra was up next, and Motega half listened as she recounted how they had now met with all of the district supervisors, but a good part of his attention was just focused on the warm shoulder touching his own.

It wasn't that he hadn't recognized how much he'd missed his sister while away, his only flesh and blood in the whole world. It was just that he had done such a great job of balling up any emotion and pushing it away into a dark place. He'd left all those years ago because he didn't feel like he was his sister's biggest priority anymore.

Her studies with Jyuth took up most of her time once they had the luxury of being somewhere safe from harm. He wasn't deluded enough to think anything had changed now. He was sure she spent most of her time with the old wizard and would do so in the future. So, at some point, he'd probably slip away again, but for now, it was good to have his sister and his friends around him.

He'd been looking in Petra's direction while she was talking, and he realized she'd finished a minute ago, and now he was just staring. She mouthed silently, "Are you alright?" and he gave a little nod as he came back to what was happening.

Alana was talking. "From what Folstencroft and I have calculated, we have Eden leading the race. Unsurprisingly. He has more than half of the nobles currently committed, more of the other merchants or independently wealthy votes than we do, and he can probably call on half of the guilds, especially the higher guilds.

"If we assume we can rely on all twenty of the merchants we've met with in the past two days, also get half of the guilds and be able to organize all twenty of the city districts to be able to vote, then we are fifteen votes behind. We think there are probably another fifty or so people who could vote. Not counting nobles currently on their way here to vote for Eden, that have yet to get their pyxie from Lord Jyuth. So, we'd have to get more than two-thirds of the undecideds. Not taking into account if other candidates drop out, their noble supporters would likely switch to Eden."

Motega watched Mareth's shoulders slump as Alana walked through the numbers. "Well, shit, Alana," Mareth said, his head in his hands now. "We're only three days in. Do you mean we're done?"

"No one is ready to quit, Mareth, but it's uphill. I think

we have to recognize that so we can address it," explained Alana. "We need to get some nobles over to our cause, and we need to get those other undecided voters. And, we still have to organize thousands of ordinary citizens to contribute to their district."

Florian whistled. "That's a lot to do. What about delaying some of those nobles on their way from the other side of Edland? We could probably stop a handful of votes for Eden."

"No," said Mareth forcefully, "that's the kind of situation where something gets out of hand and people get hurt. If that happens, we're done for."

"There is something else I don't think anyone has considered," said Neenahwi.

"What is it, my lady?" said Alana, "Folstencroft and I went through it in detail this afternoon, and I was using what Jyuth himself has been telling me."

"Well, he hasn't thought about this either, or if he has, he's decided not to volunteer it," said Neenahwi, pausing for dramatic effect. Once she had everyone's attention she continued. "The announcement said anyone who owns property within three leagues of the palace. Everyone has been focused on those in the city above ground. But Unedar Halt is within three leagues of the palace."

"The dwarves?" Mareth leaned forward. "But why would they want to be involved?"

"I don't know. But if you could give them a reason, there are probably tens of families who meet the rules. We'd have to talk to the forger and work out a deal, but it could be worth a try."

"How would we even do that?" asked Trypp. Motega knew he couldn't help himself. He loved working the angles and doing the unexpected, and while Motega appreciated that planning was necessary, he loved being in the moment, but for Trypp it was the other way around.

"I've given it some thought. Purely hypothetically up 'til now, of course," Neenahwi continued. "We can't simply go through the Mountain Gate. That would raise too much suspicion, and the dwarven guards might not let you in even if I vouch for you. But I do know of another way to access their city, a tunnel on Mount Tiston. Little more than an air vent, but used in the summers for the drake hunt. It'll be lightly guarded, but it could be dangerous. The climb down is difficult, and there may well be beasts living in those caverns."

"Could you take me, Lady Neenahwi?" asked Mareth. "I'd risk it. Folstencroft, you should inform Lady Grey I'll be gone for a few days. Let's work on the plans now, and then we leave at first light."

"Wait a moment, Mareth," said Alana. "This is not part of the plan."

"I know. But you said it yourself. We're behind. And we need something big if we're going to catch up. I think we need to risk it. Can you and Petra keep everything moving here?"

Alana looked at Petra, who shrugged. "Yes, of course. I guess we need to roll the dice."

"Exactly, Alana! We'll go, too," said Motega, excitement building in his gut to get out there and do something more than talking. He checked his comrades. Florian was nodding. Trypp rolled his eyes and shrugged. That settled it. "We'll organize what we need."

~

The circle of stamped-down vegetation was some fifty feet across, four-foot-high blades of Bhiferous grass surrounding it, named after the great roaming beasts that grazed these lands and supported the way of life of his people.

A single stone sat in the middle of the clearing and on it, cross-legged, was a man, naked except for cropped trousers and a falcon sitting on his shoulder. The tall blades of grass waved in the wind and billowy clouds swept over the pink sky faster than was natural. All was quiet. The wind made no sound through the grass. The insects, birds, and other beasts didn't stir so much as a chirrup.

Motega sat on his stony perch and breathed deeply. This place didn't smell of his homeland either; the rich earthy smell of fertility was absent. All he could detect was the long-faded residue of acrid smoke and fire.

The tall grasses parted in front of him and a large plains wolf entered the clearing. At the shoulder, it was as tall as a man, and it held its head proudly high, but the fur, so shiny grey in places, was matted in others around weeping wounds.

The wolf took four long, slow steps and stopped in front of Motega. Behind it appeared two more wolves, and then four more, and the movements of the grasses indicated many more waiting behind. The other wolves in the clearing were as tall as the first, but they showed no visible signs of injuries, and their pelts were streaked with white.

Seven pairs of yellow scouring eyes assessed the seated man, but no growl or snarl interrupted the silence. The falcon spread its wings and shrieked welcome to the other noble beasts.

Motega had been here many times before. He knew he was dreaming. Or he was at least asleep, but this was still real. The wolves shimmered in front of him, grey and yellow, blurring and stretching upwards to leave seven men and women standing before him.

They, too, were naked, standing tall and proud, long hair hanging down to the smalls of their backs. Their bodies were adorned with a variety of tattoos, monochromatic scenes of hunts or battles etched in red into their skin. The figure closest to Motega, the wolf that had first entered the clearing, was still burdened with slashes across his torso and arms. His face was uninjured though, strong jaw and broad face, with a nose, broken in the past, above a smiling mouth of sharp predator's teeth. To this man's left was another man, visibly related in features but standing a foot taller and broader in the shoulder. This man walked to the fore.

"Motega, your ancestors greet you." The tall man's voice was deep like a well. "Your people still crave vengeance."

"Greetings, my father's grandfather," said Motega, meeting the man's gaze. Though he didn't enjoy these conversations, he knew there were forms to follow. "Elkin, do you have wisdom to share with me?"

"Our people are gone. The other tribes of the Missapik are dead or enslaved or fled like deer. These outlanders, the men and their demons and the hooded ones move west to continue to conquer. They rape our land and steal our future. And you are playing games." Elkin stood with arms crossed and brows furrowed, well-experienced in chastising children.

"Chief Elkin, I am one man. What can I do? What you tell me burns my soul every day. And one day I will bring honor to our tribe."

"Grandfather, you are hard on him," said the wounded man.

"You are soft on him, Sharef."

"Please, let me talk." Elkin nodded, and so, Sharef continued. "Greetings, son. Did something happen to your hair?"

Motega unconsciously reached up to rub his hand through the short hair on his head. It felt like the fur of a rabbit.

"Hello, Father. It is good to see you. There was an accident."

"Never mind. It does grow back," he said, smiling. Motega had only fuzzy memories of his father from when he was alive, most of them from a distance. He had recently realized he spoke with him more now that he was dead than he did when alive. "You have seen your sister?"

"I have father, and she is strong. She reminds me of mother now. You cannot visit her still?"

"No, we cannot penetrate her dreams."

"I don't understand. She would have been chief when you stepped down. You should only be able to visit her."

"I know, son. We do not know the answer, though some have ventured theories." He turned his head and looked at a naked woman standing inside the circle. "Maybe her magic disciplines have taken her from us. In any case, we know she is important. You both alone are formidable. Together, you could move the stars. You have not asked, but I have wisdom for you, too."

"What is it, Father?"

"Follow your instincts, Motega. In kindness or ill. You are my whirlwind, and you will heal me. One day."

A tear welled in the corner of Motega's eye. "Thank you, Father. Thank you all. I will try."

CHAPTER 26
SPELUNKING

Dawn was beginning to break over the city as the party departed the coach house of the Royal Oak. Steam rose from the puddles of overnight rain due to the early morning heat, the humidity adding a closeness to the air unmatched by the empty streets.

Neenahwi had managed to meditate for a few hours back at her tower before meeting again, and she could see the tiredness in her companions from their late-night preparations. Motega and Florian led the way through the Red Gate at the end of the Lance, Mareth and Dolph following, and Neenahwi, Trypp, and Jules's stable master bringing up the rear.

Inhabitants of the Narrows and Four Points were beginning to move about in the emerging daylight. A poor bird needed to start the search for a worm early. Neenahwi's companions would go unremarked unless Mareth were going to be accosted by fans of his singing, but Neenahwi was concerned she could be recognized by the guards at the Cripplegate. So, she pulled up the hood of her robe and moved her horse closer to Dolph in front, hoping to be hidden by the men around her.

The Curtain Wall was soon behind them—with hardly a second look by the guards at the gate—and they flicked at the reins to bring the horses to a trot on the road already occupied with travelers seeking entry into the city. In fact, the stable master was likely to get much more attention on his way back to the city later, leading six tacked-up horses without riders, but it was a problem he didn't seem unduly concerned about.

Their route took them west from Kingshold for five miles before Neenahwi joined her brother at the head of the party to lead them off the paved road and up into the foothills of Mount Tiston.

The green hills dotted with sheep and goats were a pleasant accompaniment to the ride, her brother thankfully not wanting to engage in conversation. She could hear Mareth chattering behind her, first with Dolph, and after his lack of reciprocity, finding a more fertile partner in Trypp. But as long as she left enough space between herself and the others, she could enjoy the birdsong.

They kept their distance from the few farmsteads, following deer paths through the grass, steadily rising up and back to the east as the morning aged.

Like a pustule on the fresh face of a maiden, the mountain erupted from the land, grasses giving way to rocky, bare earth, shrubs scattered about the landscape. From here, the journey would prove too difficult for the horses. Loose footing and the incline would make it a better match for ponies or mules, but Neenahwi was grateful the horses had borne them so far.

Encumbered by their packs, weapons, and coils of solid

rope, they set off on foot as the sun reached its peak. Florian offered to carry her line for her, and though Neenahwi would have resisted in the past to demonstrate her strength, she was happy to see him lift her load. She flashed him a smile, touched his arm in thanks, and continued to lead from the front.

Neenahwi looked up and saw the falcon flying above their party, soaring on the thermals and causing a pang of longing in her to be flying again. Her brother called the falcon Per, and since they had left the city, the bird had regularly returned to his shoulder. If she didn't know better, it looked like it was whispering in his ear. Wait, she did know better, that was probably exactly what it was doing.

"So, the bird of yours," Neenahwi broke the silence with her brother, "is that what I think it is?"

"Yep."

"I thought they were always wolves in our clan?"

"Me too." Motega looked into the distance of the mountain peak as he walked and spoke. "So did Kanaveen. He's the reason why I have Per." As if on cue, the bird flew down and landed on his shoulder, Motega treating it to a thin strip of jerky.

"Go on, then. You obviously have a tale to tell. Spit it out."

"Not much to tell, sis. When I ran away—and yes, I do admit to myself that is what I did—I went to see Kanaveen. He said before I left I had to do the Quana, the coming of age ceremony, so if I died, I'd go to our hunting grounds in the next life. Apparently, that meant he had to punch me in the face, knock me out, and then leave me naked in the wild forest."

Motega told the story as he climbed up the rocky incline,

loud enough for just her to hear. "That's when the spirit came. At first, I thought I was going crazy and having hallucinations from hunger or Kanaveen tainting my water with the wrong mushrooms. It kept shifting shape from wolf to falcon until it leaped at me, or flew at me, not sure which, knocking me to the ground. I hit my head on a rock and got knocked out again. Next thing I remember was seeing myself lying on the ground, which was enough to scare me shitless and wake me up. And there was Per, staring right at me."

Neenahwi was silent listening to the story, trying to find her footing in the climb. "I've never done the Quana."

"Have you been to see Kanaveen recently?"

Her cheeks burned with the shame of not being able to answer the question. The truth was she hadn't seen the former champion of her father, the man who had saved the two of them when they were children, since Kanaveen had wanted to leave Kingshold a year after their rescue from Pyrfew. He had been like a father to her, a surrogate she then replaced with another. And why did they all have to leave?

"I'll go and see him once this election is done. Will you come with me?"

Motega reached out a hand to grasp her arm, and he smiled. "Of course, I will, sis. He'll like that. He probably won't punch *you* in the face." She smiled, too, and put her hand on his before they carried on climbing. "So, Per has seen some other things up there flying around. They're not birds. He doesn't have words, so he showed me what he saw. They look like dragons from children's books. You know anything?"

"Don't worry, Motega. No one has seen dragons for centuries. Those are drakes, probably no bigger than ten feet long. The breeding season is approaching, and that's why they're here. They live most of the year on the western seaboard across the Arz Sea from Edland, but each summer they come back to roost in the caves here. We should be early enough in the season, and our destination low enough, that we won't be a bother to them."

"A bother to them?" said Motega. "I was more concerned about those teeth and claws being a bother to us!"

THE CLIMB BECAME INCREASINGLY VERTICAL, AND SO, THE conversation died out once more. After reaching one large outcropping where the rock appeared smooth, like a melting glacier, Motega had asked what caused it.

"Fire," was all Neenahwi answered as she pushed on from the front.

Eventually, she called a halt halfway up Tiston at a ledge that looked much like five others they had seen earlier in the afternoon. The group ate their modest lunch of bread and cheese with a vengeance, washing it down with fresh water gathered at a stream at the base of the mountain. When they finished eating, Neenahwi gestured to the mountainside and an area of juniper bushes close by.

"Here's what we're looking for." Neenahwi parted the bushes to reveal a cave entrance descending into the dark. "After all the up, now we go down."

IT MIGHT HAVE BEEN A LITTLE OVER-GENEROUS TO describe the hole they saw as a cave. In fact, it was more of a vent to provide fresh air to the inhabitants of the dwarven city below the mountain. It was about four feet wide at its entrance and descended at an angle before sharply dropping off into the darkness.

There was only room for one person to move at a time, and so, it was decided that Trypp would lead the way—even though his experience of spelunking was limited, his climbing skills made him the best choice. Tying off a rope onto iron spikes driven into the cave wall, they were able to descend through the tunnel into the dark. They stopped at various natural stone shelves when possible, sometimes only big enough for one or two of them to rest at a time.

Neenahwi did pause to admire the lamps Trypp, her brother, and Florian wore on their heads. She hadn't seen a similar design before, and even though it only shed a limited amount of light to their proceedings, it was all they had.

Neenahwi's arms were tired as she descended the fifth rope and arrived at a ledge where she was again able to rest. Trypp and Florian sat there ahead of her, with the others descending behind.

"How much further do you think we need to go?" asked Trypp.

"I'm not sure. I believe we're getting close, but I have no real way of knowing," said Neenahwi.

"We have one more length of rope, and we don't know how far down we need to go. Once everyone reaches this point, I'm going to have to go and retrieve the last line." Trypp didn't look happy about the prospect of climbing down without a rope. "Hopefully without falling."

"You can do it, man!" said Florian, giving his friend a pat on the back, nearly knocking him over the ledge.

Once the rest of the group was safely on the broad ridge, Trypp climbed up the rope into the darkness, the light of his headlamp barely visible. And then, all of a sudden, the rope fell to the ledge. All was quiet as the friends waited with bated breath.

The light bobbed around above them, shining from one direction to the next as Trypp looked for the next foothold. But soon he was within sight; he jumped the last few feet to land with a little flourish.

From there, Florian led the way down the rope, Trypp following at the back, not using the cable at all, instead, untying it and letting it fall to the group below whenever they reached a safe position. It was slow going, and not without danger, but after doing it three times, they reached the floor.

They were in the middle of a vast green cavern, wide enough so they could see the walls on either side, but too long to see in which direction they should go, left or right. The ceiling was high. In fact, they could not see it either, just the ends of stalactites dripping into view. The floor of the cavern was covered with various mosses of greens, purples, and even reds, organized into neat little rectangles. Certain plots were obviously mushrooms and other fungi of strange and peculiar shapes, some reaching into the air like miniature mountains, and others pooled around the floor like melted candles.

"This is one of the gardens," said Neenahwi. "There are many of them to feed the dwarves under the mountain."

"Are they patrolled? Are we going to run into any guards or workers?" asked Mareth.

"Potentially. We should be careful. We have to keep the light to a minimum and keep our eyes peeled for any signs of people who will raise the alarm too soon." Neenahwi set off, gesturing for the group to follow her.

"How do you know which way to go?" asked Motega.

"I can feel the movement of the air. The city is still below us," answered Neenahwi.

Never had a group of ramblers, traipsing over farmland, tried to be so careful. Following Neenahwi's lead, the group tiptoed through the vegetation of the cavern, mindful of the crops for the people who lived in the city. They skirted around various squishy vegetables and sponge-like mosses. Neenahwi had tried a number of these unappetizing-looking plants in the past, and she had to admit, when they were prepared with some of the dwarven specialty slug sauce, they were close to edible.

Everyone's eyes focused on looking at the ground, making sure their footing was safe, while they passed under stalactites hanging from the ceiling, sharp pointed ends dripping salt to the ground. The end of the cavern came into view and the vegetation stopped, a barren patch of cavern floor before the vegetation resumed again a hundred yards or so beyond. Neenahwi, tired and glad of not having to watch her step, strode across the bare rock.

And that's when things went crazy.

CHAPTER 27
UNEDAR HALT

Something hit Neenahwi on the back of the head, and she fell to the floor, striking her forehead on a rock. Shouting in pain, she rolled onto her back, hand touching her brow to reveal blood on her fingers.

In front of her, the air was filled with tentacles thicker than her arm and more than twenty feet long, lashing out at the men who had followed her. Mareth was struck to the floor as a tentacle caught him in the stomach. Motega drew his axes and rolled across the ground out of reach. Dolph, sword already in hand, chopped at appendages reaching for him. In the center of the chaos was a mottled grey squid-like creature, easily ten feet tall, two eyes as big as dinner plates staring out.

And beneath it, she could see the black leather boots of Florian.

Why can't a stalactite just be a stalactite?

Suddenly, at her side was Trypp, with a look of concern on his face. He helped her to her feet, and she saw his mouth move to ask if she was alright. She didn't know if she couldn't hear him because of the shouts and grunts of battle or if the ringing in her ears had something to do with it.

A little groggy, she paused, seeing Mareth draw his sword and move to fight next to his bodyguard. She heard his voice as he sang, the words indistinguishable, but she recognized the tempo as a fight song. Motega had assessed the situation and had dived forward toward one of the squid's eyes, dodging one tentacle, chopping at another, jumping over one that reached to grab his ankle, to get within striking range.

She tried to focus her attention and divide her consciousness, but the ringing in her ears kept causing her concentration to fail. She was going to have to do this as she had as a girl. "Trypp, don't let me fall," she ordered.

She closed her eyes and tried to ignore the chaos, drawing thread after thread of the plant life around her, and feeling the modest flow of mana that she could control. Opening her eyes, she pulled one of her steel arrows from its pouch and threw it into the air. Neenahwi gathered the energy to hold the missile in the air, flying around and around above the monster and her friends, creating momentum before firing it at the squid's eye.

A rocky-looking eyelid closed, but the arrow sank into it, becoming lodged. Motega and Dolph had both managed to get close to the body of the Squiditite, causing deep wounds across its body. Dolph aimed a blow at its other eye, but his sword was caught by a tentacle, which twisted and pulled the weapon from his hand to clatter on the floor. Thankfully, though, the creature had decided this dinner wasn't worth the trouble, and two tentacles stretched high up into the air to reach other stalactites and pull itself back into the darkness.

Florian was lying on the ground, not moving and covered in slime. His face was grey, and there were small red welts on his face and arms that looked like love bites from the ugliest date he'd ever had. Motega rushed over and put his ear to his chest, heard breathing, and slapped his face about the cheeks to wake him, but to no effect. "Neenahwi," said Motega. "He won't wake; he's breathing, but he's not responding."

Neenahwi ran over to inspect Florian. After a few moments of deliberation, she turned to face Motega and Trypp, who were leaning over her shoulder. "He's paralyzed, it's some poison. Certain predators paralyze their prey, so they can better take their time to eat it. I think it's what that thing was going to do."

"How long is it going to last?" asked Trypp.

"I can't say for certain, but from other examples I've seen, once it's stopped being delivered to the victim, then it will usually wear off in time. I think all we can do now is wait." Neenahwi looked back down at him and saw the gobs of slime dripping off everything above his knees. "Well, I guess we could clean him up, too."

The group felt uneasy resting on the barren patch of earth where they knew the stalactite monster lurked above, so they picked up Florian and took him to a soft bed of rust-colored moss to one side. They sat by him and waited, not sure of the passing time in the dark underground.

All of a sudden, Florian sat up with a start, eyes wide, and open mouth sucking in a huge lungful of air.

"What the fuck was that?"

Motega laughed. "I guess the sky finally fell on your head." He helped him to his feet, and Neenahwi hugged him.

"Good job you're as tough as an ox," she said, causing his face to regain some color.

After a few minutes, the party was on their way again. Neenahwi at the front with the rest following in single file, all of them now paying more attention to the dark above their heads than the mosses under their feet.

Ten minutes of walking and they reached the end of the garden cavern, a single exit passageway burrowed into the wall in front of them. They crept down the obviously crafted corridor, the walls too smooth to be natural. It twisted and turned, and soon a faint light was visible around the corner ahead.

Neenahwi called a halt and gestured for them all to come close. "Ahead is going to be one of the entrances to the city of Unedar Halt," she whispered. "You wait here, and I'll go and announce ourselves."

"What?" said Mareth. "We've been slinking around, and you're just going to walk up to them?"

"Yes. That's exactly what I'm going to do."

She turned and walked around the corner, the passageway opening out to a small chamber with a large ornately decorated archway opposite her. Standing guard were three armored dwarves, all wielding pikes. "Hail, deep folk of Unedar Halt! It is Neenahwi, wizard, and daughter of Jyuth."

The dwarves turned, muttering something amongst themselves. They didn't call out to her. They just took a threatening step forward. Turning up the intensity she called, "I'm here to see the forger. And you would be minded to take me to him."

MINUTES PASSED. ONE OF THE GUARDS HAD RUN TO

deliver the message that Neenahwi had arrived and asked to meet the forger, the youngest of the three on guard judging by his comparative lack of grey hair. Dwarves, they were called by most above-ground people; though, in fact, they weren't much shorter than the usual malnourished resident of Kingshold.

They were a different people in appearance, though, standing around five feet tall but broad and with muscular limbs and short necks. Their eyes were typically blue—sensitized to the dark, but still unable to see in the pitch black—and their ears were larger, giving them superior hearing. Yet, Neenahwi had always thought the people of Unedar Halt were not that different from most humans in appearance, but they were quite unique in other ways—not least, they had much longer lives than the people of Edland, even significantly longer than her own people.

She had addressed the guard using the common tongue instead of their language, knowing, except for the most strident follower of Varcon, they would understand. The remaining two veteran guards were talking amongst themselves in Dwarvish in hushed tones. It was difficult for her to hear, but she could make out a few phrases.

"This is why we shouldn't be understaffed."

"Just walked right up."

"Too bloody many in the infirmary."

"Need to be ready when the Graks come again."

Her understanding of Dwarvish was pretty good, but she hadn't heard the term Graks before. Were they under assault by goblins again or some other creature from beneath the earth?

After what seemed like an eternity of standing around

(though her comrades had long since settled on the floor and rested their eyes after the exertions of the day), the messenger guard returned with a dwarf at his side. He had long, white hair, braided beard, but lacking the spectacles she had often seen him wear above ground to protect his eyes from the bright light of the sun.

"Keybearer." Neenahwi gave a deep bow and kicked Motega where he lay on the ground, gesturing for him to stand. "It's good to see you again, Egyed."

"And it's always a pleasure to see you, too, Lady Neenahwi," he said, returning a deep flamboyant bow, mischievous smile peeking out from his beard. "Without Jyuth, I see. But it seems you picked up some other waifs and strays on the way here. Can I remind you, you are allowed to use the front door? Sneaking around in the dark is liable to get you pegged for thieves and a quarrel in the guts."

"We have good reasons for wanting our visit to remain secret to others in Kingshold. At least for now," said Neenahwi. "We wish to see the forger."

"So, I heard from this young guard here. And why would that be? He's a very busy man."

"Please, Egyed, I ask that you trust me in this matter. I'll tell you both at the same time. Can we see him?"

The dwarf laughed. "Of course. I already sent word to him. You know you're always welcome after your help last year with the spectre. Come, follow me."

Neenahwi set off to follow the keybearer and gestured for Mareth and the others to follow. They passed by the guards unmolested, the surprise on Florian's face clear as he was allowed to keep his weapons as he entered the city.

"The deep people are deeply respectful of each other's

weapons. It's a great insult to touch someone else's arms," she informed him.

Walking alongside the dwarf, Neenahwi stepped through the short tunnel entrance and into a vast cavern that was the center of Unedar Halt. Its scale always took her breath away.

Though the city was much smaller than Kingshold, there was nothing else she had seen of this size that had a massive roof of stone above it, lacking any support structures. It made the primal part of her mind scream it was unsafe and the sky likely to fall on her, but she knew this space had remained unmolested for many centuries.

She suspected that though no visible columns were holding up the cavern ceiling, there were magics in place far stronger than any pillar of stone could be. The cavern ceiling was covered in a phosphorescent moss, similar to that used by Motega and his friends, providing a dim light that in contrast to the passageways they had traveled through earlier in the day seemed like daylight. She could see the looks of wonder and amazement on her comrade's faces as they followed behind; few people of Edland had ever seen the city of their closest neighbors.

They crossed a bridge over a wide river that emerged from under the cavern wall at this end of the city and flowed to disappear underground some distance away. Dwarves were filling stout barrels of water and loading them into carts pulled by teams of creatures resembling armadillos, but were the size of a pony. Egyed stopped at the crest of the bridge and turned to the gawping men behind.

"I'm sure you gentlemen haven't been here before. All visitors come through the keybearer, and I've been in this role since before your parents even knew how babies were made." The dwarf chuckled at his joke. "And so, let me take a moment to share with you the pride I have in my home."

Egyed gestured to the large area of bare earth in front of the bridge where groups of heavily armed soldiers engaged in various physical activities: combat, sprinting in armor, target practice with large evil-looking crossbows. "These are our drilling fields. All citizens spend at least one day each week in drills, male or female, from the day they start school to the day they are too old to pick up their weapon."

His arm swept to the right. "There, you see those strands of silver snaking and intersecting until they reach the ceiling? Those are chimneys that take the fumes from the forges and workshops of our city. No fires burn here underground. We use the heat from the earth itself, channeled for use by our craftsmen to melt those metals we mine far below where we stand. But we don't want noxious fumes fouling our homes.

"Away from the forges there, you see those tall buildings. They store our harvests, which provide for all of our people. We don't have any who starve in this city. All work and all live together.

"And in the center of the city, you see the two tallest buildings. On the left with the gold spire is the Smelter, the place where our council meets to make decisions for the good of all. It's called the Smelter as all of our clans come together, with their own opinions and histories, and there they are combined into one view, tempered through discussion and argument.

"Opposite the Smelter is the House of Varcon, where the priesthood lives. They're the only people who live day and night in this cavern."

Mareth was at the front of the group and was listening

intently. Neenahwi could see his mouth soundlessly word the new names of things. She supposed he was unconsciously committing them to memory. A bard was always a storyteller. "And so, where do all of the other people live?"

"Good question, sir! Glad to see you're paying attention. This is but a fraction of the whole city. Many other caverns branch off this central chamber, where all of the living quarters are. Generally, people live with their clans, and these caverns are constantly expanding as they're mined further; we're not a people to stay still, you know. And now let's be off to see the forger."

The dwarf turned and strode off down the bridge and onto the smooth roadway ahead, Neenahwi trotting to get alongside him.

"Egyed, a question as we walk," said Neenahwi. "What is a Grak?"

The keybearer turned his head and regarded Neenahwi. "And where did you hear that term, girl? Those guards back there didn't realize you're smarter than you look?" He smiled once more. "Seriously, though, that's not for me to discuss with you. Come, the forger will be getting nicely shriveled by now."

Neenahwi gave Egyed a puzzled look, but decided to refrain from asking further questions. They continued walking down the main street through the middle of the chamber, the twin spires growing in front of them as they moved closer. They passed the drilling fields and neared the workshop areas, but instead of continuing straight ahead toward the Smelter, they made a left turn onto another pathway heading to a smaller archway in the cavern wall.

"Where are we going, Egyed?" asked Neenahwi.

"As you requested," said the keybearer, disappearing into a cloud of steam. "We're going to see the forger."

~

"So, you're saying we have to take our clothes off?" asked Mareth.

"Yes. Don't you normally take your clothes off for a bath?" replied Neenahwi.

"Yes, but I don't normally meet with the leader of a city while naked."

"Don't worry. I'm sure you have nothing to worry about. Petra always seems happy enough," said Florian, laughing.

"Look, this is a good thing. We're going to have a quiet audience with the forger. Just go along with it," said Neenahwi. "And, Florian, you can't take your swords with you. Put them down."

Neenahwi slipped out of her robes and took off her underclothes, her back to the men who seemed much more embarrassed about getting undressed than she was. She wrapped herself in the blanket they had all been provided and stood there, tapping her foot until the sounds of belts being unbuckled, weapons being laid on the floor, and boots being pulled off had ended.

Egyed returned to the small antechamber they had used to get changed, and he bade them all to follow him. They entered a cavern lit by red rocks set in the wall, numerous pillars arching from the floor up to the low ceiling, and all around were pools of steaming, bubbling water.

"These are our thermal baths," explained Egyed, still content to play the tour guide. "Here the water is trapped close to the hot earth we use in our crafting. And, of course, after a long day's hard work, everybody needs a rest."

They walked past a series of pools, many inhabitants soaking in each one, male and female mixed together, most with eyes closed and a contented look on their faces. Egyed stopped at a pool much like the others, but with a solitary dwarf soaking inside.

His head was shiny, and he had a close-cropped white beard; wrinkles surrounded his eyes, but his shoulders and arms visible above the water still looked strong. Egyed dropped his blanket and slipped into the pool beckoning the others to join him.

"Master Forger, here are Neenahwi and her...ahhh... friends," said the keybearer as he eased into the waters.

"Master Forger, thank you for seeing us and granting us the hospitality of your baths," Neenahwi spoke to the old dwarf, but he had yet to open his eyes. "I come on important business. I want to introduce you to Lord Mareth Bollingsmead and potential future protector of Edland. This is his bodyguard, Dolph, and here is my brother, Motega, and my friends Florian and Trypp."

The dwarf's chest rose up and down in the water, curly white hairs appearing and disappearing under the bubbles. She counted five breaths before he opened his eyes. "Lady Neenahwi, you know it's always a pleasure to see you. But usually, you use the front door. What is this important business you mentioned?"

"My lord," interjected Mareth, "it's concerning the election of a new lord protector of Edland. We need your help. Under the rules of the election, the people of Unedar Halt can take part. The candidates who are currently standing for this position are no friends of the dwarves. They are nobles who are shortsighted and selfish.

"We believe in doing something for the people of Edland to make it a fairer society, to make it where we're not afraid of people who are different. That's why I was persuaded to stand for election, though it wasn't something I wanted to do. I believe we should have stronger ties with your people. But without your help, I'm not going to be able to get the votes needed. And we'll all be stuck with a protector we don't want."

"Hmmm. First of all, I'm no lord. We have no lords or ladies or kings or queens under the mountain. We only have people who are chosen to do the job that is right for them and our people," said the forger.

"Second of all, you people always make so little sense to us! And this election is no different. Egyed here already told us we can vote if we want to; we can pay the price of admission probably better than most of the people of Kingshold. We discussed it at the Smelter, and we've decided not to be involved, as what does this have to do with us?"

"You're right," conceded Mareth, but he wasn't going to give up yet. "You're secluded down here. But if Lord Eden wins the election, he's going to see there's some opportunity for gain in the relationship with your people. And he's going to bring war to the region. Is that going to stay away from you? I don't know."

"I don't know either, but what I do know is the council met, and the council made a decision. We will not be involved. Now it's very nice to meet you, Mareth, and I wish you well in this election if Lord Eden is as bad as you say, but I'm not minded to do anything more."

"Master Forger, can I ask you a question?" asked

Neenahwi. She needed to switch tack here. The direct approach wasn't going to get them where they needed to be. "Why were the drilling fields so empty today? Is it because the infirmary has been overly busy of late? Grak problems?"

The old dwarf's eyes narrowed. "What do you know? Egyed, have you been talking about things you shouldn't?"

"Of course not," Egyed huffed. "She's been listening, and she's smart. She's probably figured half of it out already, and now she's fishing for the rest."

"Hah. Fishing indeed. I can sense you have a problem, and it just so happens I'm very good at fixing problems." Neenahwi mirrored the relaxed pose of the forger, arms wide, elbows resting on the side of the pool. "And I know the deep people always try to help people who help them. So why don't you tell me what pickle you're in, and I'll tell you how I can help."

The two dwarves looked at each other. Egyed shrugged and said, "Why not tell her? Maybe she can help. You don't have much longer before you're going to have to make a decision that's going to make you unhappy."

The forger sighed. "I guess you're right. But listen here, girl, this stays between us." Neenahwi nodded and allowed him to continue. "There have been some of the younger dwarves who have gone missing. Except we know where they've gone. They've gone above ground. There have always been a few dwarves who get the Yellow Fever, the desire to see the sun and see the world not contained by the ground above.

"Usually, we lock them up for a while. For their own good, you understand. And then after they get hungry, they come to their senses, and we all move on. Why I think it may have even happened to me in my youth. Anyway, that's beside the point, but now we have a more difficult situation.

"It's not just one young dwarf who got the Yellow Fever, it's a whole blasted gang of them, and the leader is my son! And my son just happens to be a priest of Varcon. He and his gang are holed up in one of the cavern branches trying to dig a new way to the surface. We thought we'd just starve them out, same as we usually do, and they'd come back to their senses and their families. But my son has taken one of our Juggernauts.

"They're enchanted statues, and he's one of the few who can animate and use his mind to control it. Make it move around. Make it dig. Make it fight. And these Juggernauts are big and difficult to take down. So, for the past three months, this gang has been raiding our very own city using the Juggernaut to fight their way to our food stores, and then take what they need and return to their hidey-hole.

"Nobody wants to kill another dwarf, especially one of our youngsters, and so, each time they attack, our soldiers and guards take injuries from these dwarves and the Juggernaut. And we're running out of fit folk, and I'm running out of options. I've been holding off making the call that the next time they attack, we're going to have to stop pulling our punches."

"Sounds like a very difficult situation, Master Forger," empathized Neenahwi. "What say you that the next time this troublemaker son and his friends raid the city, we stop them? And then you bring us your votes?"

"There can be no deaths! A few broken bones are fine, but any dwarf dies, and the deal is off. His mother would kill me. And the deal is this, and this is all I can promise. Once you do this deed, I'll bring it before the council again and suggest we change our decision. But we also will need to have assurances, Mareth, that if you're lord protector, there will be no changes in our relationship."

"Master Forger, I can assure you, if you vote for me and I win, then our relationship is safe."

"Fine, lass, you've got a deal," said the forger, spitting on his hand and leaning over to shake Neenahwi's outstretched hand. "Now, let's get out of this piss pool and go get something to eat. I'm getting all shriveled."

CHAPTER 28
LIMITS OF POWER

"I took the liberty of laying out the black robes today, sir."

"Percival, all my clothes are the same. Must you make the same joke every day?" Hoskin had woken at his usual hour, early, but Percival was always on his feet before him to help him with the task of getting dressed for the day ahead.

Hoskin had dressed himself for a good thirty years from the day he told his mother's maids to leave him alone until he became lord chancellor of Edland, but apparently having someone like Percival came with the job and he wasn't supposed to argue it. Of course, most other valets weren't also acting as the treasurer for one of the most powerful nations in the Jeweled Continent. *But needs must right now.*

"I think it's always important to start the day with a smile, sir." Percival didn't smile. Hoskin wasn't sure if he'd ever seen Percival smile. "And your breakfast awaits in your sitting room."

Hoskin was helped into his clothes, and he combed his

short hair to some semblance of order before slicking it back with animal fat.

Waiting for him on the table in his sitting room was his breakfast: porridge with chopped nuts, slices of hot fatty bacon, crispy bread, cheese, sliced apples, and a tall pot of strong, black coffee. Some days, breakfast was the only meal he'd have time for, especially the past few weeks, so he tried to make it count. He sat, picking up his spoon and knife when Percival cleared his throat.

"Yes, Percival? Is there something you wish to tell me?"

"I'm afraid so. I don't think it's good news. Lady Kingsley was assassinated last night."

Hoskin spat out a mouthful of porridge. "What? Old Lady Kingsley? Always talking about her grandfather being chancellor?"

"Great grandfather, sir. And, yes, the very same," said Percival. "She was standing for election," he added unnecessarily.

Hoskin froze, not moving or talking, but a color slowly rising in his face. All of a sudden, he stood upright, pushing the chair, which toppled backward to the floor.

"This is outrageous! They can't just go around killing each other like this. There'll be no one left!" Hoskin began to pace around the table. "Jyuth," he exclaimed after his third revolution.

"Pardon, my lord?"

"Jyuth! This is all his damned fault." Wasn't the wizard supposed to be the wise one? He must have seen this would happen. Anarchy!

Hoskin took for the door, flinging it open and striding out into the corridor in the direction of the wizard's apartments. Percival ran to catch up with his master.

They made short time across the palace courtyard to the single-story, free-standing building Jyuth had called his home for longer than Hoskin could remember. Not stopping to knock, the chancellor swept through the doorway, buzzing like a swarm of bees, through the antechamber, and into the sitting room. A servant girl was clearing the breakfast dishes, Hoskin noting the wizard had been able to eat his breakfast this morning, unlike him. His breakfast would be cold by the time he returned, which only added insult to injury.

"Where is he, girl?" asked Hoskin.

The servant girl turned to face him. Hoskin recognized her as the usual young woman who attended to Jyuth, the one who had been assaulted by Aebur's agent. She didn't look afraid at Hoskin's outburst, but did suffer a bout of stutters trying to answer.

"Are you looking for me, Lord Chancellor?" said Jyuth, walking into the sitting room, which suddenly felt smaller to Hoskin.

This had seemed like such a good idea a few minutes before, but now the wind had left Hoskin's sails at the sight of the wizard standing tall, hands on hips, a frown framing his piercing dark stare. Hoskin gulped and tried to regain enough composure for his voice not to crack.

"Lord Jyuth," he began, coughing slightly to clear his throat. "Yes, I was looking for you. Lady Kingsley has been assassinated."

"Well, that's a shame," said the wizard nonchalantly, walking over to a sofa and making himself comfortable. "She was such a terribly nice xenophobe."

Hoskin ignored the joke.

Or the truth in what the wizard said. He wasn't sure which it was supposed to be, and it didn't matter either way if one looked at it from the right point of view. That being his point of view that things were getting out of control. "You need to do something about this," he implored.

"What can I do? You say it was an assassination, and it was probably a suitably expensive and professional job. And if it wasn't sanctioned, then Chalice will take care of it. You know the law, Hoskin."

"But it's getting out of control, and it's all because of your election." There, he'd said it. He'd blamed Jyuth for this mess. In for a copper, in for a crown. "I've looked at the records, to double check my own memory, and there are normally only one or two contracts for the Hollow Syndicate a year in this city. We've had three in the past two weeks, and there's still a week to go! They aren't even civilized enough to duel."

"I'm sure the good lady thinks her services are perfectly civilized," chided Jyuth as he tapped his fingers on his crossed leg. "Look, I can't do anything, and even if I could, I'm not sure I would. Lord Hoskin, you know as well as I do, it's probably good to have a few less nobles around. Present company excepted, of course." Jyuth gave Hoskin his fuck-off-and-leave-me-alone smile, the primal part of the chancellor's brain recognizing danger and instructing his feet to take a half-step backward to the door. "If you're so upset about it, you could always talk to Lady Chalice?" volunteered the wizard as Hoskin edged out of the room.

THE CARRIAGE RATTLED OUT ONTO THE COBBLESTONE streets as it left the palace gateway, Hoskin alone for the journey to the Hollow House.

He didn't feel like company right now. The start to the day had put him in a bad mood, and the response to his message for an audience with Lady Chalice had left them in a worse mood. A very brief response of, '*If you want to talk, then you know where I am.*' And even though it was obviously a personal insult that he would be the one making the journey, he didn't intend to give up this bone yet.

The ride was short from the palace, through the inner circle, and down the Lance, or it would've been if it wasn't for all of the people who had been mysteriously instructed to get in his way today.

Hoskin banged on the roof of the carriage in a vain attempt to make the driver go faster before falling back into his seat with an exhalation of frustration. He closed his eyes and wondered why he even cared about this. What did it mean to him who was going to be in charge in eight days' time? No one would thank him. But no one had ever thanked him for the service he'd done for more than a decade.

Eventually, the carriage made its way past the lined shop fronts and turned right before reaching the Outer Wall. The Hollow House was more aesthetically alike to a small fortress than the other homes in the neighborhood. High walls of stone surrounded a compound with a single gate on the main street, but there were no outward signs of guards on the walls or at the entrance. A person would have to be either grossly stupid or new to the city to consider trying to rob this particular abode. Death was an art form within, the best education money could buy.

The gate opened to admit Hoskin's carriage, and it came to a halt in the courtyard. He had been here before, many years ago, receiving a tour from the old steward, who had spent his life working for the syndicate, but had probably never killed anyone in all his days. Except through boredom.

It was the same wrinkled old fossil who greeted him as he climbed down the carriage steps. Surveying the empty courtyard, it was as Hoskin remembered.

On the west side of the compound was the student dormitory, and facing those living quarters were the classrooms and training facilities for new acolytes. There were only ever twenty partners, as the assassins were referred to, at any one time. When an acolyte had made the grade, they would either have to challenge an existing member for their position or somebody would willingly move on.

The Hollow Syndicate had become quite the place to send one's son or daughter for their education. Not firstborn, of course, maybe not even second, but for a younger child, having them taught under the leadership of Lady Chalice had the potential to be quite lucrative. Even though the percentage of candidates who'd get close to graduating was small, it had created the problem of a surplus of assassins coming through the school.

Which the good lady had solved simply by establishing new branches of the syndicate in other cities around the Jeweled Continent, seeded by Kingshold's finest. What a wonderful export Edland had. *Something to be proud of*, he considered sourly. *Not enough civilized murder in our country; let's spread it around.* True, it did prove useful that there was a certain understanding between the branches and the head office here. Made him wonder why the other cities would countenance their existence. But he supposed a score of deadly assassins had a certain special kind of lobbying power.

The old fossil beckoned him to follow. Thankfully, he wasn't going to have to sit through another tour of the various classrooms; he was going directly into the third building, the Hollow House.

It wasn't grand like the major guild houses, which unofficially was the status given to the syndicate. Solid wood, stone and pristine whitewashed walls with no decoration save a collection of portraits of past Syndicate leaders greeted Hoskin as he was led to a sitting room. He sat on one of the cushioned chairs with its back to the wall and waited.

A different door to the one Hoskin had entered through opened, and in stepped a tall woman of middling years, red hair shot through with grey, but skin betraying few wrinkles and a body strong, wound tight like a spring, clothed in riding gear.

"So, what is it you want to talk about, Hoskin?" asked Lady Chalice.

"I'm glad to see you just want to get down to business. I do have a country to run," he said. "Did the guild kill Kingsley?"

"Of course, we did," she replied. "I was quite proud of the job. Poison, of course."

Hoskin sighed, now realizing this was a fool's errand. And so, he knew what that made him. "Lady Chalice, I need you to stop taking contracts on people involved in the election."

"Ha! Why on earth would I do that?"

She still had not sat down, pacing the room like a tiger in a cage. Hoskin felt uncomfortable looking up at her, so he, too, stood, but he had to concentrate to stop his legs from shaking.

For the second time of the day, he asked himself what was he doing? Chalice reminded him of the wizard, the aura of power and confidence emanating from her made him want to wrap up this dialog. "My dear Chancellor," she continued, "this is Winterfest come early for us, and who am I to turn down gifts? And let's face it, you don't matter. In less than ten days, you'll be gone and there will be a new chancellor. So why should I help you?"

"What about we say I'm appealing to your sense of citizenship?" he tried one last time. "Stopping the country from descending into chaos? How about wanting to see if the winner of the election can be decided in a way different from the man who spends the most money with you?"

She turned and sauntered toward him. Eyes drilled into his, hands on her hips, pushing out her chest, which he found difficult not to look at. She stopped six inches from him, her proximity causing havoc in his brain. The flight mechanism screamed to be listened to, but his neglected libido wanted to stay and see what would happen.

"What a good little man you are. Wanting the competition to be fair," she said. "But let me tell you something. They are all shits. Most of the kings and queens we've had through the years have been shits, but we have all managed to survive. Whoever wins is going to be a shit, too, but we'll still survive. So, if the syndicate cuts out a few of those bloodsucking leeches on the way, then great. Especially if it fills my coffers."

Hoskin maintained eye contact, though he could feel beads of sweat running down his forehead. "The wizard said much the same thing."

She smiled. A genuine smile illuminating her face, joy that Hoskin had finally seen the light. "Now, he is a smart man. And I thought you were, too, Lord Chancellor." The smile disappeared as quickly as it had come. "Let me give you a little advice. You have more important problems to deal with. You look after your business, and I'll look after mine."

SHE WAS RIGHT. THERE WERE MORE IMPORTANT THINGS TO deal with.

Hoskin sat in the privy council chamber, Uthridge and Ridgton seated across from him discussing how they would respond in light of the information retrieved from Aebur.

The new Pyrfew fleet was both an imminent and a long-term danger to Edland, and something needed to be done about it. Hoskin couldn't help wondering if this was what Chalice had been referring to, or if there was something else, some other dung sandwich awaiting him.

"I've canceled shore leave for the fleet currently at port in Kingshold," said Ridgton. "They'll set sail tomorrow under Commander Crews. I've sent birds to the other garrisons and ports in Edland, all within three days' sail of here. Twenty ships will leave here today, and another twenty-five will join them before they cross the Arz Sea."

"That's going to leave us pretty much defenseless against an attack from the sea," said Uthridge.

"Yes, true. For a short period, at least. There are no reports of any other fleets at sea right now, but I've sent messages for other vessels, calling them away from their routes and back to Kingshold," said the admiral. "But it could be a week or more before we have a skeletal fleet in place. We'll be reliant on the smaller vessels of the tax collection fleet in the meantime. Lord Chancellor, I recommend we close the port."

"Are you crazy?" asked Hoskin. "Even a week without trade ships will cause an uproar. There will be riots if there's not work for people to buy bread. What are the other options?"

"Well, we can step up the other city defenses, the city guard needs to be made aware, and their drills need to be stepped up," said Uthridge. "I'll speak to Penshead about what he needs to do. That is, if I can get his attention. I've heard he's been focused on trying to get notable people to back him, and by some particularly unusual methods."

"I'm afraid to ask." Hoskin sighed. "And so today, I'm not going to. Just make it happen, and make sure the chain defenses are working correctly in case we do need to close the port."

A knock, and then the door opened, Percival peeking through the crack to gain his attention. Hoskin gestured for him to enter, and his man walked briskly around the table to hand him a rolled note tied with string.

"You should read this now, my lord," whispered Percival, bending close to Hoskin's ear. "It's most urgent."

Hoskin's stomach lurched. What else could go wrong with this day? He slid the string off the parchment and unrolled it, reading and rereading the single written line, and wondering what the world had against him.

Aebur has vanished.

CHAPTER 29
THE RALLY

The time between nights on the campaign and mornings at the palace was narrowing, not leaving time for enough sleep, and it was taking its toll on Alana. It helped she had basically moved into the Royal Oak now—less distance to walk to and from the palace, meals available when she needed them—but it also meant she didn't have a moment when she wasn't working.

Dawn this morning had dragged her out of bed in a fog; she couldn't remember the walk to the palace and reporting to Bertha, though she knew she had done that, the remnants of breakfast on the tray in her hands as she left Jyuth's apartment being unequivocal evidence to the fact. As she walked across the courtyard, down the steps, and through the laundry rooms to the kitchen, she was again lost in considering the permutations of how they could get enough votes.

Not necessarily enough to win. That seemed unlikely with another candidate dead and her supporters probably going to switch to the frontrunner. Enough was starting to mean a number that wouldn't be too embarrassing for them all, so they could, at least, hopefully, have some future say when Lord Eden would be declared lord protector.

There was still much to do to rally the people and excite them enough to persuade thousands of families to part with the coin they sorely lacked, even for a few days, and for them to be able to trust they'd get it back. But that wasn't going to be anywhere near enough. The guilds needed to be on their side, too, and they were falling into two camps along the traditional lines of grand vs. lesser guilds. The lesser guilds were their target, but she worried how they could be convinced later today if Mareth still wasn't back from the journey with Jyuth's daughter to the dwarves.

Alana was uncertain how she felt about Neenahwi. She'd come into their group like a whirlwind, full of confidence of the like Alana only dreamed.

Within hours of meeting Mareth, she had joined them at their table. The table where Alana felt so at home now, working with her friends on something more significant than her life as a servant. Alana knew it was a great boon to their effort that the wizard's daughter was assisting them, in particular when Jyuth was so obviously sitting out of the whole affair. But what if Neenahwi called her out as a no-nothing servant or asked her to fetch her meal when they were with her friends in the same way she'd done before when meeting with her father.

Granted, Neenahwi had always been extremely polite in how she had spoken to her, in contrast to everyone else at the palace, and especially so after their first meeting. But part of what made Alana unique before was she spoke with Jyuth. That made people listen to her. But how was she going to compete with his daughter?

She stopped walking and looked down. She was back in

the courtyard and no tray in hand. Must have been back to the kitchen without even realizing it again.

What was becoming of her?

That was why she had stood there looking like a mackerel on the docks when the lord chancellor had come in. Her dad would have said, "Shut your mouth, love, you'll catch flies."

Thinking of her dad made her smile briefly and shake her head at herself. She walked back toward the gardens and Jyuth's apartment to see if he needed anything from her. She hoped not, so she could find a quiet corner and read through more of the merchant agreements that Folstencroft had provided.

Crunch. Crunch. Crunch. Footsteps behind her on the gravel path once again brought her back to the present, and she turned to see who was following her.

"You there. Alana, isn't it?" said the armored man she knew to be Captain Grimes of the palace guard. "Is the lord wizard home? Bugger it, if he's not there after I've walked all this way to see him. Why isn't he in the palace proper to save us some shoe leather, eh?"

"Yes, sir, it's Alana, sir. And I don't know, sir; you'll have to ask him," she replied, the subtle joke passing her by in her present mental state. "But he is there, or at least he was fifteen minutes ago."

"Good, good. Lead the way then, Alana."

Alana led the guard captain to the apartments and entered the room to announce him first, Grimes looking concerned about barging in on the wizard.

Jyuth was changing into one of his looser robes he used when meditating for an extended period, and so, when Alana told him who was waiting outside, he grumbled while changing back into what he considered to be his more impressive robes. Alana couldn't tell much difference between the two types of clothing, other than the fact Jyuth belted his finer choice of wardrobe, but she didn't have the heart to tell him so. As he buckled his belt, Alana went to bring the captain to the sitting room.

"Morning, Grimes. What brings you here today?" asked Jyuth as he strode in from his bedchamber and sat on the sofa. Alana stood to one side, but didn't move to leave. The guard commander's eyes flicked to look at her, and then back to Jyuth. "You can speak freely, Captain."

"Yes, m'lord. I wanted to report that two individuals have been detained leaving the Mountain Gate, sir. Edlanders by the look of them, not dwarves, of course. They've been taken to the guard tower. You did say before you wanted to speak with anyone who used the door, m'lord."

"That's right, Grimes; I did. Good work. Take me to them. Alana, you're coming, too."

Grimes and the wizard set a brisk pace back through the gardens, both of them taller than her, which forced her to do a half-skip every few steps to keep up. The walk took them around the palace and through a number of gates, secluded terraces and, eventually, to the guard tower overlooking the clear zone before the enormous ornate brass door leading to Unedar Halt, the Mountain Gate.

Grimes led them into the watchtower and up a flight of stairs to an office where the door was wide open. Inside, sitting at a simple wooden table were Mareth and Dolph, with steaming mugs in hand talking to two guards, who were similarly equipped. Grimes's expression alternated between puzzled and angry with each passing breath.

"By the hairy balls of Arloth. Since when did guarding someone involve having a cup of tea and chat?" Grimes's voice increased in volume the more he spoke. By the end of his question, he would have been audible down in the Narrows.

"Sorry, sir," replied one of the guards, quickly standing and putting his cup down at the same time, causing half of the contents to spill. "This is Lord Bollingsmead, sir. We were just making sure he was comfortable, sir."

Jyuth looked to Alana, eyebrows raised in question. She nodded. "Not to worry, Captain. It looks like your men did an excellent job," said Jyuth. "Now, I'd like to have a moment alone with these two before you escort them from the palace."

Grimes saluted and manhandled the two guards out into the stairway before he closed the door.

"So, this is them?" Jyuth asked her.

"Yes. This is Mareth, or Lord Bollingsmead. And this is Dolph," said Alana.

"Good morning, Lord Jyuth." Mareth got to his feet and gave a bow. "It's a pleasure to meet you finally."

"Yes, yes. Likewise, I'm sure," said the rotund wizard, "but I don't think you want to be seen talking with me for long. I'm deliberately staying out of this election. Where is my daughter?"

"She's safe, as are her brother and his friends. They're staying for a few days to help us secure the votes of the deep people." Another riot of emotions hit Alana. A few more days without having to confront the reality of what Neenahwi would mean for her situation was welcome, but the news she could be securing a substantial number of votes was bad.

No, she thought, *that's a good thing.*

"Excellent," said Jyuth, nodding. "Good thinking by the

way. Wondered if anyone would consider trying to secure their votes. Now, you'd best be off. Alana, from the look on your face, I assume you have a lot to discuss with this man, so you're free to go, too."

Jyuth left, patting Alana gently on the arm on the way out of the door, leaving her alone with Mareth and Dolph, who hugged her in greeting. She looked at them both, dust and dirt on their trousers and jerkins, but the rest of them surprisingly clean.

"We've got a lot to discuss as we walk, Mareth," said Alana. "It's the ward rally tonight, and this afternoon we're meeting with the guilds. I'm glad you're back. But first, we need to get you cleaned up. And I need to talk to you about these merchant agreements..."

THE DOOR TO THE MODEST OFFICE OPENED A CRACK, AND Master Gonal put his head in, the smile of an excited child on his face. "There are a lot of people out there!" he exclaimed.

"How many is a lot, Master Gonal?" Mareth sat in the only chair left in the room, the desk and other furniture having been moved to an adjoining storeroom. He'd been sitting there for the past half an hour while Petra applied makeup to his face like a traveling actor on a feast day. She had left five minutes ago, wanting to take care of a few last-minute tasks to ensure everything ran smoothly. That left Alana in the room with Folstencroft, Mareth, and Dolph, his ever-present shadow.

"Imagine how busy the market is on Fifthday. It's that busy, but without any stalls, just people pushed in against each other. It's amazing." Gonal was enjoying being at the center of the action. Alana had probably heard him say how he wanted to do something better for the city of his birth at least five times over the past week, and now he could feel something special was happening. They all could. Gonal ducked his head out of the room without waiting for a response.

"Sounds like a lot of people..." said Mareth, trailing off and staring into space. For the first time she could remember, he looked apprehensive. Alana saw they needed to get his mind thinking about something else. There was still half an hour before the rally began.

"I'll go and investigate, Mareth," said Dolph. "We'll need safe passage to the market square. We may need a bigger escort." And the bodyguard disappeared, too.

"Don't worry about it, Mareth; you'll be fine. It's just a slightly larger crowd than you would usually have. More importantly, what are we going to do about winning over the guild masters?" she asked.

The meeting with the guild masters had taken place in the stonemasons' guild house. Master Ballard had decided not to run for the role of protector after he'd heard about Mareth's candidacy. Alana thought there was a high likelihood Lady Grey had visited him and that might have had some bearing on his decision. In any instance, his support had been extremely valuable, gathering all of the lesser guild masters along with the textiles' and merchants' guild masters of the grand houses.

In the magnificent surrounding of the circular stone chamber, guild masters seated in banks around the circumference, the meeting had been challenging.

Mareth had stood in the center of the room and tried to

appeal to the attendees' desires to be involved in running their country. He painted a picture of a more just and open society and how they could be a beacon to other nations and states around the Jeweled Continent. He was always such a great orator, it seemed uncanny, able to hook people's attention as if he was telling an epic tale to a group of children around the fireside, and the quiet at the end of his speech showed he had done it again.

At least until the guild masters had snapped out of it and began to complain.

"What is it with them? All they did was whine," exclaimed Mareth. "I didn't know what they were talking about most of the time! What's the problem with Redsmoke bacon? We're going to run out of cedar in ten years' time? Why is that a problem now? I don't think I handled the questioning well."

"My lord, you should not feel bad about this. No one expects you to know the specifics of each of these situations." Folstencroft insisted on being formal with Mareth, even in private, which she could tell the bard was having some trouble getting used to. "I think there was er...a lot of pent-up frustration in the group."

That was an understatement. After the first few guild masters had politely waited their turn to speak, the bacon issue was raised by the Butchers' Guild, which caused the Merchants' Guild to take offense and shout over Master Lean, the butchers' guild master. It had unfortunately caused others to raise grievances with one another, all at the same time.

While this happened, Mareth, Alana, and Folstencroft had stood open-mouthed in the center of the guildhall, unsure how to regain control, while the arguing continued unabated. Alana realized this had been a mistake. Folstencroft had thought they could work with all of the guilds at once, as they had Master Ballard on-side, but that was wishful thinking. She had realized they needed to get out of there.

"Yes, I think that's pretty obvious!" said Mareth. "I'm just happy you were thinking on your toes, Alana. Suggesting I plead ignorance of their specific situations, but asking them to help educate me about what they thought I should do, at least got them all to ignore each other again and write their side of the story."

"And now we need to follow up with each guild individually," she said. "I'd suggest sending Petra tomorrow. She has a way of winning people over."

"Yes, I agree," said Mareth. "Folstencroft, can you go and see to it you have a plan for this?" The secretary gave a little bow and walked from the room, anxious to not be there for further discussion of how poorly his meeting had gone.

Alana looked out of the window; she felt a lump in her throat, and her eyes teared up as she contemplated what she was going to say.

"Mareth. I wanted to talk to you. Now might not be the best time, but it's so difficult to get a quiet moment with you." She sniffed and wiped at her eyes with the back of her hand.

"What is it, Alana?" Mareth asked, getting to his feet and approaching her.

"I-I don't think you need me anymore," she blurted out. "You have Neenahwi now, and Lady Grey. They're both real ladies who know what they're doing. I'm just a silly girl, playing at games of nobility. So, after tonight, I'll just go back to the palace. I'll wish you all the luck in the world, of course." In her nervousness, she had once again said all of this to the floor; now she looked up to see a quizzical look on the bard's face.

"Hah! As if I'd let you leave," said Mareth, regarding her with brotherly affection. "I haven't forgotten you got me into this mess. You and your sister. You think I'm going to let you walk away while I'm still up to my neck?" He smiled as he continued. "And remember you're here because you know what you're doing. *You* saved the meeting today, and *you* planned all of this tonight. Which, now that I come to think about it, is an even bigger mess you've dropped me in. Maybe you *should* go back to the palace."

Alana's mood had been starting to lighten, and then it crashed back into the dark pit.

"Sorry, sorry. Too soon for jokes, I see." Mareth held her shoulders and looked her in the eyes. "Serious now. You're in this with me; we're all in this together, win or lose. Alright?"

"Alright." She sniffed again, hands moving to wipe tears and snot from her face.

"That's good," he said, giving her a brief hug. "Earlier you said we've got to talk about those merchant agreements. We have a few minutes now. Think you can explain it so a five-year-old can understand?"

"Yes. I'll go and fetch my notes. They're back there," she said, gesturing to the adjoining storeroom. She gave a weak smile to Mareth, feelings of relief but also embarrassment creating havoc with her stomach.

Threading her way through the storeroom, squeezing past the stacked chairs, desk, and cabinet, she reached where her leather satchel was hidden. The bag had been given to her by Jules in a quiet moment, a thing of shiny brown leather that gave off the unmistakable aroma of quality hide. It was the dearest thing in the whole world to her.

From this end of the storeroom, she could hear the crowd on the streets outside. They were still a few minutes' walk from the marketplace, but the crowds spilled out this far. They'd chosen to use Gonal's building to prep for the rally because it was closer to the marketplace than the Royal Oak, but if the crowds were shoulder-to-shoulder here, then it was really going to take Mareth some time to fight his way through to the makeshift stage they had erected.

She found the satchel and tucked it under her arm. She was about to call out to Mareth to tell him he'd better leave early when she heard him and another voice talking.

"...awfully large crowd out there. That's the kind of crowd where, if they don't like the show, they can tear you limb from limb." Mareth's voice. But who was he talking to?

"You don't need to worry. They'll love you, and they'll be chanting your name. And just think how those nobles will feel afterward. They're going to be scared, Mareth, scared of you with a city at your back." It took a moment for Alana to work out who was talking, as it was little more than a heavy whisper. Then it came to her. It was Lady Grey. Alana quietly crept past the furniture to the doorway of the office.

"That's a big ask, my lady. Two things most of the people in this city know for good or ill: don't get ideas above your station, and don't trust anyone when it comes to coin. I've got to convince them to forget both of those pearls of wisdom they learnt from their granny."

Alana peaked around the door and saw Mareth take a deep breath and exhale, tension evident in his stance. Lady Grey, dressed head to foot in black, took a half-step closer to

Mareth and rested her hand on his arm. They were only inches apart.

"You will be fabulous. You look like a hero. Your words will win them over," she breathed. Her hand moved up from his arm to touch his face with the backs of her fingers. "Your smile will entrance them." Alana could see their eyes locked together. Mareth didn't move as her face moved closer to his. "I think I know how to help you relax..." His mouth opened, to receive hers or to protest, Alana did not know, but it woke her into action.

Why hadn't she announced herself before? Alana cleared her throat and stepped into the office, Mareth and Lady Grey instantly both taking a step away from each other, Mareth echoing Alana's coughing.

"Alana, I didn't see you there," said Lady Grey, not appearing in the least bit flustered. Far from it. Alana sensed a look of challenge in her eyes.

"Oh, good evening, my lady. Yes, I was just working in there," said Alana, gesturing to the storeroom. "Mareth, I think it's going to take you longer to get to the stage because of the crowd. We should probably leave."

"Aye," said Mareth, looking a little flushed and slightly relieved at the interruption. He retrieved his mandolin from the corner of the room and fastened his rapier around his waist. "Let's get this over with."

IT WAS PAST MIDNIGHT, BUT THE ATMOSPHERE IN THE Royal Oak was congratulatory. Alana floated around the common room with a cup of wine in her hand, disbelieving what had transpired.

It had taken so long for Mareth to reach the stage that the district supervisors had decided to warm up the crowd and attract their attention as they got restless. Minstrels had taken to the stage as well, to sing songs, many of them Mareth's creations, and so, by the time he'd reached the platform, hundreds, if not thousands, of people were singing *Tin Man*.

That had been Petra's doing. Thinking on their toes must run in the family. In fact, growing up in the Narrows, if people couldn't think on their toes, then they were likely to end up in a box. Her sister had surprised her with what she'd been capable of these past few weeks.

Mareth had climbed the stage, and the crowd had become so quiet one could hear the inquiring questions of young children to their parents of, "Who is he?" Alana couldn't remember how long Mareth spoke, but it was mesmerizing, watching the people of Kingshold lap it up like the cat that got the cream.

And when he sang *Edlander's Choice*, she saw the tears in the eyes of the people at the front, and then like a wave moving to the back of the throng the chant of, *"We choose you. We choose you,"* rose into the warm summer night.

She looked over at Mareth, an arm around her sister's waist, and a mug of ale in the other hand, the silliest grin she'd ever seen plastered on his face. She supposed that's how she looked, too.

The inn was closed to the paying public now, except for some longer-term tenants, and some of Lady Grey's house guard was now stationed there. But she knew all of the volunteers and district supervisors who'd come back to celebrate, and they all seemed caught by the events of the evening.

By the bar, she could see Jules and Lady Grey deep in conversation, the owner of the inn nodding before the noblewoman left her and walked to the door to the back room. Alana watched Jules move around the room, exchanging a few words with Mareth and Petra, Dolph and Folstencroft before walking over to her.

"Alana, let's meet before everyone celebrates too hard. Backroom," said Jules. Alana nodded and followed her. The select few filed into the room and sat at the table where Lady Grey was waiting at the head. Dolph remained standing at the doorway, which he closed behind them.

Lady Grey looked at everyone around the table in turn before she, too, smiled a broad smile. "Well done, everyone. I think we can say that was a marvelous success. Mareth, you were inspiring; everyone in the city will have taken note now." Lady Grey bowed her head to the bard, who was holding hands with Petra under the table. "And Folstencroft, well planned. Excellent work."

"Actually, my lady," interjected Jules, "It was Alana who was responsible for tonight. It was her idea, her plan. We all did the jobs she assigned." Petra and Mareth nodded their agreement, and even Folstencroft, looking sheepish, signaled his concurrence.

Lady Grey looked at Alana. She could feel the gaze assessing her, which brought on a hard-to-contain need to squirm. It took all of her will to match her gaze and ignore the years of conditioning of avoiding looking one of her betters in the eye.

"Well, Alana, you're a constant source of surprises," said Lady Grey. "Nicely done. I assume the wizard is fully aware you're wasted at the palace?"

"I can't answer that, my lady," she said.

"Or you choose not to. Very smart." The others around the table looked at the two of them as they spoke; Mareth, though still smiling, was considering the situation closely. "Well, as I said, nicely done to all. I'm sure there's much to do tomorrow, so celebrate, but not too much. I will return home now."

"Lady Grey," said Mareth, "before you leave. I wonder, can we find time to talk tomorrow?" Mareth's eyes flickered to Alana, and she saw Lady Grey notice it. "I have been reviewing the agreements with the merchants and I have some concerns."

Lady Grey looked at Alana as she spoke. "Oh? And what kind of concerns are those?"

"Some of the agreements seem to be quite outrageous concerning what's promised," continued Mareth, "and others contradict each other. The same thing pledged more than once. I'd like your counsel as to how it would work in practice."

"Yes, yes," said Lady Grey, her attention returning to Mareth. "These are significant details we need to work through. Let's talk tomorrow." She slid back her chair and stood. "For now, you should celebrate what you've achieved so far. But remember, we haven't won anything yet. In fact, things only start to get interesting from here."

CHAPTER 30
JUGGERNAUT

The morning had been spent trying to work out a plan for how to stop the child of the forger and his gang of troublemakers. Of course, the trouble was doing so without killing them. That would have made life much easier, but then, the dwarves would probably have been able to handle that pretty well themselves.

Motega couldn't fault the hospitality of the deep people. He and his friends had slept well on comfortable beds (even if they were a little on the short side) in guest quarters at the Smelter, usually reserved for visiting dignitaries. Breakfast had been hearty, if a bit different from what they were used to, but he could go to his grave knowing giant centipede bacon was actually quite tasty.

Now, the priority was to obtain as much information as they could. Motega loved the adrenaline thrill of being in a fast-moving situation, but not having a well-researched plan was likely to leave him dead or waiting in line for the gallows, and so, he'd learnt to value the preparation.

They'd spent a considerable amount of time talking to

the forger over dinner the previous evening and now Captain Karken of the guard had been made available to them. The captain was a woman, slightly taller than the forger, and her brown hair was devoid of grey. She had a plain, broad face and, contrary to myths, she didn't have any facial hair. But she did have a sparkle in her eyes as she engaged in the planning discussions with her new comrades.

Captain Karken explained how the raids tended to follow the same approach. Without warning, the Juggernaut would charge into the city, sending guards and civilians alike scattering, upending carts, clearing barricades, and even damaging buildings with its immense strength as it moved through the city to the storage depots. Its purpose was always to create a diversion and engage any defense so a second wave of young dwarves could gather supplies into sacks.

Of course, the guards were trying not to hurt any of the youngsters, so they didn't use their highly effective crossbows. A fact which also allowed the third element of the raids to be mainly untroubled. Half of the Graks would hold the tunnel from where they came, using rocks and sometimes even crossbows to keep any city defenders at bay. The raids typically were quick—half an hour for them to come in and get out—so there wouldn't be a lot of time to respond.

The germ of a plan had come to Motega a little earlier, and he'd just finished explaining it to Captain Karken. Neenahwi, Florian, and Trypp followed along, though they'd already been through it. The captain nodded as she listened.

"Now, we need to go and see these locations to see if this is going to work," Motega said, pointing at two places on a map of the city rolled out before him. "If they aren't suitable, these places are other options I want us to consider. Captain, can you have someone take Florian and Trypp to do reconnaissance?"

"Yes, of course. Should we start on the defenses now?" asked the dwarf.

"Better to wait until after I've seen the ground and determine if we have good positions," said Florian. "No need to move big blocks of stone around more than necessary."

"The other thing concerning me right now is that we don't know how much time we have to get ready," said Motega. "Can you think, please, Captain? How often do these raids happen?"

"I gave this some thought earlier," she said. "It's not reliable. The gap between raids has been as short as six days and as long as nine, and they've been at various times of the day. It's been six days already since the last raid—"

"So, it could happen at any moment," interjected Trypp. "And if we're not ready, then we'll have to wait for the next time. Or try something much riskier, as I think we'd run out of time."

"I don't think the forger will countenance risky, Mr. Trypp," said the captain.

"Me neither," said Motega. "So, let's get going, and we can all keep our fingers crossed they've been rationing, and we have enough time to get ready."

WHEN CAPTAIN KARKEN HAD SAID ANY TIME OF THE DAY, it had taken a while for Motega to realize she really had meant any time at all.

There was no night in Unedar Halt. No natural light infiltrated the caverns; there was just the same steady light given off by the plants lining the walls, or the lanterns posted in various places lit by unknown and potentially magical means. The same light no matter how many hours had passed since breakfast.

Florian had reported back confirming the chosen areas for the ambush, and so, they'd immediately set to work on the preparations. Florian's view was the small square with bare earth by the food silos would be big enough for them to maneuver when they would engage the magical statue.

The entranceway to the caves used by the rebels wasn't ideal, as they'd have a reliable place to defend if they were organized, but there were sufficient places for a few individuals to hide. For that element of the plan, they were just going to have to depend on surprise and the rebels' naivety.

Motega, Florian, and Trypp knew each other so well they hardly needed to discuss their roles, but they did so Neenahwi would understand the plan. Trypp already had food and water gathered in a bag when they met, a pillow under his arm; he set out for his assignment as soon as they'd finished talking. Florian went to work with the dwarven team who would help build the barricades, leaving Motega to discuss with his sister what she could do.

"What are you going to do?" she asked.

"I'm going to walk the route a few times, look for ways out we haven't considered, so we can head them off. And then I'll be barricading, too."

"Well, I can build barricades. Probably quicker than you can, little brother," said Neenahwi.

"Ha-ha. I'd like to see it. You've been reading books too long; you've gone a bit soft." He squeezed her upper arm, and she punched him in the chest. "Oof, still good technique though. Ten crowns says I do more."

"Deal." And they spat and shook on it.

Motega worked the square they'd chosen, Neenahwi joining Florian back at the entrance to the city where they would create the run.

Dwarven teams of four hauled perfectly cut stone blocks on wheeled buggies to where they stacked them chest high across each of the exits from the square, leaving just one entrance open. It was backbreaking work. Each stone took two to carry it and put it into position, but they needed stone because the Juggernaut would cut through wood like a hot knife through butter.

Motega worked through the day, taking lunch with the team working alongside him, getting to know the everyday people of this city. In one of the teams was a mother of a Grak, and she was worried about what would happen to him if they couldn't stop them soon. She was a dwarf, but she was just like any other mother Motega had met when their son had gone off to war or was on the run from the guard. He'd hardly known his mother, and she was long past being around to care, but if she had been, he expected she wouldn't be too relaxed about the situations he got into either.

As dinnertime approached, Motega's team had finished barricading the square, and so, they walked to see how they could help Florian's team with their work. After all, the run was much longer than what they had to do.

Except they passed barricade after barricade. The road twisted to the left, and the streets there were all barricaded. Turned to the right and more barricades still. Barricades, and then Florian and a gaggle of dwarves sitting with their backs to a wall and a mug in each of their hands.

"Motty! Where have you been?" asked Florian, beer froth on his upper lip.

Motega stopped and looked at him, eyes narrowing to slits, hands on hips. "We've been working. How did you get done so quick?"

"Your sister. Did she say something about a bet? We fetched the stones on the buggies, and then she stacked them all. Super quick."

"She stacked them? How?" Motega asked incredulously.

Florian wiggled his fingers in the air. "Magic. She's over there resting." He hooked a thumb over his shoulder, and Motega saw his sister meditating in a secluded corner. "She told me to tell you she won."

"She cheated!" Motega cried indignantly.

"Well, I'm not going to tell her that. Come and sit down and have a drink." Motega walked over next to Florian and slid down the wall until he was seated. "Now, we have to wait."

And wait they did.

And there was nothing like waiting to make him notice the things that might have passed him by if he was busy, like the constant light of the city, the lack of shadows.

They'd been underground many times in the past, a few jobs had required investigating catacombs or strange subterranean mazes to retrieve specific items, but they were universally dark, lit only by the lanterns they brought with them. Nothing like fighting off giant spiders by the light of a couple of shuttered oil lamps to give them night terrors for a few weeks afterward.

Those adventures underground had thrilled Motega, especially in hindsight. Constant danger required constant vigilance. This particular experience was more a glacial pace.

Hours passed, and the dwarven teams went home to their families. The ale stopped. After all, they needed to have their wits about them, and Neenahwi still meditated. As best as they could fathom, night arrived, and so, they slept close to the trap they'd built.

False day followed false night. Gambling debts were settled. Instructions were passed on to new dwarven guards arriving for their shift. Weapons were cared for. And false night followed false day.

And the constant light was still taking some getting used to.

MOTEGA WOKE WHERE HE'D BEEN SLEEPING, A SIMPLE CAMP roll behind one of the walls they had built in the square. All was quiet, but he could sense they were coming. Even with Per remaining above ground, his senses were tuned to imminent trouble.

He stood and stretched out the kinks in his shoulders and back from the hard, stone floor, the city quiet without the noises of crafting from the workshops. Then there was a sound, a shout from the direction of the entrance to the city where they knew the rebels would come from.

He gave a snoring Florian a kick with his boot and said, "It's time."

Motega climbed up to the flat roof of the squat stone building next to him and scampered across neighboring rooftops to get a view of the run they'd created as more cries went up and a steady *thum, thum, thum* reverberated through the streets.

Noises of wood splintering and stone smashing against stone came to his ears. He squinted to be able to get a better view down the street, his distance vision blurry from the curse he'd received as a child, but he made out the figures of the dwarven guards falling back in line with the plan.

In front of them was something huge. He couldn't make out the details of it at this distance, but its feet moved in time to the *thum, thum, thum*.

It picked up speed and charged the dwarven guards, sending two flying into the wall opposite. Behind the Juggernaut, because that was what this must be, he saw a dozen dwarves slowly following, keeping their distance. They would reach the square in minutes.

Motega ran back the way he'd come and climbed down into the mouth of their trap. Florian was there waiting, twin swords drawn and a smile visible beneath the helm he'd obtained from somewhere. Ten guards stood with him, war hammers in hand.

Motega pulled his war axes from their holsters and saluted his comrades as the remaining dwarven guards from the street rushed into the square and formed a second line. Six left, so another six were likely destined for the infirmary. He heard a whistle and saw his sister standing on the roof of the building opposite, hidden from view of anyone outside the square. She gave a ready signal.

The Juggernaut was a second behind the dwarves, stopping in the entryway to the square as it surveyed the closed-off route to the grain silos and the troops arrayed before it, Motega positioned in the middle front.

He could see it clearly now. The Juggernaut was a stone statue of a dwarf come to life. It stood twice as tall as Motega and was the same width again. Carved from one piece of stone, a dwarven warrior in full plate armor, gauntlets and a helm with thin slits for the eyes where two green lights shone. It was a thing of beauty, delicate details etched into the armor, carved chainmail between stone plates flowing like fabric. And though it didn't wield a weapon, the clenched gauntleted fists were as big as wine casks.

Motega scanned the Juggernaut, looking for weaknesses and finding none.

And then it charged.

MOTEGA SAT CROSS-LEGGED ON THE STONE IN THE CENTER of the circle, pink skies overhead, the fake-land silent as ever, empty except for the scarred man standing in front of him. His father had come through the grasses as the ravaged wolf, but this time he was unaccompanied. This night there were no more of his tribe's ancestors.

"Where are grandfather and the others today?" asked Motega.

"They hunt," said his father. "Winter is coming, the Bhiferg pass through the planes, and so, they hunt."

The world around Motega shimmered and changed, the grassy circle giving way to a hilltop overlooking green plains under a blue sky, but Motega and his stone seat remained constant. On the planes below him, he could see a herd of Bhiferg, a hundred head or more of the grazing beasts.

In between him and the herd were human forms. The Bhiferg were large, at least four times larger than the cattle he'd seen in the fields of Edland. Motega had never seen the Bhiferg in person, but he dimly remembered how the preparations for the hunt, and then the inevitable work afterward, would consume the attention of the tribe for weeks.

"This is the annual hunt of the Bhiferg," said his father.

"This herd travels through our lands once a year, as they have done for centuries, moving from east to west in autumn, and then west to east in the spring. They travel thousands of miles, always moving to new grass. We are blessed for them to come before winter. The hide makes our armor, and it makes our houses, and the meat we kill today is dried and salted and feeds us when there is little to hunt, and nothing grows from the fields.

"But we must be careful to think of the future, even though we hunt this herd, we are stewards of their wellbeing. So, we only hunt before winter. In spring we leave them be, for if we hunt too much, then there will be nothing left for next year or for other tribes that live in this world. We are also selective, for there is but one bull for this whole herd and if we kill it, then the herd will die out. Come, let us move closer to look at them. Your eyes are not damaged here, but it is still difficult to clearly see."

Motega stood and followed his father down the hill and through the knee-high grasses to where a group of his people stood. One figure was unmistakably his grandfather, though he was a young man and did not look at their approach. Motega called, "*Ho,*" in greeting, but no one turned.

"They cannot see you, Motega. This is but a remembrance of what happened in days gone by. My memory of when I was a child. See there..." Motega's father raised a scarred hand to point at a boy of teenage years looking intently at his grandfather as he talked to the hunting party. "That is me." And Motega could see the resemblance immediately, the shrewd eyes and leaner build than many of his people, but with strength in the wiry muscles.

Motega looked around at the shadows of his tribe. He

could see the anticipation and excitement on their faces, he could see the muscles flexing ready for the hunt.

So that's where he got it from.

He turned his attention back to the herd. Now that he was closer, he could see them more clearly, and he'd been wrong in his initial impressions. They were much more significant than he'd initially thought. Each cow stood twice as high as one of the hunters, and they were twice as long as they were high from snout to tail. They were powerfully built; massive legs, thick necks, and covered in black fur of some kind. He scanned the herd, and his eyes rested on an even bigger creature, half the size again of the cows with wicked-looking horns as long as any spear held by the hunters, covered with shiny chitinous plates.

"That is the bull," his father said, seeing where Motega was looking. "The bull is the strongest and is fiercely protective of the herd. He will attack the hunters if they attack his family."

"So how do you get to hunt if the bull attacks, but you can't kill it?" asked Motega.

His father smiled. "We dance! Look, they are heading out to hunt. See how your grandfather is moving directly toward the bull. He is the dancer. The others will move into position, but not strike until he has the bull's attention. Observe and learn, Motega."

His grandfather walked purposefully across the grasslands, circling the herd to come at the bull face on. He was wearing light leather armor, itself made of Bhiferg hide, and he held a wooden club in each hand, each no longer than bicep to hand.

Stopping fifty strides from the bull and assuming a ready position on the balls of his feet, his grandfather struck the clubs together in rapid succession, causing all of the herd, including the bull, to stop grazing and look at him. From a pocket at his belt, he drew a fist-sized rock and threw it at the bull's head, striking it above the eye.

It blasted a note of anger and charged.

His grandfather did not move as the beast lowered its head, horns catching the light as it quickly closed the gap. Motega held his breath, certain this was how his grandfather had died; this was the lesson he was supposed to learn.

The beast was an arm's length away when his grandfather leaped to one side, an arm flinging out to strike the bull around the snout before he tucked into a roll and came to his feet. The bull charged past, skidding to a halt, turning to go around at its attacker once more.

This time, it moved forward more deliberately and inexorably, head swaying causing the sharp horns to weave in the air much like Florian would achieve with his blades. His grandfather circled the bull, and then he let out a howl and charged the beast. Darting one way, and then another, he stepped inside the horns and struck the creature twice about the face.

Its mouth opened to bite at him, and Motega saw large front fangs appear, as long as knives that must surely retract for grazing. His grandfather dodged the open maw, planting one hand on the base of a horn and using it to flip over and above the beast. Motega noted the clubs had leather ties about their handles enabling the dancer to release the weapons and use his hands for evasion.

From the corner of his eye, he could see the others in the hunting party had now closed in on a handful of cows and were attempting to take them down with spears. The rest of the herd ran away, kicking up high clouds of dirt and dust, but three were encircled.

The bull had turned to where his grandfather had vaulted, but he was already gone, running around the back of the beast, striking at areas of the flank not protected by the plate-like armor on the way. The clubs beating on the side of the creature sounded like drums, and they were joined by bellows of frustration from the beast.

It tried to turn faster, but his grandfather had already grabbed the bull's tail and used it to haul himself up onto its back. Though it twisted and turned, he ran along its spine, as sure-footed as on land, until he reached the massive neck. He clamped his thick, strong thighs around the neck, dug his heels in under the plates protecting the shoulder, and proceeded to beat the bull rapidly around the back of the head. Motega could tell he was causing no lasting damage to the beast, but it was sure going to have a headache when this was done. It tried to rear up and buck him off, but it was no wild horse. Its weight that made it so formidable worked against tossing its new passenger.

One cow went down, and then another, moaning, deep mournful noises as the life fled them from the many spear wounds. The bull turned once more, and Motega could swear it was looking at its sisters and daughters dying.

It bellowed again, a voice of farewell, and then it ran after the herd making for the horizon, his grandfather still beating it on the head and shoulders as its hooves thundered across the plains. His grandfather grew smaller as they moved further away, but he could still make him out as he stood on its back, arms raised and loosing a triumphant howl of his own before somersaulting off the beast.

Motega realized his father was looking at him, and so,

switched his attention. His father rested a palm against his cheek and said, "Remember, Motega, the dance is in you."

THE JUGGERNAUT CHARGED, ARMS AS BIG AS PILLARS raised above its head ready to squish the bug in front of it.

The dance is in you, his father had said.

When he had that dream, on board the ship carrying them to Kingshold, it had faded from his memory the next day. While developing the plan for how they were going to deal with this magical construct, he had reassured everyone he'd be able to keep it occupied, but he hadn't known why he'd said it. Now, as the giant stone dwarf charged, he remembered the dream entirely.

He could dance.

It was faster than he had thought it would be, hands crashing down toward him before he was completely ready. He threw himself out of the way, landing on his side and knocking the wind from his lungs. He wasn't going to have as many style points as his grandfather so far.

He scrambled to his feet as another hand came crashing down where he had just been. Instead of moving away from it, he closed inside and leaped, smashing his axes against the stone helm before darting away and behind. Now, the Bhiferg didn't have arms longer than a poleaxe that could flatten him with a single blow, so that was a mark against Motega's chances, but then again, his grandfather didn't have the kind of help he did.

On the roof above the square was Neenahwi, arms outstretched, conducting unseen music. Her focus was unflinching, and Motega could see and sense her work. The light from the cavern ceiling dimmed. The humid underground air became dry and easier to breathe. And under the Juggernaut's feet, the dirt began to turn to mud.

Motega ran headlong at the construct, dodging to the right, and then the left to avoid concussive blows, before peeling away and behind it. He noticed the stone dwarf's head followed him as he moved.

The pilot must have to use those green stone eyes to see!

He circled the Juggernaut at speed. Its feet moved much slower in a circle than in a straight line, especially as the mud beneath its feet grew deeper. Motega switched direction, jumping over a leading arm that spun around, before leaping toward the Juggernaut, ax striking over his head to hit one of the stone eyes and causing it to crack.

The follow-through of his blow carried him into the Juggernaut, and he hit with a thud before bouncing down into the mud, his legs instantly sinking. The stone dwarf had to turn so its good eye could see Motega, and as soon as it saw him wallowing, a hand swatted down. Motega tried to throw himself clear, but his right boot was caught in the mud. The hand caught him a glancing blow, strong enough to send him flying across the square, leaving his boot behind.

His shoulder hurt like hell. It might have been dislocated, but the adrenaline was pumping. Around him, Florian was fighting regular-sized flesh and blood dwarves. Motega saw one go down from a blow with the flat of his blade, but he didn't seem to be getting much help from the dwarven guard. Their hearts weren't in it. They weren't losing ground, but they weren't pushing the attack either.

Motega couldn't give it more than a moment's consideration, though. The Juggernaut was trying to extricate itself from the mud, one foot on the solid ground as it attempted to lever itself out from what was now a thick quagmire. Motega ran forward, jumping up onto the stone knee and scrambling up to sit astride its shoulders. He rained blows on the stone helm of the Juggernaut, not sure if it caused any real distraction or damage other than the small shards of stone sent flying in the air, but it sure did make him feel better.

The arms of the Juggernaut couldn't reach up and over its head, the carved armor and its intimidating vambraces restricting its movement. From his perch, he could see few of the rebels still standing. A few more crumpled bodies lay at Florian's feet, but others had fallen, too. Had the guard finally decided to take the fight to them?

The construct lurched around, and Motega saw another rebel slump slowly to the floor, and then he realized his sister was taking care of what Florian couldn't handle, putting them gently to sleep.

The pilot of the giant stone dwarf suddenly realized its comrades were falling, and it stopped trying to dislodge Motega. Once more, it began to lift itself from the mud pit, ignoring the pounding about its head until it had regained a solid footing. Then it backed up to the wall of a neighboring building, and Motega realized he was going to be caught like wheat at the mill, so he jumped off the Juggernaut's back and rolled to his feet near Florian.

The Juggernaut took one step toward them, and another, but it didn't charge.

It reached down and picked up one unconscious dwarf and draped it over a stone shoulder like a sash before picking up two more prone figures, one in each hand. Then it turned, and half ran, half lumbered back the way it came.

"It's getting away," exclaimed Motega. "Trypp needs more time!"

Motega dashed after it. Though it had a head start, it wasn't moving at full speed in its encumbered state, so, slowly, Motega was able to close on it. His arms pumped as he ran, his shoulder burning like a hot poker driven into his armpit. Ahead of him he could see the long road ending at the entranceway to the tunnel.

There was a face-off, another dozen rebel dwarfs armed with crossbows staring down city guard, taking cover behind the defenses they'd built yesterday. Motega was within two horse lengths of the fleeing Juggernaut when he ran up a stepped wall onto the flat roof of a single-story building.

He knew that if the stone dwarf made it back to the entrance, then their plan was going to fail, and Trypp would be in grave danger. He jumped from one building to another, coming almost alongside the Juggernaut before he leaped off the roof and drove both feet into the back of the stone dwarf's helmet. Once more, Motega bounced off what was effectively a walking wall, his legs jarring with the impact against the statue, and his teeth biting into his cheek with the impact as he hit the floor. But the Juggernaut was off balance, and it fell face first, sending the dwarves it carried skittering across the pavement.

The Juggernaut moved its arms underneath it and lifted its immense weight to a kneeling position. Its head turned, good eye looking at Motega less than an arm's span away from it.

Motega's head swam. There seemed to be two giant stone dwarfs. Both of them raised an arm as if to strike. The images coalesced into one, but it was too late as a clenched fist flew toward his face. Motega faced what was coming to him with open eyes, ready to see his father again, when the bright green light in the eyes of the Juggernaut flickered and went dead. The statue went immediately immobile, freezing in position, stone fist close enough to Motega for him to see the seams of the rock.

"Nice timing, Trypp," he muttered, and then collapsed onto his back.

CHAPTER 31
ASSASSIN IN THE NIGHT

"Can I tell you something?"

"Of course." Petra's words were slow and drawn out. It was the middle of the night, and Mareth had been unable to sleep, even after their lovemaking. Petra was beginning to drift off though when he felt the need, the urgent, burning need to confide in her.

"And whatever I tell you, you won't think less of me?" he asked.

This got her attention, and she lifted herself up onto her elbow and tried to shake the sleep out of her brain as she pulled the sheets up to her neck. "Of course, Mareth, what is it?"

"I don't know what I'm doing. This whole election, I have no idea how to win or what to do. I'm just doing what I always do and using the *charm* to say what people want to hear."

"That's not true, darling," she said. "You know life isn't fair; you've seen that for a long time. And now you want to do something about it."

"But what do I do about it? I have no idea how to run a country. What would it be like if I was lord protector?"

"Shush, it's normal to be nervous about doing something new. Were you nervous the first time you performed? The first time you were in a battle?"

"I was shit scared each of those times!" said Mareth, throwing his hands up in the air.

She smiled. "But you were brave each time. Being scared and brave is the best combination from what I've seen. I've seen people who don't get scared, and they're typically not too bright. Most of them are dead now, too, because they didn't know better."

"It's probably not going to matter, anyway, because I'm not going to win."

"Hah! Scared of winning, but you'd hate to lose?" she laughed. "Don't count yourself out of it, Mareth. I've never seen anything like the rally yesterday—there were thousands of people calling your name—except on royal feast days, and normally it's because there's free ale. Those people were doing it because they're starting to believe in what you represent. In all of us."

Mareth sat with his back to the headboard, remembering how it had felt to see all of those people. By Arloth, he'd been scared. It was the kind of crowd he'd always dreamed of performing in front of, but these were a different kind of tale he was telling now. Petra took his silence as needing more encouragement.

"And the meetings went well with the guilds I saw today. They're all very reasonable old men, you know," she said.

"Maybe to you."

"Yes, maybe to me," she conceded, "but their grievances

seem reasonable. They want to be heard, too. Though I might not understand all of the details."

"And that's it!" he exclaimed, throwing his hands in the air again. "I can't even keep these deals straight. If it weren't for Alana, I wouldn't know what was happening. Some of the deals just don't even make sense. If I do win, then there will be some unhappy people who don't get what they were expecting." He shook his head. "You know Alana is a godsend. Like you. Why was I so lucky to have Alana and you sent to me?"

"Because you're a good man, Mareth. Even if you're less handsome now that the beard's gone." She dug her elbow into his ribs at the joke.

"Have you spoken to Alana recently?" asked Mareth. He knew he was also not sleeping well because he felt terrible for what had nearly happened with Lady Grey before the rally. What had he been thinking? Had he even been thinking? He'd been lost in his nerves and then... she was there. He hadn't felt attracted to her before. Well, he might have in the past, but why would he now when he had Petra? Someone smart, beautiful and caring, and best of all, she pushed him. He hadn't had anybody like that before.

At least Alana had been there to stop anything wrong from happening.

"We spoke today about the guilds, and also about Danley in Bottom Run," she said. "We've heard he's not well-trusted by many of the people down there. Not with their money, anyway. I think we're going to need to find somebody else to cast a vote for that district. Why do you ask?"

"Oh, it's nothing," he said and quickly changed the subject. "Can you believe what we were doing? You know, all I wanted was to be famous for a so—"

The inn had been quiet, given the hour and Jules's restrictions on the number of guests and customers. In fact, the common room wasn't open to the public at all now, and only a handful of guests were staying overnight, all in the opposite wing of the inn. But from the corridor outside, Mareth could hear a commotion.

"I just want to get to my room!" slurred an unknown voice.

"It's not here, sir. Must be on the other side. Turn around," said one of Lady Grey's guards stationed outside his room. Just one of the security enhancements that had been forced on him. More guards than just Dolph, and a bedchamber with bars on the windows. Not a lot of freedom for this songbird, but it would be over soon.

"Get out of my way! I's down at the end of the corridor." It seemed the guest must've had a glass or two too many.

"What's going on out here?" Mareth heard Alana's voice, the commotion waking her. She was still getting up at the crack of dawn to go to the palace and attend to the wizard. Her few hours of sleep were precious to her.

"I should go and see what's happening; maybe I can help," Mareth said to Petra.

"No. Stay here. They can handle it."

"It's fine. I want to help Alana."

Mareth got out of bed and pulled on his trousers. Opening the door to the corridor, he saw one of the guards talking to a man, well-dressed though looking a little worse for wear. He was clean shaven and of medium height and build, and the wall seemed essential in keeping him vertical. The inebriated fellow struck a chord with Mareth. It all seemed quite familiar to him. Alana was standing outside her bedroom door dressed in a nightgown with hands on hips.

"Look here, sir," said Mareth, "I'm sure there's something we can do to help you. Let the man take you to your rooms."

The drunk man turned to face him, and his eyes narrowed. Time seemed to slow as Mareth saw him stand up straight, no longer leaning on the wall for support, and his hands moved under his coat. There was a glint of steel from the reflected lamplight on two long wicked sharp knives suddenly held in the drunk's hands.

The guard didn't stand a chance, the drunk moved forward in a flash. Punching the guard in the face with the butt of one knife, and then ramming the point of the other up and under his ribs. Blood bubbled at the corners of the guard's mouth, hands stopping as they sought his blade before he slumped to the floor between Mareth and the assassin.

Alana screamed.

The drunk moved his complete attention to Mareth, no sign of any inebriation in the way he acted or moved now. Mareth scrambled back into his room, his sword was still in the sheath, hanging on a chair in the corner of the room. Not old Betsy but the stupid rapier he was supposed to wear now. It struck him that he hadn't exactly had the time to practice with it, and if he got through this, it would probably be a good idea to stop making excuses and get started.

Mareth managed to slam the door into the drunk's face as he ducked back into the room, buying him the seconds to reach the blade. The drunk burst into the room, malice in his eyes as the rapier came free from the hilt with a hiss.

This was not like the stories though. The assassin wasn't going to deliver a message about how Lord So-and-so wished he could see the look in Mareth's eyes before dealing the deadly blow. No, the drunk was all business and no talking.

One, two, three steps, and the assassin closed the ground between them, right hand slashing high into Mareth's face. He parried in time, but the left came toward his stomach, which he had to twist out of the way to avoid. The blows came right, left, right, right. Mareth hadn't the chance to draw his parrying dagger, and so, only armed with the rapier, and in close quarters, Mareth was at a clear disadvantage. And that was before taking into account their comparative skill.

Mareth had always prided himself on being an adequate swordsman, at least with his old sword. The rapier was a different matter, though. All about sticking with the pointy tip. Not having the weight or being able to slash like he could with Betsy. But he just about held his own, parrying killing blows, but he took cuts to the face, to the forearms, another one to his leg, and all in less than a minute from when the drunk had first attacked. He knew he wouldn't be able to keep the defense up. The assassin was too good and would eventually get through.

So, Mareth tried to drive him back.

Attack with the pointy end. Give him something to think about. Pushing off his front foot, Mareth feinted toward the assassin's gut, and then switched to thrust the rapier toward his eye. The assassin parried the attack easily, catching Mareth's blade on the guard of one knife, and then trapping the rapier, sandwiching it with the other knife. The drunk twisted both blades at once, and the rapier was torn out of Mareth's grasp. A kick to Mareth's stomach doubled him over, and another to his face sent him sprawling to the floor.

He knew then, that was the end. Another minor obstacle eliminated. A footnote to history before the grand regime of Lord Protector Eden.

The formerly drunk assassin smiled as he raised the knife to strike, but then something or someone grabbed hold of his arm. The assassins other arm lashed out, knife still in hand, and the distraction was disposed of.

Mareth saw him prepare to strike once more when a roar came from the doorway. A naked man, broadsword raised, charged into the bedroom.

The assassin turned, but too late as the sword swept through the air, slicing through the arm and into his neck, almost severing head from shoulders. Blood erupted around the room, covering Mareth in gore to add to what his wounds had bled out. It took a moment for Mareth to realize who had rescued him.

Dolph.

Petra was screaming at the top of her lungs. Mareth thought to try to reassure her he was fine, but he realized she wasn't looking at him. She was standing on the bed and looking at a figure curled on the floor, blood pooling around them. Petra screamed.

He rushed over to the prone figure and saw it was Alana. At first, Mareth thought her throat had been cut, but he could see she was still breathing, though it was quite shallow. She, too, had saved his life.

"She's alive," Mareth shouted. "Quick, give me the bed sheets." The wound was wicked looking, long and deep, but luckily it had cut across her collarbone and not her neck.

But she was still bleeding out. He pressed a ripped bed sheet to the wound to staunch the flow of blood while Petra cradled her sister's head in her lap, tears streaked down her face, a low keen escaping as she rocked back and forth. All of a sudden, there were more guards around them, many voices, but none of them clear to him, the chaos leading to a cacophony he couldn't understand. Then Jules was kneeling beside Petra and Mareth, concern etched on her face. He realized, at that moment, that he, too, was crying. He wouldn't let this girl, who meant so much to Petra, and to him, die for saving him.

"Jules! We need a doctor fast. And a good one."

CHAPTER 32
I PREDICT A RIOT

The massive brass doors opened at a waved command of the old dwarf, and the bright sunlight of the morning began to shine into the faces of the assembled crowd. Neenahwi stood next to the forger—her brother and Florian a couple of steps behind.

Florian was mostly unhurt from the fight of the previous evening, but Motega was showing signs of some stiffness. But at least his head was still on his shoulders.

When he had the bright idea to run after the Juggernaut, Neenahwi had run across the buildings on the opposite side of the street, half wondering what her maniac brother was doing and half wanting to see what help she could provide. But it had all moved so quickly.

She'd hesitated initially because she didn't want to harm the rebels being carried by the Juggernaut, remembering the terms of their agreement with the forger, and then, all of a sudden, the statue had been about to squash Motega before she could do anything. In truth, she'd also felt quite drained from her exertions beforehand, so it was a massive relief when the Juggernaut had stopped with seconds to spare, Trypp succeeding in his mission.

It had taken them and the guards just a few more minutes to subdue the remaining conscious rebels, the fight going out of them once they'd seen the Juggernaut stop in its tracks, and Florian bat a few of the quarrels out of the air as he had approached them, swords in hand.

Trypp had appeared from the tunnel where the rebels had come, dragging an inert dwarf behind him. This one was dressed in robes like others of the priesthood, Trypp pulling him by the feet with the dwarf's head bouncing along the ground, the robes unfortunately gathering up around his chest and exposing his arse.

The tall black man had a big grin on his face, likely enjoying moving around again after more than twenty-four hours waiting in a bolt hole for the attack to occur and for the rebels to go past him in the tunnel. His cue to sneak down to find the ringleader, hoping there wouldn't be any further guards. They had all been lucky the coast had been clear, and the priest was deep in a trance when Trypp closed up behind him and used a handkerchief soaked in chloroform to knock him out.

The dwarves had been joyous to have the situation resolved. Neenahwi had never taken the dwarves for great huggers, but she had more than a few embraces from men and women alike as their sons and daughters were declared safe and sound and locked away in the cells for a while so they could have a good long think about what they'd done.

She had struck while the iron was hot, as the dwarves themselves liked to say, and called the forger to assemble the council and discuss their petition. Twenty clan leaders met with her and the forger, and now twenty clan leaders, fathers and mothers of large families, stood with them at the Mountain Gate to Kingshold.

It hadn't been easy to convince them, even though their gratitude was deep as their mines, but the forger was true to his word and called them to stand together. She wasn't sure whether the forger was supporting them because he'd taken a liking to Mareth, or whether he was doing it because she vouched for him, but at this point, she didn't care.

The gloaming of Unedar Halt gave way to the blazing sun of the surface, and Neenahwi had to shield her eyes as they adjusted. The dwarves all around her wore their spectacles with colored lenses, as was common when they ventured above ground. Those glasses capped off their appearance, adorned as they were in their most beautiful armor and carrying their ceremonial maces and small chests with the required gold. She wondered if the guards were going to buy the explanation of them all having ceremonial maces.

The forger and Neenahwi in the lead, they marched out into the clear ground and across to the guard tower marking the entrance to the palace grounds. Standing on this side of the tower were less than a dozen figures she couldn't make out, the sun was on her face, and they were in the shadow of the tower. She could see a commotion on the top of the tower, calls of alarm and confusion.

As they approached she could make out the figures in the shadows, Mareth, his bodyguard, and Trypp, whom she'd asked to sneak out and send word during the night, accompanied by a handful of guards dressed in the house uniform of Lady Grey. Mareth, flanked by Trypp, walked to meet them in the open space. He didn't look in good shape either. He walked with a limp, favoring his right side, and he had a stitched wound on his chin and above his eye.

"Good morning, Master Forger," Mareth said in greeting as he shook the dwarf's hand. "And Lady Neenahwi, thank you for bringing these fine friends on a wonderful day like today." He was trying to be jovial, but Neenahwi could sense a simmering anger under the facade.

"Lord Bollingsmead," said the forger. "The council listened, and we're here to lend you our support, for good or ill."

"What happened to you, Mareth?" she said.

He shook his head and didn't comment. She looked to Trypp and raised her eyebrows questioningly.

"Probably a conversation for later," said Trypp, "but you're not going to like it. Not one bit of it."

"I think we should be getting along, don't you, Lady Neenahwi?" said Mareth. His bodyguard signaled the other guards to flank the procession from Unedar Halt. She nodded, and they closed the distance to the tower when an order to halt came from a figure running across the nearby palace courtyard.

"What's going on here?" said Captain Grimes. "Who's in charge and who says you can just waltz into the palace? Oh, it's you again," he said to Mareth. "Guards!"

"I would be the one in charge here, Captain," said Neenahwi, stepping in front of the Bard, so she was clearly visible. "These are my guests, and we're going to meet with my father."

"Lady Neenahwi, I didn't see you there," said the grizzled old soldier, softening somewhat. "Of course, you can go and visit your father, but they can't be walking in here all armed up."

"Oh, you're mistaken, Captain," she said with a straight face. "These are not vicious studded metal clubs they carry.

No, they are ceremonial maces. It is a grave insult to ask a clan leader to give up their ceremonial mace."

"Ceremonial. Mace." Grimes gave this some thought. "Right. I actually meant those guards. They'll need to either stay here or leave their weapons at the tower."

"Lord Bollingsmead, I think you can have your men remain here. We'll be quite safe. Captain, you may escort us to my father's apartment."

Neenahwi didn't stop for a response from either of the two men. Things were too complicated for so early in the morning, and she wished to get this over with and have a chance to rest.

From the clatter and sound of boots on gravel, the rest were following behind her as she led the way. Of course, she didn't need Grimes to show her the way to where the wizard lived. She'd spent nearly half her life living in the palace, but having palace guards walking with them would hopefully stop any more unfortunate interruptions.

The palace gardens were beautiful at this time of year, the scent of snapdragons and jasmine filling the air, fountains and bubbling streams calming her nerves.

At least until she walked right past a thin shadow of a man, hair now more grey than black, who had evidently been expecting her to stop. She heard him trot to catch up with her.

"Lord Hoskin, fancy seeing you here," she said.

"Yes, how surprising to see me in the palace, Lady Neenahwi." She noted how his tone had become much more acidic in the past few weeks. Neenahwi sensed the influence of her father rubbing off on this one. "What are you up to?"

"I'm just going to see my father."

"With a score of dwarves in tow? For what purpose?"

"Lord Chancellor, I'm becoming short on patience. That's what happens when I exert myself and don't get enough rest. But I still have more than enough energy to shut you up if need be. If you want answers, then you can follow along and observe, but I have no interest in explaining myself to any who ask."

He gave her a second look, and then stopped to let her walk on ahead. She heard him greeting the forger behind her and was grateful for a few moments of peace before they reached their destination.

She strode into her father's sitting room ahead of the rest of the trailing parade, expecting them to wait to be announced or ushered in. Jyuth was sitting at a table eating breakfast, later than usual.

"Ah, daughter," called Jyuth, "you're back. How did it go?"

She walked over and grabbed a sausage from his plate. Food was a good substitute for sleep or meditation at times like these. "Good," she mumbled between bites, mouth full as she spoke, "I've got some visitors for you."

"Do you now? Haven't even finished breakfast, but I suppose that will have to wait. Breakfast was late, can you believe it?" He looked incredulous. "Place is going to the dogs. No Alana again this morning, either." He rose to his feet and stretched, a few miscellaneous joints cracking as he did so. "Let's go out there and see them."

Neenahwi grabbed a slice of fried black pudding and ate as she walked alongside her father, out into the gardens abutting his residence, to meet the small crowd. Jyuth walked over to the lead dwarf and grasped his hand in both of his.

"Master Forger, it's good to see you."

"Master Jyuth, it's always a pleasure. Though not as pleasurable as visits from your daughter." The dwarf gave a big smile, and the two old men embraced. Jyuth moved to shake hands and greet by name each of the other clan leaders who had accompanied them, and he nodded to Hoskin, Grimes, and Mareth. Neenahwi noticed Motega, Florian, and Trypp standing to one side. Her brother looking as much like a teenage boy in trouble for climbing the wrong trees as he used to when he, too, lived in these apartments and was caught doing exactly that. Jyuth saw him, walked over and took him into a bear hug. The wizard whispered something into her brother's ear she couldn't hear before shaking the hands of each of his friends.

"So now we've got all of the pleasantries out of the way, what's all this?" Jyuth was interrupted by the sight of four men striding across the lawn toward them. "Well, well, it's all go here today. Eden, what are you doing here?"

Mareth visibly prickled as he turned to look at the nobleman walking across the grass like he owned the place already. The bard's hand moved to his blade, but his bodyguard held his arm. Neenahwi began to realize that once she had this situation dealt with, there were probably going to be other messes to address. Was there any chance of retiring with her father, she wondered?

"I'm here to observe what's going on, Lord Jyuth," said Eden, coming to a halt between the dwarves and her father, slightly off to one side. Behind him stood an armored knight, seven feet tall with a long sword strapped to his back. "And I'm ready to put a stop to anything untoward if needed. I almost didn't make it here. The city is even more unruly than usual today."

Hoskin was standing close to her, and she saw him call Grimes over, a look of exasperation on his face, and ask him to have someone find Penshead. It seemed the lord chancellor was having one of those days, too.

"Well, you're free to observe, Eden," said her father, "but I'm the arbiter of fair play in all this. Don't forget it. Now, Master Forger, what has brought you and the council to see me today?"

"Master Jyuth. In line with the proclamation announcing all those living within three leagues of the palace of Kingshold, who own property and are heads of their households, we're here to cast our votes in the election for lord protector." Each of the clan leaders pulled purses from the chests they carried, bulging with coin. "And we all have a thousand gold coins to prove our worth."

"Outrageous!" bellowed Eden. "These are dwarves! They're not part of the realm."

"Now, now, Eden, a man of your age must take care of the balance of his humors. You are going decidedly pink." Her father looked as if he was enjoying riling Eden further. "The rules are clearly laid out as the Master Forger described them. Unedar Halt is definitely within three leagues of the palace, and there's a long history of our people having agreed to common policy around such things as trade and working together in times of war."

Eden looked like he had something stuck in his throat. He fiddled with his buttons to free the top one. "Well, those gold coins are probably not even crowns. Let's see them."

The forger clenched his teeth at the insult and dug into his purse for a wide, gleaming gold coin, as big as the palm of Neenahwi's hand. "These are our gold coins. Pure gold, not mixed with copper. And they're bigger than your crowns. Two of these would be equivalent to ten of yours, but still, we each brought the requisite number."

"See, Eden. Everything is aboveboard," said Jyuth. "Bring me the gold, and you shall have your demons."

Mareth hadn't said a word since Lord Eden had arrived. His eyes flicked between the procession of dwarves handing the chests of gold to Jyuth and the nobleman in front of him.

Soon, her father was twenty thousand gold coins richer. Jyuth gestured in the air and clapped loudly twice, a pointless display of showmanship as far as Neenahwi was concerned, but her father had his ways, and twenty small pink humanoid creatures appeared on the ground in front of each clan leader.

"Take these pyxies with you, and before the solstice, tell them for whom you wish to cast your vote. I can assure you, your vote will be tallied fairly," said the wizard.

The forger looked around at the other clan leaders, many of whom were visibly uncomfortable about being so close to the creatures that Neenahwi thought looked like shaved rats.

"We will not allow any demons, even ones as small as these to enter our halls," said the forger. "We shall vote now." Each dwarf knelt in front of their pixie and said, "Lord Bollingsmead," and the pyxie disappeared in a little puff of acrid smoke.

Now, Mareth smiled. He smiled and limped over to each of the clan leaders, shaking their hands and giving his thanks.

"Two nasty surprises in one day, eh, Lord Eden?" said Mareth. "I'm sure seeing me alive was quite a shock."

"I don't know to what you're referring, but I'd tread lightly if I were you." Eden was close to purple now, and the big knight clanked a half-step forward to stand ahead of his lord.

"Of course, that's what you would say, but you better be ready for the consequences when I win," goaded Mareth, all eyes on him and Eden. The mutual disgust almost tangible.

"Don't kid yourself, lordling. You're still going to lose. Even with your stunted little friends."

~

NEENAHWI, MARETH, AND TRYPP ESCORTED THE DWARVES back to the Mountain Gate and said their goodbyes, thanking them again for their help. Motega and Florian had remained behind to talk with Jyuth.

After seeing Lord Eden firsthand, the dwarves had seemed even more pleased with their decision to throw their lots in with Mareth. The forger was particularly incensed by Eden's parting comment and had to be restrained from going all ceremonial with his mace. Once the doors had clanged shut, Neenahwi stopped Mareth and Trypp from walking directly back to the palace.

"So, tell me what's been happening. What happened to you, Mareth?" she asked

Mareth was still quite tense and wasn't the talkative individual Neenahwi had met recently. The silence stretched to the point where Trypp felt he had to fill it.

"From talking to Jules, it seems like it's been all go the last few days while we were underground. He's apparently the new savior of the common people after the rally the other night," Trypp pointed a thumb at the bard, "and then last night, there was an assassination attempt."

"What? Targeting you, Mareth?"

"Yes. In the dead of night, he came. Apparently, he'd been undercover, staying at the inn for a week. That's how I got these," Mareth said, pointing to the wounds on his face, "and this," rolling up the sleeve on his left arm to show a bandage that seeped blood through the bindings from wrist to elbow. "And I'd be dead if it wasn't for Alana and Dolph."

"Where is Alana?" ask Neenahwi. "My father hasn't seen her this morning."

"She's back at the Royal Oak," said Mareth. "She was gravely injured. She attacked the assassin when he had disarmed me. He tried to cut her throat. She lost a lot of blood, but if the blow had been an inch higher, she'd be dead already. But she's still asleep, and the doctor doesn't know if she will recover."

"Foolish girl. Brave, but foolish," she said. "Take me to her, and I'll see what I can do."

"Wait," interrupted Trypp. "There's more you need to know. Tell her, Mareth."

Mareth again was silent, looking up at the mountain and not meeting either of their gazes.

"I'll say then," said Trypp. "When we were coming up to the palace to meet you, Mareth gave another little speech. He clambered onto a cart near the gate to the Inner Circle and sang a song of how Eden had tried to have him killed to whoever was standing around. A couple of score of people were probably there when he began, and by the time he finished—folks had been coming out of wherever they were—there were a couple of hundred. All baying for blood.

"And here's the weird part. I wanted revenge, too. When he sang, I could feel it. In my bones. In my heart. Like I needed to do something about it. And those people, they all ran when he finished, stopping to tell others. The news will have spread like wildfire, doubling and tripling in the telling."

Neenahwi considered the bard, eyes narrowing. "You

were at the Bard College. Do you know of the song weavers?"

"What's a song weaver?" asked Trypp, looking at Mareth and Neenahwi in turn.

"A song weaver is a bard whose words spin enchantments," she said, not taking her eyes off Mareth, looking for a tell to give him away. "They're rare. Hasn't been one in generations."

Mareth regarded her in return, face impassive. "I don't know what you're talking about."

"Like hell, you don't," she snapped. "You have a responsibility with a gift like that. There's going to be fire tonight if you don't do something about it."

"So, what?" said Mareth, steel in his voice. "Let there be fire. Let the nobles be scared for once. Let them see what it's like to live in fear every day. They deserve it."

CHAPTER 33
A DIFFICULT KNIGHT

Night approached, which only served to draw attention to the lights coming from the city. Kingshold didn't sleep at night. It maybe took a brief nap between the hours of three and four in the morning, but what Hoskin saw wasn't usual behavior. It looked like half of the city was spilling onto the streets. He reflected on the fact that a mob armed with firebrands was probably the situation most rulers least wanted to happen, but took some solace that he wasn't the target of their ire.

Hoskin stood on one section of the palace wall with Captain Grimes and Percival, and from their vantage point, they could see considerable crowds forming in the Upper Circle and moving slowly, inexorably toward Eden's estate.

Eden's guards were prepared. They had already assembled and aligned across the major thoroughfares to his manor house. But what bothered Hoskin most was where was the city guard? These were private soldiers with swords drawn and shields raised, and things were likely to kick off soon. A few burly commoners had already tried their luck to get to the manor, but had their skulls bashed, and for now, the fear of imminent danger for the people closest to the guards was keeping the crowd at bay.

Captain Grimes leaned on the palace wall and stared down at what was occurring, shaking his head and grumbling.

"Captain, Percival," said Hoskin. "Come with me. Let's determine if we can see any signs of the city guard from the other side of the palace."

Hoskin led the way around the top of the battlement, through the upper chamber of the gatehouse, nodding to a guard sergeant who had a slightly worried look on his face. Hoskin shared the same concern. He didn't want any crowd anger to spillover to him and those behind the palace walls.

They exited the gatehouse and onto another stretch of battlements looking southwest, the city falling away down the natural incline to the sea. As they walked, Hoskin could see three figures standing ahead, but it was difficult to make out who they were in the reduced light. They could easily be guards at their stations. Grimes obviously had better eyes, though.

"Lord Chancellor, there's your commander of the city guard," said the captain of the palace guard, disdain dripping from his every pore.

Hoskin quickened his pace, lifted his head, and straightened his back to stand at his full height as he approached the armored knight.

"What the bloody hell are you doing here, Penshead?" asked Hoskin. "I warned you this afternoon this was going to happen. Where's the guard?"

"Ah, Lord Chancellor, I do believe everything's in hand,"

Penshead said. “Why don’t you run back to your library, and I’ll take care of the city?”

“With all due respect, sir, who the fuck do you think you’re talking to?” Hoskin felt his blood boil. “You need to have the guard down there, taking care of this mess, or I’m going to hold you personally accountable.”

“Ha. Do you think I’m scared of you, Hoskin?” The knight turned to face the lord chancellor for the first time, standing at full height to look down on him. “You’re pointless. In days, you’ll be gone. No one who wins is going to keep you around. I know I wouldn’t. Now, the way I see it, it’s Eden who doesn’t know what the fuck he’s doing. Before long, there’s going to be a bunch of dead commoners, and then a whole lot of angry commoners, and it’s going to be his fault.

“Who’s going to want to vote for someone who’s likely to bring an uprising? Or, instead, are they going to want to vote for the brave knight who brought peace at the end of the long night of fighting? I know who I’d choose.”

“Listen, you jumped-up pikeman,” said Hoskin, jabbing his finger into Penshead’s breast plate, “you’ll do what I say, or I’ll replace you.”

“I’d like to see you try. You don’t have the balls,” said Penshead, turning back to look at the mobs in the streets below.

Captain Grimes placed a hand on Hoskin’s arm and turned him to face the way they’d come, before firmly guiding him back to the end of the battlement.

“What are you doing?” said Hoskin through clenched teeth. “Are you turning on me, too?”

“No, m’lord. I’m just going to need some men.” Grimes turned and looked at the guard sergeant they’d previously passed. “Sergeant. I want you back here in three minutes with ten men. And send ten men up to the other end of the battlement, too. Sir Penshead has, how should I put it, temporarily lost his senses. And so, he’s going to spend the night in the dungeon. Because I care about his condition, I want you to know if someone was to try kicking some sense into him, just once or twice, you understand, I think it would be good for his mental health.”

Hoskin smiled. He liked Grimes.

The sergeant rushed down the stairs, and they heard him shouting for troops. The three of them went back out onto the battlement and waited and watched as the score of palace guards seized Sir Penshead and dragged him toward Hoskin.

“Good night, Dickhead,” laughed Hoskin. “It looks like your plan is not going to work out after all.” Hoskin couldn’t remember if he’d ever had more fun.

The knight screamed, and roared, and bellowed as he was led away.

“Grimes, you’re now commander of the city guard, too. What are you going to do about this mess?”

“Well, let me begin, Lord Chancellor, by saying how happy I am to receive this auspicious post at such a favorable moment in the city’s history,” said Grimes. “I do love to clear up the shit.”

“Yes, yes. Hardly ideal, I know. But I don’t think you want an angry mob knocking on our door in the middle of the night either.”

“Well, first of all, we need to get Penshead’s captains here, so they know the chain of command. And then the plan is containment.”

"Containment?" asked Hoskin, the afterglow of his little triumph fading fast.

"Aye. People are going to riot. It's too late to stop it. They'll have made plans. Pitchforks, torches, babysitters, that kind of thing. What's important to remember with a riot is it's like a wildfire. Things are going to get burned. We just need to make sure the whole place doesn't go up."

Hoskin suddenly realized that without Penshead around, there would be no one to blame if this all went awry.

"It should be alright, Lord Chancellor," continued Grimes. "But it's probably best to make peace that there's going to be some smoke come morning."

THE CARRIAGE CLATTERED OUT ONTO THE STREETS FROM the palace gate. The roads were clear enough now to take him toward the Lance. Hoskin sat alone in the carriage brooding over what he was doing.

Why wasn't he tucked in bed, at least trying to get some sleep, even though it had been in short supply in the past few weeks?

Had Penshead gotten to him with his remark about his love of books?

In some ways, he could even see the logic of that buffoon. Eden was the target of the ire of the crowd, why not let him taste the repercussions, for once? But he knew the situation could quickly get out of control, and the crowd could turn on the city guard and the palace. How he detested Lord Eden, the man was too cocksure. Eden thought this was going to be a procession to his coronation or whatever kind of ceremony they were going to have.

It was well past midnight, and the city wasn't quiet. Instead of the usual bands of drunks and petty robbers, the place looked under siege. Shouts and calls and screams reverberated through the cobbled streets. Barricades had been formed with carts and tables, claimed by the guard from private citizens, armored men sheltering behind.

He had watched through field glasses from atop the palace walls how the guard had attempted to bring some control to the matter. The rioters were initially focused on Eden's soldiers. Barrows of stones had been wheeled to the front of the angry lines, and the bombardment of Eden's soldiers followed. In some ways, Hoskin commended their restraint; they didn't charge and attack for a good thirty seconds. Then it was a mess. Armored soldiers fared well against an unarmed commoner, but not so well when surrounded by ten armed with the tools of their trade.

It took the arrival of Grimes and the guard, driving into the little space between the two groups, indiscriminately deploying their clubs to the heads of both sides to break them apart. The city guard had greater numbers than Eden's private army and so the rioters fell back. Again came the missiles. Rocks and lit bottles of spirits by the look of the resulting fiery streets. Bands of rioters would gather and try to rush the guards, but they were repelled and slowly forced backward.

Hoskin had lost sight of what was happening as the conflict moved further away from the palace, and he had to rely on messengers for news. Now, it seemed that Grimes's plan of containment had worked, creating two main areas of the city where the trouble remained.

And so, Hoskin was heading to the Judiciary, to see with his own eyes what was happening.

The carriage slowed to a halt near one barricade, rioters with torches and whatever weapons they could find visible beyond. Hoskin step down from the carriage and called out. "Grimes!"

The commander broke off from the man he was standing with and approached the lord chancellor.

"Commander Grimes. Report if you please," said Hoskin.

"We have the firewalls in place, and the trouble channeled. The guards have responded well, m'lord. Only one captain refused to follow orders, and so, he's been replaced. This here is one of the hotspots. We're trying not to engage them anymore, sir. There's been plenty of looting and fire, but we're going to let them run out of steam. Most of the civilians have gotten out of the cordon and, in fact, we'll be letting the rioters out, too, as long as they leave in ones and twos. I think this will have all died down here by dawn."

"Good. What about the other hotspot?"

"I don't know, my lord. I was just about to go and check in with it," said Grimes.

"Get in. Let's go see together."

Grimes spoke to the driver, and then climbed into the cab, sitting opposite Hoskin. It rumbled back the way they had come and into the Inner Circle. The other mob had been contained with their backs to the Inner Wall, but three entire city blocks were under their control.

"This is the situation we have to be worried about, my lord," said Grimes. "There's no release valve for this mob right now. No way for them to slink back home with whatever they looted. That's when the kettle can explode."

The horses slowed to stop a few hundred feet from the barricades, across the broad street named after the Inner Wall.

It looked like hell. The tall buildings opposite the wall were all on fire. At the barriers near the inferno, people were trying to escape from inside the cauldron, and on the other side of the barricade, there was pitched fighting between the men of the mob and the guards. Cobblestones were flying through the air and raining down on the heads of the armored troops as they tried to keep the rioters contained.

"Shit," exclaimed Grimes. "Lord Chancellor, please wait here. You need to stay safe." Grimes climbed down from the carriage and ran over to his men.

Hoskin waited, aware that watching a riot from the safety of your own high walls was quite different than being a stone's throw away. The horses skittered and whinnied at being so close to the fire. They would rather be somewhere else, too.

He saw figures being dragged clear of where the fire was burning, pulled out into the quiet streets, where they collapsed. Some of them not moving. Others shrieking as flames on their clothes were beaten out.

Hoskin felt useless.

He cursed Eden for starting this.

He cursed Bollingsmead for riling the crowd.

But he found his choicest curses were reserved for the wizard. Yes, as he had said, Randolph had been a useless king, but was this any better? Was this an augury of what was to come? Hoskin was interrupted from his litany of muttered profanity by the returning Grimes.

"I've given the order to abandon the far barricade and fall back, Lord Chancellor. I'm going to hope a good bunch of them will run for the Feast Gate, and then we'll try to split them up. If we leave them here, there's going to be too many dead. Commoners *and* guards. If you disagree, my lord, I can release command."

Hoskin considered the situation. The anger and adrenaline of facing down Penshead had long since passed. Now he just wanted to be somewhere else. "Whatever you think is the best, Commander. You have my full support. I shall be heading back to the palace now."

"I'm afraid there's one more piece of news, m'lord."

Hoskin's heart sank even further, bad news always followed bad news.

"The building there," Grimes said as he pointed to a building in flames, "that's a whore house. A fancy whore house, mind you. But it seems Admiral Ridgton was visiting this evening. He was trapped in the fire."

"Is he dead?" asked Hoskin.

"Not yet. But he's badly burned, and it looks like he took a beating as he tried to escape. I'm sorry, my lord."

Hoskin sighed. "Not your fault he couldn't have just used his hand for one day." He closed the door to the carriage, and spoke through the open window, "Carry on, Grimes. At least it'll be dawn soon."

CHAPTER 34
ARREST

The vibe of a few nights past, the celebratory atmosphere after the rally in the market square, had gone. Mareth sat at the usual table in the common room of the Royal Oak, but it felt different.

The inn was in lockdown. After the events of the last two nights, Lady Grey had wanted him to move into her mansion, but he had refused. He didn't intend to run. But Mareth didn't complain when Jules sent all of her remaining customers to other establishments, or when Lady Grey beefed up security even more. It was also reassuring to see Motega and Florian back in the building.

The day had been a strange one after a strange night. Mareth hadn't slept a wink. The sounds of crowds in the street, clashes between the people and the city guards, babies and children crying from fear, had helped to keep him awake. He knew he'd acted rashly yesterday, even before Neenahwi had pointed it out, but the anger that had consumed him had made him unable to recognize it. At the time he wasn't sure what effect the song would have. He knew he could weave something to make people angry, but it had never spread to other people who weren't physically there, like it did yesterday. Thinking about this had been another cause of his insomnia. The only explanation Mareth could settle on was the combination of barely hidden, simmering resentment that most people just accepted, combined with how close it was to when many of the people had been at the rally.

His wounds were sore, but his pride was wounded even more. Mareth believed in fair play. That was how they were trying to compete in this election, and if he lost, then they'd all accept it. At least for now. But Eden wanted to take the competition out and not care about the damage he inflicted on people's lives. Alana had nearly lost her life saving his. It had driven his anger, and he now admitted it, at least to himself; he'd felt an intense satisfaction yesterday when people took up his cause. Today, all he felt was empty.

The morning had been quiet. People were focused on cleaning up and not moving about the city. Nobody wanted to be far from their homes and loved ones. Mareth had paced the floors of the common room until Jules had told him he was wearing it out. So, he went out into the city, pacing the neighborhoods and meeting with people, some of whom who had lost all of their meager possessions to fire or looting.

The guilt was a crushing weight, far different from his conceit of yesterday. He said sorry to them for what had happened, but they told him not to stop. All day he heard messages to go and win, to become lord protector, even as a strange summer fog rolled in over the city making Kingshold appear even more otherworldly. The words of encouragement brought tears to Mareth's eyes as he walked back to the

Royal Oak. He didn't want to disappoint anyone. But how could they win?

Mareth's remembrances faded away as his friends, old and new, gathered around their customary table. He forced a smile, first for Petra who was already sitting next to him, and then for the rest. Jules, Motega, Florian, Trypp, and Neenahwi, along with Lady Grey and Folstencroft, took seats at the table.

"Neenahwi, how's Alana?" asked Mareth.

"She'll be fine. I healed the cut, and then removed the stitches. She won't even have a scar," said Neenahwi, "but she's going to sleep like the dead for a few days. The healing depletes a person's energy, and she'll need to recover. I'll let my father know he'll need to have some different help for a little while."

"Thank you, so much," said Petra earnestly.

"Yes, thank you," said Mareth. "That lifts my spirits considerably." He looked around the table. "So, what news?"

"The curfew has been announced; everyone is to be off the streets by the eighth bell," volunteered Trypp. "From what I heard, there were at least three dozen people who died in the troubles last night. And I heard the city jail is overwhelmed. That means probably a couple of hundred detained."

Mareth felt Neenahwi's eyes drilling into him, or maybe he imagined it, and it was just the guilt.

"The loss of life is sad," said Lady Grey, "but the message last night sent to the whole city was a powerful one. It could yet work out to your advantage."

"I'm not thinking about that now," said Mareth.

"Well, you need to. People took to the streets last night because they believe in you. And I heard they told you the same thing today. However, the curfew is a constraint on our ability to operate."

"Yes, you're right," he said to Lady Grey. "You are right. And you were right, too, Neenahwi."

"About time you recognized it, Mareth," said Neenahwi. "I hope you remember my other words about your responsibilities, too. That kind of action is not one I want to see repeated."

"Yes, I remember. And I'll do better," said Mareth, hoping he hadn't damaged this new relationship. He turned his attention back to the table. "I agree, we need the curfew to end. We only have three days left to organize the districts and to get more guild support. Folstencroft, in Alana's absence, do you have a good view of where we are in potential votes?"

"Yes, my lord," said the secretary. "The votes of the people of Unedar Halt, already cast, make it very close by my calculations. But the death of Lady Kingsley sent some of her supporters to Eden, so he's still in the lead. With a number of merchants and other wealthy families still undeclared, there are likely ten votes between us. And of course, this assumes we can still organize all of the districts in the time we have left, but we have a much larger group of volunteers now."

"That is good news. But we're still behind. So how do we make up the difference?" Mareth asked the group at large.

"The interesting thing will be if any of the nobles change their votes through fear of commoner uprising," said Neenahwi.

"I agree," said Lady Grey, "and there may be one obvious candidate for you, Mareth. Your father arrived in the city this afternoon."

Mareth considered this piece of news. He wasn't surprised the real Lord Bollingsmead was coming to the city. In fact, Eden had thrown it in his face ten days past. He hadn't seen his father in more than fifteen years, and they didn't part on the best of terms. But every vote was vital, so he'd have to give it a try.

His thoughts about his father and family were interrupted by a steady banging on the door of the inn.

"Open up! City guard!" came a voice from the street.

Mareth looked to Lady Grey, who remained impassive, and then to Jules. She shrugged and walked over to the door to let them in. Motega and Florian silently pushed back their chairs from the table, ready for trouble.

Through the door, and out of the fog-filled street, walked an armored knight whom he recognized to be Sir Penshead, accompanied by a dozen city guard. Lady Grey's men in the inn fell back to the edges of the room, allowing the visitors ample space.

"Mareth Bollingsmead," said the knight, "I'm arresting you for inciting the people, assaulting the city guard, and destruction of private property. You'll come with us."

"I don't think so, sir," said Mareth. "Where's the signed writ? This is obviously politically motivated."

"I don't need a writ to make an arrest," he said. "These men here, and more waiting outside, say I can take you to jail where formal charges will be made. You are considered a danger to the peace."

"And who is it, Sir Knight, who considers our Lord Bollingsmead to be a danger?" asked Lady Grey. "I assume it's not you. Because, I have it on reliable information, you were relieved of your duty last night and you're not the commander of the city guard anymore."

Mareth couldn't hide the surprise from his face. Lady Grey had more ears in private places than he could imagine. Jules was still standing by the door to the inn. She opened it again and took another look outside. She closed it, and then shook her head toward him.

"You have some balls, Sir Penshead," said Mareth. "Do your men know you have no authorization to do this?" From the anxious looks between them, he could see some of them did not. But that wasn't going to matter much if it came to a fight; they'd surely stand by their comrades. "And I don't think you have enough men with you to get out of here in one piece. There's no one outside."

Motega and Florian stood and moved in opposite directions around the table, Dolph came out of the shadows, and Lady Grey's guards drew their swords. The city guard mirrored their actions.

"We'll see about that," said the knight as he, too, drew his sword.

"Hold, all of you!" Neenahwi stood, arms above her head, a brilliant light shining from her hands and illuminating the whole of the inn, drawing everyone's attention. "Listen."

Everyone stopped. Mareth was waiting for her to say something about how this was stupid, we're all Edlanders, or some other inspirational speech, but she didn't say another word.

Then he heard it. Bells ringing in the night. Not just one, but many, and they weren't tolling the hour. It was a constant pealing, irregular from one bell to another.

"Why's the alarm being called?" asked Mareth. He ran out of the inn, past the knight and his guards, who didn't try to stop him. They just stood there open-mouthed, trying to listen to the sound themselves. Mareth turned the corner to see to the east where the sound came from.

The fog was thick. Usually, he would have been able to see all the way to the market square, but the next corner was hardly visible. Though the visibility was poor, there was enough to be concerned about. Great blooms of orange light reflected in the fog, coming from the direction of the harbor.

And the bells still tolled.

Was Kingshold under attack?

CHAPTER 35
RUNNING TOWARD TROUBLE

Motega was a few steps behind the bard as he ran for the door, a couple of things at the forefront of his mind. First, he, too, was concerned what the tolling of the bells meant. He'd never heard the city alarm rung here in Kingshold, but he'd experienced it before in other cities around the Emerald Sea, and it was never a good thing. Secondly, he didn't trust these guards, who were apparently operating without authority, not to attack Mareth from behind.

"Get out of the way, man!" he called out to a guard who was about to follow Mareth out onto the streets, and, surprisingly, he stepped aside. Outside, the fog was thick, but Motega heard the sounds of chaos in the night. He caught sight of Mareth disappearing around the corner, and so, he pelted after him, almost colliding with the bard who had stopped dead in the street, looking at the blooms of yellow and gold reflecting in the fog bank.

"What the fuck is going on?" Motega asked the world at large.

"I don't know. Doesn't look good. Are we under attack?" said Mareth incredulously. Motega heard the others run from the inn, and then slow to a halt beside them.

"What in the name of Arloth is that?" asked the knight, the standoff of moments earlier seemingly forgotten. At least for a while.

"We've just covered that," said Motega. "We don't know." He whistled, and Per flew down and landed on his forearm. Instructions were whispered into its ear, and then it took flight and disappeared into the fog. The bells were still ringing, coming from the harbor but, thankfully, the peeling hadn't extended further into the city. No bells from the Curtain Wall hopefully meant there wasn't an army outside the gates. But what was going on?

"So, do I remember rightly the bells weren't ringing last night during the riot?" Motega asked all, and no one in particular.

"Correct, little brother," said Neenahwi. "I've never heard the bells ring like this before. There's something bad going on, and it's that way. I suggest we stop gawping and we get to looking."

Motega turned to face his sister. She had a look of concern, but she also seemed tensed and ready to be released, the glow in the night sky reflecting on her face. She met his gaze, and he nodded.

"You heard her," said Motega. "Let's go." And he sprinted off, with Neenahwi only half a step behind.

At the rear, he heard Trypp call out a question, "Why are we always running toward trouble?"

They skirted the northern end of the Cherry Tree District before cutting to the south and toward the direction of the market square. It was a little out of the way from how the falcon would fly, but he wanted to keep to major streets and avoid ending up in dead ends or unexpected twists from heading through streets he didn't know so well.

"I thought you could turn into a wolf?" he shouted over to his sister, his feet pounding the pavement, but she didn't struggle to match his pace.

"I can," she had to shout back to be heard, "but it's pretty embarrassing later when I change back, and I'm naked. Or you'd need to carry my stuff around."

"Good point. You don't want to excite Florian too much, not when he's going to need to focus soon."

The street was getting crowded, people trying to move in the opposite direction from where they were headed. The looks of fear, and glances over their shoulders, told Motega they were getting close as they reached the paved expanse of the market square. Motega and Neenahwi paused to catch their breath. He was surprised to see he needed it more than she did. How did she stay so fit if she sat around reading books all the time?

Florian, Mareth, Dolph, and Trypp caught up shortly afterward. The guards who'd been at the Royal Oak followed behind, with Penshead lagging last of all. Plate mail was not made for running, and Motega gave the knight credit for being able to keep up in any way at all.

As everyone gathered themselves, Motega closed his eyes and stepped into the body of Per. The falcon was flying low through the streets. It was too foggy to be able to see up high above the roof level, but he was flying too fast to be able to work out where he was. He saw bands of skirmishers, maybe marines, lightly armored, running through the streets, making barricades and attacking small groups of Edlanders.

Motega returned to his body, Florian and Trypp looking

at him expectantly. They had come to rely on him and Per to tell them what they were about to step into.

"The city is definitely under attack," said Motega. "I don't know how or why, but there are a lot of fighters that way. Lightly armored but moving fast and looking to build defenses."

"Defenses? That means they're looking to hold instead of pushing further. At least for now," said Florian. He played the part of fearsome fighter well, but Motega was no longer surprised by his sharp tactical brain.

"Maybe there are going to be more reinforcements?" suggested Trypp.

"Makes sense," said Mareth. "In that case, we have to see what happened to the sea defenses and see if we can stop whoever it is from landing more troops."

Penshead was trying to get air back into his lungs, observing the conversation among the four of them, seemingly puzzled by how Motega knew this information when he hadn't been able to get that far in front of him. "You know this because of magic?"

"I guess you could say so," Motega said.

"Did you see where these barricades were?"

"I don't know exactly. But it was a broad street. Straight. I would guess Ships Row. It would make sense they'd try to block the major approach way."

"Then I say let's go that way," said the knight, pointing to the northeast corner of the market square. "Through the Warehouse District where the streets are smaller."

Motega shrugged, as did the others, and they ran out across the stone slabs, weapons drawn.

~

An overhand blow from the curved saber arched toward Motega. He blocked the strike with one ax, before bringing his other up and under his attacker's small leather buckler. His target was lifted into the air with the impact of the weapon hitting his chest and biting through the leather armor. Eyes bulged as Motega wrenched his blade free.

Another skirmisher was ahead of him, attention focused on the big armored knight who had led them blundering into this squad of invaders. Motega struck the man in the small of the back and spun to meet another attacker coming from the alleyway.

They needed to ditch this walking bucket once this fight was over; he was a liability. Why on earth had Motega even followed him in the first place?

The invader in front of Motega was a big man, bald head, and holding a long spear, a sharp blade and a vicious looking hook combined at the end, that he waved in the air toward him. The spear probed forward in short stabs, Motega blocking them as he assessed Baldy. Another thrust, this time at his face, and he quickly deflected the attack upwards, but the spear came back down, the hook sticking into the back of Motega's shoulder. It didn't hurt too much, nothing he couldn't handle. A few inches of steel in his body seemed to happen with disturbing regularity.

Baldy looked like the cat who had got the cream, pulling Motega toward him and forcing him to his knees. But Motega was grateful for the help. Now, he was inside the reach of the spear. One ax hooked Baldy's foot from under him, and he fell on his arse, the other weapon burying itself in his groin.

Motega stood and looked around. Florian was helping the knight to his feet. The squad of invaders were down, and so were a couple of the guard, but all of Motega's crew were safe. But not for long. It seemed like they'd charged into the snake's nest. Coming toward them was another squad, with bows drawn, ready to fire.

"Run! Archers!" called Motega, pulling his sister as he fled back the way they'd come. Now Motega led the way, twisting and turning through narrow streets until he burst out onto the broad strip of Ships Row, connecting the market square with the harbor. Two score of city guard stood in the center of the street, surveying a barricade ahead of them, more archers standing on top, daring the guards to advance.

He stopped and waited for the others to catch up. "We need to get close to the harbor, and up high ideally, so we can see what we're dealing with."

"No. We should join with these guards and push through these barricades," said the knight.

"Look, you can do what you like," said Motega. "In fact, I think this is what *you* should do. We'll go and find out what we're dealing with."

"I know a place in Dockside, a tavern called the Salty Hull," said Trypp. "It's got a roof with a view of the harbor. And it's a warren down there. We're well and truly cursed if we run into any more of these soldiers in Dockside."

"You know, I'm not sure these are soldiers," said Florian. "Did you see the way they were armored? It was all a mismatch. And no markings or insignia."

"Sorry, Florian, I was too busy trying to stop them sticking me to look at their outfits," said Trypp. "You want to try for the Salty Hull or what?"

No one else seemed to have a better idea. "Let's go," said Florian, but he turned to Penshead first. "You do know if it weren't for me, your brains would be covering the street back there, don't you? You owe me. Don't forget it."

The knight nodded.

Motega thought Florian put more stock in Penshead's honor than he would.

THE JOURNEY THROUGH THE FOGGY GARDEN DISTRICT was uneventful. Unfortunate people clothed in rags rummaged through piles of pungent discarded vegetables and fruits not good enough to sell at market anymore, but good enough to eat when they didn't have anything else. A worm or two provided extra protein.

The food stores gave way to ramshackle wooden buildings, the order of the street layout disappearing around the same time the fog started to thin. Trypp led the way, eventually leading them to a dilapidated two-story structure, with a shingle hanging outside: the Salty Hull.

Dockside inns in any city were usually a place Motega only frequented when given no other choice. The regularity of brawls, and the various maladies that patrons and workers were afflicted with, made sure their lives were in more danger than strictly necessary to get a pint of pissy beer. Trypp walked past the main entrance, where the door was closed, likely barred shut, and skirted around the corner to come to a small door in the rear. *Knock, bang, knock, tap, knock.* His hand beat out a signal on the door, and he waited. Nothing happened, so he did it again, and this time the door opened a crack.

"Who is it?" came the voice from inside.

"Thorley. It's Trypp. Let me in."

"Nope. He's dead."

"I was dead, but I'm back to haunt your old bones. And to pay you those three silver marks I owe you."

The magic words spoken, the door swung open and they were ushered inside quickly.

"You're looking pretty good for a dead 'un," said the old man, blessed with little hair and fewer teeth, who must be Thorley. "You want to hide? I got a room full of folks doing likewise. But they'll be ready to fight if those bastards try to come in here."

"We need to get up on the roof. See what's going on here," said Trypp.

"Heh. Think yourself a hero now, do ya? Well, go ahead. Just keep your head down. I don't want you attracting attention to us."

Trypp led the way up narrow, rickety stairs to the widow's watch. The inn was taller than the surrounding shanties, so it had a good view out over the harbor. The six of them stood by the railing and looked out. To their right was the entryway to the harbor between the stone walls of the sea defenses and in front was the wide-open space of water beyond the docks. There floated more than twenty anchored galleons, releasing smaller longboats rowing troops to shore. Many of the vessels moored along the dockside were on fire.

"That's odd. They don't look like typical warships," mused Motega.

"Yep," said Mareth, shaking his head. "They look like corsairs to me."

"How can you tell?" asked Trypp.

"I recognize some of the ships. I'm familiar with the North Sea Corsairs."

About to ask the bard how familiar he was with a bunch

of pirates to know what their ships looked like, Motega turned to look at Mareth. But the thought left him as his attention was drawn down the line of waterfront buildings toward the Warehouse District. Even with his poor eyesight he could see an island, bigger than the market square, in the harbor where none had been before. A humped island with buildings on the back of it, with what looked like a tower at the tallest point.

"Look," said Motega, pointing at what he'd seen.

"How did that get here?" asked Neenahwi. More invaders were running to and from the island, close enough to shore to use gangplanks. Motega couldn't make out any details, so he reached out to Per once more.

The falcon soared high above the harbor, the fog clear here, like being in the center of a smoke ring. He swept over the corsairs' ships and beat his wings to fly close to the invaders' island. Motega wondered what manner of construct it could be to float a whole town, even one as ramshackle as this. Then, as Per swept in front of the island, closer to shore, Motega saw a massive reptilian head, chin resting on the cobbled street of Wetside, and suddenly things made sense.

Well, actually, they made no sense at all.

Straight out of the story books, that was a Draco-turtle.

CHAPTER 36
AMBUSH

The owl descended through the fog, wings outstretched to slow its descent, talons gripping something long and thin about the middle. Gliding down toward an open window of a building in the palace grounds until it landed on the floor of a bedchamber.

Air warped, colors merging, a faint sizzling sound, and where the owl once was stood Neenahwi, naked as the day she was born, stretching the kinks out of her body. *Owl eyes were always the best at night*. She'd picked out Jyuth's bedroom and could hear him talking in the next room.

"What's going on, Hoskin?" asked her father. "Are you going to make me have to go and look for myself?"

"I don't know what's happening! I came here to ask you what the fuck was going on!"

"Now, now. Is there any need for that language?"

"You swear all the time. And I'm fucking sick of this job," said the chancellor. Neenahwi agreed he did sound sick of it.

"I only swear when it's appropriate. For effect. You, however, don't swear. It doesn't suit you."

Neenahwi grabbed a robe from a hook on the wall and sauntered into the sitting room, surprising the two men standing there. Hoskin looked quite shocked at her state of undress beneath the robe. "Father, do leave him alone. There are more fucking important things right now," she said.

"See, she can curse," said Jyuth, nodding to Hoskin. "She has the right presence."

"Lady Neenahwi," pleaded Hoskin, "save me from this old lunatic. Do you know what's going on?"

"Pirates. Pirates and sea monsters," said Neenahwi, shaking her head, more to herself than anything else at the ridiculousness of the story she needed to tell. "I kid you not. There's a flotilla of galleons in the harbor. Hundreds of corsairs on the streets, behind barricades they've built, and then to top it off, there's a whole town of pirates on the back of a Draco-turtle. How on earth did this happen? Where is the navy?"

"Most of them are sailing across the Arz Sea right now," said Hoskin. "They're trying to intercept a new Pyrfew fleet."

"Well, somebody knew that was going to happen. Because I don't think these pirates just happened to be stopping by, saw the open port, and thought, *I know, let's pop in and borrow a cup of sugar.*"

"Do you really think they're invading?" Hoskin turned and called out of the door, "Percival, has someone found Grimes yet?"

"I have no cunting clue," said Neenahwi in answer to his first question. She looked at her father, who had yet to say a word. "You've been very quiet."

Jyuth's eyes stopped staring into the middle distance and focused on her. "I was trying to sense the Draco-turtle. I haven't seen one in centuries. I thought they'd all died. They have powerful minds that are usually very obvious to us. But I can't sense anything."

"Father, I'm not lying."

"Of course not. But it becomes stranger and stranger."

"We have to go and help. My friends are down there. Motega is down there. They can't stop that thing alone," she said.

"Yes, of course, my dear," said her father. "Hoskin. Get Uthridge and Grimes and organize the defenses. And get out of here; you don't need to see this."

Hoskin backed out of the room, nodding, eyes wide, looking like someone who'd had one kick too many to the head. Once he'd left the room, Jyuth pulled his robe over his head and placed it on the floor, then his amulet beside it.

"Do you have the stone with you?" he asked.

"Yes, here in a pouch."

"Good. You'll need it. Let's go."

She undressed, too, as her father shimmered into the form of a golden eagle. It hopped over and clutched his belongings in taloned feet before launching itself through the doorway Hoskin had just departed and out into the night sky.

THE TAWNY OWL FOLLOWED THE EAGLE, FLYING ABOVE THE low fog, unable to see much of the city beneath her except where it dissipated near the harbor, the floating town visible.

An eagle.

Her father was always so ostentatious.

Neenahwi carried her belt of pouches and the robe this

time, she had no intention of fighting pirates or the Draco-turtle in the nude. She'd previously left her clothes behind on the tavern rooftop in her rush to get to the palace, only taking her leather belt and its valuables. But the extra weight and size of the robe caused drag, slowing her flight, and so, she fell behind the wizard in front. Tawny owls weren't made for carrying so much. But it wasn't much further to go.

Out of the fog came a bolt of bright orange fire that she only just adjusted her flight to avoid, heat singeing feathers.

What was that?

She beat her wings to gain altitude and more time to react. The blast had appeared almost out of nowhere because she was so close to the fog. A second eruption of flame quickly followed the first, and this time it caught her in the chest, suffocating her with hot air as her feathers erupted. She transformed back to human as she fell, the acrid smell of burnt feathers in her nostrils, belt and robe knocked from her grip and falling down into the fog. She followed them, dropping like a stone.

There were seconds before the ground would meet her. This was where the years of study and meditation came in, along with what Neenahwi liked to think of as natural talent. Hedge wizards and witch doctors might be able to do magic with hours of preparation and a handy sacrifice, doing it in a split second with the earth about to give you a hard embrace was entirely different. She divided her mind and called on her own energy, drawing from her precious reserves, causing the air beneath her to turn thick, the viscosity slowing her fall.

She still hit the ground with a *thud*, knocking the wind from her lungs and bringing sharp pain to her knees and hands as she landed on all fours.

Shit.

Neenahwi stood and dusted herself off. The street around her was deserted. Fog limited visibility to twenty feet or so, but she could see across the way where her belongings had landed, hanging from a broad ancient oak tree in a small patch of green grass of what passed for a park in Kingshold.

From the fog stepped a tall, well-dressed man, flanked by four guards. The man smiled as he approached. Neenahwi tried to shake some sense back into her head after the fall. *Gawl Tegyr! What's he doing here?*

"Hello, Neenahwi darling. I'm so glad I got your attention."

"You fired at me?" she demanded. Gawl Tegyr was known to her, the Pyrfew ambassador to Kingshold was often in the city. The on-again, off-again, nature of the Edland and Pyrfew conflict meant there was as much gamesmanship through diplomacy as on a battlefield. She also remembered hearing that Gawl had been particularly animated after Jyuth had rescued her and Motega from the emperor's captivity.

"I just wanted to talk to you, my dear," the ambassador spoke as if he was an old family friend. "I know you must be hurting inside, what with the old fool saying he's going to leave you."

"How do you know that?" she screamed. "How did you do that? You're not a sorcerer."

"What, just because you and your father didn't know? There's more than one type of magic. And I have knowledge you could only imagine. But I want you to know the emperor still has only the warmest of feelings for you. Even after you ran away."

She took one step toward the ambassador, fists clenched by her side and teeth gritted. "Don't talk to me about him!"

"He's missed you, my dear. It's time for you to go back and sit by his side." Behind him, she saw two of the guards carrying coils of heavy ship's rope, which began to unwrap and rise in the air like snakes rearing to strike. Gawl Tegyr didn't move, didn't shift his gaze from her face. The ropes leapt forward faster than she could react, her composure gone, swept away by the storm of his words. One rope coiled around her middle, pinning her arms to the sides of her naked and bloody body, the other around her legs, causing her to topple to the ground.

"Don't worry. Once we're away from this abominable little city, and we have a chance to talk, you'll be unbound. I've arranged transport." Gawl began to walk forward, his guards remaining where they stood, motionless.

Neenahwi closed her eyes and blew a deep breath, attempting to re-center herself. Her belt was not too far away. *It's just the same as if I held them in my hand*, she told herself. The sounds of the city subsided, the noise of battle and fire and screams from ahead of her faded away, and she was able to part her mind. One piece of her felt the steel from afar, then another, and another still.

Three short razor-sharp arrows burst free from a pouch on her belt and flew into the air, buzzing between her and Gawl Tegyr, causing him to stop his advance. Those sharp silver blurs changed direction and swooped down to her prone figure, the razor fletchings slicing through her bindings before climbing into the air to strike again. The thick ropes required many cuts, and the closeness to her skin left her with a crisscross of slices in her flesh. But in seconds, the lines fell away in pieces, such was the speed of the steel arrows.

"You won't take me," she said with determination as she

opened her eyes and climbed to her feet. Gawl Tegyr looked at her in amusement. It only stoked the fire inside. "You won't take me."

Neenahwi stood and raised her arms. The steel missiles, a gift from her father, hovered in the air above her head. She brought down her hands, and they flew across the gap between her and Gawl faster than the eye could see.

If the arrows were a blur, then Gawl's hands were a flash. Left raised to the first bolt; it was deflected away, an inch from his palm. Right moved to meet the second arrow to similar effect, before the third, too, was stopped. She fractured her mind further, one piece of her seizing a chunk of cobblestone, another a piece of jagged metal, another pulled a knife from the belt of one of the guards who didn't respond. All were added to the maelstrom of missiles flying at her attacker. But he blocked them all.

She felt thin, hardly present in the world any longer. Her mind shattered like a mirror, and she could see a hundred smaller images of herself. She'd pushed too far and had to stop.

The debris fell to the ground as she reeled back in the line she'd wantonly cast out. Only the arrows remained airborne now, but they were still, unmoving, waiting by her elbow.

Gawl Tegyr's arms resumed their relaxed position by his side, his head cocked to one side as he regarded her. "Why do you subscribe to Jyuth's way of doing things? You're not a juggler, or a court fool, tossing around axes. Why not simply use force?" A wave of invisible pressure hit her whole body, pushing her back a step and lifting her unbound hair behind her. Her missiles flew across the street, embedding into the far wall.

"Why not just take what you need? And simply kill if you need it," he said. Neenahwi's magic eye could now see the thin threads leading from the four guards to Gawl Tegyr. The conduits became bright red as the guards willingly gave their lives, their energy, to the wizard, before they crumpled to the ground.

Gawl raised a hand, and a blast of green energy enveloped her. The pain was immeasurable, more than she'd ever dreamed possible. She screamed. She screwed her eyes shut, but tears still poured down her face as she fell to her knees.

"Of course. I don't mean to kill you," Gawl continued pleasantly. "That would be rather against the point, wouldn't it? Yes, I don't suppose you can answer right now. I hope you'll remember I did ask you nicely to come along."

Neenahwi couldn't see him anymore, but she could hear him gloating. Her limbs felt like they were on fire. Her teeth were iron spikes driven into her jaw. Her lungs rebelled at every breath. And when he touched her, putting his hand gently on her face, it felt like acid melting her flesh.

Her eyes opened, bulging.

She had to do something. Desperately, she reached out for mana to combat his. Her mind was a thousand groping hands, seeking something to take in this stone-dead street, anything to keep her alive.

And then she found it, and she took all it had. And, it was such a lot of power, too. It felt old and great.

Her face erupted in a brilliant flash of light, eradicating the darkness of the night for a split second with the brightness of the sun. She saw Gawl's face, less than an arm's span away from her, illuminated first in surprise, and then pain as he brought his hands up to shield his blinded eyes.

From the wall behind Neenahwi, her steel arrows pulled

free, spun and shot toward the ambassador. Thudding into his body, one after another.

Gawl Tegyr slowly fell to the ground, hand reaching to the steel arrows protruding from his flesh before he was still.

The green energy around Neenahwi disappeared. The pain, too, as if it had never been there. In relief, she lay back on the floor and breathed deeply. Opening her eyes, she saw the boughs of the ancient oak tree above her, the one living thing she'd found. The once bright green leaves of the summer were now an ashen grey, and one by one, they fell around her.

She allowed herself a few precious seconds of rest, but thought it best not to be lying unclothed in a city being invaded by pirates, so she stood and retrieved her robe from where it had fallen. Neenahwi also collected her belt, tied it around her waist, and checked the contents of the remaining pouches. Everything seemed to be in place. But she needed to get her arrows back.

Turning to face where Gawl Tegyr had fallen, she saw the body spasm.

It twitched again, and the chest bulged. The neck swelled from something moving below the surface. And then the ambassador's face split open.

CHAPTER 37
NOT PREPARED

His chair felt reassuringly familiar. It wasn't luxurious, as it had once belonged to his father, and he was a man for whom substance was more important than form. But the worn oak and his tired body were old friends, and its sturdiness grounded him. He had thought he was so close to being able to see the end of the tunnel and leave this behind. He hadn't asked to run this country since the king's death. He'd been told to do so by the wizard, and the Hoskin of a little more than three weeks ago didn't have the balls to say no. Now, he'd tell Jyuth to stick it up his magical starfish. At least, he liked to think he would.

The clay cup of hot coffee helped, too. It brought some spark back to the brain.

Percival must have brought him here to his office because he couldn't remember the walk. And put the cup in his hand. Good man, that Percival. What a find. Where had he found him? He had the makings of a damn fine treasurer, too. *Wonder if he was any good at marshaling the defenses of the city.*

Unfortunately, it was something he had to do. But as his

father would have said, when life gives you a beating, kick it in the ballsack. So, he had to organize some kicking.

"Percival!" he called to the open door in front of him. "Are you there?"

Percival stepped into the doorway, looking slightly harried, the first time Hoskin could remember him not looking perfectly composed. "I just returned, my lord."

"Good. I need Uthridge and Grimes now."

"They're just behind me, my lord. I'm sorry it took me so long to find them."

The general royal walked into the office first, followed by Commander Grimes. Both were wearing breastplates and chainmail. While Uthridge gleamed and wore an immaculate tabard over the top, by comparison, Grimes followed his name. A long night of fighting fires and firebrands, and now invading pirates, were evident in the soot and smoke that tarnished him.

"Ah good. Thank you, Percival," said Hoskin. "You may close the door. I'll call if I need you." Hoskin looked at the two men standing before him and let the silence drag out for a minute. "Gentlemen, how rude of me not to offer you a seat..." Uthridge was already moving to sit, hand on the back of the chair in front of him, pulling it away from the desk, "but I don't think that will be necessary. It seems to me there's been too much sitting around on the job, don't you?"

They both stood stock still, eyes forward, reverting to the skills they would both have mastered as young soldiers. *When the boss is pissed off, don't say a word unless you have to.*

"So, do either of you know what the hell is going on?" asked Hoskin when it was clear neither was going to volunteer anything.

Uthridge looked to his left to Grimes, signaling he

expected him to go first. "It seems like we're in the middle of an invasion, my lord," said the guard commander.

"What amazing insight!" said Hoskin. "Who are they? How many? How did they do this?"

"I'm afraid I don't have too many details, my lord. I've been on the streets with the guard; I've seen them, and I don't recognize any colors or markings to identify them. They're lightly armored, skirmishers more than real soldiers. No idea of the numbers right now either, my lord. The fog has made it so you can only see them when they're right in front of you."

"They're pirates!" Hoskin thumped the desk. He couldn't remember ever hitting a desk before in his life. "Lady Neenahwi saw them firsthand. A whole fleet, at least twenty galleons. How many men would that be?"

"If they really are pirates, then I wouldn't expect more than three hundred men on one of those ships," volunteered Uthridge.

"Six thousand men! Within the walls of Kingshold! And, apparently, they have something called a Draco-turtle. Do you know what that is? No? Me neither, but it doesn't sound good."

"I assure you, my lord, six thousand men cannot hold Kingshold," said Uthridge.

"Agreed. That's not even enough to take the palace with the walls we have here. I've also ordered the Inner Wall gates closed," said Grimes.

"It might not matter," said Hoskin. "She also said they've set up barricades around the harbor. That's probably what you've been running into as well, Grimes. They aren't advancing, at least not yet."

"Don't worry, Lord Chancellor," said the old general. "I

have the garrison being mustered as we speak. We'll drive them back into the sea once morning comes, assuming the fog clears."

"The morning? *If* the fog clears? We're just going to give them free rein down there until then?"

"I'm afraid we just don't have that many soldiers sitting around waiting in armor. They're at home with their families and have to be called and organized. That will take some hours."

Hoskin sighed and looked to Grimes. "What about you?"

"I have five hundred city guard and two hundred palace guard. We can try to contain them if they want to move beyond their barricades, but they have the men. The guard aren't real soldiers. There hasn't been an invasion in living memory."

"Don't they train for this? Practice. You know drills?" asked Hoskin.

"I'm sorry, my lord. They should, but I've only been on the job for a day. Isn't much I can do about it now."

Hoskin cursed himself for not worrying about these things before. Penshead was not his choice, but the safety of the city was still his responsibility. Why would he ever think this would happen, though, when Edland had the strongest navy on the seas to hide behind?

His hard chair was not so comfortable now. The weight of the palace, the people of this city, pushed down on him from above, crushing him against the unyielding oak. Hands planted, palms down on the desk in front of him, he closed his eyes and breathed. "I want them gone by noon, fog or no fog. And you two need to protect the people down there. Don't raze our own city, Uthridge."

CHAPTER 38
THE SALTY HULL

Mareth could feel Neenahwi's robe draped on his arm, but his eyes remained closed. Motega had drawn everyone's attention to the beast in the harbor, which had resulted in Neenahwi disrobing, which was not the reaction Mareth had been expecting. And after the recent incident before the rally a few nights past, screwing up his eyes had seemed like the most honorable course of action.

It also had the secondary benefit of not being able to see the invading force of pirates anchored in the harbor, which had been bringing back some uncomfortable memories. However, Mareth's hearing wanted to try to make up for the self-inflicted loss of the other sense, and so, he could hear only too starkly the cacophony of chaos in the city: shouts, screams, tolling bells, steel on steel carrying across the water. And then a flapping noise, followed by a buffeting of air.

"Can I open my eyes now?" asked Mareth.

"It all depends on what you're trying to avoid looking at," said Trypp. "The beautiful naked woman or the thousands of men who'd be happy to gut us and throw us in the harbor? The first one has gone, but the others are still there, unfortunately."

Mareth opened his eyes. "The first. Where did she go? What was she doing?"

"My guess is she went to get Jyuth," said her brother. "That is one big fucker out there, and I don't know what we can do about it. I guess you've never seen her transform."

"Still haven't, thank you very much. Why did she have to get undressed?"

"Ever seen an owl wearing a robe? No, me neither," Motega replied.

Everyone went back to looking out over the railing at the harbor. Mareth counted twenty-two ships, big ones. The steady stream of longboats ferrying men to shore continued. *What are they doing here?* He'd never heard of North Sea Corsairs banding together in such large groups. Three or four, even five crews, he'd heard of coming together to take down more lucrative, but highly guarded, targets. But this was something else. Pirates didn't care about conquest, and he'd never heard of them turning mercenary. They preferred to intimidate, not fight.

"What are they doing here?" Mareth said out loud, still really talking to himself.

"From my years of military service, I'd say this is what they call an invasion—" started Florian.

"Hilarious, big man. You want to explain to me why it's dark now?" spat Mareth. He was losing patience with the jokes. These three new friends had been invaluable, and usually he appreciated their banter, but how could they joke at a time like this?

"Actually, I was going to say this would be an invasion if

these ships would be getting out to let more in. Or if there was a force outside the gates. But I don't think there is. And there aren't enough men here to take the city. They must know that."

"So, what are they doing, Florian?" asked Trypp.

"Good question."

Mareth saw small groups of pirates wandering along the dockside, but they didn't seem interested in venturing too far into the neighborhood. He wouldn't be surprised if these crews had berthed here before, maybe even drunk in this same tavern, so they'd probably know their location well. He watched as longboats rowed back to the galleons, bobbing in the water. The lamps at the prow and stern of those boats cast strange shadows on the planking area in the middle. No people sat there, but they weren't empty either. Mareth followed the line of their progress back to shore where they'd come from. There. He saw other figures moving crates into the longboats.

"By Arloth!" Recognition hit him. "This is a raid."

"A raid?" asked Motega. "This is not some fishing village."

"I know. But look over there," said Mareth, gesturing to what he had just seen. "They're loading something onto those boats to take back to the ships. And look over there, you can make out them hauling it up onto the deck."

Silence as everyone squinted to see in the darkness.

"It does look that way," said Dolph, nodding.

"Bastards," said Mareth, shaking his head. "This is the way we attacked Hulmouth. Five ships to raid that poor town."

"Pardon?" said Trypp.

"I said that's the way they do these raids. Hulmouth was

a town in northern Pienza. There wasn't a lot left after the corsairs had taken slaves and anything of value."

"No, that wasn't the question," said Trypp. "What you said was *we*."

All four of them stared at Mareth.

"Fine!" he said. "I may have been a pirate for a little while. But I didn't want to be, believe me."

All four of them stared at him some more.

"Ha!" said Florian, punching his shoulder and almost pitching him off the roof. "You're going to have to tell us that story."

"Later. I promise."

"You'd better not let anyone else hear it, Mareth," said Trypp. "I don't think folks will want an ex-pirate for a lord protector. Even those numbskulls down in Bottom Run."

"I'm aware of that. That's why I don't usually talk about it," said Mareth, a little sheepishly. "But look, I know these people. I think I know what we can do."

After a brief discussion, they descended to the common room of the Salty Hull. Pushing past locals standing in the hallway to enter the long, smoky room, Mareth remembered how roughly a score of people had been sitting in there when they arrived. Now the place was standing room only. He looked over his shoulder to Trypp, and Thorley was grinning his toothless grin next to him.

"We recognized youse when you came in, Lord Bollingsmead," said the innkeeper. "Might a bin a few folks went out and told some others."

A motley collection of men and women, hardy souls with

hard muscles from years of laboring at the docks. Most with drinks in hand, and all with their eyes on him. Motega and Florian cleared some men from a table nearby with hardly a grumble. Mareth thought he'd like to see them do that on a usual night. Then again, he doubted even the most hardened nut would pick a fight with Florian, and Motega had the wild eyes of someone anyone would generally regret starting something with. Mareth climbed onto the table.

"Good people!" he called.

"Where?" called some wag at the back of the room, earning a few chuckles, but more than a few scowls.

"Good people," he tried again. And he poured his heart into his words. Like he did the morning after the visit from the assassin, like he did when in front of thousands in the marketplace. There was no song, but he could still weave the words with this small a crowd. He made sure to make eye contact, just a second or two for each person, but it was like creating a binding line from them to him.

"Our city has been attacked by pirates! Low scum and thieves have come to our home to steal from us. They're taking our people as slaves, our food, and our treasure!"

Cries of, "No!" and various curses rippled across the room, *"Corpse fuckers,"* being one particularly original utterance from an old lady sitting in front of him.

"Yes! And when they're done, they'll set our city on fire and flee into the night."

Heads shook in the crowd. "What can we do?" called a tall skinny boy off to the side, pimples on his cheeks, and a mustache of beer foam.

"We're going to stop them," shouted Mareth. "They're thieves, and thieves are cowards!"

Trypp had taken offense at that statement back on the

roof. It seemed like the three of them had some tales to tell, too. But Motega had understood right away. What was it he had said? *"Nothing worse than someone screwing up the exit."*

"They don't want to take over the city. They don't want to fight more than they have to. No profit in death is their proverb. They want to go back home with their plunder. So, what will we do?"

Silence. He could have heard a rat fart. He knew he had them. They all hung on his words, waiting for the grand plan.

"We burn their ships!" called Mareth. "Without their ships, they can't go home. If two or three ships go up in flames, fear will take them! Fear that they'll be the ones left behind, ready to be crushed by our soldiers. But if we wait for the soldiers, they'll take what they want and get away."

"Burn them!" called the wag at the back. And the chant was picked up around the room. Mareth stood on the table, hands on hips, looking at what they had to work with. It would work. It had to. He raised his hands for the cheering to stop and smiled at them.

"I need your help," he said in a conversational tone. "I need lamp oil and pitch. Rags and kindling and coals. And a few small boats. And we need volunteers."

And then the room was abuzz with calls to assist, Dolph, Trypp, Motega, and Florian fanning through the room to organize.

CHAPTER 39
PARTIAL REVENGE

She remembered when as a child, she, her brother, and Kanaveen fled their homeland after her family, her entire life had been destroyed. They'd traveled east, hoping to find other tribes to warn about the invaders. But it soon became clear they were heading to the source of their enemy because these destinations had already been visited. It was a familiar sight each time: whole tribes slaughtered, buildings nothing more than smoldering embers.

But in one village, she'd seen a child, a girl who looked to be about her age, cowering against a tree with her back toward them. She'd gone to see the child, to reassure her they were there to help. The smell as she neared, sweet like rotten fruit, should have made her realize something was wrong. Neenahwi had spoken soothing words, reaching out tentatively to touch the girl's shoulder and turn her, so she could see her face. The body, unbalanced, had slipped to the ground, the light touch enough for the child's stomach to burst open. Thousands of maggots erupted, spilling onto her bare feet.

She remembered this as the body of Gawl Tegyr began to contort and bulge, before the man's face split like an overripe peach and something pushed out. Round, multifaceted eyes and clicking mandibles on a long skinny neck emerged from the ravaged head of the man she had just fought. The head reached down and attacked the cadaver's torso with sharp mandibles, cutting through bone and flesh like a tailor's scissors. The chest cavity opened like a book, a book of children's nightmares, and from it, the creature climbed. The insectile head sat atop a shiny chitinous black body, steel arrows still embedded in its center. Multi-jointed arms ended in wicked scythes of bone, and though it seemed impossible, skinny, furry legs unfolded from the body until they alone were as tall as Gawl Tegyr had stood. Ichor made the creature shiny, and its initial stumbling as it found its feet reminded Neenahwi of a newborn foal.

She slowly stepped backward away from the foul issue. *Another demon.* Its head tilted as it regarded her, mandibles clicking.

"I've known you a long time, Neenahwi," the demon spoke through its insect mouth in a rasping hiss. "You know you're almost a daughter to me. Do you remember me now?"

It advanced as it spoke, still a little unsure on those long legs, and she backed away some more. What was it about this creature that seemed familiar? She couldn't remember ever having met it in the past. And then it came to her. In her demon stone-induced vision on the mountain. She'd seen the same head atop a different body murder her family.

What to do? Her stomach burned at the sight of the hellish apparition responsible for destroying her life. But little mana remained in this area for her to draw for her power, her weapons were lost, already lodged in the demon's body without any apparent untoward effect, and it now approached menacingly.

An arm flashed out, blunt side of the razor-sharp appendage hitting her squarely in the stomach and sending her flying across the street into the wooden shingles of a building. She crashed to the street and attempted to gasp great gobfuls of air back into her lungs. The demon advanced on her once more.

"You don't need to be in one piece for this, Neenahwi. We have ways of keeping even a broken body alive."

She scrambled to her feet and fled. Bare feet slapped against the hard cobblestones as she pumped her arms and ran away down the closest street. From behind, she heard it pursuing her. A wet, squelchy sound and from the corner of her eye, she saw it spit a gob of liquid from its mouth. She flung herself to the side and down an alley, the putrid liquid hitting the ground where she'd been moments before, sizzling as it scoured the stone. Acid.

Neenahwi ran harder than she ever had before, giving her all to escape when all she wanted to do was turn and fight and kill this monster. The pouches on her belt rose up and down, striking her legs as she ran. She burst from the alley into a street of brown brick warehouse buildings, avoiding more volleys of acid. The twisting nature of her path had given her a slight advantage in her flight, the demon struggling to negotiate the sharp turns.

Now she had a plan.

And she was done running.

Drawing on her own life, she used a tiny sliver of energy to make the nail on her index finger grow long and sharp. She raked the wolf's claw across the palm of her right hand, slicing deep into the flesh. Skidding to a halt, Neenahwi fumbled with the drawstring of a pouch as the demon entered the street behind, it slowing to a walk as it saw its prey no longer fleeing.

The blood from her hand made undoing the strings difficult, but she created a small gap and was able to shove her right hand in to grasp the contents.

She felt the demon stone in her hand. And then a rush of energy up her arm and into her body as the gem made contact with her bloodied palm.

It was like nothing she'd ever felt before: the power available, she could beat anything. Hairs all over her body stood on end. Fire danced across the fingers of her other hand, and the world became brilliantly stark as if it was the brightest day. She pulled her hand from the pocket, gem in her fist, and it too was encased in red and purple flame that gave off no heat.

The demon continued its advance, hunched over on its long spindly legs like a grotesque crone. Its body lifted upright and then jerked forward to spit gobs of acid in her direction. Without thinking, flames leapt from her hands to catch them midflight, the caustic spittle exploding in white flashes.

"You feel the power. It flows through you, yes?" rasped the demon, mouth clicking. "It's about time for you to embrace your heritage."

She didn't know what it meant. Her people didn't have these demon stones. Was it referring to Jyuth? It seemed unlikely, considering how Gawl had referred to her father before. Of course, it could likely mean nothing, just trying to put her off guard.

"It's time you paid for what you've done!" she yelled. Twin bolts of fire arced from her outstretched hands toward the demon. It parried them with bony appendages, but its arms burned, and it gave a high-pitched squeal.

"Don't you want answers?" it asked, a note of desperation in its words.

In her hand formed a ball of fire. She had only needed to split her mind once to draw on the never-ending thread of energy from the stone. To pull, and pull at it, weaving this tainted mana into the form she needed. One aspect to arm herself and the other to fire. The demon bolted to the side to avoid the grenade that exploded against the brick building behind it. It scrambled up the warehouse that ran along the length of the street, long reach and pointy appendages helping it to scale the surface like a spider. It paused at the top of the wall, its insectile head turning to look completely behind it at Neenahwi.

"Don't you want to know why they all had to die? Why I was there?"

The demon skittered along the building as it called out, reaching a chimney on the outside wall. An arm, still smoldering from the flames it had parried before, smashed into the stack with immense force, bricks and clay and mortar showering down onto Neenahwi and the street around her.

She tried to raise her defenses, throw up a wall of fire, but her aspect was occupied with offense, and she was a second too late. Chunks of masonry, half bricks and sharp chimney pot smashed into her body, dust clouding her vision before her conjured shield evaporated any debris coming into contact with it. Pain flared, briefly, across her body, and she jumped back in alarm, but as she looked down, it appeared she had suffered no real damage. The demon stone had protected her.

Through the dust-filled air and her conjured shield came

the horrifying insectoid face of the demon. It had launched itself from its perch and slammed into Neenahwi, knocking her to the floor. On all fours, it arched over her, the head twisting as it observed her on the ground, and she could see herself, scared and alone, reflected a thousand times in the compound eyes.

"Don't you want to know why *he* wants you? Why he had me tear you from your family?"

Closing her eyes, she saw her mother—her body impaled by the demon's talons—screaming at the injustice of life. She saw her mother and screamed for the orphaned child she had been. She screamed, and the gem answered, feeding on her pain, and her wail became a torrent of flames smashing into the demon and heaving it into the air and back against the damaged building.

Neenahwi clambered to her feet, her eyes still closed, though she could sense her foe. The demon struggled to rise from under the pile of rubble, knocking aside debris as it did so. Purple ichor dripped from weeping sores across its torso. "Please, Neenahwi, you can't know if you kill me!"

In her mind she saw the assault on her tribe again and again. She saw her father, this demon, cowering before her, holding him aloft by the head. A wicked jerk and his neck snapped before he was thrown away like a chicken carcass.

She saw her father die again, and she became fire. Neenahwi was a gateway for all the never-ending fire the stone could pour. The demon screamed again, the most exquisite music she'd ever heard. And the stone cried in joy within her heart, shared delight at the suffering of this vile creature. It was ablaze, limbs withering and igniting of their own accord as it tried to crawl toward her, but she didn't stop her assault. A blackened stump of an arm reached out, and it tried to say something before it fell, unmoving to the ground.

Neenahwi collapsed. She dropped the gem and rebuilt her internal walls to hold back the torrent of power. She was in control this time, though it had been close.

But the power's absence created a void filled with the pain of her wounds and the pain in her soul. Tears slipped down her cheeks as she released the sobs of grief she'd carried with her for more than fifteen years. Minutes passed until the pain eased and her weeping ran itself out. And then she allowed herself to recollect what had happened, and what the demon had tried to say at the end.

You look so much like her.

CHAPTER 40
FIRE

Creeping across rooftops had never been Mareth's strong suit, and carrying a metal pail of hot coals wasn't helping his balance or his attention, either—the heat only just bearable through his gloved hand. Motega, Florian, and Trypp moved like cats, apparently in their element. At least Dolph had the good grace to seem more uncomfortable than he on the pitched roofs. The Salty Hull was too far from the dockside for what they needed to do, and so, they all followed Trypp as he led them along a path above the streets, trying to minimize the number of small, but still terrifying, leaps across alleyways.

They reached the front row of buildings, and he could see more clearly the groups of fighters patrolling the broad dockside street known as Wetside. Trypp and Motega conferred ahead before moving again—not the right position yet. Motega carried his unstrung longbow in his hand, Trypp having retrieved it for him from the Royal Oak while they got everyone organized. Hopefully, the plan was in motion.

Trypp brought them to a halt again on a flat roof,

evidently the right place, as Motega had already begun to string his bow. Mareth placed the bucket down, relieved for the level footing once again. Once the bow had been readied, Motega's falcon flew down to land on his outstretched crooked elbow.

"This is the only flask of Goblin Fire I've got," said Trypp. "Are you sure Per is going to be able to carry this? It's bigger than the liquid fire we used before."

"Don't worry," said Motega. "He may look small, but I've seen him carry off a wolf cub before." Motega took the offered glass bottle, about the size of a brandy bottle, and looped a leather tie through the eye-hole handle. He held the leather loop up, and the falcon flapped its wings to rise and grasp it before taking off into the air. Motega beckoned for Mareth and Florian to come closer.

From the big fighter, he took three strange-looking arrows, the tips modified. There was a typical arrowhead, but it was fixed to a small metal cage, which opened at a hinge. From the pail, Motega used tongs to sort through until he'd found the right size coal and dropped it into the metal cage, securing the door with a tiny latch.

"I hope you realize how expensive these are to have made. We'll be sending you a bill if you become lord protector," said Motega to Mareth. "Did you both see what I did?" Motega asked Mareth and Florian, who both nodded. "Good. I need you to do the same again with the other two arrows when I need them."

The bowman turned to look out over the harbor, arrow nocked, but not drawn, Trypp holding his arm tight. Mareth looked out across the port, too, but he couldn't see the bird in the darkness. And the ships seemed impossibly far away, easily three hundred strides.

"Are you sure you can hit them?" asked Mareth.

"Shhh, he's not with us right now," said Trypp. Mareth peered around at Motega's face and saw his eyes rolled into the roof of their sockets. "And he can do this. Just watch."

Seconds passed. Mareth held his breath, as did everyone else on the roof, as Motega lifted the bow and drew back the string. "Per dropped the flask. Right on the aft deck," said Motega. And then he loosed the arrow. It disappeared into the night, too dark to follow its path.

Whoom!

Even from a few hundred yards away, Mareth could hear the noise as the fire erupted. He had heard about Goblin Fire before, but never seen it in action. Some people said it was made with the piss of a hundred goblin maidens. He wasn't sure about that, but it did make him wish they'd more than the one flask of the stuff. The flames on board the ship had quickly moved up the mast, catching fire to the unfurled sails. Pirates who must have been close to the drop of the flask were running around, engulfed in flame. He saw one hurl himself over the edge to get to the water.

"We need to move. Now!" said Trypp. "They'll start looking for who's responsible."

Trypp led the way again across the rooftops. This time, they were moving away from the city, toward the harbor entrance where, hopefully, they could find a position facing the rear of the ships. Across one roof, the careful passing of hot coals before he leaped over another alleyway, before dashing across more pitched roofs, until Mareth came to an abrupt stop behind Trypp.

"This place is no good, Trypp. Keep going." Motega waved his hand to continue the way they were going.

"Mot, look in front of us. What do you see?" said Trypp quietly.

Mareth had been focusing on his footing, and when he looked up, he saw roughly a dozen figures dressed in black, short bows in hand.

"Oh, fuck." Motega sighed. "Can't we get a break?"

One figure detached itself from the group and took a few steps toward them. The tight-fitting black clothes and athletic body of the leader made it impossible to work out who they were. But she raised her mask to unveil a lithe and mature face, red hair tied behind her head.

"Hello again, Florian," she said.

Trypp and Motega looked at Florian. He shrugged as if to say he didn't know who she was either.

"I'd meant to say thank you again for the workout a couple of weeks ago. It was the best sparring I've had in years."

"Ahh, it's you," said Florian. "I don't really have time this evening. You know, what with the harbor full of pirates and everything."

She smiled. "I'm afraid I don't either. But hopefully some other time." Then she turned to face Mareth. "Lord Bollingsmead, isn't it? Not normal to find your type out on the Sky Road."

"Er, I seem to be at a disadvantage. Who are you?" he asked.

"Oh, you know me, Mareth. After all, you sent me a letter and a gift in a wheelbarrow, not four days past." The gears clicked into place. This must be Lady Chalice. Not high on his list of people to meet at the moment. Given the imbalance in numbers, he hoped she didn't take offense about how he had her assassin returned.

Mareth decided that bravado was the best course of action. "Excellent. How nice to meet you, Lady Chalice. I assume you're here to try again? May I suggest you wait in line behind the pirates?"

"Let me assure you that if I had a contract on you, then you'd be little more than a pin cushion right now," said the lady assassin. "What are you doing up here? The rest of the nobles are quivering in their beds. Did you have something to do with that out there?" She gestured to the blazing ship.

They were interrupted by shouts and bellows and the sounds of many people running. They both looked over the edge of the building to see a healthy-sized mob of people waving clubs and boat hooks as they closed in on a patrol of corsairs. *That* was more of a diversion than they had planned. The good people of the Salty Hull must have gathered some additional friends.

"Look, Lady Chalice," said Motega, "we have to be somewhere, and quickly. Are you here to stop us, or do you want to help?"

She regarded him for a moment. "So, you have more Goblin Fire. Do what you have to do. How can we help?"

"Diversion," said Mareth immediately. "And stop any of the corsairs from getting to this end of the docks."

She nodded once at him, and then turned and nodded once more to her black-clad team to head the way Mareth and team had come. "Good luck," she called. And then the assassins ran lightly across the rooftops past them and disappeared. Trypp signaled for their team to follow him again, and they, too, continued where they'd been heading.

Trypp led them across two blocks of buildings, Mareth switching the pail between hands regularly as the heat continued to sear his skin through the gloves. Eventually,

Motega called a halt. "This should do," said Motega. "Look out for the signal. Should be those two ships there. And get those arrows ready."

Mareth worked with Florian to prepare the missiles, opening the miniature steel cages, and selecting coals of the right size.

"There," said Trypp pointing out into the harbor.

Motega notched one of the arrows and drew the string back to his chin. "Per can see them. This one is in position. Just waiting for them to get clear."

No one spoke as they all watched Motega hold the drawn bow, muscles in his neck and back straining. And then the arrow flew out into the dark.

Seconds ticked by. There was no immediate effect this time.

"It hit," said Motega. "Where's the next boat?"

Concern hit Mareth like a punch in the gut. If he hit the boat that was supposed to be full of kindling, lamp oil and pitch, why had it not burst into flames? Another foolish idea of his that had no chance of succeeding? Just like this whole sorry joke of running to be lord protect—

Boom!

A massive eruption of fire against the new ship, flames licking up the side of the galleon, quickly drawing cries of alarm just audible across the water.

"Where is the other one?" Motega muttered urgently.

"Crap," said Florian, pointing to a different ship than the one they were expecting. "It's over there. I just saw it come alongside that ship." This ship was further toward the center of the harbor, not one of the original targets. The volunteer must have got turned around in the night. This ship looked to be nearly five hundred strides from where they were.

Motega moved to climb down the outside of the building they stood on. "When I get to the bottom, drop me the arrow," he said to Mareth. "And give me some cover." Motega climbed down the two stories faster than a cat after a mouse. Mareth dropped the arrow, point first, and Motega caught it around the shaft before it struck the ground.

Motega ran to the dockside, jumped onto a fishing boat and, with one foot resting on the side of the vessel, pulled back his bow. Florian was down in the street already, twin swords drawn, looking for anyone who might interfere. *How does an armored man move so fast?* Mareth wondered. But it seemed like the patrols were busy with the locals, and the arrows coming from the rooftops, as no one came to intervene.

And then the arrow was gone, the final fiery missile loosed. Mareth didn't see how it was possible for Motega to hit a target at such a distance. But this time, just seconds later, there was another explosion, and fiery oil was blown across the rear of the galleon. Mareth mouthed a silent, "Wow," and scrambled down the building, behind Trypp and Dolph by the time he dropped the last six feet or so. They all stood and watched as the harbor was lit by the sight of the three burning ships.

Moments passed, and then a horn blew, and then another, and then a final deep note came from the direction of the turtle town. "That's the call back to ships. We did it," Mareth said gleefully, grabbing Motega and squeezing him with all his strength. A feeling of intense satisfaction filled his bones. He could see the pirates coming back to the harborside more quickly than before, leaving the city streets.

But behind the fleeing invaders, fire rose into the air. This time in Kingshold.

Out of nowhere, there was an ancient cry of anguish, and the Draco-turtle lurched forward. Even from this distance, Mareth could see it trying to clamber ashore, enormous legs as big as mature oaks clawing at the cobblestones for purchase. It opened its mouth, and a huge blast of steam and fire belched out. Bolts of red and blue light came back at the monster as an answer, and it howled in pain. The long neck and draconic head whipped around, streams of flame gushing forth to envelop its attackers.

"Neenahwi!" shouted Motega, dropping the bow as he sprinted toward the monstrous carnage. Florian ran after him, a few steps behind. As Mareth, unthinkingly, went to join them, he felt a firm grip around his wrist.

"Can't let you do that, boss," said Dolph. "Lady Grey wouldn't be happy if I let you get barbecued."

CHAPTER 41
THE DRACO-TURTLE AWAKES

Neenahwi picked herself off the ground once she felt she could stand without falling again, and she walked toward the harbor. She was dazed, not noticing her way was free of corsairs, or the flickering red flames enveloping her from head to foot. In actuality, the two were very much linked. Roaming bands of pirates and others that manned barricades fled at the sight of what they later named in song as the Crimson Banshee. The demon stone clenched firmly in her fist again, she picked her way through abandoned ramshackle fortifications, and past small fires burning unattended, until she eventually stepped out onto the broad harbor side street of Wetside.

Once again, she saw the galleons anchored in the harbor, looting pirates running back and forth to long boats. Some stopped to look at her standing plainly visible in the street, most going back to their tasks, but some running off in a new direction with a purpose in mind. She heard a whistle and turned to her left.

She saw the Draco-turtle, wallowing massively in the

water, hundreds of strides long with a ramshackle assortment of wooden buildings perched on its back, bigger than many market towns of Edland. The shell of the turtle had only a slight pitch to it, but it still peaked some fifty feet above the water. At the center of the carapace was a tall tower, not unlike the watchtowers of Kingshold, but surely made of wood, like the other buildings clustered around it.

There was the whistle again and she saw a figure crouching behind a wall of oaken barrels. Her father. She ran over and ducked down next to him.

"Where did you go?" he asked. "And do you realize you're on fire? It's not helping the hiding, you know."

She looked down and saw the flames for the briefest moment. As soon as she was aware, they shrank away. "It's a cold night. I didn't want to catch a chill." She forced a smile, not wanting to discuss what had just happened to her. Maybe not ever wanting to discuss it at all. "What are you doing?"

"I am trying to talk to the turtle."

"How's that going?"

"Not well," he said. "I met this one once before, a long time ago. She didn't have any interest in attacking cities back then. Ships were fine sport, but not armored fortifications. And she sure as shit wouldn't have let people live on her back. I thought she was dead." He paused, and then pounded his fist into his palm. "And she might be because I'm knocking on her mind, and she's not answering the door."

"You're obviously the expert when it comes to Draco-turtles," she said, "but she doesn't look very dead to me."

"I would concur with that assessment. Sod it. We're going to have to get into the town and see what's controlling it—"

Fwoom!

Out in the harbor, one of the ships stood out in the darkness like a candle, flames quickly licking up the masts to the furled sails, figures leaping from the burning deck and into the water below. Everything around them froze for a moment, pirates on the wetway stopping suddenly to see the beacon casting flickering light onto the other ships. And then, “Sound the alarm!” and “We’re under attack!” before cries of “Stay in your troops!” and “Ready your bows!” brought some order to the chaos, and many more pirates to the street around them.

Neenahwi looked at her father. “I bet that was Motega.”

“Hmph. Well if so, he’s made it a lot more bloody difficult for us now.” Jyuth peeked his head over the barrels. “There are bowmen everywhere now, too bloody many.”

Neenahwi risked a glance over the cover, too. “We could take them.”

“Of course, we could, or probably, anyway. You never know if a lucky arrow has your name on it.” He turned to look her in the eye, hand gripping her forearm. “But we kill them, and more will come, and then we’ll have to kill them, too. Is that what you want? Father and daughter of destruction, feared throughout the world?”

“They’re invading Kingshold, Father. This is different.”

“They’re not invading. Use your noggin, girl. They’re raiding.” He looked sympathetically at her. “Look, I know you’ve your gem now, but I’ve had mine a lot longer. They’re different, but they’re the same in many ways. I’ve used my power to kill hundreds in the past, before I knew better, or since then, when I thought I really had to. But it leaves you thin. The best of you wears away and leaves the bad behind. It takes a lot of time to repair those threads.”

"So, what are we going to do?"

"We wait. And be ready only if we absolutely have to."

She stared at her father, who held her gaze, while she weighed the options. The gem was nagging at the back of her mind, calling her to use it. She'd felt it when fighting the Gawl-demon, and quite frankly, it scared her. She nodded in agreement and they ducked back into the safety of their hideaway, listening and risking small looks to see what was happening. From toward the dockside area of town, where she'd left her brother and his friends, she heard a new sound. An amalgamation of roars and insults yelled at the top of the lungs. The sound traveled clear down the far distance of the curved Wetside street and out across the water.

"Soldiers?" asked Jyuth, squinting into the darkness.

"I don't think so. Nor city guard. I could have sworn I saw someone swinging a broom—"

And then the explosions came, first one, and then a minute or two later, the second. Screams after each blast, carrying across the harbor, and battle cries returned as pirates ran to meet those newly arrived defenders of the city.

A moment passed and then a long, deep horn note sounded from the floating town, and squad captains called, "Fall back!" and "Prepare to withdraw." Corsairs flooded out onto Wetside from the streets that joined it, but they moved away from where Jyuth and Neenahwi hid, toward the many longboats and the mob trying to arrest their escape. Sensing their moment to act, Neenahwi and Jyuth stepped out from behind the barrels, just as the huge wedge-shaped head of the Draco-turtle, green-scaled and coated in barnacles, swung in front of them on its long neck. The mouth opened, revealing rows of wicked fangs as big as a grown man, before a huge cloud of steam gushed out followed by torrents of burning fire.

Father and daughter looked at each other.

"I guess we better go do something, girl."

CHAPTER 42
TURTLE TOWN

The clear ground quickly disappeared as Motega ran toward the monster that had set about lighting up the city. He drew his axes as he closed on a ragtag mob of locals, dockhands, and laborers, swinging shovels and long hooks into the faces of pirates who had quickly realized they were outnumbered. He could sense the reassuring presence of Florian a few steps behind him. The brother he'd never had, always there for whatever craziness he got them into.

And then people were all around as he and Florian pushed through the locals, and then leaped at the corsairs in front. A thick-set woman with dirty-blonde braids and a gap-toothed smile swung a sword overhand. Parrying with one ax, he smashed her in the face with his other fist, not enough room in the melee to reliably swing his other weapon. She went down, and a man, no, closer to a boy, just a few whiskers sprouting from his chin, stabbed forward with a long, serrated dagger. The ax that had parried the previous blow followed through into the side of his head above the ear, face crumpling and blood exploding into Motega's eyes. He felt a moment of sorrow for the boy. But then life was a bitch. And his sister was fighting a dragon-turtle-pirate-town thing.

After he took the last shot, he was still using Per's eyes when the bird had circled back around to the city. There he'd seen Neenahwi and Jyuth standing in the street, and then huge torrents of fire and steam belching from the beast's massive head. Motega had only just got her back, and now he realized how much he'd missed her. And formidable though she was, he couldn't see how her metal arrows were going to do much against that thing, and putting it to sleep was surely going to be harder than a few dwarves. No, now was the time to beat a graceful and hasty retreat, and if he had to pick her up to do it, then so be it.

He broke through the line of pirates, some clear pavement in front of him, though more of the invaders were coming to support their own against the mob. Motega realized once the numbers were evened out, the locals were going to have real concerns, but that needed to be someone else's problem.

Florian caught up, bloodied swords in hand, and shouted over to him, "Mot! What's the plan?"

"We've got to save Neenahwi."

"Aye," he replied. "Let's try to kill a few of these arseholes on the way." Instead of running around a pair of pirates coming toward them—their focus on the pitched battle Motega and his friend had just left—Florian swerved to meet them at a run. They didn't stand a chance. Motega had never seen anyone as good with a blade as Florian, and with two, he was twice as wicked. Florian pointed to a group of four for both of them to engage, but as the two friends adjusted the course, their prey suddenly fell to the floor, arrows poking out like spines on a porcupine. Motega and Florian skidded to a halt.

"Where did they come from?" asked Motega. Running into lightly armored pirates armed with swords was one thing. He'd fancy his chances every day, but running headlong into bowmen tended to fall into the fatal mistake category.

Florian looked around and pointed up to the roof of the customs house that ran parallel to Wetside. Motega could just make out some shadowy shapes as they moved.

"Up there," said Florian. "Looks like our friends from back on the rooftops. Come on." And he set off again at a run. "You know, I think she likes me."

"Who?" asked Motega.

"The assassin lady."

"She's near twice your age, Flor. She was with Jyuth when he rescued Neenahwi and me from Pyrfew."

"She's a hell of a fighter, and she looks pretty good for an old lady. Hey, did you say we were going to rescue your sister? Looks like she's handling herself to me."

They were closing in on Turtle Town, but he couldn't make out the details from how far they were away. All he could see was the bright light of the Draco-turtle's flame, but then he noticed streaks of red and purple light moving toward the beast.

"I can't see that far! What's happening?"

"Looks like she and Jyuth are fighting back. Holding their own, at least." Their feet pounded on the street as they ran the more than a mile of Wetside to get to where Turtle Town had taken residence. "Whoa! One of them just flung up water from the harbor and into the fire breath."

Motega pumped his arms and legs, gulping down huge lungfuls of air as he increased his speed. As they got closer, he could feel the heat on his face, smell burning wood from the buildings on fire. They slowed to a walk, mouths hanging open at what they saw. Neenahwi was a few hundred strides away, throwing balls of red energy at the reptilian face. Some would explode on contact; others would glance off and ricochet into Turtle Town, creating fires mirroring the conflagration of the harborside. Jyuth was standing closer, back toward them, water flowing unnaturally up from the harbor and toward the raging fires at his command while he, too, fired purple darts in rapid succession that would sink into the long neck, penetrating through the hard scales like hot needles. Jyuth looked over his shoulder and saw them.

"Get back!" he called, waving them away. "You want to melt like a candle? Actually, stay where you are. I need your help." And he stepped slowly back toward them. "Something is controlling this Draco-turtle, up there in the town. Find it and stop it."

"I came to get Neenahwi," said Motega, feeling a little foolish as he saw his sister in action.

"She doesn't need your help with this. But she'll need your help tomorrow; she's going to have one hell of a hangover. But you getting toasted isn't going to be helpful."

Motega didn't respond, caught in two minds. He knew Jyuth was right, but didn't want to admit it, didn't want to be taking his orders again.

"Look," said the wizard, "this is the chance for you two to be the heroes. Save the city." Jyuth was nodding at them like they were simpletons. Motega and Florian nodded back. "Well, get fucking moving then!"

THEY STOOD TOGETHER ON THE END OF A WOODEN PIER. Motega stripped off the few extraneous items he felt he didn't need. Quiver, boots, and bandolier of knives placed carefully in a pile. He secured his war axes with leather ties and looked across at Florian, who regarded him with mild interest.

"Are you ready now?" Florian asked.

"Yes," said Motega. "You're swimming in the chainmail?"

"Yep."

"And your boots?"

"Yep."

Motega shook his head. "Mad. Nothing worse than wet boots."

"Your stuff might not be here when we come back," said Florian, looking at the pile of Motega's belongings. "I've heard there are thieves around."

"That's alright. We might not come back."

Motega dove into the harbor, pushing through the dark water before he surfaced and made a course for Turtle Town. Glancing back, he saw the strong arms of his friend plowing through the harbor waters as if he wasn't carrying an unnecessary, extra twenty pounds. *Show off.* He'd be more tired for it, though.

As he approached Turtle Town, Motega could see a small wooden jetty protruding from the side of the shell, a long boat moored against it where pirates disembarked. The two swam alongside the wooden structure, which looked like it could be pulled in when not in use, and pulled themselves up. A man approached, wisps of white hair with a face that had seen many days in the cruel sun of the open sea. One eye gave Motega a bead, the other looking off in a different direction, before the stranger reached over and grabbed him by the forearm and helped haul him up. Motega shook off the water like a shaggy dog and helped Glass Eye pull up Florian.

"You fellah's missed the boat, eh?" the old man chuckled to himself at his joke.

"Argh, m—"

"Yeah," said Motega, interrupting Florian and shooting him a dirty look. "We got a message for the boss, and we were told not to hang around. You know where he is?"

"He'll be up on the hill, I'd wager," said the pirate. He squinted and gave them some more concentrated one-eye attention. "I don't know you. Haven't seen your faces before."

"Likewise. But not like we do this every week, eh? Raiding fucking Kingshold. Boss has balls," bluffed Motega.

"Heh. He does indeed. Alright then, fuck off and do your job. Once we torch this shithole, we'll be out of here."

Motega winked at him and punched his arm jovially. Florian did the same and almost knocked Glass Eye into the now empty boat.

They latched onto the rear of the squad walking up the narrow lane toward the tower on top of the *hill*. The path, no wider than to allow four men walking abreast, was still something of a thoroughfare, dark alleys branching off at angles. The structures were two or three stories high, each construction supporting another as beams linked roofs, or one building would go up, and then over and down on top of its neighbor. Building materials were clearly salvage, but it certainly had the feel of a real town, a shithole of a town, as they passed shops and a tavern with a sign hung from a mermaid figurehead called the Tasty Tit.

Blending into the crowd, looking as dirty and disheveled as the smelly men and women around them, they passed as other pirates. Once Motega was comfortable they were going unnoticed, he nudged Florian with his elbow and gave him the kind of look he'd been on the receiving end from Neenahwi a hundred times.

"Argh?"

"That's what they say, isn't it?" asked Florian.

"From now on, I do all the talking."

The ground moved beneath their feet, lifting into the air, and then coming back down with a *thud*. Motega had to steady himself on the bearded pirate in front of him, who took the turtle quake in stride. The pirate turned, Motega noticing he was wearing a lacey pink nightgown, belted at the middle, with a saber tucked away. "Fuck off!" he spat in Motega's face, the pirates rank breath making his eyes water. Motega decided to let that one pass.

Upping the pace and pushing through the crowd to reach the top of the hill, they saw a wide area without the chaotic sprawl of tottering hovels, all except for a tall, wooden tower built in the center of what must be Turtle Town square. On a stage made of wooden packing crates a tall man, well-dressed in clean scarlet trousers and coat, beard trimmed short, addressed groups of scurrying pirates.

"Torch it, boys! Let Kingshold burn, and then we shall depart!"

"Aye, aye, King Kolsen," came answering calls.

"Karr," called the pirate king, addressing a lingering skinny lad armed with a crossbow. "Go and find that puffed up toad Tegyr and tell him we have to go. If he's not done, we're leaving without him."

"Where should I look, Captain? I mean, King," stammered the lad.

"Ashore, lad! Just make an effort, pass the word. But don't get left behind yourself."

A ball of red flame lit up the night as it looped up into the air from down below Turtle Town, exploding on to the bare shell of a nearby street, scattering flame some distance.

"And put out those fires!" shouted the pirate king, pointing. "And don't forget what we came for. Profit first!"

"Death last!" came in answer from the corsairs continuing about their business.

Avoiding the assemblage, Motega led Florian up to the door of the tower and opened it a crack. Inside were at least five men that he could see, lounging in seats and playing cards by lamplight at a table. Around them were stacked, sealed crates, the profit from this or another recent entrepreneurial adventure. Motega closed the door quickly and quietly.

"There's a lot in there," he said.

"How many?" asked Florian.

"At least five, but probably more."

"Well, we need to get past them."

"I'm aware of that," said Motega, rubbing his chin in thought. "I hope this isn't a terrible idea."

"It probably is, but I don't have anything. So, go ahead."

Motega nodded, and then flung back his shoulders and puffed himself up to his full size. He pushed the door open wide with a bang.

"Oi, you fuckers!" shouted Motega. "What do you think

you're doing? Get off your lazy arses and get those crates over to the king."

The swarthy-looking men snapped upright in their seats, pipe dropping from the mouth of one into his lap. The brave or the stupid one opened his mouth to answer, "But we just brought them i—"

"Did I ask you to speak? Does the king ask you to think? Do you want me to go and tell him this fuckwit is too busy playing cards to do what he's told?" Motega turned to walk out of the open door.

The pirates scrambled to their feet and made for the crates.

"No problem," said Mouthy hurriedly. "We're right on it."

Motega and Florian watched nine corsairs in total load their arms and thread their way out into the square. Florian closed the door behind them. Looking around the room, they saw wooden steps in the corner leading upwards and in the center of the room a curious length of glass pipe that dropped from the double height ceiling above and disappeared into the turtle shell floor.

"You know we're screwed when they figure out what we've done and come back," said Florian.

Motega shrugged.

They ran up the stairs around the inside of the tower until it reached a trap door. Opening it a sliver to take a look, the pair quickly climbed out into the room at the top of the tower. Open windows on all four sides allowed the orange light of fire in the night to cast a sickly glow over the room. Its sole inhabitant was a skinny young man, pale complexion, and wire-rimmed spectacles perched on his nose. He stood at a table full of alchemical equipment. Flasks of different-colored ichors, an oil burner, and series of glass beakers and jars arrayed before him.

"I don't need anything right now," the alchemist squeaked without turning. "Leave m— Wait, who are you?"

Florian sprinted across the room in three long bounds and grabbed Mouse around the chest, bringing the blade of his sword to his throat. "Don't try to shout," he said with a growl.

Motega stalked forward, looking at the equipment on the table and the timid captive with fear in his eyes. "How are you controlling the beast? I want you to stop it. Now."

"No way," stammered Mouse. "Kolsen will kill me."

"Don't worry," Florian whispered into his ear. "You'll die before then if you don't help us."

A wet patch appeared on Mouse's trousers, and he whimpered before nodding emphatically. "It's the green one." His eyes flicked to the green flask on the table. "Five drops, down the tube, and it'll stop the fire."

"Now, that wasn't so hard, was it?" said Motega as he picked up the glass container and poured all of it down the glass pipe disappearing into the floor. And with his ax, he smashed the glass tube and the bottles of different-colored liquids that hissed as they came into contact with the table.

"You fool. What have you done?" said Mouse. "We'll all die now. I won't be able to control it."

"No way we're letting you have your toys," said Motega. "What happens now?"

All was still for a moment. Turtle Town had stopped moving, and the roar of the draconic fire that had been a dull noise in the background ceased. *Bang*. The trapdoor was flung open and through it climbed the pirate king and the men they'd sent on a wild goose chase.

Florian regarded the ten pirates in front of them, swords drawn and spreading out across the room. He turned to Motega. "Called it. Royally screwed."

"They made me do it, Kolsen, sir," squeaked Mouse.

The pirate king Kolsen ignored the alchemist, regarding the interlopers intently. "Kill them," he ordered, and his men began to move forward. Motega drew his other ax.

From the window behind Motega and Florian streaked a ball of outstretched talons and feathers into the pirate king's face. Per! Kolsen screamed and flapped his hands at the falcon clawing his face. And then the ground moved again, synchronized with great agonized bellows audible through the open windows. The world lurched to the left as Turtle Town pushed off against the street of Wetside and turned back out to the harbor. The pirates stumbled and looked to the king in confusion, unsure whether his last order still stood. But he was still trying to fight off the tearing beak and razor-sharp talons making a bloody mess of his face.

In times like these, Motega always thought, it was best to go with what you know. So, he and Florian, still clutching Mouse, dove from the window and into the night sky.

CHAPTER 43
NAMING AND SHAMING

From the shadows of a doorway at the rear of the throne room, Hoskin could see the assembled crowd. The room hadn't been used since the death of the royal couple, and it seemed strange to him now to see the vast chamber in use. In fact, if there had been a viable alternative, he would have taken it and avoided using the room, but he had to admit to himself it did also reinforce a particular message.

The room was three times as long as it was wide, a raised dais at one end where the thrones rested along with his usual seat, three steps down, reserved for the lord chancellor. Commander Grimes stood by that chair, and noticing Hoskin, he gave him a small nod of recognition. At the other end of the room were the double-height twin doors through which the assembled good people of Kingshold had passed momentarily before. The guild masters who weren't nobles stood furthest away from the throne close to the entrance, next to them were the senior priests of the various religions observed in Edland, and the open nature of the country meant there were rather a lot.

Lining the sides of the chamber were the collected nobility and their attendants, clustered amongst the pillars supporting the upper tier that was mostly empty today. Each noble family stood in their appropriate places, the same whenever the court was in attendance, determined by an unclear method of self-selection, which inevitably made the jockeying for position a national pastime. The central floor was typically where supplicants, ambassadors, or others addressed the king and queen, and this was where his primary audience—the remaining candidates for lord protector—had been guided to wait.

Standing there was Sir Penshead and Lords Eden, Uthridge, Fiske, and the new Lord Bollingsmead. Each of them had brought a handful of attendants, who stood off to the side, and Hoskin caught sight of some familiar faces. Sitting on the steps of the dais in front of the assembled candidates was the wizard Jyuth, forearms resting on knees with back straight, chin up, and eyes closed, ignoring the hubbub of collected murmuring around the room. Hoskin thought he'd probably waited for long enough, no need to let them get too restless.

Striding out from the back of the dais, Hoskin walked past the two carved wooden thrones and descended the steps to his usual seat, but he didn't sit. The noise of chattering continued. He nodded briefly to Grimes who signaled two guards, armed with halberds, to strike the heels of the wooden shafts of their weapons on the ground. The noise reverberated around the stone chamber, and all eyes looked forward.

"Friends and fellow Edlanders," began Hoskin, "I've asked you all here today because we need unity after the events of the past few days. Our fair city has suffered at the hands of invaders and our own people." Hoskin regarded the candidates in front of him. "One of you will rule Edland in just a few short days. Your role is to protect the people of our nation so they can lead good and prosperous lives, and I don't envy the burden one of you will inherit. The world has changed in this past moon cycle. The cart has started rolling down the hill, and I fear there's no stopping it now. I know some of you have been calling for war, some for expansion, and others for retreating inward and ignoring the outside world. You'll soon find so simplistic a view is naive."

He paused and looked around the room. Muttering between neighbors had begun again, and some of the nobility seemed vexed. In particular Eden. But Hoskin didn't care. They might not want to listen to him, but they were going to. In the past, he wouldn't have been so bold as to speak his mind publicly, but the past four weeks had changed him, too, and it seemed there was no stopping that particular cart either.

"But who rules is for you to decide," he continued. "I'm neither a candidate nor going to vote. For now, I give thanks to those of you who helped Kingshold and Edland last night. I cannot award titles or rewards, but I can make this known to you all."

"Sir Penshead, I heard you worked tirelessly with Commander Grimes, the two of you organizing the city's guard and defenses. And you personally led assaults against the barricades. You've rediscovered your bravery and your priorities. I salute you." Hoskin's nod to the armored knight was mirrored in return.

"Lord Bollingsmead. And I mean the younger, of course."

A murmur of laughter rippled around the room as many looked down the hall to the recently arrived elder Bollingsmead.

"It appears it was you who led the defense of the city. It was you, and your companions, who attacked the ships, you who rallied the people of the city to defend it and send the cowardly pirates running for the open waters. And I have it on very good authority," he said, looking down to see Jyuth nodding as he gazed up at the vaulted ceiling, "that your companions, Motega and Florian, risked their lives to board the monster burning our city and cause it to leave."

Jyuth began to clap loudly, singularly at first until more hands joined his, and applause filled the throne room. Bollingsmead gave a small bow while the two fighters Hoskin had named stepped out from under the gallery and raised their arms in triumph. Though Hoskin considered their smiles to be the silly grins of youth, the pair indeed looked tired from their exertions of the previous night.

"As I said, I can grant you little gift other than my appreciation. Without you, even though Kingshold is scorched in places, it would be in even more dire straits. But I can do one other thing. I can let all know who it was, when the city was in greatest need, that did nothing." The apprehension of what he was about to say, and to whom, made him feel a little nauseous, but it also conjured an intense feeling of pleasure in the back of his mind. "Who was it, Lord Eden, who did nothing last night? Who locked their compound and ordered their guards to see to their own personal protection instead of the city? I wonder if you would be able to tell us all?"

Eden's jaw clenched, his complexion flushed, and a vein bulged in his temple while his eyes fired hot needles into Hoskin's flesh. Hoskin met his gaze and held it with a smile on his lips now. It was only the sight of Lord Bollingsmead turning to look at Lady Grey that distracted Hoskin. The young lord seemed visibly shocked Eden had not helped last night. Hoskin considered it a sign of his naivety, and he saw him mouth a word to the lady, who had so clearly become his sponsor. *Coward.* So easily readable for Hoskin, and also it seemed for Eden, too, who had followed the chancellor's distracted attention.

Eden took a step toward Bollingsmead. "How dare you call me a coward!" he roared. "I've proven my worth to the realm countless times! I'm the liberator of Redsmoke!"

"I believe it was called Redpool when you liberated it, my lord," said Bollingsmead, regarding his verbal attacker quite calmly. "And I've heard stories about that campaign."

"What are you blathering on about, boy?"

"The official story goes you're a master tactician and orator, who during parley, goaded the installed governor of Redpool to open the doors and meet you on the field. The real story is a little different, isn't it? You actually had a squad infiltrate the city and murder his family while you were under the white flag."

"How dare you!" Now Eden really exploded. Flecks of spit flew from his mouth, and he moved within feet of Bollingsmead. "Liar! You may have no honor, lying with common tavern wenches and behaving like an entertainer, but I won't stand to be called a coward! A liar! A murderer of children!" He turned and looked again at Hoskin. "I demand, by my rights, to settle this by duel!"

Bollingsmead regarded Eden, his eyes taking him in. Eden was tall and still muscular for a man in his late forties, and Hoskin remembered him as quite the duelist in his youth. Bollingsmead turned to face Hoskin, too, smiling and spoke a single word. “Agreed.”

Hoskin sighed. So much for bringing people together in unity. Now, there’d be blood on the throne room floor.

“I name Sir Frederick as my champion,” said Eden.

And a tall knight in gleaming plate armor strode forward to stand by his side, loosing a shield worn on his back and drawing a long sword. Bollingsmead’s smile disappeared. It seemed the savior of Kingshold was naive in other ways, too, if he thought Eden would actually fight himself.

CHAPTER 44
DUEL

Mareth was dead on his feet throughout the lord chancellor's speech. It had been a long night. There had been holdouts of corsairs, the ones left behind, he'd helped to subdue, and the sun was rising by the time the last of the fighting had stopped. And then there were fires to quench. The people who'd come to his aid, to be the front line of taking the fight to the pirates, became bucket chains. They'd probably still have been fighting those fires if Neenahwi and her father hadn't used magic to make the waters from the harbor flow into the burning structures. As it was, he only had time to wash and shave before traveling to the palace after receiving the summons.

He knew he should probably have held his tongue when Eden rose to the charges Hoskin announced, but he couldn't help himself. He really disliked the man, someone he once thought was a hero of the realm cared nothing for the people. That Eden was still the favorite to become lord protector had Mareth considering where he was going to have to move. And when he challenged him to a duel,

Mareth's sleep-deprived mind imagined Eden dead at his feet and the path to victory open. He didn't exactly feel comfortable fighting with the rapier hanging at his hip but, surely, he could take an old man.

Then the big bastard-knight stepped forward, and Mareth's head spun. Of course, Eden himself wasn't going to fight, and his champion was probably going to cut his thin blade in two before doing the same to him. Mareth took a deep, ragged breath, and the blood drained from his face.

"Lord Jyuth, you must do something," said Hoskin. "There has been enough blood spilled."

The wizard had appeared to be only paying partial attention for most of the proceedings, but now he became present. "I can't do anything with fools, Hoskin. Law is the law. Loser either dies or is banished. It's been this way for centuries, though I'll make it clear, it was never something I agreed with."

The brief moment of hope Mareth had grasped for disappeared like a lost love partially seen in the crowd. He heard Neenahwi ask the same favor of her father, but she sounded distant to his ears, like he was under water and the sound was muffled. He'd been in fights where he could have died many times. Shit, he'd seen his friends cut down by men and monsters, and his foolishness had been responsible for leading some of them to the grave. But now, faced with his own death, he felt an overwhelming weight of despair that he'd let everyone down, all of those people who'd believed in him.

A hand touched his shoulder, and Mareth noticed the lord chancellor standing in front of him, the grip on his shoulder providing an anchor back to the throne room.

"Lord Bollingsmead," Hoskin spoke clearly and slowly, eyes locked on Mareth's, "do you name a champion?"

Name a champion? The thought hadn't even occurred to him. But how could he ask someone to take the blade in his place? He turned to look at his companions. Lady Grey's mouth was pursed, and her eyes betrayed the anger she contained. Mareth quickly looked on, unable to bear the look, his eyes resting on Dolph. Dolph had been his shadow for the past three weeks. He'd fought at his shoulder last night, but now he shook his head.

"I will champion you, Mareth." Florian stepped forward. A few moments before, he was basking in the applause of the great and good of Kingshold, and now he looked sober. And tired, too.

"No, Florian." Motega made to pull back his friend, but Florian shrugged off his attention. "You're exhausted. I'll do it. He looks like another Juggernaut, eh?"

"No, Mot. It's not like the Juggernaut. I know Sir Frederick, and he'll beat you in single combat. I'll do it. I can win." His last words sounded to Mareth like he was trying to convince himself. "No arguments, Mareth. I do this willingly."

Mareth nodded and turned back to Hoskin and Eden. "I name Florian as my champion."

THE SILENCE IN THE THRONE ROOM DISAPPEARED AS THE crowd anticipated the bloodshed to come. Palace guards strode forward to stand in front of the attendees, forming a rectangular ring for the duel. Mareth and Eden stared across the ring at each other, the ill will palpable in the air. Sir Frederick placed a shining steel helm over his head, covering his long curly blond hair and chiseled features, and clanked into the ring. On his left arm was a shield bearing Eden's crest, and in his right, he gripped a broadsword.

Florian bounced in place opposite the knight, stretching the muscles in his arms and back, rotating his neck. He had stripped off his tunic to reveal chainmail underneath, but he wore no helm, nor carried a shield. In both hands, he held what Mareth had never seen him without. One sword was long and plain, lacking adornment or engraving, but made of solid steel. The other blade was slightly shorter, with a curve to the point, filigree etched along its length.

The lord chancellor stepped between the two fighters and looked at Mareth and Eden in turn. "Lord Eden. Lord Bollingsmead. Do you withdraw your desire for a duel?"

"Never," spat Eden.

Mareth shook his head.

"Then, in the witness of these fine people, may Arloth guide the winner and show pity on the fallen. Begin!" And Hoskin quickly ran to the side ducking behind the palace guard.

Sir Frederick strode directly at Florian, shield in front of him with sword close, held at chest height. Florian skirted to the left, trying to keep his distance as he assessed his foe, but the rectangular fighting area naturally brought them closer together. Sir Frederick moved like quicksilver, striking in rapid succession, which Florian struggled to parry. Each of Florian's blades only just moved in time to deflect the knight's strikes. Florian looked exhausted, his breathing already labored through his open mouth.

Florian swayed back from another strike and tucked into a roll to try to give himself some distance, but it wasn't fast enough. As he regained his feet, the knight was already upon him. A flurry of blows, low and high, each one forcing Florian back toward the crowd, who in turn shrank back to safer vantage points. Sir Frederick's shield lashed out, smashing into Florian's face and chest and sending him sprawling across the floor.

"Hah! That's what you get for consorting with tavern scum, Bollingsmead," laughed Eden. "This won't take long."

Florian got to his feet and wiped the blood from his mouth with the back of his hand. Frederick hadn't followed up. He was clanging his sword on his shield in time to calls of "Eden, Eden, Eden." A man who certainly enjoyed his work.

Florian waited, swords pointed at the stone floor until Frederick decided he should finish the job. Once again the knight sauntered forward before quickening his pace for the final approach, his blade slicing through the air. Florian's left sword parried one strike high, the follow-up pushed low with his other weapon from across his body.

The plain sword held Sir Frederick's blade wedged against the stone floor, the muscles of Florian's arm rippling as it pushed against the knight's long sword. It only bought a fraction of a second, but it was enough for Florian to spin, stepping inside the knight's guard, bringing his other weapon slicing down onto the gauntleted hand. The force of the blow, and the precision of the strike, ripped the gauntlet from Frederick's hand. It fell to the floor along with the knight's sword and a couple of fingers.

Florian's turn continued, all one fluid movement, and he pushed into the shield with his broad shoulder, knocking Sir Frederick backward with all the force his legs could launch. The knight struggled to hold his balance, and he toppled to the floor. The clatter of steel on stone mingled with the knight's screams as his brain recognized what had happened to his hand. Florian's left sword flashed down, completing the spin, threading above the gorget and pushing through the chainmail protecting the knight's neck.

Sir Frederick's screams turned to a gurgle as he thrashed on the floor, trying to bring his hands up to help him lift his helm, but his ruined hand and bound shield didn't help. Florian took a few steps back and watched as the life bled from his opponent.

Mareth exhaled, realizing he'd been holding his breath for who knows how long. The throne room was completely silent for a few moments until there was the sound of hands clapping. Lady Chalice applauded, regarding Florian with the eye of a sailor in a whore house. "Bravo," she called. Eden stared at her, looking as if he had a chicken bone caught in his throat.

Lord Hoskin made to step into the ring, but Jyuth put an arm across his chest to hold him back. "Let me," he said quietly. The wizard strode into the clear space, and his voice boomed out, "By the grace of Arloth, Lord Bollingsmead is the victor. Lord Eden, you've been found wanting. And so, in line with the law, you are stripped of your lands, your titles, and you must leave Edland. You have twenty-four hours."

"This is outrageous! You can't do that," shrieked Eden. "My lands were granted by the king. Only the king can strip them."

"I think you forget yourself, Eden. I was the one who stripped the throne from the king. I suggest you hurry and pack. In twenty-four hours, if you're still on Edland soil, then the customary bounty will be honored."

Eden's retinue approached him as he gasped for air. One person on either side helped support him before he fell and escorted him out of the throne room, all eyes following them out.

Jyuth snapped his fingers, and Mareth's attention jerked back to see the wizard pointing at the corpse of the armored knight on the floor. "Can someone please clean up this mess before tomorrow?"

CHAPTER 45
GOODBYES

The bed felt the same as she remembered, even though it had been ten years since she last slept in here, since she'd bought her own place in the city, after the palace had become too constricting. But now, waking in her old bed in her father's apartments made her surprisingly content. Sunlight slanted through the shutters. Was it still evening, or had she slept through to the morning? After the excitement of the throne room, she had made sure Florian was uninjured, and then went to sleep as quickly as she could.

Climbing out of bed, dressing in the robes she'd worn the prior day, she walked through to the sitting room to see her father at the table, breakfast arrayed before him.

"Good morning," he said.

"So, it is morning then. I wasn't sure."

"Well, it's actually past lunchtime, but we both needed the rest." He patted the seat next to him. "Come, join me for breakfast."

Neenahwi sat and looked at the spread arrayed before

her. Yogurt and figs with honey, hard boiled eggs, thick slices of ham, hard cheese, still warm crusty bread, and sliced apples, pears, and peaches. Her stomach told her eyes to stop gawping and get stuck in. She ate with gusto and without a need for either of them to talk. Once they'd eaten their fill, they leaned back in the chairs, drinking tea from delicate cups.

"Are you really going to leave?" she asked. "It's all fucked up."

"Yes, I am."

He looked regretful to Neenahwi, but she knew him, maybe knew him better than she knew her brother, and once he made up his mind, he'd follow it through.

"Maybe I'm the source of the chaos," he continued. "We'll only know once I leave. And I'm still tired."

"Hah! Tiredness again, old man? You look better than I feel this morning."

"That's different. You have more vitality than me. The things I've done over the centuries, they've left me thread-bare and thin."

She looked at him, and for a moment, she saw an old man slumped in the chair, but the familiar facade came back as he smiled a warm smile at her.

"When are you leaving?" she asked.

"Tomorrow, after the votes are tallied. I'll slip away during whatever celebrations are planned to happen."

He sighed a deep sigh and reached over to take her hand in his. "I'm truly sorry to leave you, Neenahwi. You've been one of the few moments of light in my long life. And I'm so proud of you! You've grown into a very formidable woman. I don't need to protect you anymore." Then the smile disappeared to be replaced by a look of granite. "And I'm sorry for what you're going to have to face. You can sense it. Tomorrow, when a new lord protector walks into the palace, it's not going to be the end of the troubles. And Gawl Tegyr won't be the last to meddle in the affairs of Edland, or to come for you."

A blubbery snort erupted from Neenahwi. Tears flowed down her cheeks. Was this goodbye forever or just for a while? One father had been taken from her, and afterward, she'd felt an absence that hadn't been filled until she'd grown to love this old man. How could she manage without him?

"Believe in yourself, child." He embraced her until the sobs slowed, and then wiped her tears with the back of his hand. "Keep Motega close to you, and his friends. I have some gifts for you. Stay here while I go and fetch them."

Neenahwi watched her father open a box in the side room that housed the chests of gold he'd been gathering in exchange for pyxies. He took a rectangular leather case, placing it on the ground, and then removed four other items, putting them alongside the other. The first wrapped object he lifted back into the chest, closed the lid, and rose from his knees, holding all of the gifts with some difficulty. He placed them on the table and sat opposite Neenahwi.

"First is this." And he handed her a small box made of ebony. It was unadorned and without an obvious way of opening it. "Here, place your hand flat on the lid." He guided her hand onto the box, and after a few seconds, it *clicked*, the top rising up a fraction of an inch. "That'll only work for you, and me, of course. I did have to put what's inside in there."

She lifted the lid off the box, and inside, resting on red velvet, was a pendant on a golden chain. Holding the necklace before her, she saw the delicacy of the work in the chain and the outside of the pendant, vines of roses wrought in gold and silver, twisting as they formed an empty oval. He reached up and turned it to show the rear of the pendant where a sharp silver thorn jutted out.

"Do you have your demon stone?" he asked her.

She pulled the red gem from a pouch, and it rested in her palm, the shifting and swirling shades of red visible through the smooth surface. She offered it to him.

"No, it's not for me. Insert it into the casing." She did so, and like a magnet, the stone clicked the final fractions of an inch into place. It looked terrifyingly beautiful. "The spike on the back creates the connection to your blood, the same way it did two nights' past. But no matter what, don't wear this all the time."

"Thank you so much, Father. It's beautiful."

"Beauty isn't relevant here, but I do take some pride in my craftsmanship. And you're welcome. There are two more things." He handed her a scroll, sealed with wax. "Don't open this until I've gone. Tomorrow night before you sleep should be fine. Promise me."

"OK, Father, I promise."

"And a final gift for you. These are my journals." Jyuth placed on the table ten thin, soft, leather-bound books, collected together with a leather strap that looked like an old belt. "Back when I used to keep them. Probably the first fifty years or so of my studies. Maybe there'll be something useful in there for you."

Neenahwi sniffled again. "Thank you, Father. I look forward to reading them."

"And here's one more gift. For Motega." He undid the wool wrapping to reveal an unstrung, long bow made of a single piece of horn, larger than any she'd seen in the past. "Tell him I love him, too. This is dragon horn. Ancient. I was going to give it to him when he came of age, but didn't have the chance."

The old man drooped. Past failures remembered were such a weight. Neenahwi stood and embraced him once more. It felt good. Comfortable.

"Ahem." Jyuth rose to his feet. "Now, let's not be maudlin. We have one last night together. What shall we do?"

Without a moment's hesitation, Neenahwi knew. "Let's fly, Father."

CHAPTER 46
VICTORY

Petra's hand, held in hers, felt reassuring as they walked through the palace grounds. Alana was still uneasy on her feet, and she wasn't sure she'd have been able to do this without assistance. The past week had been a haze, moments of wakefulness when she ate, only to sleep more, interspersed with vivid dreams she could now just remember as phantoms.

The last thing she could clearly recall was trying to stop the assassin, and Arloth knows what she was thinking at the time, but apparently it had bought Mareth valuable seconds. And then there was black. A few of Alana's dreams had remained with her, visions of her mother and father sitting by her bedside, holding her hand and mopping her brow, as well as scenes of vast, unspoiled grasslands where, laughing, she ran barefoot. Was that the next world? Had she come so close to dying?

This morning, Neenahwi had told her she should stay in bed, but Petra had woken her specifically to receive a letter.

A personal invitation from Jyuth, and she didn't want to miss this occasion.

The two of them walked through the entrance to the palace and down the long hallway to the throne room, Trypp a step behind them, their volunteer for escort duty. She noticed the staff of the palace going about their business the way only a former servant would, last-minute preparations for the influx of people attending this momentous event. As she passed, they saw her, too. Alana could sense their unvoiced questions of why she was there, dressed like one of her betters, in a gown she knew she had only borrowed that morning.

Ushers guided them up marble stairs to the gallery. They found an open spot by the wooden railing and looked down at the throne room. Below her, the most important people in the country waited, nobles, priests, merchants, guild masters and, for the first time, the district supervisors, standing in groups, all intently looking forward to the dais at the end of the room.

Jyuth stood there next to a great black chalkboard, a small, naked pink pyxie sitting on his shoulder like a monkey with the organ grinder. A succession of pops heralded the appearance of a series of tiny demons near the chalkboard. Each, in turn, picked up a small piece of chalk and made a tally mark below the name of a candidate before disappearing. The tiny demons resembled shriveled newborns to her eye, but they stood upright on their sharp-clawed feet, their mouths full of needle-sharp teeth and eyes so much like a cat it gave her the willies. Alana wondered which of the pyxies belonged to the district supervisors, the fruits of their planning and hard work paying off today.

"Are you sure everyone was able to cast their vote?" she asked Petra.

"Yes. I'm certain. I told you I was with them when they received their demons from the wizard," Petra replied. "I must admit, all of the supervisors had never seen as much gold as they handed over today. If it weren't for Florian, Motega, and Lady Grey's guards watching over them, I wouldn't have been surprised if some of them would have disappeared. But we promised everyone would get the money back tomorrow, and so, we weren't going to let anything happen to stop that." She paused for a moment. "You know, we didn't give as much thought as to how we would get everyone their money back."

"You kept records, didn't you?"

"Of course! But there are still thousands of people who'll be depending on getting their money back."

"Don't worry, Petra." She smiled and squeezed her hand. "I'll be there to help tomorrow."

Alana looked at the chalkboard and saw the names of the candidates across the top. She noticed Eden's name was still there, even though he was disqualified. And worse, he had many tallies below his name, less than she'd been projecting just a week back, but still more than two score.

"Do you see how many votes Eden has?" said Alana. "That's going to be trouble."

"Don't worry," said her sister. "Mareth is in the lead. How can he lose now?"

"She's right," said Trypp, who'd been strangely quiet the whole journey. "It's not going to affect the result today, but the question is how many of those votes were cast before he was exiled. If people still support Eden and voted for him anyway, then it'll create problems later. I heard he didn't leave the country right away. He and his retinue were seen heading to his estates in the north yesterday. Is he going to run after packing, or start a fight?"

She looked at her sister and saw her gazing down at Mareth standing with Lady Grey, and so, let the thought pass. She could see them laughing and smiling, and she knew what Petra was thinking.

"Don't worry, Petra. You know he wanted you to be there with him, but you're up here helping me." Petra smiled back at her, not commenting on what they both knew was a lie.

The past four weeks had changed their lives. They'd done things they never expected. They now counted influential people as their friends that they could never have dreamed of, but still, there were limits. Motega and Florian were there with Mareth, but they were formally there as his bodyguards. She and Petra were but commoners, a servant girl and tavern maid, and from the Narrows, at that. Those kind of marks were hard to scrub off.

The wizard stood silently at the front of the chamber, watching the little demons do their work. The successive *pops* as the pyxies appeared and disappeared began to slow, the board filling with tally marks. After a few moments, no more of the pink creatures materialized, and Alana saw Jyuth say something to the pyxie on his shoulder. It shook its head. Jyuth nodded before the little monster vanished, too, with a tiny *crack*.

Jyuth raised his hands in the air and clapped three times. The murmuring of the crowd ceased.

"Lords, ladies, and gentlefolk of Kingshold, the tallies are in. I, Jyuth, here at the founding of Edland, certify these results as being true and accurate." He paused and looked around the chamber, daring anyone to contest the fact. The silence stretched in anticipation. "It's clear for all to see, the new lord protector of Edland, until the day he dies, is Lord Bollingsmead. Let's welcome him!" he boomed.

Throughout the hall, there were cheers and applause, cries of "Victory," "Bollingsmead," and "The Bard!" Petra grabbed Alana in a tight hug, squeezing hard until she remembered the wound her sister had recently received.

"Oh no, I'm sorry. Are you okay?"

"I'm fine, Petra; don't worry. No stitches, remember?" Alana replied. "We did it! I can't believe it!" And Petra held her again, lights dancing at the edge of her vision, caused by the strength of the embrace or her incredulity that this was indeed happening, she wasn't sure.

Down below, she could see Mareth swamped by well-wishers. Lady Grey had grabbed his face and kissed him on both cheeks. Mareth and Florian were shaking his hand so hard it seemed like his arm might fall off, while Dolph tried to impose some order around them before the palace guard arrived in more significant numbers. And Mareth accepted it all with a look of bemusement on his face.

An old man pushed his way through the crowd to try to get close to the new lord protector, calling something inaudible over the din to the palace guards who had now formed a cordon. Eventually, he was face-to-face with Mareth, and they looked silently for a moment into one another's eyes before the old man embraced him, Mareth looking slightly uncomfortable.

"Who is that?" asked Petra, also surveying the scene below.

"I think it's Lord Bollingsmead. His father."

CHAPTER 47
YOUR NATION CALLS

Standing off to the side of the dais, Hoskin listened to Jyuth's announcement with a combination of relief and resentment. Relief, that in one more day, it would all be over for him. Once Bollingsmead was crowned, or whatever it was they were going to call it—and he wondered what ceremony Percival had settled on—he'd be free of responsibility, at last. Free to be with his books, his writing, and free again to walk in the green hills of his childhood home. But a nagging part of him was also furious that Jyuth hadn't so much as thanked him for his service this past month. Yes, there had been a few incidents, but they were hardly his fault. He'd like to see what it was going to be like without him.

The part of him that wanted to be free won the internal battle. Who cared if no one recognized him? Pretty much no one had his whole life, even though he'd supposedly been one of the most powerful men in the kingdom for the past decade. No, it was better to be able to leave without much fanfare. He breathed deeply as he watched the crowds moving to congratulate the new lord protector, realizing he should probably do the same.

Grimes stepped forward and walked alongside him.

"Are you well, my lord?" he asked.

"Yes, Grimes, never better. And how about you?"

"Nice to not have anybody killing each other today, my lord," he replied, and then added, "Well, at least not yet."

Hoskin smiled. He'd miss Grimes. And Percival. He wondered whether Percival would come with him and be an aide in his studies, as Grimes cleared a path through to Bollingsmead. Or as he now realized, Bollingsmeads plural, as the son stood with the father; Lady Grey and those two fighters who'd fought off the monster stood close by.

"Excuse me, my lords, I hope I'm not interrupting this reunion?" Hoskin said as the two men broke from their embrace.

"Not at all, Lord Hoskin," replied the younger Bollingsmead.

"You must be very proud," Hoskin said to the elder.

"Over the moon, Lord Chancellor," he replied in a gruff voice, bristled cheeks quivering. "I always knew he was destined for great things, you know."

Hoskin noticed the confused look that passed over the younger's face, his brow furrowed as he considered what his father had said. Hoskin realized there were probably a great many other things said in the past, which would be quickly forgotten by at least one of these two.

"And congratulations to you, my lord," he said to the younger. "You'll make a fine lord protector. I want to reassure you that I will, of course, do whatever is needed for an orderly transition before I return west."

"Return west? What?" said the new lord protector, confusion giving way to surprise and concern.

"Why, back to my family home, of course. I assume you'll be looking to put in place your own structures?"

"You're leaving? We need to talk more." The younger Bollingsmead laid his hand on Hoskin's shoulder. "Don't rush off anywhere, please. I think you've done a great job. I was hoping you might stay around. I have need of people who know what they're doing."

Those few words hit Hoskin like a punch in the gut. Recognition. *But what about the books and the hills?* said the part of him that wanted to get away.

And the other Hoskin laughed.

"Thank you, Lord Bollingsmead. I'll give it some thought this evening... Now, I have taken enough of your time; enjoy your celebrations."

Hoskin turned and walked away, his face a picture of shock only noticed by a few onlookers.

HOSKIN SAT IN A COMFORTABLE ARMCHAIR IN HIS quarters, dressed in a cotton nightgown, with a book in his lap. He considered his accommodation. More significant than most, but more modest than he could have justified. These rooms had become his own and felt like home. Would he miss them if he went back to the house of his childhood? Could he even remember what his rooms looked like there? Since the death of his mother and father, he'd now have the master chambers, which he'd rarely been allowed to enter.

These thoughts had intruded on him as he worked his way

through the book the wizard had given him: *Bethel the Red.* The queen used to frighten children if they wouldn't go to sleep. The stories of her inquisitorial squads pulling families apart, chopping blocks working day and night, were known by all. But this account was slightly different, or at least provided context.

He never knew the extent to which Pyrfew had infiltrated Kingshold with agents, apparently high-born and commoner, rich and poor, many of the cells not knowing about the others. It was tinder packed under the very foundations of Kingshold that would have been ready to be lit at a moment's notice. Given the past few weeks' experience, Bethel's actions began to make some sense to Hoskin.

A knock at the door interrupted his reading once more.

"Yes? Who is it?"

"It's Percival, my lord. May I come in?"

"Of course."

The door opened, and the familiar face of his assistant peeked around the door.

"My lord, I have Lady Grey here to see you." And without waiting, he opened the door wide to let in the woman, her features hidden under a hooded black coat. Once inside, she pulled down the hood to reveal her handsome face, and Percival closed the door behind her. Percival remained outside.

"What an unexpected pleasure, my lady," said Hoskin by way of greeting. "It's not often I'm visited in my nightgown by a beautiful woman." He chuckled at his attempt at flattery.

"I know," she replied flatly. "I know all about you, Lord Hoskin. How are you? You looked quite ill after talking with Lord Bollingsmead earlier."

"Yes, it did take me a little by surprise. Probably just the shock on top of the tiredness from the past few weeks. I was rather looking forward to retiring, you know. But if my country needs me, then I guess I'll have to put it on hold."

"I was afraid you might say that."

"Pardon?" Hoskin paused. His visitor's previous words only just sinking in as being a little peculiar. This whole meeting suddenly seemed quite out of the ordinary. "What did you mean about knowing all about me?"

"Sit on the bed," commanded Lady Grey, ignoring his questioning.

"You can't come in here and order me around, my lady!"

"Sit. On. The. Bed." As she spoke the words, a force compelled him to stand, walk over and perch on the edge of the bed. He tried to fight it, but his legs wouldn't obey him. "I'm sorry it's come to this, Hoskin. I truly am. You may not realize it, but you've been most helpful."

"Percival! Come quick!" he called.

The door opened slightly, and Percival's head appeared around the door once more.

"I'm afraid I can't help you, my lord," said his trusted assistant. He slipped into the room, closing the door behind him. "But it was a pleasure working with you these years."

Lady Grey and Percival advanced on Hoskin, now unable to move any of his limbs, his jaw clenched shut by an invisible force against his desire to scream for help. Lady Grey pushed him gently back onto the bed, and Percival picked up his feet from the floor, so he lay comfortably. Lady Grey pulled a small vial from a pocket of her coat and held it up for him to see.

"This poison is quite painless," she explained. "I believe it's the type of thing young lovers drink when they're kept apart. Gentle sleep, and then your heart will stop. I don't think it will come as a great surprise to anyone that you'd take your own life in such a romantic fashion."

She bent over the lord chancellor, smiling at him the way one would to a sick child when about to administer medicine. One hand gripped his nostrils as his mouth opened involuntarily, and she poured the sour poison down his throat. He tried not to swallow, but he was going to choke and drown if he didn't. The liquid slipped down his gullet and, slowly, black crept in from the corners of his vision until the light of the room became pinpricks.

And then darkness.

CHAPTER 48

ONE LAST NIGHT

"Mareth, do we have to have so many guards here tonight?" called Jules from across the common room. She wasn't happy, threading through the roomful of armored palace guards sitting around, talking, playing cards, but not consuming any beer.

"Yes!" answered Dolph. "Tell me again, Mareth, why we're not staying at the palace tonight?"

Mareth leaned back on his chair, feet on his favorite table, and a grin plastered on his face that seemed like it would never come off. He took a sip of foamy beer and rocked forward. "Because I don't start the job until tomorrow. And they might not let reprobates like you lot into the palace." Mareth winked at Trypp.

"Who are you calling a reprobate?" said Jules, putting down a tray of drinks and cuffing him playfully around the head. There was a scrape of chairs behind her, and three members of the guard got to their feet. "Sit down, you pillocks," she called back at them, and they sheepishly returned to their seats.

Jules sat at the table after passing around the drinks, and Mareth took a moment to look at the friends around him. It's true, he might have had a few drinks so far, but it wasn't the ale causing the giddiness. He felt a genuine warmth for his companions.

"And I also wanted to be here one last time," said Mareth, looking at his mug. "One more time when we could pretend we were going to try to change the world without the reality of having to do so. I have so much to thank you all for."

He looked at Petra to his right. They held hands under the table, and she squeezed his knuckles harder than he'd expect for someone of her size. Her blonde hair was tied in a braid that fell down the front of her dress. She looked beautiful. Jules had helped her with an outfit fitting for the palace earlier that evening, and no one had a chance to change. Her cheeks were flushed, probably from going pint to pint with him, and her eyes glistened as if she was on the verge of tears.

"Petra, my love, you've been the dawn of my life. Without you, I'd still probably be sitting here this evening, but having done nothing of worth in the meantime. You believed in me when no one else did, and you were the first link in the chain that binds all of us who are around this table."

Petra smiled while a tear escaped her eye. She leaned over and grabbed Mareth by the collar and pulled him into a long kiss. Alana's cough interrupted them, and Mareth turned his attention to her. He couldn't believe she was up and about when last week she was bleeding out on the inn floor. But there she was, actually looking stronger than she had earlier today (obviously the healing power of ale) and with not even a scar to show above her gown.

"Alana. Where to begin? Without you, I'd be six feet under. Without you, we wouldn't have known what to do. And without you, half of this table wouldn't have come together. Thank you so much for driving us all forward."

Motega, Florian, and Trypp were spread around the table. Motega and Florian had their customary smiles, and Trypp was trying hard not to enjoy himself. These three had been essential to what had been done, and they'd hitched their wagon to his solely on the basis of adventure. He was going to need to keep them around, but maintaining their interest would be the challenge.

"Motega, Florian, and Trypp, more people who have saved my life. I probably need to be a little more careful about that in the future. But seriously, you guys are an amazing team. I don't know how you do what you do, but keep doing it. And do it for Edland, please."

"Lady Neenahwi." Mareth looked at her sitting quietly at the opposite end of the table. She'd been uncharacteristically quiet since the announcement, lost in her own thoughts. "Thank you for joining our cause, too, and not just thinking of us as a group of beer dreamers. I hope you'll guide us in the future.

"My dear, lady Jules." He looked at the landlady of his favorite inn, his former crush, and now someone he thought of as a big sister. "How on earth you let me stay around all of these years amazes me. How you've turned away business for the past two weeks to house us has astounded me. From now on, all visiting ambassadors will be *encouraged* to stay at the Royal Oak!"

"Shut up." And she cuffed him around the head again. "That's not why I did this, and you know it. No one cares about personal gain—"

"Well, we were expecting protection from prosecution out of this deal," said Trypp with a straight face.

Everyone looked at him and, after a moment, laughed.

"No, I mean it," he insisted.

Mareth turned to Folstencroft. "Where is Lady Grey tonight? I wish she were here. Without her support, both financially and in lending us credibility, we'd have been laughed out of all meetings. Besides the ones that were brokered by Petra anyway."

The secretary sat upright, drinking water from a clay cup. Apparently, not everyone was going to let their hair down tonight. "I'm afraid she had an appointment, and then wanted to get an early night, my lord."

"I've told you. You don't need to call me 'my lord' when we're all together. Well, we all appreciate you, too, Folstencroft. You stepped in and organized when Alana was laid low. And I'm looking forward to hearing about your system for paying back all of the voters. Zzzz." And Mareth pretended to fall asleep. Everyone laughed again except Folstencroft. Florian whacked him on the arm.

"That's funny, man! Laugh! You won't break anything."

The secretary cracked the barest of smiles.

"We all here are a chain," continued Mareth. "We have links with each other now, some of them go back years, others weeks. But they're forged from steel, not from tin. "

His friends nodded, and they looked at each other in silent reflection. Motega broke the quiet. "So how are you feeling, Mareth?"

"Oh, I'm shit scared. Don't any of you think you're running off. You're chained to me now."

"We're all with you, Mareth," said Neenahwi. "But as my father would say, don't fuck it up!"

“I think it’s already fucked up. Isn’t that why we did this? I hope it can’t get any worse,” he replied. His hands rested against the worn oak tabletop, and he again considered his friends gathered around it. “Jules, I love this table. Can I take it with me?”

EPILOGUE

Jyuth rolled back and forth with the gait of his horse as it walked with little guidance from its rider over hills of what would be a verdant green in the daytime, but were now a dull grey in the moonless night. Kingshold was visible behind him in the far distance, nestled between Mount Tiston and Deepwater Bay. If he'd looked back, he would have seen it twinkling in the dark, lights in the city that would continue through the night as people celebrated the solstice and the new lord protector. He didn't look back, though. Jyuth examined a book he held, able to see it even without a source of light. He held the book close, then at arm's length, and then turned it sideways. The cover, embossed with gold letters, read *Sexomnicon*.

"This is very interesting, Horse," he said, for that is what Jyuth had called all of his horses for more than eight hundred years, having run out of names of a more personal nature. "Who knew you could do that? Maybe this retirement is going to be more interesting than I feared."

Horse didn't reply. But Jyuth didn't expect it to. Horse

rolled on, following a simple trail that continued in a south-westerly direction from the capital city. Horse paid little attention to the three metal discs, constructs of Garlick the smith, as big as wagon wheels that trailed along just behind it, hovering in the air. On all three discs rested wooden chests, bound with iron, almost as long as the diameter of each circle. On one of the floating platforms, accompanying a big chest, was a smaller duplicate, an eighth of the size of the larger container. Horse thought those chests looked heavy. He was glad he hadn't been required to pull them himself like a cart horse.

Pop.

A small pink demon, fluorescent in the dark, appeared on Jyuth's shoulder. It peered down at the book being inspected by the old man and gave what could only be described as a dirty little chuckle.

"Heh, heh, heh," said the pyxie, nudging Jyuth's head with his elbow.

"Yes, very," said the wizard, turning his head. "Did you take the gold back to the people as I asked?"

The demon nodded.

"Good. I have no interest in an angry gaggle of dwarves on my trail. Or for those district supervisors to all be strung up come the morning." Jyuth stroked the pyxie under the chin, which it stretched forward like a cat. "The others, though, they won't miss it. Well, not too much."

Jyuth stopped stroking the little pink creature. It looked a bit mad that it had been distracted like a pet.

"Where is our share?" it said with a deep voice unsuited to its small frame.

"The chest there. As agreed." Jyuth pointed to the small chest on the third flying disc.

"Good."

"Before you go, Basharaat, a question. Was everything counted fairly?"

"Ah, I see," said Basharaat, "you wish to believe everything happened fairly. Make you feel good."

"Actually, I want to know. I find belief to be quite useless in most situations."

"Know? I don't know. But belief helps in the dark night when thinking about it. I think it was done fairly. Now, accurately, I don't know." The little creature smiled. "Not all of my people can understand the common tongue too well. But they do their best."

Jyuth chuckled. "I guess it turned out alright anyway. Thank you, Basharaat."

The demon grabbed the wizard's bearded cheek and planted a kiss. Then the pyxie, and the small chest, disappeared in a puff of smoke.

HORSE PLODDED DOWN THE DUNE TO A SHELTERED COVE, pinned between rocky outcroppings. At least one of those stone abutments continued far out under the sea by the signs of the shipwreck clinging to the rocks, left there as a warning to other sailors to be careful of what was happening under the surface. Something Jyuth had always found to be sound advice in all walks of life.

The sun was just beginning to rise, but it was still early in the morning, even though the days would shorten now. Flotsam and jetsam littered the beach on the right side, at least what had been left behind by the wreck pickers, predominantly that too big (in the case of the rusty anchor) or not worth it (wooden shards, empty, broken crates, and barrels). But Jyuth expected, given time, what was left would even be put to good use, if he knew his countrymen well enough. To the left of the beach was why he was here. A small catboat, beached and secured to a metal ring set into a massive boulder of granite.

Jyuth carried his bags from Horse and put them into the boat. The chests floated over and rested on the ground nearby. He needed to launch the vessel before he loaded the heavy cargo if he wanted to get it off the beach. He braced his legs in the sand and leaned over to push the vessel into the gentle waves of the bay when something caught his attention rising from the surface.

From the sea, dripping in water, walked a figure, female from the waist down, judging by its nakedness, but with the broad chest, long-taloned arms, and the head of a black panther. Eight feet of soggy cat, and it didn't look happy as it waded through the shallow water to the shore, flinging away pieces of weed attached to its fur. Jyuth stood and walked across the sand to meet the creature, apparently unnoticed.

"Ahem." Jyuth coughed politely to get its attention.

The feline face turned, eyes narrowing as it now regarded its surroundings. "What do you want, old man?" it growled. *Sniff, sniff, sniff.* "Wait. You smell of her!"

Jyuth sighed. "I feared as much. Where are you heading?"

"That way." The creature pointed the way Jyuth had just come, and where Horse was already picking its way home. "How far is she?"

"Oh, she's much too close. And she needs a rest. I did promise I would stop being involved, and that probably includes letting her clean up her own messes." Jyuth seemed to be talking to himself more than the demon, considering his options.

"What are you wittering about, old man? So far, I've let you live, but maybe you should be breakfast. I've run far."

"Yes, that will work," said Jyuth, coming to some internal agreement. "She does need a rest after all."

The wizard pulled a thread from his robe and began to wrap it around his index finger. Behind the beast, which walked toward what it thought was a helpless old man, the iron chain attached to the washed-up anchor rose out of the sea. Each link, as big as a man's hand, showed signs of rust, but it still held together, and it lashed forward like a whip, wrapping around and around the panther beast. Jyuth picked the wrapped thread off his finger, rolled it up, and flicked it forward. Like a puppet controlled by the wizard's thread, the anchor lifted into the air, flying back in an arc before launching itself forward into the sky. The chain dragged along behind with the captured demon, a screaming tail to the metal comet. The iron-bound package sailed across the bay until it disappeared into the sea with a splash.

Clapping his hands at a job well done, Jyuth walked back to his boat and set about the business of sailing off into the wild blue yonder.

CALL TO ACTION

Thanks for reading the adventures of Mareth, Alana, Neenahwi and Motega. I hope you enjoyed it. The story continues in Tales of Kingshold, Book 1.5 of the Wildfire Cycle.

I would appreciate you leaving a few remarks or comments on Amazon or Goodreads, and of course, telling your friends the good old fashioned way. It's this reader led communication that helps to spread the word and get others interested in trying this book.

You can sign up for my newsletter to be notified of future releases, opportunities to become a beta reader, and behind-the-scenes discussion of what went into the making of Kingshold. Also, if you want to drop me a line, please do. My email address is dave@dpwoolliscroft.com.

GLOSSARY

Groups

Higher Guilds:

Engineers
Law
Merchants
Moneychangers
Shipwrights
Weavers
Hollow Syndicate (Unofficial Status)

Lower Guilds:

Artists
Bakers
Brewers
Butchers
Craftsmen

Doctors and Druggists
Ironworkers
Saddle Makers and Tanners
Stonemasons
Twilight Exiles (Unofficial Status)

Kingshold Districts and Supervisors

Fishtown - Eldrida
Warehouse - Gonal
Central Market - Aldo
Docks - Colbert
Garden - Hertha
Cherry Tree - Jules
Fourwells - Win
Golden - Geary
Lance - Row
Redguard - Ifig
Whiteguard - Garet
Inner Narrows - Dyer
Outer Narrows - Lud
Four Points - Lowell
Garmond - Yetta
Bottom Run - Denley
Woodton - Odam
Randall's Addition - Nara
Arloth's Acre - Paine
Beggar's Point - Medwyn

Cast of Characters

AEBUR: Spymaster General

AGNES: Old lady, lives on the Farm Road
ALANA: Palace maid, sister to Petra
ARTUR DANWEAZEL: Merchant, dealer of under-the-table wares and giver of extraction jobs to Motega, Trypp, and Florian
BALES: Lord Hoxteth's steward
BALLARD: Guild master of the Stonemasons' Guild
BARAX: Demon queen, trapped in the mortal world by Neenahwi
BARTHOLOMEW: Artisan of the subtle arts of persuasion and inquisition
BASHARAAT: Demon king of the pyxies
BENEVAL (Lord): Commander of the palace guard
BERTHA: Head maid at the palace
BOLLINGSMEAD (Lord): Father of Mareth
CADAWA: Childhood playmate of Neenahwi
CARNEY: Resident minstrel of the Griffon's Beak Inn
CHALICE (lady): Managing partner of the Hollow Syndicate, rescuer of Neenahwi and Motega
CREWS: Naval commander under Sea Marshall Ridgton
DAVITH: Urchin, pickpocket
DOLPH: Bodyguard to Mareth, employee of Lord Hoxteth
DUKE OF NORTHFIELD: Brother of King Roland, Pienzan duke
DYER: District supervisor for the Inner Narrows
EDEN (Lord): Savior of Redsmoke, war hero, richest man in Edland
EGYED: Dwarf, ambassador of the deep people, Keybearer of Unedar Halt
ELDRIDA: District supervisor for Fishtown
ELKIN: Former chief of the Wolfclaw tribe, Motega and Neenahwi's great grandfather

FISKE (Lord): Guild master of the Law Guild, head judge of the realm, candidate
FLORIAN: Friend to Motega and Trypp, originally introduced by Jyuth. Veteran of foreign wars, including the liberation of Redpool, mercenary for hire
FOLSTENCROFT: Administrator, employed by Lady Grey
FORGER: Elected leader of the dwarves of Unedar Halt
FREDERICK (Sir): Knight, bodyguard to Lord Eden
GARLICK: Smith in the Four Points District
GAWL TEGYR: Bearer of Light, Bringer of Peace, Ambassador of Pyrfew
GNEEF: A thief in need of a dentist
GONAL: Merchant, friend of Mareth and connection to Hoxteth
GREY (Lady): Lord Hoxteth's wife
GREYTOOTH: Shaman of the Wolfclaw clan
GRIMES: Captain of the palace guard under Beneval, but everyone knows who to go to if there is a problem
HOSKIN: Lord Chancellor of Edland
HOXTETH: Lord Treasurer, merchant, Merchants' Guild leader
HUTH: Hoskin's deceased father, former Lord Chancellor
JULES: Owner and landlady of the Royal Oak
JYUTH: Wizard, founder of Edland, adopted father of Neenahwi
KANAVEEN: Wolfclaw champion and protector of Neenahwi and Motega after the flight. Lives in the wilderness of Edland
KARR: Pirate
KARKEN: Captain in the Unedar Halt guard
KING RANDOLPH: Father of Roland

KING ROLAND: Final King of Edland, husband to Queen Tulip
KINGSLEY (Lady): Candidate
KOLSEN: Pirate King
LLEWDON: Emperor of Pyrfew, wizard, ancient
LUD: District supervisor for the Outer Narrows
MAMA BATTY: Producer of world famous blood pies
MARETH: Son of Bollingsmead, bard, former adventurer, former pirate
MOTEGA: Warrior and archer of renown from the wild continent, brother to Neenahwi, mercenary for hire
MRS. SKRUD: Neighbor to Alana and Petra, busybody, gossip, heart of gold
NEENAHWI: Of the Wolfclaw clan, wizard, adopted daughter of Jyuth and older sister to Motega
ORLAN (Lady): Chair of Kingshold University, candidate
PENSHEAD (Sir): Knight and Commander of the City Guard
PERCIVAL: Personal assistant to Lord Hoskin
PETRA: Bar maid at the Royal Oak, sister to Alana
QUEEN TULIP: Final Queen of Edland, wife to King Roland
RIDGTON: Sea Marshall of Edland
SHARAVIN: Mother of the Twilight Exiles
SHAREF: Former chief of the Wolfclaw tribe, Motega and Neenahwi's father
SILAS: Former father of the Twilight Exiles
SPINNET: Master of wardrobes for Lady Grey
THORLEY: Owner and landlord of the Salty Hull
TRYPP: Friend to Motega and Florian, former thief with the Twilight Exiles
TUFT: Neenahwi's cat

UTHRIDGE: Lord General of Edland
WHITE: Guild master of the Bakers' Guild
WIN: District supervisor for Fourwells
WREN: Guild master of the Moneychangers' Guild
ZAFF: A minstrel

ACKNOWLEDGMENTS

Writing Kingshold has been a labor of love, and it would not have been possible without the love and support of my wife, Haneen and daughter Liberty.

I'd also like to thank Jaya Balasubramaniam, Robby Craig, Erin Duncan-O'Neill, Ryan Ehrlich, Joe Smith and Bernie Zimmermann for their immense help as beta readers. They were the first to read any of this writing and their positive feedback and great suggestions have been invaluable. It is not an exaggeration to say that had they not liked the book, my writing career would likely have proved very short.

Thanks to Ronesa Aveela, Tim Marquitz and Therin Knite for their editing assistance and for helping a first time author with the things that he's long forgotten from secondary school.

And last but not least, Jeff Brown, the illustrator and cover designer, produced stunning work that really brought the city to life for me.

Thanks again to everyone.

D.P. Woolliscroft
April 2018

ABOUT THE AUTHOR

Born in Derby in England on the day before mid summers day, David Peter Woolliscroft was very nearly magical. If only his dear old mum could have held on for another day. But magic called out to him over the intervening years, with many a book being devoured for its arcane properties. David studied Accounting at Cardiff University where numbers weaved their own kind of magic and he has since been a successful business leader in the intervening twenty years.

Adventures were had. More books were devoured and then one day David had read enough that the ideas he had kept bottled up needed a release valve. And thus, rising out of the self-doubt like a phoenix at a clicky keyboard, a writer was born.

Kingshold is David's debut novel and *Tales of Kingshold*, a series of companion short stories are flooding onto the page as fast as David can write them. You can keep up-to-date on all new releases at www.dpwoolliscroft.com.

David, his wife Haneen, and daughter Liberty all live with their mini goldendoodle Rosie in Princeton, NJ. David is one of the few crabs to escape the crabpot.

ALSO BY D.P. WOOLLISCROFT

Tales of Kingshold

I am Mareth and I collect tales - tales that do not make the official histories. Join me and learn the secret stories of those who sparked the wildfire. Stories from our past, from that fateful summer and its aftermath.

If you loved Kingshold, discover the next installment in the epic Wildfire Cycle.

Tales of Kingshold, Book 1.5 of the Wildfire Cycle, includes four novelettes and six short stories.

NOVELETTES:

Of Buccaneers and Bards (previously published separately)

All That Shimmers

Hollow Inside

Visions

SHORT STORIES:

Twin Lies

Narrowing It Down

The Working Dead

From Father to Daughter

Jyuth on Magic